"I WANT TO HAVE AN AFFAIR WITH YOU, DIANA."

Rhys's voice was husky, insistent. "You know as well as I do that the physical attraction between us is as powerful as ever. You're a mature beautiful woman now, and I want you. Tonight. In this house."

For a wild sweet moment Diana was tempted. To submit to the passionate glory of his lovemaking...! But there was Belinda, her daughter...and his. The daughter he didn't know he had. She couldn't ignore her responsibility.

"What's the point of my saying I don't want you? We'd both know I was lying." She raised her head defiantly. "But we're not going to become lovers again, Rhys."

Then, somehow, they were locked in each other's arms. Somehow she was eagerly returning his hungry kiss....

JOCELYN HALEY
is also the author
of these SUPERROMANCES
11 – LOVE WILD AND FREE
31 – WINDS OF DESIRE

These books may be available at your local bookseller
or by writing to:

Worldwide Reader Service
1440 South Priest Drive, Tempe, AZ 85281
Canadian address: Stratford, Ontario N5A 6W2

JOCELYN HALEY

SERENADE FOR A LOST LOVE

A SUPERROMANCE FROM
WORLDWIDE

TORONTO · NEW YORK · LOS ANGELES · LONDON

Published March 1983

First printing January 1983

ISBN 0-373-70054-7

Printed in Canada

CHAPTER ONE

FOR DIANA IT ALL BEGAN AGAIN one warm August evening the summer she was twenty-seven.

As she and Alan drove from her apartment to Mount Royal and wound up the hillside past the cemeteries and Beaver Lake to park the car, she had no inkling that the past was about to catch up with her. No inkling that what would transpire that evening was to set in motion a train of events that would change her life irrevocably—even more irrevocably than it had been changed ten years ago.

Even at dusk the park was crowded with tourists, yet it was these very crowds that gave Diana and Alan a certain anonymity; as they stood on the grass verge looking out over the vast sprawl that was Montreal, they could have been alone. Below them lay the massed buildings, the skyscrapers and church spires of the city; they could still distinguish the silvery band of the St. Lawrence and the arc of yellow lights that was Jacques Cartier Bridge.

A breeze, light and cool, teased Diana's ash-blond hair. She lifted her face to it gratefully, for the day had been a long, hot one.

And then, abruptly, Alan spoke. "Diana, will you marry me?"

Her head swung around, her gray eyes wide. He was standing about a foot away from her, his long, lean-limbed body unaccustomedly tense, his shoulders hunched. His face, like the rest of him, was long and thin. A scholarly face, a thinker's face, redeemed from overseriousness by a mouth that smiled readily and by laughter lines radiating from the corners of his light blue eyes. As she watched he adjusted his gold-framed glasses on his nose, a gesture that told her more clearly than words that he was nervous. She said faintly, "Did you say what I thought you did?"

"I asked you to marry me."

"Oh." A party of tourists, talking loudly about the marvels they had seen in St. Joseph's Oratory, jostled her, and she moved farther onto the grass. "Alan, I—"

"I've taken you by surprise, haven't I? Sorry. But I thought you knew I was working up to it."

She could only be honest. "I did—you're quite right. I guess I'd just never worked out what I'd say."

"That's easy. Say yes."

He was half-joking yet at the same time deadly serious, and she knew she had to choose her words carefully. "You know how much I care for you, Alan. I've made no secret of that."

"And I love you, Diana. I want you to be my wife."

It was one thing to tell him she cared for him, another to use the word "love." Even after all these years she shrank from it. "If I married anyone, it would be you," she said helplessly.

Darkness was falling rapidly and it was hard to distinguish his expression. "We've known each other for over a year now, Diana. We get along well, we have a lot of the same interests—and Belinda likes me."

Belinda, her nine-year-old daughter, who that very morning had left for a music camp in Ontario.... "Yes," she repeated softly, "Belinda likes you. And that's very important to me, Alan, as you know."

He took her arm. "Come on, let's walk while we talk." They wandered along the path, Diana's flared yellow skirt ruffled by the breeze, her silk blouse molded to her figure. "Maybe I'm doing this all wrong," Alan went on. "Maybe I should be showering you with red roses or kneeling at your feet and making impassioned speeches. But—"

She couldn't help the laughter that gurgled in her throat. "I'm glad you're not. This way you're the Alan I know...and am so fond of."

His steps slowed. "'Fond of,' 'care for.' Good words, I suppose, but not really what I want to hear. What's wrong with telling me you love me?"

In her whole life Diana had told only one man she loved him. What she felt for Alan was very different, and she had welcomed the difference, for he would never use her, consume her and then throw her aside. But to call it love? "I don't know what that means," she said, trying hard to be truthful. "'Love'—the word terrifies me, Alan."

"You love Belinda."

"Of course I do, but she's my daughter. It's not the same."

"Did you love her father?"

She closed her eyes momentarily. "I don't want to talk about him."

Once again Alan turned to face her. "I think we must, Diana. Because we never have, have we? The only thing you've ever told me about him was that it was a very brief affair, that he doesn't know of Belinda's existence and that you never want to see him again. Why not?"

"Alan, I don't want to talk about him," she said more forcefully this time.

"Well, we're going to. I love you and I want to marry you. And I think you love me—but for some reason you're scared to say so. I have a feeling that reason has something to do with Belinda's father."

Again he was right; he was far too intelligent for her to deceive him, even if she wished to. No, she couldn't lie to Alan. But to tell him about Rhys? How could she do that when she had never shared with anyone the full story of the three days that turned her world upside down, of the months that followed, filled with pain and fear and a loneliness more horrible than anything she could have imagined?

"I've never told anyone about it," she said, more to herself than to Alan. And that was true. Will and Celia had guessed the connection, of course, for it was they who had introduced her to Rhys. But she had sworn them to secrecy, and not even her own parents knew the identity of Belinda's father.

"Then it's time you did. You can trust me, Diana. Anything you tell me will go no farther, you know that."

"I do trust you, Alan, of course I do!" Ridiculous that he should even think he had to say that. "But that's not the point."

"The point is you're keeping something locked up inside you that would be better shared. You said you knew I was going to ask you to marry me. Since things have gone that far between us, you can't hope to keep something that was so important to you a secret any longer. I need to know about it, darling—for both our sakes."

"I can't tell you his name!" she blurted. "Truly I can't. He's famous, you see—internationally famous now. Not even my parents know his name, nor does Belinda."

"I can do without that. It's the rest I'm interested in."

Once or twice before Diana had run into this stubborn streak in Alan, and she knew he was quite capable of persisting until she gave in from sheer exhaustion. It was the same stubborn streak that in his research had led him to make several brilliant breakthroughs where a lesser man might have admitted defeat.

"You were very young at the time," he was saying calmly. "Presumably he was older. Were you still in school?"

"No...no, I'd had a year of art school. I think I told you once that I left high school early because of the scholarship I was awarded to study art."

"Was he one of your professors? Or another student?"

"No." Her voice ragged, she cried, "Alan, do we have to talk about this?"

"Yes, we do."

She stared at the pale blue cotton of his shirtfront and, desiring only to get it over with, said tonelessly, "I met him in Montreal. I fell in love with him—desperately, catastrophically in love with him as only a seventeen-year-old can. We had three days together, the happiest days of my life. Then he left, and it was over. Or so I thought. It was only later I realized I was pregnant...." Her voice trailed off as she discovered that telling Alan even that much had left her shaking.

"Why didn't you let him know? Surely he'd have married you?" Alan demanded.

She started walking again, gazing sightlessly out over the panorama of city lights. "No, he wouldn't have; I'm convinced of that. Anyway, I was far too proud—and hurt—to go begging for help. And I was right not to, because I've managed to make a good life for myself and for Belinda." Almost as though looking for reassurance, she added fiercely, "Haven't I?"

"Yes, you have," he replied slowly. "But I'm beginning to wonder at what cost to you. I don't think you've ever really dealt with that long-ago affair, Diana; you've simply buried it as though, apart from Belinda, it never happened. Let's face it, since then I'm the only man you've ever dated more than half a dozen times, aren't I?"

"Yes," she whispered.

"Why?"

"I didn't want to get involved. So as soon as anyone showed any signs of getting serious, I backed off."

"Why was I different?"

"I don't know, you just were. Lower-key, maybe.

Not so demanding. Wanting time to yourself as well as time with me.'' She shrugged irritably. ''I can't explain it.''

''I think you've explained it very well. Are you still in love with this man?''

''No!''

''No? You sound much too vehement to me.''

''How could I possibly be in love with him? I haven't seen him for nearly ten years.''

''Which has absolutely nothing to do with it, as you well know.''

''I'm not in love with him!'' she snapped. ''That's a ridiculous thing to suggest.''

''So will you marry me, Diana?''

Her nerves jangling, she said unevenly, ''I don't know, Alan.''

''I'm sorry, Di—I've been badgering you, I know. But I'm trying to understand what's going on, and it's pretty obvious that any information about this fellow has to be dragged out of you. Does he still live in Montreal?''

''I have no idea where he lives. He travels a lot.''

''So it might be difficult for you to get to see him.''

She stared at him blankly. ''Why on earth would I want to do that?''

''To lay a ghost to rest, my dear. Look, at a very young and impressionable age you met a man who obviously swept you off your feet. You had an affair with him. I think that affair has left you emotionally scarred ever since. It was ten years ago, Diana! You should have got over it long ago, fallen in love with someone else and married him.''

"Not everyone wants a woman with an illegitimate child. A woman who's an artist, to boot, and involved in her career."

"You're begging the question and you know it." For the first time there was anger in his voice, and involuntarily she shivered. Noticing her reaction, Alan said more gently, "Come on, let's go back to the car. I'll buy you a coffee and one of those gooey pastries you're addicted to at the Café Decelles."

He tucked her hand into his arm, keeping his fingers over hers. "Your hand's cold. Here, give me your other one." Rubbing her fingers to give them warmth, he said quietly, "I've upset you, haven't I, Di? I didn't mean to do that—I only want to make you happy."

Inexplicably Diana felt like crying. Freeing one of her hands, she reached up and touched his cheek. "I do love you, Alan. You've been a true friend to me and Belinda, so good to us both. I knew you were going to ask me to marry you, and when I looked ahead into the future I always had this image of the three of us together. But now that you've actually asked me...I can't explain it, it's as though there's something holding me back."

"Someone, not something. Belinda's father."

Her gray eyes perplexed, she gazed up at him, oblivious of the passersby who were staring at them as they blocked the path. "Perhaps you're right." She shuddered. "I couldn't see him again, Alan. I couldn't bear that."

"I think you may have to, Di. Or else wear him around your neck for the rest of your life like the proverbial albatross." He brushed a strand of hair back from her face. "Whether you like it or not, he's here between us now. And he'll remain here until you lay him to rest. I want to start a new life with you, hon, but we won't be able to do that until the old one is dealt with. Am I making sense to you?"

Far too much sense.... She nodded dumbly, knowing instinctively that he was right. Her long-ago love affair had come between them even though she didn't want it to; for Alan, she was sure, was everything she wanted in a man: kind, considerate and decent, intelligent and fun loving. And Belinda liked him. "Will you let me think about all this?" she asked in a low voice.

"Of course. There's no rush." He smiled down at her, deliberately changing the subject. "Let's go— that piece of Black Forest cake is waiting for you at the café!" Even though her laugh was a bit forced he didn't complain, and hand in hand they hurried down the slope.

In the café, by mutual consent, they kept to other topics: her painting, his latest invention. Alan was a professor of mathematics at McGill University, and his field, differential equations, Diana could not even begin to understand. But his capacity for abstract thought was balanced by another talent. Without any apparent effort—in fact, he did it for fun—he invented mathematical toys and puzzles for both children and adults. A number of his games were on the market, including a couple he had thought up especially for Belinda on rainy Saturdays when she was bored. Already they had made him a great deal of money; perhaps only Diana knew that he was faintly appalled by the income he was getting from what was essentially a hobby. Almost certainly only Diana knew how much of it he gave away to various carefully chosen charities throughout the city.

Now, using a stub of pencil he produced from his pocket—about the only claim he had to being an absentminded professor was his propensity for losing pens—and the paper serviette on the table, he sketched out his latest idea, a diabolically clever puzzle that necessitated two more cups of coffee and for Diana a second piece of cake before she solved it.

It was nearly midnight when he drove her home along the tree-lined streets of Westmount to the red brick house that belonged to her parents; she had a self-contained apartment upstairs at the back, overlooking the garden. As they drew up to the curb, she asked, "Will you come in for a while?"

"No, thanks. I've got one of the computer terminals booked for seven o'clock tomorrow morning—only time I could get it—so I'll have to be up with the birds. But I'll see you to the door."

Her parents were already in bed, for the house was in darkness. Diana and Alan walked along the driveway, where the air was heavy with the scent of roses, then up the newly painted stairs to her own door, white with glass panels and a brass knob. Earthenware pots of geraniums and petunias brightened the small porch in front of it.

Taking her key from her pocket, Diana unlocked the door and stepped into the hallway, Alan following her.

"Will you mind being alone?" he asked.

"I miss Belinda when she's gone, no question of that. On the other hand, it's rather nice to be relieved of the responsibility for a while. And I know she always has a marvelous time at music camp." Dutifully she raised her face for his usual good-night kiss.

But tonight Alan's thin fingers gripped her shoulders with unaccustomed strength and his face was very serious. "There's something else I've been wanting to say for quite a while, Diana. As this seems to be the evening for letting it all hang out, I might as well say it now." He hesitated, kissed her once gently, then a second time with more force. His hands slid down her back to draw her closer.

For a moment sheer surprise held Diana rigid before she could consciously make herself relax. This was Alan, who was very dear to her. Whose kisses were always warm and pleasurable, reassuring her that she was a normal woman without at the same time making excessive demands on her. However, this time was different. Instead of releasing her as he normally would, he pulled her more tightly until his arms were like bars around her. His mouth held her captive, helpless to protest, and she was filled with unreasoning panic, as though she were about to suffocate. When his hand found the fullness of her breast through the thin silk of her blouse she gave a whimper of protest, her whole body negating his touch.

He must have felt her reaction, for he raised his head. Both of them heard the harsh expulsion of her breath and realized that she was trembling, near tears. He said heavily, "I've never made sexual

demands on you, Diana. Not because I haven't wanted to, believe me. I'm a normal male and you're a
very beautiful and desirable woman. But I've always
been conscious that you wear a hands-off sign—
Look But Don't Touch—and up until now I've never
tried to buck that." Absently he pushed at his
glasses. "This man who fathered Belinda—was he
physically cruel to you?"

Cruel.... Oh, God, she thought in agonizing recall, nothing could be farther from the truth. "No,"
she said.

His mouth tightened. "Did you enjoy making love
with him?"

It was impossible to lie. "Yes."

"And you've made love with no one else since
then?"

"That's right."

He dropped his hands to his sides, looking around
him almost as though he wasn't sure where he was. In
swift remorse she cried, "Alan, I'm sorry! I didn't
know I'd react like that, with you of all people. I just
panicked, that's all."

"You sure did," he answered grimly. "I've
learned one thing—rape's not my specialty."

"Oh, please don't say things like that!" She put
her arms around him, holding him tightly, knowing
that she had hurt him and wanting only to repair the
damage she had done. Sliding her hands up his chest,
she drew his head down and kissed him. Then, guid-
ing his hand to her breast, she held it there against the
softness of her flesh. This time, perhaps because she
was the instigator and hence in control, there was

none of the irrational fear of a few minutes ago. That there was equally no stab of desire, no drive to go farther, she chose to ignore. Against his lips she murmured urgently, "It will be all right. You just took me by surprise last time. I wasn't ready."

"One of the reasons I want to marry you is to make love to you," Alan replied. "I've wanted that for a long time. But you have to want it, too, or we'll be in trouble."

She released him, moving back a step. "For a woman who's twenty-seven years old, I seem to have a lot of things to sort out, don't I?"

He caressed her cheek. "Rephrase that. *We* have a lot of things to sort out."

She shook her head. "It's sweet of you to say that, Alan, but it's not really true. It's *my* problem, isn't it? I'm the one who's afraid of love, I'm the one who panicked when you kissed me. Yet I want to marry you, truly I do."

"Which is why I think you have to try to see Belinda's father just once more—so you'll know that's over and done with, dead, finished." He shoved his hands in his pockets, giving a humorless laugh. "At least I hope that's what you'll find out. I could be all wrong, couldn't I? Maybe you'll meet him again and pick up where you left off."

"I'd never do that, Alan—never!" she said passionately.

"I hope not. You're very precious to me, Diana, and I don't want to lose you. But as it stands right now, I don't think I really have you." He made an effort to smile. "I should certainly know the mathematical odds of a gamble, shouldn't I? It might be just that—a gamble. That after seeing him again, you'd come back to me.''

"Not a gamble—a certainty.''

His smile was more convincing this time. "I'm going to believe you because I want to. And now I must go. I'll give you a call tomorrow morning—around eleven, probably. Sleep well, hon.''

"You, too.'' She kissed him on the mouth, trying to express through her embrace all the affection she felt for him. '' 'Night.''

"Good night.''

He let himself out and she bolted the door behind him, hearing his footsteps go down the stairs, then a minute later the revving up of his car engine. Absently picking a couple of grapes from the bunch in the fruit bowl, she went through the kitchen to her bedroom. It was a large room at the back of the house, its square-paned windows overlooking the garden and brushed by the tallest branches of the birch trees. Because it faced east, she got the full benefit of the morning sun, one of the reasons she loved the room. Over the years since Belinda was born it had become a haven, the place she went to when she needed to be alone.

Bookshelves flanked the small fireplace, in front of which stood two very comfortable armchairs upholstered in a faded Chinese cotton. The carpet was a soft pale green wool, the bed queen-size and heaped with brightly colored cushions. An oak desk, cluttered with the paperwork from her last show in Toronto, stood against the far wall, while two of her own paintings, favorites that she had not wanted to sell, hung on the walls—one over her bed; the other, a portrait of Belinda, over the fireplace.

On the polished surface of the dresser there was a colored photograph of her daughter. Diana picked it up, seeing for the thousandth time the long dark hair, so unlike her own, and the serious blue eyes. It was little wonder she had never forgotten Belinda's father, she thought bitterly. How could she when in front of her was a constant living reminder of the man? Rhys's hair, like Belinda's, had been dark and thick and silky; Rhys's eyes the clear blue of a winter sky. And more than that, Rhys had even bequeathed his musical talent to the daughter he had never seen.... No, she had not been able to forget Rhys, nor would she as long as Belinda lived.

Rhys...she didn't want to think of Rhys. She wouldn't think of him. But inexorably the memories came back. In the first few weeks after he had left Montreal, had left Diana, the nights had been the worst time. Her body, so untutored before she met him, so thoroughly and complexly knowledgeable after he had left, had ached for his presence. For the fierce ruthless glory of his lovemaking. For the touch of his hands, those sensitive musician's fingers that had drawn from her responses and emotions she had never guessed she was capable of.

But he had gone. And with the new maturity that was his legacy to her, she had known he would not be back. Frightened and confused and alone, she had taken the only course open to her: she had fought back her body's demands, buried the tempestuous memories of their coupling, vowing that never again would her body betray her into the terrible beauty that was love. She was helped in this by the inevitable physical changes that pregnancy and childbirth brought, and by the time Belinda was only a few months old, Diana had succeeded in her aim. The hands-off sign, as Alan had called it, was firmly in place, and the emotions Rhys had called forth were unknowingly being channeled into the care of her tiny black-haired daughter and into a ferocious ambition to succeed as an artist, to become as well-known in her field as Rhys was in his.

Now, all her movements mechanical, Diana replaced the photo and drew the curtains, then undressed for bed, forcing her mind back to a protective blankness. Although she was tired—the emotional strain of the evening with Alan had taken its toll on her—it was a long time before she slept.

CHAPTER TWO

MORNING WAS ALWAYS Diana's best time, and the next morning was no exception. She awoke about nine and lay back in bed, feeling deliciously lazy—no Belinda to get up for, no pancakes and bacon and eggs to cook. The sun was slanting through the gaps in the curtains, barring the carpet with gold, and idly she watched its slow-moving pattern.

The small amount of information that she had shared with Alan about her affair with Rhys seemed to have opened a crack in her defenses. Maybe she had succeeded in caging herself away from her own sexuality.... But there had been more to those three days than lovemaking. Intertwined with it, inescapably part of the attraction, had been many other elements. Shared laughter. A flow of conversation that had ranged across the whole spectrum of human concerns. A meeting of minds, an intuitive understanding that had needed no words. And lastly a deep commitment, more easily expressed on Rhys's part because of his greater age and experience, to the demands and rewards of the artistic life. So many things to miss after he had gone.

It was doubtful if Diana had forgotten anything Rhys had ever said to her. It was all there, stored and waiting, wanting only the slightest invitation to bring it out into the open. This morning she had woken up remembering one thing in particular: a remark he had made that last evening they spent together at the apartment. He had touched her cheek with his finger and said, ''If in ten years' time you think you want to see me again, you can always get in touch with me through my lawyers, Moncton & Gillespie, here in Montreal. It's Martin Gillespie I usually deal with. But not before ten years, Diana—remember that.''

At the time she had vowed she would never get in touch with him, not if it was the last thing she did, and nothing that had happened in the intervening years had changed that vow. Nothing, that is, until last night, when Alan's proposal had brought her face to face with the past. Alan thought she needed to see Rhys one more time, that she would not be free of him until she did so. Over the months that she had known him she had developed a respect for Alan's judgment, and in the clear light of morning she was more than half-convinced that he was right. If she could see Rhys again, even from a distance, she would know that the love was dead, the affair buried under the many long years that had fallen between. And she would be free to marry Alan and begin a new life with him. He *was* right; she couldn't marry him as things stood now. She had to deal with the past in order to clear the way for the future.

Before she could change her mind she reached for the telephone book on the bedside table and leafed through the yellow pages until she found the number for the firm of lawyers whose name Rhys had given her. Dialing quickly, she found that her heart was thumping and her palms were damp on the receiver.

"Moncton, Gillespie & Sons. Good morning."

"Good morning." Diana licked her lips. "I wonder if I could make an appointment with Mr. Martin Gillespie?"

"One moment, please." During the long pause Diana had time to wonder why on earth she was doing this. "There's a cancellation at three forty-five today, so you could see Mr. Gillespie then, if that would be convenient."

"That would be fine, thank you. The name is Diana Sutherland."

"Fine, Ms. Sutherland. Three forty-five. Goodbye."

So that was that. She had committed herself at least to finding out where Rhys could be contacted. And if she chose to go no farther, she didn't have to, she thought firmly, trying to slow the beating of her heart by taking a couple of deep breaths and flexing her fingers to rid them of tension.

When Alan phoned at eleven—one of the nicest things about him was his dependability, she had long ago decided—she was able to tell him what she'd done.

"Good for you, Diana. That's a big step to have taken. But I'm sure it's a step in the right direction."

"I wish I was as sure," she heard herself reply.

"It'll turn out all right, you'll see. Look, I'm tied up this evening—I think I told you we have a couple of visitors from France at the department, didn't I? Tonight's the night we take them to meet the president."

"Have fun!" she said heartlessly, knowing full well how Alan hated protocol.

"Thanks a lot. How about lunch tomorrow, Di? Are you free?"

"Sure—I'm on holiday, remember? No daughter, and a show just finished."

"Okay. How about that little restaurant near Place Ville Marie, the one we went to a couple of weeks ago? Around twelve-thirty?"

"That'd be lovely. See you then."

Somewhat heartened by this conversation, perhaps because Alan was treating the whole matter so calmly, Diana did some routine housework around the apartment, made a salad for lunch and then got ready to go downtown. Thoughtfully she regarded the contents of her wardrobe. Four or five years ago, when she had first started to become known, she had added to her innate sense of style a touch of outrageousness, a hint of the bizarre. Protective coloration? A means of hiding the real Diana Sutherland? Perhaps. Or perhaps it was just an appreciation for fabrics that were a little out of the ordinary, for color combinations that startled and amused rather than soothed. Today, however, because of the nature of her errand, she wanted something more correct. Respectability was the effect she was striving for, she decided mischievously.

A couple of hours later, when she entered the lobby of the thirty-story building that housed among other concerns the law firm of Moncton, Gillespie & Sons, she was dressed very sedately in gray and white. However, there was no disguising the elegance of the light gray linen suit with its scalloped jacket and below-the-knee culottes. Her blouse was a froth of white ruffles, her stockings white mesh, her shoes of soft gray suede. She looked cool and expensive if somewhat unapproachable, and more than one pair of eyes followed her progress across the lobby to the elevator as her heels clicked on the marble flooring.

She pressed the button, wondering why elevators were always on the fourteenth and fifteenth floors when she was on the first, and waited. Her eyes idly watched the red numbers on the dial, but her mind was preoccupied with what lay ahead. The elevator arrived and she filed in with the others who had gathered. Smoothly and silently she was carried upward to the eleventh floor.

She walked across the carpeted foyer and through the double mahogany doors to the law firm's reception area. There the artificial cool of air conditioning was refreshing after the stifling heat of the city streets. More mahogany. Tastefully arranged flowers. And a carpet so thick her feet sank into it. Mr. Moncton and Mr. Gillespie were obviously doing very well for themselves, she thought wryly.

The receptionist was as decorative as her surroundings. To her Diana said, "I'm to see Mr. Martin Gillespie at three forty-five. My name is Diana Sutherland."

"Mr. Gillespie is expecting you. Come this way, please."

They went down the hallway to another mahogany door, where a highly polished brass plate announced that Martin Gillespie was within. Diana was ushered inside, and the door closed behind her. A man of perhaps sixty was seated at the desk, and Diana's two main impressions were of immaculate grooming and disconcerting intelligence. She stood still for a moment in the full glare of light from the ceiling-high windows behind the desk.

An untrained observer would have seen her beauty and gone no farther than that. It was not the vapid beauty of a Hollywood star or of a fashion model, for the cheekbones were too imperious, the chin too firm and the fine gray eyes too direct for that. But it was beauty, nevertheless. Bone deep, a matter of line and coloring and pride of bearing; beauty, moreover, with the added patina of success. It would have taken a more careful observer—and Martin Gillespie had been a highly skilled lawyer for many years—to have seen that the woman standing so quietly by the door was nervous, that the self-confidence was, at the moment, a facade. The long slim fingers were clutching her gray suede purse rather too tightly, and tension underlay the soft sensuous curve of her mouth.

He stood up, extending his hand across the desk. "Good afternoon, Miss Sutherland. Do sit down, please. Before we begin, may I say how delighted I am to meet you? I've been an admirer of your work for several years and a few years ago purchased two of your pieces at a showing here in Montreal. *Bridge at Night* and *Street Scene No. 3*. I'm glad to see that you're finally getting the national recognition you deserve."

Faint color touched Diana's cheeks and her mouth relaxed into a smile. "Thank you," she said simply.

"It's very kind of you to say so." She was never quite at ease accepting compliments of this nature, for she had always recognized that by some fluke of genetics she had been born with her talent. Certainly she had worked at it over the years, perfecting her technique, striving for new ways to express the visions that claimed her. But the basic gift was just that—a gift.

Mr. Gillespie was still talking about her work, and she forced herself to concentrate and make the appropriate responses. Finally, however, a small silence fell, and she knew the time had come to state her business. At home she had rehearsed what she would say. Now she swallowed and began with assumed calm, "Mr. Gillespie, about ten years ago. . . ." Ten years ago to the very month, she thought painfully, swallowing again.

"Yes?"

"Exactly ten years ago I met Rhys Morgan, the concert pianist, when he was in Montreal on a Canadian tour. We became friends but shortly afterward went our separate ways because of the exigencies of our careers." At home that had seemed a fine phrase; now it merely sounded stilted. "The arrangement was that in ten years we would get in contact again. At that time he gave me your name as his legal representative, saying you would always know of his whereabouts." A tiny pause. "I wonder if you could give me his address, please? Or at least some way I could reach him, if he's currently on tour." There, it was out. Let him think what he may.

With great care Martin Gillespie was adjusting the angle of the leather-bound blotter on his desk. When he looked up, his manner was completely impersonal. "I'm afraid that won't be possible, Miss Sutherland."

She said blankly, "I beg your pardon?"

Patiently he repeated, "I'm afraid I'm unable to grant your request."

About to ask why not, she suddenly saw a terrifying abyss open in front of her, black as a pit. Her face drained of color as she whispered, "He's dead."

"No, no, Miss Sutherland. I'm sorry to have frightened you; that was not my intention. Mr. Morgan is very much alive. But we have recently received instructions from him that we are not to reveal his whereabouts to anyone. And that, I'm afraid, includes you."

Forgetful of her normal reticence, she demanded, "Did he by any chance mention me by name?"

"I'm not at liberty to reveal that, Miss Sutherland."

She stared at the imperturbable face across the desk in utter frustration. "I don't understand."

"I'm sure you don't—and I regret that I am unable to help you."

She had the insane urge to throw the exquisite Venetian crystal inkwell at the window or to tip the neat pile of folders onto the floor. Anything to disturb Martin Gillespie's magisterial calm. "There's no point in your keeping his address from me. All I'll have to do is contact the company that does his recordings or the agent that arranges his tours. I'll find out that way."

"You are certainly free to do that. But I think you

will find that they have received identical instructions from Mr. Morgan.''

"I see.'' She sat back in her chair, for the first time realizing he meant every word he was saying. It was crazy...a world-renowned pianist like Rhys Morgan couldn't simply disappear. "I'll check the newspapers and find out where he's performing,'' she said stubbornly.

The lawyer was adjusting the blotter again. "I think you're rather missing the point here, Miss Sutherland,'' he said carefully.

"Oh? You mean there is a point?'' she responded with barely disguised impatience.

"Yes. The point is that Mr. Morgan doesn't want to be found.''

If she had not been so highly strung, she would have realized that herself. "Why not?'' she demanded baldly.

"I am not a party to his reasons; naturally they're his affair. I can only presume that they seem adequate to him and that they necessitate this guarding of his privacy.''

She was up against a brick wall, and she knew nothing she could say or do was going to make the slightest dent in it. The only thing that remained was to get out of the lawyer's office with some semblance of dignity. She stood up, extending her hand and saying with complete untruth, "I understand. I'm sorry to have bothered you, Mr. Gillespie.''

"Not at all, Miss Sutherland. I do apologize for my inability to be of use to you. And again may I add how pleased I am to have met you.''

An exchange of handshakes and of smiles, hers rather perfunctory. Then she was leaving the office, nodding at the receptionist, descending the elevator. Once outside again she was struck by the heat, tangible and odor laden, with its never ending backdrop of the screech of tires, the blast of horns and the jostling of crowds on the sidewalk. Suddenly unable to stand it, she ran to the curb and flagged down a taxi. Giving her address she subsided into the back seat with a sigh of relief. Home...she'd go home, and then she'd decide what to do.

However, it was as the taxi battled its way west against the late-afternoon traffic that Diana's memory supplied her with an answer to what had seemed like an insoluble dilemma, that of locating Rhys Morgan. Her diary, she thought, suddenly sitting up straight in the seat. That was it! Her diary would lead her to Rhys.

She still kept a journal in which periodically she jotted down events or insights that seemed particularly significant to her. But at seventeen she had slavishly kept a daily record of her doings, and her affair with Rhys had received more than normal coverage. She could smile at that younger Diana now, for at times she seemed almost like another creature, no relation to the woman she had become. But the younger Diana had loved and been happy, had wept with the pain of abandonment, had borne a child—and had used her diary as confessor and solace and friend. If there were any clues as to Rhys's present whereabouts, they would be found in her diary. Her resolve to find him appeared to have been strength-ened rather than weakened by Martin Gillespie's lack of cooperation.

The taxi seemed to take forever to reach her parents' house, but eventually it did. She tipped the driver lavishly, favoring him with a brilliant smile. As she ran up the driveway she was unsurprised to find the family car missing—her father and mother must have gone to the Laurentians for the day. Entering her own apartment, she hurriedly stripped off her suit and blouse, grabbing a pair of jeans and a man-tailored shirt from the closet. Then she pulled out the ladder and clambered up to the attic, armed with a flashlight.

It took several minutes of concentrated searching to locate the boxes she was looking for, and then longer to open them and find the carefully packed diaries, four stacks of them. The one she wanted had a green cover.... With an exclamation she seized it from the pile, carefully replaced the others and closed the box. A couple of minutes later she was standing in the kitchen surveying her prize.

Now that she had it in front of her, she was oddly reluctant to open it. Putting it down on the table, she washed her hands and made herself a pot of tea. Carrying the tray into the bedroom she perched on the bed and, with the sense of doing something consequential, opened the diary at the entries for August. Before she had finished the first page she was transported back into the past; it was as if the present ceased to exist.

CHAPTER THREE

THE SUMMER SHE WAS SEVENTEEN, Diana had already left home. She had finished one year of art school and was enrolled in a series of private lessons with William Gates, one of the country's foremost representational painters. Considering her youth, it was an indication of her potential that Gates should have taken her on, for he was notoriously fussy about whom he chose to teach. And, Diana soon found out, he was a notoriously hard taskmaster. But she had never been afraid of hard work, and at seventeen she was brimming with energy and enthusiasm. By midsummer the gruff white-haired Gates and the vibrantly beautiful young girl had hammered out a working relationship that pleased them both, based as it was on mutual respect. It was Will Gates who introduced Diana to Rhys Morgan.

Will came into the studio early one day to find Diana already there, taking advantage of the morning light to work on a meticulously crafted still life. "Got three tickets to a concert," he said with his usual economical mode of speech; he hid an incisive intelligence under a somewhat homespun manner. "Try a touch of burnt umber in the lower left corner there. And for God's sake do something with that shadow—it looks as if you could trip over it.''

Diana sighed inwardly, acknowledging the justice of his criticism. "What kind of concert?''

"Pianist. Rhys Morgan, the one who won the Tchaikovsky Competition in Moscow recently. Damn lucky to get tickets; the concert's a sellout.''

The troublesome shadow was forgotten. The girl swung around, her gray eyes wide. "I'd love to go! I've got both his recordings and I was just reading recently how brilliantly he played in Moscow. When is it?''

"Not for a couple of weeks. Celia got the tickets—I refrained from asking how. We're invited to the reception afterward. You might even get to meet the man.''

"Really, Will? That would be fantastic!''

For the next two weeks the thought of the concert was never far from Diana's mind. Rhys Morgan... she was actually going to meet Rhys Morgan! She had read about his Welsh ancestry, his lonely troubled childhood as a ward of court, his introduction to the piano at the age of thirteen in the last of his foster homes. From then on there had been no stopping him. When he was sixteen, the city in which he was living had raised money to send him to the University of Toronto's Faculty of Music. By the time he was twenty he was studying in Europe. Now twenty-eight, his career as a concert pianist was just getting established; the results of the competition in Moscow would open doors for him all over the world.

On the back of one of her records there was a black-and-white photograph of him at the keyboard, and if Diana had had to use only one word to describe him it would have been "intense." His concentration on what he was doing was absolute. That was something she could understand, for she brought the same concentration to her art. And now she was going to meet him.

She gave considerable thought to what she would wear. She didn't want to appear before him as a gauche unsophisticated seventeen-year-old, for she was not yet mature enough or wise enough to accept herself as she was. In the end she spent considerably more than she could afford on a long white dress with dramatically wide sleeves, a nunlike neckline and virtually no back. Her only jewelry was the diamond-spray brooch her grandmother had left her. On the day of the concert she went to the hairdresser's and had her long hair pulled back from her face into a smoothly looped coil on the back of her head, a style that added years to her age. In the adjoining salon she was professionally made up, and when she finally looked at herself in the mirror she was delighted with what she saw. No one would possibly guess that she was only seventeen.

When the Gateses came to pick her up at the student residence where she was living—a place whose casual lack of rules was the despair of Diana's mother—she was waiting for them in the downstairs hall, a gloomy room of duns and pallid greens, with metal-framed furniture and a permanent aura of cigarette smoke and overcooked meals. In these surroundings the girl's appearance was like a jolt of electricity, for she was incandescent with excitement, glimmering with vitality. Will Gates had seen many beautiful women in his lifetime and had never wavered from his belief that his wife Celia was the most beautiful of them all. But something that was both blazingly alive and appallingly vulnerable in the girl in front of him brought him to a halt. "Well, Diana," he said inadequately. He cleared his throat. "Shall we go? Celia's in the car."

She took one step toward him and then halted. "Will, do I look all right?"

He had had time to recover. "You'll knock him off his feet," he responded dryly. "Is that the idea?"

She blushed entrancingly, her indignation sounding false to both of them. "Of course not! He won't even notice me."

One eyebrow rose in faint derision, Will offered her his arm and they went out to the car. Celia was also in a long gown, hers a rich burgundy taffeta, a perfect foil for the pure white hair that framed her face. Her bone structure was exquisite, age having merely refined her features down to their essentials. A woman of wit and wisdom with occasional flashes of earthy humor, she was already fond of Will's young protégée, as aware as her husband of Diana's formidable talent and equally aware, after her long marriage to an artist of stature, of the many pitfalls that might lie ahead for Diana. "You're looking very lovely, Diana," she said. "Is that a new dress?"

They chatted companionably as Will drove to Place des Arts, where they joined the crowds thronging around the entranceway, catching snatches of conversation in both French and English. Their seats were excellently placed. "I have my connections," Celia said darkly. Once they were seated, Diana buried herself in the program, discovering that the entire first half of the concert was devoted to Chopin, while after the intermission came sonatas by Mozart and Beethoven.

The houselights dimmed and the audience subsided into silence. The lid of the piano had been raised and on its lower surface were reflected the parallel lines of the strings, rich brown on shining black. Fascinating to paint, the girl thought. Then the audience started to clap and she had her first glimpse of Rhys Morgan.

He was much taller than she had expected, well over six feet, and there was nothing in him of the willowy effete stereotype of the concert pianist. Far from it. The highly civilized garb of evening shirt, bow tie and tails somehow emphasized his rugged broad-shouldered build; he looked as though he would be as much at home in a logging camp as on the stage. He bowed to the applauding audience, his face set and unsmiling, and without fuss or delay sat down at the bench and began to play.

Afterward Diana had no recollection of time passing, for the music caught her up, suspending her in a world without time. She stayed in her seat at intermission, unwilling to break the almost mystical spell that had been woven around her by the waltz's rhythm, the polonaise's vigor and the severe precision of the sonata, which had ended in a dazzling display of virtuosity. And when, after the Beethoven *Appassionata*, the final burst of applause sounded around her, she was not ready for the music to end.

Rhys received a standing ovation but played no encores; across the rows of seats that separated them she thought he looked exhausted, utterly drained.

It was nearly an hour later that he arrived at the reception, a gathering of some two hundred of the city's elite, who had been filling in the time by sipping champagne and eating hors d'oeuvres. Diana saw the crowd shift at the far end of the room, and when she noticed a dark head overtopping most of the others, she knew he had arrived. To her dismay he was immediately surrounded.

"Don't worry," Will said calmly. "We'll wait until some of the fuss dies down and then we'll go and say hello. I've met him twice before, you see. But I don't feel like battling that crowd, so just be patient."

Embarrassed that Will had been able to read her thoughts so clearly, she took another gulp of champagne, enjoying the tickling sensation in her nostrils, and schooled herself to wait. Her neighbor, an accountant on the board of directors of the Montreal symphony, seemed intent on divulging to her all the financial difficulties he labored under, and she listened politely, one eye always on that shock of dark hair.

The crowd was thinning somewhat, and she smiled at the waiter as he filled her glass, knowing she needed all the false courage it was giving her. She had the half excited, half fearful sense of something momentous about to happen. Rhys Morgan was barely fifty feet away now, listening to what Diana was sure were fulsome compliments from a plump and beringed matron with startlingly mauve hair. He looked, she thought, as if he had heard it all before. His face was a polite mask. Then, as though sensing her eyes on him, he looked in her direction, and for the first time she saw that his eyes were a brilliant blue. He stared straight at her for what might have been five seconds, then boldly raised his glass to her in a silent toast and dutifully bent his head to the mauve-haired lady again.

Diana stood quite still, shaken to the core. The accountant, whose name had fled her mind, had asked her a question, and she stammered, "I beg your pardon? I—I'm sorry, I missed what you said."

She tried to concentrate, tried to negate in her mind the effect of that one searing glance, all the while noticing how Rhys Morgan was steadily and purposefully working his way around to the corner of the room where she, Will and Celia were standing. Every so often his eyes would meet hers and again there would be that shock of instant communication, almost as if he was actually speaking to her: *Wait for me—don't go away. We both know we want to meet each other, don't we?* An unspoken promise, an outright demand. Both, at one and the same time.

Finally he broke free of the group nearest to them and strode across the carpet, allowing his eyes to run lightly over Diana before he greeted Celia and Will, whom he obviously remembered. She waited, as she had waited all evening. Now that the moment had come to meet him she was suddenly, fatalistically calm.

Will and Celia had been complimenting him on his performance, and then Will said, "Mr. Morgan, may I—"

"Rhys, please. Let's not stand on formality."

"Very well, then. Rhys, I'd like you to meet my protégée, Diana Sutherland. Remember her name—it's going to be famous one day."

Rhys looked over at her. "I'll remember it," he said as though he was making a private vow to her. He held out his hand and she laid her fingers in his.

For Diana the world shrank to a pair of piercing blue eyes that seemed to see into her very soul and a warm strong handclasp that was the only thing that kept her from falling. She had never felt anything that could be remotely compared to what she was feeling now: an elemental response to a man's touch that was as powerful as it was primitive. She had dated a number of students during her year at art school, been kissed by a few of them and been mildly disturbed to find herself almost unmoved by the experience. Now Rhys Morgan had merely shaken hands with her—a conventional social gesture, nothing more—and she was trembling and dizzy. Her eyelids dropped to hide her confusion and she pulled back her hand. Instantly he released it, saying smoothly, "If you're studying with Will Gates, I'll be willing to bet you're working very hard. What medium do you prefer?"

Ridiculous, her brain cried. *Are we to talk of oil paints and tempera panels when all I want to do is ask you to hold my hand again and never let it go?* From a long distance away she heard a voice that she recognized as her own say with creditable calm, "This summer I'll be working mainly in oils. But in the fall when I go back to college I'll be taking courses in watercolors and printmaking."

"You have the best of teachers." He turned to Will again and the conversation became general.

Diana listened and smiled appropriately, feeling all the while like a mechanical doll. Apparently the feelings that had seized her when he had held her hand had been hers alone; he had not shared them. If he had, how could he be carrying on an intelligent discussion with Celia about a medieval book of hours and Elizabethan miniatures—more or less ignoring Diana, besides?

Then as if she was in a dream she heard him say, "I must finish my rounds—nearly done, thank God. Let me take the three of you for a drink afterward?"

Celia answered. "That's very kind of you, Rhys, but I'm afraid Will and I have to get home. Our two grandchildren are staying with us for a week while their parents are away, so we have a baby-sitter." She smiled up at her husband. "At our age!"

Rhys looked over at Diana. "What about you, Miss Sutherland? Surely I can persuade you to join me?"

"That would be lovely," she faltered. "Thank you."

He nodded at her. "I'll be back in a few minutes."

Once he was out of earshot, Will said meditatively, "Now that's a high-powered man, Diana—you take it easy, hmm?"

"Will!" Celia cried in protest.

"Just a word of warning," he mollified her. "I guess we'd better be going, hadn't we? See you to-morrow morning, Diana—nine o'clock sharp."

"Yes, boss," Diana said meekly. "Good night, both of you—and thanks again for bringing me." As Rhys had been cornered by the earnest accountant she had been talking to earlier, Diana went to the ladies room, where she tidied a hairdo that didn't need tidying and carefully retouched her lipstick. Her face was very pale, her eyes feverishly bright; she was rather wishing she hadn't drunk quite so much champagne.

As she went back into the reception area Rhys detached himself from the last group of stragglers and came over to her. "Do you have a coat?"

"No."

"Let's go then."

Unable to think of a thing to say she followed him through the far door and down a series of corridors to a back entranceway. A green sports car was parked outside. Diana was not mechanically minded and could not have given the car a name, but she did know it looked expensive and well-bred, with a subtle intimation of power under its sleek exterior. Rhys opened the door on the passenger side, waited as she settled her long skirts and closed it, all without laying a finger on her. He got in the driver's seat and put the key in the ignition. Then he turned to face her.

Because she was endeavoring to look calm and poised, her hands were lying loosely in her lap. Moving very deliberately he picked one of them up in his own, turning it over and tracing the lines in her palm.

She could no more have stopped the sweet ache of longing that swept through her than she could have stopped breathing. She fought for control, so that outwardly the only signs of her discomposure were the leap of the pulse in her wrist and an involuntary curling of her fingers.

He said very slowly, "So you feel it, too?"

Wide-eyed, she gazed at him as she took in all the implications of what he had said. "You mean... you do?"

"I felt it the first moment I saw you across the room. But you looked so cool and virginal in your white dress, I wasn't sure you...."

Her eyes dropped to their linked hands. To her utter amazement she saw a faint tremor in his long fingers. He was as affected by her as she by him.... It seemed impossible, and once again she searched his face for clues.

He had been watching her and said softly, "Oh, yes, I want you, Diana—I want you more than I've ever wanted a woman before. I'm just a little more adept at hiding my feelings than you. You can put that down to age or experience or whatever you like." He added abruptly, "How old are you, anyway?"

It was, she knew, the moment of choice. If she told him the truth, that she was seventeen, he would immediately whisk her back to the residence and she might never see him again. She didn't think she could bear that. On the other hand, if she lied.... She didn't know what would happen if she lied, but whatever it was, she wanted it with all the rash hunger and impatience of youth. She said evenly, "I'm twenty."

"You must be in your senior year, then?"

"Will only takes on senior students," she said; until she had come along that had indeed been his rule.

"I see." With the ball of his thumb he was stroking her wrist gently and repetitively as if he wished to learn by heart the fragility of the bones, the pulsing of the blue veins beneath the softness of her skin. She knew she was lost, that her need for this man, untutored as it was, far outrode any considerations for truth. But he was speaking again. "And your lovely white dress—is its message deceptive?"

"Virginal" was the word he had used earlier. Instinctively she sensed that if he knew her to be completely without experience, he would go no farther. Her decision to gamble on this knowledge took only a flash of time. With a rather brittle smile she said, "I'm afraid it is—would you prefer it to be otherwise?"

He hesitated, his expression very serious. "Oddly enough, in one way, yes...and why that should be so, I can't explain. Were you in love with the man?"

"At the time I thought I was." She shrugged with what she hoped was an air of sophistication. "Now I'm not so sure."

He dropped her hand and shifted in his seat, gazing out of the windshield. "We have two choices, Diana. I can drive you home and we can forget this ever happened. Or I can drive you to the apartment where I'm staying and we can make love."

She blinked. "You're very...forthright."

"We both know that's what we want—don't we?"

"Yes," she whispered.

"So which is it to be?"

"You're asking me to decide?"

He banged his palm against the steering wheel. "That's not very fair of me, is it? Particularly as there are certain conditions." Again he swung around to face her. "You called me forthright a moment ago. I'm going to be just as forthright now. My career is the most important thing in the world to me right now. I want to make it to the top, Diana—and since Moscow I'm beginning to think that might even be possible. Which is simply a way of saying I want no personal commitments. I'm not about to fall in love or to marry. I'm sorry to sound so unromantic but that's the way it is, and if you do come with me, it must be without any false pretenses."

Body and mind in a turmoil, she gazed at him wordlessly. Her brain heard what he was saying, but the heavy beat of her blood cried over and over again, an exultant refrain, *he wants to make love to me, he wants to make love to me.*

"This is Tuesday. I leave for Vancouver Friday morning, and from there I go to the States. So once Friday comes, anything between us is over, Diana. Finished." He smiled crookedly. "Hopefully a lovely memory, but that's all. Do you understand what I'm saying?"

He wants to make love to me.... "Oh, yes."

His smile was less guarded now, his eyes openly caressing. "So what do we do, my beautiful Diana?"

Her lips curved in seductive response, but with a wisdom beyond her years she kept silent.

"We'd be fools to pass this up," he said more roughly. "Do you know how rarely this kind of chemistry happens between a man and a woman? A hell of a lot less often than you might think."

"Has it ever happened to you before?" It suddenly seemed important to know.

He hesitated. "No. No, I can't say it has happened quite like this before."

"Nor with me," she said with absolute truth.

The moment of decision had arrived, yet in a strange way Diana knew the decision had already been made. Even as they had been talking, the message of their bodies had been paramount. Rhys said quietly, "Whenever I'm in Montreal, a friend of mine lends me his apartment. He travels a lot—he's in California right now. Shall we go?"

She nodded, quite unable to speak, and he reached for the ignition. Then, as if he could not help himself, he leaned over to her, his hands reaching up to cup her face. Her body swayed toward him as his lips brushed hers. That single delicate movement was all it took. His arms went hard around her, straining her close. His kiss burned her mouth and the fire leaped through her body, brilliant, molten, until there was nothing in the world but a desperate need to lose herself in him, to give him everything that was hers to give, to become one with him. . . .

With infinite slowness they separated, and the mark of that kiss was to be read in each of their faces. Diana's lower lip, soft and full from the imprint of his mouth, was quivering; she could hear his harsh rapid breathing, see the raw hunger in his eyes.

He said huskily, "We'll go to the apartment. I want to undress you and learn every inch of your body and cover it with kisses. I want to see you tremble with longing...and hear you cry out with fulfillment in my arms. I want to make you mine."

That he should speak to her with such naked honesty seemed the most natural thing in the world, and any lingering doubts she might have had had been dispelled in the conflagration of that single kiss. "I want you, too, Rhys."

He pressed her shoulder quickly and started the car.

She didn't bother following their route, for their ultimate destination had little to do with districts or streets or apartment blocks. She couldn't help noticing, however, that it was a very opulent building. They drove into the underground parking lot and took an elevator to the sixteenth floor. With a key he took from his pocket, Rhys opened the door of apartment 1609, allowed her to go ahead of him and closed the door behind them.

The lighting was subdued and indirect. The floor was inlaid oak, highly polished. The single painting on the mushroom-colored walls was a Klee, and with quick interest Diana went closer to it, examining it minutely. It gave her something to do, for she and Rhys had not talked much during the drive and now a constraint seemed to have fallen between them. From a few feet away he asked formally, "Would you like a drink?"

She replied with artificial brightness, "I had rather a lot of champagne at the reception. A coffee would be nice."

He disappeared into the kitchen and she wandered into the living room, her long skirts swaying as she moved. The decor was stark and modernistic, more so than she cared for. There were a lot of mirrors and shiny black surfaces, in which the artfully arranged potted plants were reflected and re-reflected. Not a cheap decor by any means, she knew, noting with her eye for detail the suede-covered chaise longue and the impressive collection of silk-screen prints.

Rhys was taking a long time over the coffee.... In the mirrored wall across from the long bare windows that overlooked the city she saw a tall slim figure in white, head held high, body a taut line. What was she doing in this apartment, that girl in the long white dress? Why was she here?

Suddenly struck by the enormity of what she was doing, Diana stood very still. She must have been mad to have come here with Rhys Morgan. Mad, bewitched, moonstruck....

What would her parents think if they could see her now, if they knew she had come here deliberately, of her own free will, to make love to a man she had met only a couple of hours before? In her mind's eye she could see them both quite clearly: her plump, pretty mother with her sweet trusting smile and her curly blond hair that owed more to artifice than to its natural state; her father's blue eyes, baffled as they so often were when confronted with the vagaries of his only child, who had chosen to be, of all things, an artist. There was something not quite respectable about that in Roger Sutherland's eyes. Nice girls went to university and studied languages or English literature, and then got married, settled down and raised a family.

They would be appalled, both of them, Diana knew. As would Celia and Will. Will had warned her against this very thing, and rightly so.... She must have been crazy to come.

She turned around sharply and headed toward the hallway again.

"Given up on me?" Rhys said easily, coming out of the kitchen balancing two cups of coffee. "It still takes me a while to find things."

"Rhys, I—"

"Here, take this and I'll get the cream and sugar." He passed her one of the cups, and as she automatically reached out for it their fingers touched and held. Her eyes, full of conflict and uncertainty, flew up to his face. She shivered as violently as if those same fingers had stroked the whole length of her body.

"Are you all right?" he demanded.

"Yes...but I—"

Abruptly he put the two cups on the steel-edged glass table. "This is nonsense," he said roughly. "What the hell are we doing drinking coffee that neither of us really wants? We know what we want, don't we, Diana?"

She made one last valiant attempt to extricate herself, dragging her eyes away from that mesmerizing blue gaze. "I shouldn't be—"

He interrupted her, his voice gentler. "Are you afraid I'll think you cheap or wanton if you respond to me, if you show your feelings?" he said. "Is that what you're trying to say? That you shouldn't be so open? Diana, that's the way I want you to be. There's no point in our trying to hide it, is there? I want you—my God, how I want you! And you want me; don't ever be ashamed of that. Not with me." With a strange deliberation he took her chin in his palms, his long fingers lying lightly on her cheeks. "I want to make love to you, Diana," he said quietly.

Her fears and doubts vanished, and with them the bewildered reproachful faces of her parents and all of Will's admonitions. "And I want to be with you," she replied very seriously, for it was almost as though they were exchanging vows. The words that he had said earlier in the car about his departure on Friday and his lack of commitment dropped farther to the back of her mind.

Briefly his lips brushed hers, light as gossamer, and that was all it took. His arms went around her and he swung her up off her feet, carrying her across the living room to a door in the far wall, which he kicked open impatiently with his foot. All Diana was to see of their surroundings before the next morning and the arrival of daylight was another long uncurtained window through which the diffuse glow of the city lights cast soft shadows in the room. She was flung onto the softness of the bed, her skirts disarranged to reveal the slender line of ankle and calf and knee. Rhys's jacket dropped to the floor and then he lowered himself on top of her, his weight crushing her into the mattress.

For Diana the rest of the world dropped away. There was only the surface of the bed, only the searing reality of kisses that made her faint and dizzy

with longing, of hands that found her breasts under
the fabric of her gown. Only a man's hunger and her
own all-encompassing need of him. She heard him
breathing harshly in her ear and heard her own voice
gasp out his name as she felt all the throbbing demand of his masculinity. Her body arched to receive
him.

Her convulsion of pain he must have mistaken for
desire, for in rhythms as old as time she sensed his
release. Then through his shirt there was the pounding of his heart under her palm; his dark head lay on
her breast, his breath rapidly fanning the hollow in
her throat. He lay very still, and almost shyly she
cradled him in her arms, glorying in his weight, all
thought suspended in physical sensations that were
totally new to her.

It was a minute or two before he spoke. "Sorry,
darling," he murmured ruefully. "There was nothing
very subtle about that, was there? Am I too heavy for
you?"

"No," she whispered, tightening her hold a little.
"I like it."

There was a thread of laughter in his voice. "I'm
not usually so—abrupt. I kissed you that first time
and I was lost. I had to have you...."

She was trying to ignore the implications of that
little word "usually." Then he began nuzzling his lips
against her throat, and she forgot everything but
sheer pleasure. His hands circled her neck, finding
the clasp on her dress, undoing it and very slowly
edging the material away from her body. His lips
stroked the fragile line of her collarbone, buried

themselves in the hollow of her throat where the pulse was beating against her skin, found the valley between her breasts. With a boldness that sprang from sure knowledge of his desire for her, she guided him to the very tip of one breast, where her flesh hardened to his touch in a wave of unbelievable sweetness.

Her fingers began fumbling with his shirt buttons. As his lips continued their leisurely exploration of places no other man had ever seen, let alone touched, he gradually slid her dress down over her hips and divested himself of the rest of his own clothes. Finally there was nothing between them. His chest was dark with hair; she ran her fingers through it, delighting in the smooth planes of sinew and bone that lay beneath. Then he gathered her into his arms and she felt the whole length of his body against hers, the hardness of muscle, the roughness of hair against her own more subtle curves and smoothness. They began kissing, and time dissolved until for Diana there was nothing but the slow inevitable gathering of desire, of an almost unbearable tension that was at one and the same time pleasure and pain. With exquisite control, using all the gifts of his body and intellect, Rhys gave her all that he had not been able to the first time. And like a finely tuned instrument she responded to his every touch, her slender frame quivering and shuddering with all the harmony and dissonance that he evoked. It could have only one ending. The rhythms pounded through her veins, her fingernails dug into his back, leaving, she afterward discovered, tiny oval indentations in his skin. From a long way away she heard a voice that was her own cry out his name, once, twice. The fulfillment was total and absolute, both death and rebirth, an ending and a beginning. It left her limp and exhausted yet filled with a strange kind of peace that, far from severing them, bound her to him more closely than before.

Gradually her heartbeat slowed. She murmured drowsily, "That was beautiful, Rhys, more beautiful than I ever dreamed it could be. Thank you...."

"It was beautiful for me, too, Diana." He kissed her gently, without passion. "Here, let me cover you." He pulled the sheets over her, leaving one arm to lie heavily over her body. "Will you sleep now?"

"Yes...I'm sure I will." Her last thought as she sank into a deep dreamless sleep was that he must love her to have treated her with such care and consideration. With the glow that this engendered curled warmly around her heart, she fell asleep.

CHAPTER FOUR

DIANA AWOKE to a strange bedroom, a room she had never seen before. She was naked, lying in a tangle of sheets. And she was alone.

The bed was on a raised dais, a mirror at its head. The walls were black, the carpet bone white. The furniture was built-in; it looked, she thought dazedly, like ebony. A crystal statue, of a man and woman embracing, stood in an alcove; blushing, she averted her eyes, and memory returned.

Now that she was more fully awake, she noticed other things: her dress, neatly hung over a Plexiglas chair, her shoes side by side on the carpet. She had no recollection of taking them off. . . .

The doors opened and Rhys walked in, a towel wrapped around his hips, his hair damp and curly. Hurriedly she pulled the sheets up to her chin and her eyes dropped.

"Good morning, Diana," he said, amusement quirking his mouth. "The bathroom's all yours. Breakfast'll be ready in about fifteen minutes."

He sounded far removed from the passionate lover of a few hours ago. She said stiffly, "Can you lend me a dressing gown?" He had casually let the towel fall and was taking a pair of trousers out of the ebony wardrobe. She dragged her eyes away from the smooth play of muscles in his back and added even more stiffly, "Please."

He turned back to the bed, doing up the zipper on a pair of beige slacks. "I won't see anything I haven't seen before."

"Rhys!"

Relenting, he threw a dark blue robe onto the bed. "There you are. Don't take too long, okay? We've got to be out of here in three-quarters of an hour." He was buttoning up his shirt, clipping on gold cuff links.

"Why?" she asked blankly.

"Because I have four hours of practicing to get in this morning and a master class to teach this afternoon," he said briskly. "And you must have classes, don't you?"

She thought of Will's last words, "Nine o'clock sharp." "Yes...yes, I do. What's the time?"

"Seven-thirty."

He was so businesslike, so detached. She felt her heart constrict with fear. Was this his way of saying goodbye? Of saying he didn't want to see her again? Without stopping to think, for if she had she would probably never have spoken, she blurted, "Wasn't I any good? Don't you want me anymore?"

He stopped in the middle of knotting his tie. "Whatever gave you that idea?"

"You seem so...so cold and remote. I thought—"

He sat down on the edge of the bed. "Diana, there's one thing you'd better learn about me, and the sooner the better. When I've got music on my mind, you can forget about me—I'm off in another world. I'm sorry, but that's the way it is. I'm already wondering how I'm going to improve the coda of the Beethoven, so I'm not really here at all. It's got nothing to do with last night. Last night was wonderful for me. And tonight, if you want to come here again, could be even more wonderful."

"Oh. . . ." Unconsciously she expelled her pent-up breath, seizing on his last words and ignoring the warning in his first. "I'd love to be with you again tonight," she said shyly.

"Why don't I pick you up at your residence—say, seven o'clock? We'll have dinner somewhere first."

Her smile was dazzling. "Lovely! Now if you'll get out of here, I'll get up."

Although he smiled, there was still a question in his eyes. "Sometime you must tell me about this other man you were in love with. If I hadn't known better, I'd have said your experience was minimal, to say the least. And look at you now—you're behaving as if no one's ever seen you without your clothes on before."

Her fingers tensed under the sheets as she forced herself to meet his eyes guilelessly. "My experience has never included anyone like you," she said with perfect truth. "And I still feel shy in front of you—I'm not going to apologize for that. So, if I'm going to be ready in time, you'd better let me get up."

Apparently he was satisfied with her answer, for he grabbed a lightweight jacket from the wardrobe and left her alone. Hurriedly she wrapped the robe around her and went to the bathroom. Her hairdo had suffered in the night; her eyes were blue shadowed. Will would have to take only one look at her to know exactly what she had been doing.... Turning on the taps, she swathed her hair in a towel and stepped into the shower.

Three-quarters of an hour later Rhys dropped her off at the front door of her residence. He had talked very little during the drive from the apartment, nor, keeping his earlier remarks in mind, had she expected him to. Now all he said was, "Have a good day. I'll see you at seven." He leaned over and quickly kissed her cheek, an almost impersonal gesture, as if he had been married to her for years.

"All right—bye," she said, trying not to show that she minded his withdrawal. Purposely she didn't watch him drive away but ran quickly around to the side of the building, letting herself in the door with her key. She had no desire for the woman on the front desk to see her in her evening gown. Up in her room she changed into jeans and a brightly colored smock, brushing out her hair and applying rather more eye makeup than usual before leaving for Will's studio. She was ten minutes late, but she need not have worried about being interrogated about her date with Rhys. Will had just discovered that one of his paintings currently on a western Canadian tour had been vandalized and he had no time for Diana; he was already planning to fly out there to discuss the damage. Quietly she began work on the still life.

Even at seventeen Diana had the gift of complete concentration when it came to her painting; she blocked out the night's events as if they hadn't happened. The day passed quickly and it was not until she was on her way back to the residence that she allowed herself to think of Rhys. She was going to meet him again, she thought exultantly, her heart singing. And tonight they would make love once more. Her whole body tingled with delight and she was humming to herself as she hurried down the sidewalk. It seemed a perfectly natural extension of her happiness that a thought should click into her mind. As she raced up the residence steps she realized that she was in love with him. Never mind that he was ten years older and a world more experienced. No other word could explain the joy and anticipation that flooded her when she thought of him. She was in love with Rhys Morgan. And in just over an hour she would be seeing him again. She must hurry. She had a lot to do, for she wanted to look her best for him.

Their second night together was all and more than Diana could have asked for. As her companion in one of the city's finest restaurants, Rhys was relaxed, witty and intelligent. His conversation was stimulating, avoiding cliché and generalization; his interest in her was unforced, bringing out the best in her. Then, back at the apartment, as her lover he was generous and sensitive. As he had predicted, she became less shy and inhibited, delighting in pleasing him and thereby herself. That she was falling more and more deeply in love with him as the slow hours passed, she kept to herself. It was all so beautiful, so much the realization of all her fantasies, that she scarcely wanted to sleep. Every moment was to be savored.

On Thursday she completed the still life, which even to her hypercritical eye was more than satisfactory: it was good, perhaps the best piece she had done so far. It was too bad Will was away and wouldn't see it until Monday. She cleaned her brushes and left the studio, hurrying back to the residence to change. Rhys was to cook dinner for her at the apartment that night.

When she arrived there, her hair in a severe chignon, her dress—a new one she had bought that day—a provocative silk jersey with an extravagantly full skirt and a recklessly plunging neckline, he put down his wineglass quite deliberately. With a note in his voice that she had come to recognize, he said, "Well, my beautiful Diana, dinner can wait. Come with me."

Her eyes shining with happiness, she stood very still while he undressed her. When he had done so he unpinned her hair and drew it forward over her shoulders and breasts. It was very long, as pale as ripe grain, shining as if sunlight had been trapped in it. "You look about sixteen with your hair down like that," he said half-jokingly. And then for quite a while they said nothing at all, content to make love in an intuitive silence, by now knowing what pleased the other well enough that words were unnecessary.

It was only later when they were back in the kitchen, Diana in Rhys's blue robe—it smelled illusively of his skin and for that reason she loved wearing it—that they began talking again, catching up on each other's day.

"Would you mind washing the spinach and slicing the mushrooms, Diana?" Rhys asked. He never called her by anything but her full name, and she was glad of it. "Di" seemed rather juvenile to her; her father called her Di. "I had a hell of a day," he went on. "Practiced for five hours, drove over to the university for the master class and found they were expecting me to teach two rather than one."

"Don't you ever relax and do nothing?" she asked, taking a sip of the martini he had mixed for her. She had come to know him well enough to marvel at his energy.

"Once a year I go to Newfoundland. I have a summer retreat there in a little place called Woody Point." He grinned at her. "I only practice three hours a day when I'm there."

"How disgustingly lazy!"

"Does a day ever go by that you don't paint?"

"Not very often," she admitted.

"Well, then.... One thing I did do today. On the way home I dropped in to the gallery—the one you told me has three of your paintings," he said, starting to fry some bacon. "Each in its own way was a fine piece of work, I thought, although I particularly liked the one with the glasses of wine. You caught the light refracting through the liquid perfectly."

She blushed, pleased by his praise. "Today I finished the still life I've been working on all week. At the risk of sounding conceited, I feel good about it. No doubt Will will tear it to shreds—metaphorically at any rate—when he gets back."

"You do a lot of still-life painting. I'm surprised he doesn't encourage you to get outdoors more."

She was paying more attention to the mushrooms than to what she was saying. "Oh, that comes a bit later—probably not until my third year. Pass me the paring knife, would you?''

He said quietly, ''But you've just finished your third year.''

With her hand outstretched for the knife, she stared at him in consternation. To support the fact that she was supposed to be twenty, she had told him she was in her final year—*oh, damn.*

In a flash she made a decision. Because she loved him, she wanted there to be no deceit between them. And she felt secure enough in the relationship now to reveal to him her true age. After all, he had made it quite clear that he enjoyed being with her, so why should it matter to him that she was seventeen, not twenty? He didn't appear to have found her lacking, either as companion or lover....

Looking him straight in the eye, she said levelly, ''I lied to you. I've just completed my first year.''

He made the connection instantly. ''How old *are* you, Diana?''

''Seventeen.''

''I see. So that's why you wear your hair up so much—to make yourself look older. You must have laughed at me when I told you how young you look with it down.''

''No, I didn't laugh at you.'' Her eyes fell. ''I was sorry that I'd deceived you.''

''So you realized that first night that if I'd known you were only seventeen I'd have taken you straight home.'' There was repressed anger in his voice.

She said calmly, ''That's right.''

''Seventeen! Dear heavens, Diana.''

"What's the difference?" she cried, goaded into defending herself. "What does age matter anyway? You said yourself we'd be crazy to turn our backs on the kind of...of physical attraction that's between us. What does it matter if I'm seventeen or twenty or twenty-seven?"

"It may not matter to you but it matters to me—I don't make a habit of robbing the cradle. What the devil would your parents say if they found out?"

Her chin lifted defiantly. "That's why I'm living in residence and not at home—because I want to be independent and live my own life."

"And what about this other relationship you had—is that as much an untruth as your age? Was I the first one, Diana?"

Her denial was instinctive. "No. There was a student...last winter. He graduated in the spring."

Rhys suddenly reached out and gripped her wrist, his fingers like a steel manacle. "I don't know whether to believe you or not. I remember thinking more than once that there was something virginal about you, as if you'd never been with a man before, had no idea what to expect."

This was getting worse and worse. "I only slept with him two or three times."

"Two or three times. You mean you can't remember?"

"Three times. Do stop, Rhys—it's not important! Nothing to do with you and me."

"You're wrong there, my dear," he said silkily. "Because, you see, believing you to be twenty, and a sophisticated twenty at that, I assumed that you'd have taken...shall we say, precautions? Now I'm beginning to wonder.''

She could no more have stopped the flood of color in her cheeks than she could have stopped breathing. ''Of course that's looked after,'' she lied. ''I'm not that naive.''

''I hope you're right. I may not have many principles, but one of them does happen to be an aversion to leaving illegitimate children behind me. I have too much respect for life to do that.''

''Well, in my case you don't have to worry,'' she said, adding waspishly, ''although I can't speak for the rest of your women.''

Some of the anger faded from his eyes, to be replaced by faint amusement. ''Jealous, eh?''

She had done enough lying for one evening, she decided in self-disgust. ''Yes,'' she answered simply.

He nodded slowly. ''Strangely enough, I find myself disliking the idea of this student friend of yours—even if it was only two or three times.''

She risked pulling a rude face at him, and he laughed, tweaking a long strand of her hair. ''Get on with the salad, woman, or it'll be midnight before we eat. I've got to get up early tomorrow. My flight leaves at some ungodly hour like six A.M.''

She stared at him aghast, for his casual words had introduced a reality that, consciously or unconsciously, she had been striving to ignore. ''You mean you're still going?'' she stammered.

He was turning the bacon, his back to her. ''Of course,'' he said with faint impatience. ''I'm on tour, remember? I have a concert on Saturday night in Vancouver.''

Without thinking she whispered, "Take me with you."

He turned to face her, a faint frown on his face. "What did you say?"

"Take me with you, Rhys."

Her hands were stretched in front of her in a gesture of pleading. He took them in his own, gently chafing them. "I can't do that, Diana. You know it as well as I do."

"Why not?"

"A hundred reasons." He smiled at her, although his blue eyes were watchful. "Come on, let's finish with dinner and then we'll go out for a walk."

Her mouth was dry and her heart was pounding as if she'd been running. Forgetting all her pride and her carefully cherished independence she repeated, "Please, Rhys—let me come with you. I won't be a nuisance. I'll stay out of the way when you're busy. But don't leave me here without you."

"Diana, it's impossible—it can't be done."

"You don't want me."

He sighed. "It's not that. There are just too many other factors involved."

"Tell me what they are," she said evenly, reaching over and turning off the element under the bacon.

"You're really serious about this, aren't you?"

With all the passionate intensity of seventeen, she said, "I've never been more serious about anything in my life."

"For a start, you're eleven years younger than I am." When she started to say something, he added, his face softened by an emotion that could have been compassion, "Don't interrupt, Diana, let me finish.

Secondly, there's my career. The first night we met I told you that it was the most important thing in the world to me. That hasn't changed. I want to make it to the top, which means that for me right now marriage or any other kind of commitment isn't on the books. I don't have the time or the energy, and the kind of life-style I lead wouldn't be fair to any woman. We'd end up in the divorce courts in no time, and I'm old-fashioned enough not to want that.

"And lastly, Diana, there's your career." His face sober, he rested his hands on her shoulders; they felt very heavy. "You're going to make it to the top, too— I feel that in my bones. You're extraordinarily talented. But you're also very young, which means you have years of study and work and travel ahead of you to develop that talent. It would be as wrong for you to commit yourself to another person now as it would be for me. Can't you see that? The timing's all wrong, Diana, for anything other than what we've had."

She felt very cold. His arguments, all so logical, all so undoubtedly right, had fallen on her like blows. She said the only thing left to her. "But I love you."

He winced, his eyes closing briefly. "Oh, God, Diana—I warned you against that, remember?"

"How can you warn someone against falling in love?"

"I suppose you can't...."

"Please don't leave me, Rhys—I need you."

"You only think you do, Diana. You're too young to know the difference."

"Don't patronize me!"

Patiently he tried a new tack. "Look, let's make a

deal. I said the timing was wrong, didn't I? Let's give ourselves some time—ten years, say.'' He ran his fingers lightly down her cheek, apparently not noticing that for the first time she flinched away from his touch. ''If in ten years' time you think you want to see me again, you can always get in touch with me through my lawyers, Moncton & Gillespie, here in Montreal. It's Martin Gillespie I usually deal with. But not before ten years, Diana—remember that.''

Ten years... it sounded like forever. ''What you're really saying is that you want me out of your life,'' she flailed. ''But you don't have the courage to say it outright, so you're offering me some kind of a palliative. Ten years! Why not make it twenty? Or never?''

Distraught as she was, she could still see the effort he was exerting to control a growing anger. ''You'll be surprised how fast ten years can pass, particularly when you're involved in something as demanding as music or painting. I said ten years and I mean ten, Diana.''

She made one last attempt. ''Rhys, I love you— you can't just leave me!''

''You're in love with love,'' he said, intentionally brutal.

She drew back, her face agonized. Then suddenly she whirled and ran for the bedroom, Rhys following hard on her heels. Forgetful of modesty or dignity, she flung the robe on the floor and picked up her lacy underwear from the chair, aware of nothing but a frantic urge to be gone from there.

''What are you doing?'' he demanded.

Too upset to realize what a foolish question it was, she said unevenly, "I'm leaving." She fumbled with the front closure of her bra, her movements awkward and uncoordinated.

He came closer. "Here, let me do that."

She struck away his hand. "Leave me alone!"

"Diana, let's sit down and talk about this rationally. I don't want you leaving like this—"

"That's too bad!" She pulled the dress up over her hips. "I'm sorry I'm upset. I'm sorry I was stupid enough to fall in love with you. But I will not sit down and talk about it rationally." Thrusting her feet into her shoes, she added with vicious emphasis, "Nor will I get in touch with you in ten years' time. I never want to see you again, Rhys Morgan—never, do you hear me?" Frantically she looked around for her handbag.

He had picked it up from the floor and was holding it. When she made a grab for it, he seized her wrist. "Diana, please don't go until you've had a chance to cool down. This is all wrong—"

"You mean that for once things aren't going your way? That I'm letting emotion clutter up your tidy little scheme for a three-day affair? At least I'm not afraid of emotion, Rhys—I'm not afraid to say I love you."

He had released her wrist and she snatched the bag from him, avoiding his eyes as she went to pass him. But he stepped in her path, put his arms around her, and kissed her firmly on the lips. "Ten years, Diana."

She wrenched free, her breathing ragged. "No,

Rhys—never.'' Clutching her handbag, she ran for the door. This time he did not attempt to stop her.

The taxi ride back to the residence passed in a kind of dream. It was not until she was alone in her own room with the door locked that Diana gave way to the held-back tears. She threw herself facedown on the bed and sobbed her heart out, crying until there were no more tears to come, until sheer exhaustion, like an anesthetic, deadened the pain.

But not the hope.... There was a telephone by her bed and she found herself staring at it through tear-swollen eyes, willing it to ring. Surely he would reconsider? He had not been totally indifferent to her, she would swear to that; now that she looked back on the scene in the kitchen, she could see that he had been more than patient with her, a restraint that could have come only from caring and concern. *Make him change his mind,* she prayed inwardly. *Let me go with him wherever he goes....*

But the phone remained obstinately silent. She drifted in and out of a sleep haunted by nightmares, her eyes burning, her body restless. And then she woke with a jump to find that the clock by the bed-side table said quarter to seven. His plane had left at six. So he was gone....

She buried her face in the pillow. He was gone and she would never see him again.

CHAPTER FIVE

THE TELEPHONE RANG. Diana jumped, staring at it as if it were a venomous snake about to bite her. Disoriented, jerked from the past yet not fully back to the present, she had the crazy notion that when she picked up the receiver she would hear Rhys's voice.

Ridiculous. She had not heard from him in ten years and was not likely to now, particularly after Martin Gillespie's disclosures. Wherever Rhys was and whatever he was doing, he obviously wanted to be left alone. Gingerly she stretched out a hand and picked up the phone as it rang for the third time. "Hello?"

"Alan here, Diana. You sound very faraway—are you all right?"

She had been faraway, farther away than he could guess. "Yes, I'm fine."

"Just called to see how you got along this afternoon with the lawyer, before I leave for the president's reception."

Briefly she recounted what had happened. "But I think I know where he may be," she concluded. "At least, it's the only lead I have. He had a summer retreat in Newfoundland, in a place called Woody Point. If he's gone there for a rest, that would explain why he doesn't want the address given out to anyone.''

''It seems a bit of a long shot to me. You might go all the way over there for nothing.''

''That's quite possible, I suppose. But it's the only thing I can do, Alan. I think you're right, you know—I do need to see him one more time. If he's not in Newfoundland... well, at least I've tried.''

''I see.... When are you thinking of going?''

''As soon as I can—it's a good opportunity with Belinda away. In fact, I think I'll call the airlines right now.'' There was silence on the line. ''Alan, are you still there?''

''Yes,'' he replied hastily. ''Sorry, hon. I guess now that you've come to the point of actually making arrangements, I'm wondering if I was crazy to have suggested the idea. I don't want to lose you, Di.''

''Alan, you won't, I swear you won't!'' Her voice was filled with conviction. ''If anything, this will be the means of our truly finding each other. I'm sure of it.''

''I hope you're right.''

''I am.'' She laughed with intentional lightness. ''Don't be such a worrier!''

''Okay, I'll try not to be. You'll let me know your plans tomorrow?''

''Of course I will. I'll see you then.''

They exchanged goodbyes. Briskly, not letting herself dwell on Alan's doubts, Diana took an atlas from the bookshelves, discovering that Woody Point was on the west coast of Newfoundland and that the nearest airport was Deer Lake.

She phoned the airlines and booked a seat on 'the first flight to Halifax the following Saturday, with a connection to Deer Lake. Then she phoned what was, she discovered from the telephone operator, one of the few guest houses in the village and reserved a room for two nights—that would be long enough, she decided. And finally she made arrangements to rent a car in Deer Lake.

All this activity banished her mood of nostalgia. She was a very different person than she had been ten years ago, she thought grimly, and a lot of that change was directly attributable to the relationship she had had with Rhys. She was no longer a romantic and idealistic seventeen-year-old. She was a woman successful in her own field—practical, levelheaded and in control of her life. And if indeed she was to meet Rhys Morgan, she would do it not as a young girl bowled over by his reputation and charisma but as an equal.

A fine resolve, and one she was still carrying in the forefront of her mind on Saturday as she drove to Woody Point in the small blue Pontiac she had rented. From the crowds and confusion of Montreal's Dorval Airport, with its ever present scream of jets, she had landed in Deer Lake with its little cluster of buildings, its few private planes lined up on the tarmac, its single ticket counter and hand-lettered board of arrivals and departures. She had picked up her car, found a tourist bureau and obtained a map and was now within a few miles of the village where she might or might not find Rhys Morgan.

At first she had found the scenery disappointing—

scrub forest on low-lying hills. But then on her left she had passed the vast lake called, according to the map, Big Bonne Bay Pond—she was to discover that a pond in Newfoundland could be ten miles long and half as wide. And on her right the hills had grown more and more spectacular. She had turned left at Wiltondale, entering Gros Morne National Park. Now on her right were the sparkling tidal waters of an arm of Bonne Bay, with the road curving along the shoreline.

The scattered communities she passed were small, not overly prosperous, and Diana found herself wondering what it would be like here in winter... surely an almost total isolation from the outside world? After she passed Birchy Head and Shoal Brook, she saw the village of Woody Point spread in front of her. At the crest of the hill she pulled over to the side of the road and got out.

It was late afternoon, warm and sunny with a light breeze coming off the water. Rounded white clouds flecked the sky to the north, casting shadows on the high wooded hills that entirely surrounded the bay, their cliffs plunging into the water's depths. Farther west she saw the bare slopes and vast plateau of Gros Morne Mountain, so distinctive in size and shape that she had no trouble recognizing it from her perusal of the tourist literature she had picked up. On the far shore was the little settlement of Norris Point, linked to Woody Point by a white-painted car ferry that was now chugging its way across the bay. And lastly there was Woody Point itself, a cluster of brightly painted houses on the lower slopes of the mountain, with a lighthouse, and fishing boats moored along the shore. The whole scene was punctuated by stands of poplar trees that stood like sentinels, guarding a place too peaceful to need them.

Peaceful it was, quiet and remote, a world as different from the one Diana had left that morning as could be. A car drove by her, and as the sound of its engine diminished she could hear only the wind sighing in the trees, the distant drone of the ferry engine, children's voices drifting up from the beach. A gull flew overhead, the rhythm of its wings coming to her distinctly with a beauty all its own.

Quite suddenly she was glad to be where she was, filled with an anticipation for she knew not what. The object of her search, to find Rhys, dropped into the background; she felt a childish urge to run headlong down the hill and join the boys on the beach who were throwing rocks in the water. Smiling to herself, she got back in the car. Perhaps she'd stay longer than two nights, she thought. After all, she had her painting gear with her and this looked like an eminently paintable area. She'd have a busman's holiday. No cares, no responsibilities, only herself to look after.

The guest house was on one of the narrow paved streets that ran more or less parallel to the shoreline and was painted a somewhat startling ultramarine blue with white trim. It was flat roofed, set in a primly arranged garden with cherry trees, a wooden swing and a hedge of tall delphiniums whose blue clashed with the house. Carrying her suitcase, Diana walked up the shale path, which was bordered with rounded beach stones painted alternately white and blue. The whole place seemed to echo her earlier mood of childish gaiety. It was also, she noted gratefully, very clean.

The landlady, Mrs. Bairns—"Call me Stella, dear"—was an American. "I came up here from Philadelphia ten years ago, dear, and I've never spent a summer anywhere else. I winter in Florida, of course. Just sign here. So you're an artist, are you? That must be nice."

Diana grinned to herself. Her fame, such as it was, had obviously not reached Woody Point. "Yes. In fact, I'm already so impressed with the scenery here I'm wondering if I might stay longer than the weekend?"

"No problem. Let me show you your room. Dinner's at six."

The room was at the front of the house and overlooked the bay. It had frilly net curtains, white lace doilies on every possible surface and a hand-crocheted bedspread in shades of violet and green—as fresh and naive as Stella herself. Diana supposed her landlady was about sixty, a widow, as it transpired, who liked to open her home to visitors in the summer, "for the company, dear." Yet in the time that Diana stayed there she never forced herself on her guest; she managed to combine tact and discretion and even a streak of genuine business sense with an equally genuine kindness. She was short and firmly corseted, given to wearing brightly colored cotton dresses that did not always coexist comfortably with her blue-rinsed hair.

Now, having shown her new boarder the bathroom across the hall, Stella left her alone. Diana unpacked and went down for dinner: delicious broiled halibut steaks with fresh vegetables from the garden, followed by lemon meringue pie. As she sipped her coffee, Diana realized she should ask her landlady about Rhys; if anyone would know his whereabouts, Stella would. Yet something held her back. A reluctance to reveal the real purpose of her visit? More likely, a reluctance to discover that perhaps her trip had been in vain?

After dinner, with no set plan in mind, Diana went out for a walk. She went down the hill to the shore, inspecting the shops, the tiny post office, the ferry wharf. There was a public telephone in a little booth by the side of the road, and suddenly wanting very much to hear her daughter's voice, Diana checked her watch. Just gone seven; Belinda should be at the residence. Impulsively she dialed the operator.

The call went through with no trouble, and across the miles Belinda's clear treble piped, "Hello?"

"Hi, darling! Mom here. How are you?"

"Fine! We had barbecued chicken for supper and all the ice cream we could eat—I had four helpings."

"Only four?"

"I was full." Belinda sounded faintly surprised.

Suppressing laughter, Diana asked, "And what about the music?"

"Oh, that's going fine, too," Belinda said unconcernedly. "I'm learning a lot. My roommate's name is Jennifer. She's really nice."

She chattered on, responding to the occasional

question, until finally Diana said, "I've got to go, love—this is costing me a fortune. I'll call you again in a couple of days. Glad you're enjoying yourself."

"Okay, mom. Bye."

Diana replaced the phone, pleased that she had followed her impulse. No worries about Belinda pining away without her, she thought wryly. The child was flourishing in her absence, and a good thing, too. Belinda came by her self-reliance honestly enough, of course; her father was the most self-reliant of men.

Which brought her back to Rhys, who at this very moment might be within a mile or two of where she was standing. The smile slowly fading from her face, Diana began to walk along a narrow dirt road that led past some fishing shacks, following it until she came to a rocky beach, where dried seaweed lay in pungent-smelling heaps at the tidemark. A fishing boat was offshore, its motor a low guttural growl, its two occupants, both in yellow oilskins, working their way along a fishnet anchored with bright orange buoys. Puzzled, Diana watched them. They were hauling the net out of the water, striking it rhythmically with sticks, then letting it fall back before pulling up the next section. She itched for a sketch pad to catch the stoop of their figures and the long sweep of the net, wanting to transfer to paper what her intuition told her must be back-breaking labor.

Eventually she walked back past the fish shacks. A fisherman was just leaving his boat and he smiled at her, gap toothed. Impulsively she described what she had just seen and asked the reason for it.

"It be a salmon net, maid," he replied, his accent so thick she had trouble understanding him. "The runoff makes it dirty, like, and they be beatin' it clean." He was obviously quite prepared to stand and talk to her, so she asked more questions and learned about the drastic reduction in the amounts and kinds of fish caught, about the capelin run in the spring and the squid jigging by lantern at night. His speech was interspersed with "maids" and "my dears"; his manner was so leisurely, the twinkle in his eye so inoffensive that she was disarmed and finally got up the courage to say, "I've heard that there's a famous pianist who sometimes lives here at Woody Point. Do you know if he's here now?"

"I do believe so. The missus'd know more about that, now. But that's 'is place up there on the 'ill, maid. Don't know but what that's 'is car right now."

She followed his pointing finger with her eyes. High on the hill, above all the other houses and distanced from them, was a long low cedar bungalow. A white car had just driven up the track toward it. The car stopped and someone, a man, got out. Even as she watched, he came around the hood of the car and gazed out over the bay.

From that distance she could scarcely distinguish his features; besides, it looked as though he was wearing dark glasses. But she did not need to see his face to know him. She could see the crop of dark hair and the long rangy body—that body that she had known so intimately so long ago—and she could have picked him out of a crowd anywhere. Rhys...after all these years, it was Rhys.

"Might be 'im. Then again, might not. They comes and they goes, the summer people." Philosophically the fisherman wadded some strong-smelling tobacco into his pipe.

Rhys had disappeared from sight now. She said weakly, "It looked like him. I'd better go now—I enjoyed talking to you. Goodbye."

She walked back the way she had come, scolding herself for allowing the mere sight of Rhys to affect her. For affect her it had, no question of that. The only question, she thought dryly, skirting between two houses to get back on the paved road, was what she was going to do about it.

Somehow, back in Montreal, she had thought no further than arriving in Woody Point and finding out if Rhys was there. Now she knew he was. So what next? Did she walk calmly up to his front door and say, "Hello, Rhys. Long time no see"? Did she wait until she bumped into him accidentally in the village, which in a place of this size was bound to happen sooner or later? Or did she simply turn around and go home now that she knew he was alive and well?

The sun had sunk behind the hills, leaving sky and water tinged a lurid orange. If she painted it like that, she thought whimsically, how vulgar it would look. But that had absolutely nothing to do with her dilemma. Dropping into the one-room library, which was still open, she browsed for a while, then bought herself an ice cream at the restaurant nearby. She was tired now and, without actually having thought it out, knew she would go back to Stella's, go to bed and in the morning make a decision.

She did not sleep well. It was strange to know that Rhys was so near to her physically—less than half a mile away—yet so far from her in any other way. At some point in the night it occurred to her that he might be at the end of his stay, might be gone in the morning. The panic that the thought produced gave her the answer she had been looking for: she had to go and see him. Having arrived at that conclusion, she was able to sleep.

In the morning it was merely a question of mechanics, of how best to do it. Should she telephone first and announce her arrival, or should she simply arrive? Somehow the prospect of hearing his voice on the phone terrified her. If the meeting was to take place, it must at least be face-to-face. So she dressed with care, leaving her hair loose around her shoulders and choosing a pair of slim white trousers with a tunic-style blouse, navy blue cotton lavishly embroidered in white. A simple outfit yet undeniably elegant, it gave her courage. After putting on navy thonged sandals, she knew she was ready, as ready as she'd ever be. She looked at herself gravely in the mirror, wondering what changes he would find in her.

It was another beautiful day, cloudless, in fact, with the leaves hanging still on the trees, their shadows sharp edged on the ground. Diana began walking in the direction of Rhys's house, climbing steadily but stopping every now and then to get her breath or to engage in conversation with a man building a porch onto his house or a housewife hanging out the wash. Delaying tactics, maybe, but pleasant ones nonetheless.

Finally, however, she could delay no longer, for she had come to a long graveled driveway that led to the cedar bungalow. She began to walk along it, her footsteps sounding very loud; almost as loud as her heartbeat, she thought ruefully. She rounded a curve, and there parked in front of the bungalow was the white car—a Jaguar, she noticed. Rhys could well afford it, she was sure. In the ten years since she had met him, he had indeed made it to the top. Much as she had tried to avoid any notice of him, she had not always been able to; in newspapers and magazines, on radio and later television she had heard of his meteoric rise to international acclaim and then, possibly more difficult, his maintenance of that position.

She had reached the front door. Although the lawn was neatly mowed, there was little attempt at a formal garden. She found the boulders and casually placed shrubs more in keeping with the surroundings than flower beds would have been, anyway. Taking a deep breath, she raised her hand and pressed the door bell. From inside came the double note of chimes and then a woman's voice calling, "I'll get it, Rhys."

So Diana was at least partially prepared when the door swung open. The woman was young, five years younger than herself, Diana guessed, and very beautiful. Her hair was blond, too, but fine and straight, falling nearly to her waist. She was petite, thin rather than slim, attractively dressed in a flowered sun dress, with an intricately designed gold ring on the hand that rested on the door frame. Her eyes were blue, but something about them bothered Diana. There was a vagueness in them underlying the surface politeness, something unfocused, even a touch distrait. Her voice, however, was pleasantly light, high-pitched. "Yes? May I help you?"

The world had rocked under Diana's feet. But the past few years had brought her more than one reversal and she had acquired a poise and self-control that often stood her in good stead. She said calmly, "I wonder if I might see Mr. Morgan for a few minutes, please?" Purposely she did not give her name—she wanted to be able to watch his face when he saw her for the first time.

"Just a moment, please. Do come in and I'll close the door, otherwise the flies get in." The woman disappeared down a hallway to the left as Diana deliberately moved into the patch of shadow by the door.

So Rhys was married. Fairly recently or surely she would have heard of it—although she and Belinda had spent a month in France in the late spring, and it could have happened then. One thing it did account for—his longing for privacy. Who could blame him with such a beautiful young wife?

The girl drifted back into the hall, looking disproportionately distressed. "He was here a minute ago. I don't know where he—oh, there you are, Rhys." To Diana her relief seemed equally disproportionate.

Rhys had emerged from the back of the house and didn't see Diana. His whole attention was on the younger woman. Putting a hand on her shoulder he said gently, "I was down in the basement. Is something wrong?"

She smiled up at him with something so utterly

trusting in her expression that Diana felt a lump in her throat. "No...no, nothing's wrong. But there's someone here to see you."

"Who?" The voice lost all its tenderness, was suddenly sharp.

"I don't know." She passed a hand across her forehead. "I'm sorry, Rhys. I didn't think to ask."

Again that concern in his manner. "It's okay. I'll look after it. Maybe you should go and rest for a while. You know you didn't sleep well last night."

"All right, I will," was her submissive reply. "Wake me for lunch, though, will you?" She went back down the hallway and Rhys turned to face the door, his first long-legged stride forward suggestive of an intense impatience with whoever the visitor might be.

Diana stepped out of the shadows and said composedly, "Hello, Rhys."

He stopped dead in his tracks. His face was very tanned, but even so she could see every trace of natural color leave his skin. He said, more to himself than to her, "Diana?"

She said nothing, for indeed she could think of nothing to say. Earlier she had wondered if he would find her changed. Now she was seeing changes in him. Some things were the same: his height, his lean muscular build, all too evident in the casual jeans and white T-shirt he was wearing. His hair was as thick and silky as it had ever been, but there were flecks of gray in it, and there were new lines in his face, scoring it from cheek to chin, radiating from the corners of his eyes. But that wasn't all. As he pulled himself together and began to walk toward her again, she saw a new ruthlessness in the line of his mouth, a grimness in his expression that surely had not been there ten years ago. Or was it directed toward her? Certainly it had not been evident when he had spoken to his wife. . . .

With an attempt at levity that did not quite succeed he said, "Well, you're a ghost from the past."

"No ghost," she responded just as lightly. "Very much alive. How are you, Rhys?" Briefly she considered holding out her hand, but she suppressed the urge. It seemed a ridiculous gesture for someone with whom she had once shared far greater intimacies, and besides, she was not at all sure she wanted to touch him.

He hesitated fractionally, the blue eyes as piercing as she remembered them. He said guardedly, "I'm well, thank you. And you?"

They were talking like actors in a bad play, she thought wildly. "Fine," she said with false brightness. There was a silence, actually only a few moments long, although to Diana it felt like forever. It became obvious that he had no intention of asking her to sit down and have a cup of coffee or a drink. She said untruthfully—anything to break the silence—"I was in the area and heard you were here, so I thought I'd just drop by and say hello."

It was as if the words were being dragged out of him. "It's been a long time."

"Yes."

Between them, for a brief moment openly acknowledged, lay all that had gone before. Then in what had to be a deliberate reversion to the trivial, Rhys said, "Are you doing any painting here?"

"I plan to. The scenery is marvelous."

"An artist's paradise," he said dryly. "You've done very well, Diana. I read the article about your work in *Arts Canada*, and I saw last year's show when it was in Calgary. I'm sure your reputation will grow in the future."

"Thank you. You've done even better, Rhys—you made it to the top. Besides which, I gather congratulations are in order."

She could hear his harsh, indrawn breath. "Your choice of words is hardly felicitous."

"What do you mean?" she faltered, completely taken aback. "Marriage surely can't be that bad?"

"Marriage!"

"Well, yes—that was your wife who came to the door, wasn't it? She's very lovely, Rhys." What on earth was wrong with him? He looked as if she'd taken a brick and hit him over the head.

"Kate..." he said dazedly, rubbing his forehead with his fingers. "Yes, of course. I'm sorry, Diana— I guess seeing you after all these years has been a bit of a shock. What about yourself? Are you married?"

"No, I've never married," she said evenly, for it did not seem the appropriate time to talk about Alan.

"The men in Montreal must be blind. That is, if you're still living in Montreal."

"Yes, I am."

The words were all very correct. Why then did she have this feeling that he was willing her to leave? Did he not want his wife to know who she was? Or was she simply an embarrassment to him, a reminder of an episode he would prefer to forget? A ghost from the past, as he had said—dead but inconveniently not buried.

Drawing on a social poise that, while it might be insincere was nevertheless useful, she said, "I must be going. I'm glad to have seen you again, Rhys, and to have found you well and happy. I hope your career will continue to progress. Do you plan to go on tour again fairly soon?"

"I'm. . . taking a short rest."

"I see. Well, goodbye, Rhys."

"Goodbye, Diana." No words of regret that their visit had been so short, no invitation to come back.

She turned and opened the door, looking back over her shoulder to give him a last quick smile. But it faded instantly, for his face was tight lipped, grim—he couldn't wait for her to be gone. Then there was gravel beneath her feet again, and behind her the front door closed.

CHAPTER SIX

IN CASE RHYS WAS WATCHING, Diana walked briskly down the driveway until its curve and the slope of the hill hid her from sight of the bungalow. Only then did her footsteps flag. On impulse, instead of going back the way she had come, she headed straight for the rocky beach where she had watched the fishermen the evening before. She slipped off her sandals when she reached the rocks, glad to find the beach deserted. Walking a distance along it, she sat down on a big boulder, checking first to make sure she was out of sight of the bungalow high on the hill. In front of her the waves slapped on the stones, the seaweed surging back and forth, back and forth. Idly she watched it, allowing herself to consider all the implications of that devastatingly brief meeting, a meeting for which she had traveled hundreds of miles.

Her initial reaction was of pure anticlimax. She had traveled a long way to see Rhys again, in more ways than one, and what had it meant? Nothing. There had been no true meeting at all. No warmth, no sense of welcome, no desire on his part to know more of her life in the years that had gone by. Beforehand she had rehearsed what she would say should the subject come anywhere near the possibility of Belinda's existence—how foolish she had been! Rhys could not have been less interested. . . .

She rested her chin on her palm, gazing out over the placid waters of the bay, the heat of the sun burning through her blouse as she grappled to understand what had—or rather had not—transpired. He had changed, she thought, a faint frown on her forehead. Certainly ten years ago he had been ruthless about his career—that, after all, was why he had sent her away. But he had not been ruthless in other ways. Far from it. He had given her warmth and laughter and joy, so much so that, unable to resist him, she had fallen in love with him. Where had all that gone? When had he retreated into the guarded silences, the total disinterest that had characterized him today? Perhaps, she thought wryly, that was the price of success. If so, she had better beware.

Then there was his marriage to the beautiful Kate. Something was wrong there, off-key, though she couldn't have said what. Had Kate been ill? Did that account for her being slightly off balance, for her thinness and the exquisite pallor of her skin? If so, perhaps it was worry that had carved those new lines in Rhys's face. . . .

Further speculation seemed useless, for it was obvious she would never know the answers. Which brought her back to herself and her own feelings. Anticlimax. . . yes, she had felt that. But now that she was away from Rhys and the dreaded meeting was over, she was becoming conscious of a new feeling— freedom. She was free of him, she thought with incredulity. The Rhys she had known and loved no longer existed; a cold-faced stranger had taken his place. That he was also married was undoubtedly a factor, but it was not the prime one. She had been in love with a dream, with a man who no longer existed—and now she was free of him, able to throw away the chains that had bound her to the past.

Alan had been right. This meeting with Rhys had been the best thing in the world for her. With a faint incredulous smile on her lips she got to her feet. She must phone Alan right away and tell him.

Glancing at her watch, she saw it was eleven-thirty. Ten o'clock in Montreal, then. With a bit of luck she'd catch him in his office. Reluctant to make the call from Stella's, she went to the same pay phone she had used to call Belinda. The connection was made and she heard his familiar and very dear voice. "Ingram speaking."

"Alan, it's Diana. How are you?"

"Ten times better for hearing your voice! And you?"

"Fine." Smiling to herself, wishing she could see his face, she said, "Alan, do you still want to marry me?"

His laughter was reassuringly normal. "Sure do! Are you thinking of accepting?"

"Sure am!"

"That makes me very happy, Diana. I hope I'll be able to make you as happy." He paused. "You must have seen your friend. How did it go?"

"He was like a different person, Alan. Not the man I knew at all. Besides which, he's married."

"How do you feel about that?"

"I don't seem to feel anything very much," she said honestly. "It's very peculiar."

"I'll refrain from saying I told you so."

"You just did," she chuckled. "Alan, this is a beautiful place. I think now that I'm here I'll stay around for three or four days and do some painting. I'd like to explore more of the park, too. You can't join me, I suppose?"

"I really can't, Di. We've got assorted visitors here all week and I have to be on deck. It's too bad. But give me a call when you make your return reservation and I'll meet you at the airport. I want to get that engagement ring on your finger!"

It was so like Alan to let her know that he wanted to see her yet at the same time allow her to make her own decision about her return. In a rush of gratitude she said, "I love you, Alan. And I look forward to seeing you."

"I love you, too. Take care of yourself."

"I will. Bye." She replaced the receiver, a smile still on her face. Dear Alan. . . . Giving herself a little shake, she looked at her watch again. It was lunchtime, so she'd better get back to Stella's. Right after lunch she'd gather up her painting gear and take off.

Despite her talk of visiting the whole park, Diana got no farther than five or six miles from town those first few days. West of Woody Point, between it and the Gulf of St. Lawrence, was an area known as the tableland. She had noticed the strange-colored, flat-topped mountains on her drive to the village and had wondered at their lack of vegetation and their distinctiveness from the tree-covered hills that surrounded them. In her tourist literature she discovered that geologically these were ancient rock formations dating back hundreds of millions of years. Minerals such as iron and magnesium gave them their brown color, whereas the lack of other essential minerals inhibited plant growth.

Armed with this knowledge and her painting gear, she set out to explore. From the left-hand side of the dirt road that traversed the area the strange ocher cliffs rose to the sky; on the right was the meandering course of a river, obviously much visited by salmon fishermen. And rising above it, clad in trees and shrubs, were the weathered gray slopes of the Long Range Mountains, nearly a billion years old. A divided landscape, the road an incongruously modern note. A landscape that increasingly fascinated Diana.

For the better part of two days she hiked and sketched, clambering over the heaped-up yellow boulders, walking along the empty streambeds carved in the mountainside, listening to the roar of the waterfalls that tumbled, ice-cold, from the heights of the plateau. In these bleak and barren hills a strange sense of time began to seep into her bones; she was a mere speck of dust, transitory, already defeated by the agelessness of her surroundings. And as she painted, her series of watercolor sketches became more and more abstract, more deeply imbued with a stark recognition of the slow inexorable passage of time. The last two sketches she would keep, she knew; they were good. The rest had served their purpose as mediators between her and the landscape.

She fell into bed that night and slept deeply. When she awoke the next morning to the patter of rain against the window she turned over, feeling deliciously lazy, and went back to sleep again. It was mid-morning before she got up. After showering and washing her hair, she went downstairs to join Stella for lunch, pleased to notice that the rain seemed to have passed, a brisk wind clearing the clouds from the sky.

Stella served the meal, a seafood casserole in a creamy sauce topped with puff pastry and accompanied by a green salad, then sat down across from Diana. "You didn't tell me you were famous, Miss Sutherland," she said ingenuously.

Diana hid a smile. "Go easy on the Miss Sutherland," she said. "I much prefer Diana."

"Miss Carson at the library showed me a magazine article about you." Obviously quoting more or less verbatim, she went on, "It predicted a brilliant future for you."

Diana murmured a noncommittal reply, hoping Stella wasn't going to embarrass her, as one or two others had in the past, by asking her to paint their favorite pet or their house. But Stella had other things on her mind.

"That makes two famous people here in Woody Point," she said with naive pride. "You and the pianist."

Since it was probably all over the village that she had visited Rhys three or four days ago, Diana said resignedly, "Yes, I've met Mr. Morgan. And his wife."

"Wife? Oh, he doesn't have a wife, dear. Never married, as far as I know."

Diana stared at her blankly. "But I met her—a very attractive blond woman. Kate was her name."

Stella settled down for what was plainly to be a cozy gossip session. "That's not his wife, dear, that's his cousin. From out west somewhere—Regina, perhaps. A recent widow, I understand. All very sad."

"His cousin," Diana repeated, confounded by this piece of news. Why had Rhys allowed her to think Kate was his wife?

"That's right. A sweet little thing, although she acts a bit strange at times, you know—as if she's not quite sure where she is or what's going on. But I suppose that's understandable under the circumstances. Mind you, maybe he will marry her." Stella gave a romantic sigh. "It would be very nice for her if he did, very suitable. When you're used to being married, it's not easy being on your own."

Impulsively Diana patted Stella's hand. "I'm sure it's not." It had been devastatingly difficult for Diana to have been left on her own after three days with Rhys. How much worse if she had been married to him!

"She must be company for him. With his hand, and all. That was a terrible thing, wasn't it, dear?"

Diana carefully put down her knife and fork. "What was a terrible thing?"

Stella's eyes widened. "I thought you said you knew him. You must have heard what happened."

"No," Diana said with commendable patience.

"A car accident, last spring. Not his fault at all,

they say—I guess the other driver was drunk. Really, some of those people shouldn't be allowed on the roads, should they, dear?"

"What happened to him, Stella?"

"His left hand was injured." She paused dramatically. "He'll never be able to play again, they say. Not on the stage, anyway."

Horrified, Diana said sharply, "Is that true? Are you sure?"

"Oh, yes. It was in the papers. An 'enforced retirement,' they called it."

For Stella it was clear that the printed word was gospel truth. But Diana had no reason to disbelieve her. In fact, she thought, looking down at her plate unseeingly, her appetite quite gone, it fitted all too well. As clearly as if he was in front of her she could see Rhys's grimly lined features, his cold bleak eyes. If the career to which he had devoted most of his life was gone, finished, ended in a senseless accident, little wonder he had looked as he did. And she, blithely ignorant of what had occurred, had asked him about his next tour and had wished him well in the future. Oh, God, no wonder he couldn't wait to be rid of her!

"I'm surprised he didn't tell you, dear. As you're a friend of his." There was veiled curiosity in Stella's voice.

Once he had realized Diana did not know of his changed circumstances, the last thing he would have done was tell her. He would see that as a bid for sympathy and would despise it as such. She knew him well enough for that.

"I hadn't seen him for years," Diana murmured. Although she liked Stella, she knew the older woman's imagination was given a very free rein, and she had no desire to figure as heroine to Rhys's hero. In an effort to deflate the situation and to divert attention from the shock she had suffered, she began to eat again, chewing and swallowing with a determination to appear normal, and changed the subject to less charged topics: the weather, always safe; the ferry schedule; the duration of the lobster season.

The meal eventually ended, and Diana went up to her room to brush her teeth. This time she did not bother with makeup or changing her clothes; the jeans and cotton sweater she was wearing would do. The climb up the hill did not seem as steep today, perhaps because it was cooler, with a brisk wind blowing off the bay and whipping her thick sun-streaked hair around her head. The Jaguar was parked in front of the bungalow in the same place as before. Heading for the front door, Diana heard a voice hail her, a light high voice that she recognized immediately as Kate's.

The younger woman was sitting in a sheltered spot in the back garden near the rectangular swimming pool, and she waved to Diana to join her. "Hello," she said as Diana got close enough for conversation. "I didn't introduce myself the other day—I'm Kate Pemberton. I was asking Rhys about you after you'd gone and he told me you and he had once been friends in Montreal. Do sit down." She indicated the other chair. "You're an artist?"

Although Diana was anxious to see Rhys, there

was something vulnerable about Kate that made her unable to refuse this offer of hospitality. In the bright sunlight she could see more clearly the marks of a recent illness in Kate's face, for there were faint blue shadows under her eyes and her cheeks were unfashionably thin. She seemed to be pleased to have another woman to talk to and was surprisingly well informed about the contemporary art scene in Canada; after only a few minutes Diana felt the beginnings of a genuine liking for her.

They were discussing the current crop of coffee-table art books, including their outrageous prices, when Diana became aware that Kate was becoming uneasy, shifting in her chair and glancing over her shoulder at the sky. It was those backward glances that gave Diana a clue. For some moments she had been aware more or less subconsciously of the distant mutter of an airplane engine, and now she could see a small biplane with pontoons, the sun glinting on its wings as it came closer. Kate had given up any pretense of making normal conversation. She stood up and stared at the plane, her arms folded tightly to her breast in a gesture of defensiveness. Diana, too, got up, sensing that this was no time for politeness or prevarication. "Kate, what's wrong?" she asked bluntly.

Kate looked at her as if she'd never seen her before. Her eyes were so blank and unfocused that Diana was suddenly frightened. She touched the other woman's sleeve. "Tell me what's wrong."

Almost irritably Kate shrugged off her outstretched hand. By now the plane was almost overhead, its motor a guttural roar, and Kate's thin young face had become distorted by an inner struggle so intense that Diana was terrified for her. The wide blue eyes were agonized; one hand was pressed against her mouth and tiny whimpers were coming from her throat. Instinctively offering the only comfort she could, Diana put her arms around her and felt the tension suddenly collapse in a storm of bitter weeping as the smooth blond head was pressed into her shoulder. Then she saw Rhys running toward them from the back door and knew in a rush of relief that he would know what to do.

Swiftly he took charge. Giving Diana a quick nod of acknowledgment he detached Kate and picked her up, saying in a low voice, "I'm going to take her in— it's the plane that's upset her. Follow me."

Half-running to keep up with him, Diana held open the back door. Kate's sobs were muffled now, her face buried in Rhys's shirtfront as they went through the kitchen and down the hall. Rhys pushed open a door with his foot and carried Kate across to the bed, carefully putting her down. She clung to his hand. "Don't go away, Rhys."

"It's okay, Katie, I won't." His voice was gentle, his hands equally so as he removed her sandals and covered her with the eiderdown that was folded at the foot of the bed. "Go to sleep, now. Everything'll be all right when you wake up." He stroked her hair back from her face, and again Diana caught a glimpse of that trusting smile of Kate's.

Feeling like an interloper, very much redundant, Diana waited by the door. Rhys might not be married to Kate, but she was almost prepared to swear he loved her or at least cared for her deeply. The contrast between the way he was treating Kate today and the way he had treated herself a few days ago was ludicrous.

While Rhys sat patiently at the bedside waiting for Kate to fall asleep, Diana let her eyes wander around the room. It was a very pretty room, with blue-and-white-flecked wallpaper, filmy white curtains and a white-painted fireplace. The fabric on the canopied bed matched the wallpaper; the carpet was white. But however long Kate had been here, she had imposed nothing of herself on the room. It was abnormally tidy. There were no books or clothes lying around, no personal photographs or any other of the knickknacks that might have given a clue to Kate's personality.

Finally the girl fell asleep and Rhys stood up, withdrawing his hand. In silence Diana followed him out of the room and across the hall to the living room, a large airy room with picture windows that overlooked the bay. It, at least, looked lived in, with its laden bookshelves, its magazines and bowls of flowers, its pleasant air of untidiness. "Can I get you a drink, Diana?" Rhys asked formally.

So she was to be permitted to stay for a few minutes this time. "That would be lovely, Rhys, thank you." In deliberate challenge she smiled up at him. "I'll have my usual, please."

Something flickered in his eyes. "And if I've forgotten what that is?"

"Then I'll have to remind you, won't I? But I don't think you've forgotten."

"A very dry martini with two olives."

"Right."

"So one thing about you hasn't changed, at any rate." With casual insolence he let his eyes run over her figure, from the firm high breasts revealed in the close fitting sweater to the long slim legs in their well-cut designer jeans.

Damn him, anyway. She should have known better than to attempt to put him off balance. Fighting back a tendency to blush she said lightly, "And do you still drink Glenfiddich on the rocks?"

"Indeed I do. Is your memory as good in other areas?" Again that suggestive downward glance.

She said coldly, "Some things are best forgotten, Rhys."

"Do you think so? I might be prepared to argue that."

"Oh, do stop," she said crossly. "I didn't come here to trade innuendos with you."

"Why did you come, Diana?"

The martini was forgotten as she countered his question with one of her own. "Why didn't you tell me about the accident to your hand?"

"So you've found out," he said in a clipped voice. "I wondered if you would."

"Yes, the landlady at the guest house where I'm staying told me. I would have preferred to hear it from you."

Neither of them had sat down. Across the width of the coffee table the air between them sang with tension.

"Once I realized you didn't know, I couldn't get

you out of here fast enough. I don't want your pity, Diana—yours or anyone else's.''

"So you run away from the whole situation instead.''

"I deal with it my own way; not quite the same thing,'' he said with dangerous calm.

Fighting to keep her brain clear, she said equally calmly, ''I was not about to offer you pity. Sympathy, maybe, but not pity. They're two quite different things.''

"I don't want either one of them, Diana. I'll look after myself.''

The blue eyes were ice-cold, ice hard. Ten years ago Diana would have flung herself at them regardless. Now all she said was, ''I really would like that martini, Rhys.''

Briefly she saw he was disconcerted, thrown off balance by her prosaic request. "I'll be back in a minute. Make yourself at home.''

He left the room and she drew a couple of deep breaths, trying to relax the tension in her muscles. It seemed very important to her to break through the barriers Rhys himself had erected to find the real man within, to have him expose some of the frustration and anger he must be feeling. Yet she was not at all sure she would be able to, for he would fight her every inch of the way.

Idly she watched a couple of fishing boats round the promontory where the lighthouse stood. Behind her she heard Rhys come back in, and she said casually, "It's been a long time since I've been in a place as beautiful as this. I've spent the last two days painting in the tableland. Incredible scenery." She turned. He had a glass in each hand and she went on to say without any change of inflection, "Those scars on your hand—did they come from the accident?"

His fingers tightened around the glass and the white lines that marred the back of his hand stood out lividly against the tanned skin. "Yes," he said harshly.

When he held out the martini she took the glass, subconsciously avoiding touching him. "Can you not play at all?"

"I'll never again play for the concert stage."

"There's no hope of improvement?"

"None. No miracle cures, no marvelous operations, nothing. It's over, Diana. Finished."

"But you can still play for yourself?"

"I have no idea. I haven't tried and I'm not going to."

"But, Rhys, you can't cut yourself off from your music—it's been your whole life!"

"Then I'll have to find something different, won't I? You could say I'm one of the lucky ones—I've made enough money the last few years so that I never need to work again."

"Perhaps that's not so lucky." She hesitated. "You can't act as though your life is over, as though you'll never contribute anything more—you're not even forty."

"I'll do as I please, Diana. My musical career is over, and that's that. Now can we talk about something else?"

She was shrewd enough to know when to retreat,

even if only temporarily. "All right." She crossed her legs, taking a sip of the martini and feeling its bite. "Why did you let me go away under the impression that Kate was your wife?"

"Oh, for God's sake," he said irritably. "I suppose because I wanted rid of you."

"Why was she so upset this afternoon? You said it was something to do with the plane, didn't you?"

He took a long draft of his whiskey and put it down on the table with the air of a man who has made a decision. "Diana, I'm going to be honest with you. Kate's problem is a long story, an unhappy story—and there's no point in my telling you about it. You won't be seeing Kate again, because I don't want you coming back here. Is that clear?"

Her mouth was dry. "Why not?"

His somber blue eyes looked straight at her. "We've got nothing to give each other, you and I. The timing's as wrong now as it was ten years ago. I want you to leave here and forget you ever knew me."

"So you can stay here alone and wallow in self-pity?" she said with intentional cruelty.

His lips tightened. "So I can work out my life my own way."

She made one last attempt. "Rhys, we've not really talked about what happened ten years ago, have we? But I know one thing—lovers we were, certainly, but I also think we were friends, that we liked each other and that there was genuine caring involved. I'd like to feel I'm still your friend. You're in trouble now. You're unhappy, I know that. Please—won't you let me help? I'll do anything I can." Feeling oddly shaken, she sat back in her chair.

"Neither you nor anyone else can help this." He gestured at her with the scarred hand, the fingers clenched into a fist. "So there's only one thing you can do for me, Diana—leave here and don't come back. I don't want you back in my life. I've got nothing to give you."

Feeling as if her limbs were as brittle as glass, as if they would shatter if she moved too quickly, she stood up. "I'm beginning to wonder if you ever did," she said. "I threw myself at you ten years ago, didn't I? And now it would appear I'm doing the same thing again. Some of us are slow learners, Rhys—but I think after today I've learned my lesson. You're sufficient unto yourself. You're scared to let anyone close to you because you might have to give something of yourself, and you don't know how to do that."

He was standing still like a man in a pillory, but something drove her to finish what she was saying. "I'm sorry for you because somewhere along the way, as you made it to the top, you stopped being a man. You're an automaton, a machine. No emotions, no ordinary human needs and responses." Her breast heaving, patches of color in her cheeks, she finished, "Don't worry—I won't be back."

He, too, had stood up. "You're wrong in one thing, Diana," he rasped. "I'm a man, all right—man to your woman." With the vicious speed of a striking wildcat he seized her by the wrist. "I don't think you'll argue that."

His fingers had encircled her arm, his nails digging into her skin. Numbly she looked down at them and she was back in another time, another place, when those same lean sensitive fingers had known all her body's responses and had played upon them with devastating effect. Heat scorched her face as she snatched her wrist away. Filled with impotent fury, even her words an echo of other words, she cried, "I never want to see you again, Rhys Morgan! Go to hell your own way—see if I care." Turning on her heel, she fled to the front door, let herself out and began to run down the gravel driveway as if he was actually in pursuit.

HE WAS NOT. He had gone very slowly to the picture window and watched her until she disappeared around the curve of the driveway. His movements awkward and uncoordinated, he next picked up the two glasses, neither of which was empty, and carried them to the kitchen. Then, as if pulled by a force stronger than himself, he went down the hallway past Kate's bedroom to a room at the far end of the house, a room Diana had not seen. It gave a contradictory message of space and clutter, for while its dimensions were generous, its contents were many and varied. Books overflowed from the built-in shelves, some shoved in at angles, others in piles on the floor. A collection of framed autographed photographs took up another wall. A huge cherry-wood desk bore letters and papers in roughly sorted heaps, while more papers overflowed onto the velvet-covered chesterfield. In one corner were music stands, and a cello stood mutely, the afternoon light gleaming on its polished amber surface. But the room was dominated by the grand piano. Black and shining, its lid was closed.

He walked toward it and stood looking down at it. Raising the lid, with his right hand he struck a single note. It resounded in the room, full and pure, and then slowly died away. He struck another, and another, and each time the note was swallowed by the sunlit silence of the room.

He sank down on the stool, staring at the keyboard as if he had never seen it before. Then his fist struck a dissonant, overloud chord, a travesty of the beauty he had once been able to produce. His forehead dropped to the polished wood and his eyes closed.

CHAPTER SEVEN

DIANA'S FEET CARRIED HER not back to Stella's but rather down to the shore. Sitting on a patch of rock above the lighthouse, the grass stirring softly around her, she gazed at the far shore, her chin resting on her hands, her lips compressed. She was a fool, she thought roundly. As soon as Stella had told her about the accident she had rushed up to Rhys's without even stopping to think. And why? What had she hoped to accomplish? If she had been laboring under the delusion that Rhys needed her, she couldn't have been more mistaken. Rhys didn't need her; he didn't need anyone. Was she never going to learn that?

As a flock of sandpipers skimmed over the surface of the water, her eyes followed them. It was time she went home, she thought suddenly. Back to Montreal, where she belonged. The wild beauty of this place was not for her, any more than Rhys had ever been for her. Home...and Alan.

With a guilty start she realized this was the first time she had given a thought to Alan all day. Here among the weathered mountains and the deep cold waters of the bay he seemed very far away, remote in more than the physical sense of the miles that lay between them. Three days ago, after her first meeting with Rhys, she had felt herself freed of the burden of the past and of her long-ago affair. Now she was wondering if that sense of freedom had not been an illusion, for today she had flown back to Rhys instinctively, without thought. That she had once again been rejected was almost immaterial. It was her own actions that in retrospect frightened her....

Yes, she thought fiercely, she must go home. Home to Alan and to Belinda. Home to her parents and her friends and to the security and love they represented. She'd leave first thing tomorrow morning.

Somehow this resolve seemed to settle her mind. After supper she told Stella she would be leaving the next day and then went up to her room and did most of her packing. There was still an hour or two of daylight left, so she grabbed her painting gear and went down to the car. One last trip to the tableland before she left wouldn't do any harm.

But when she had parked at the side of the road and had climbed part of the way along a dried-up streambed, she was not in the mood for painting. Instead she found herself gazing up the valley at the vista of tumbled yellow rocks and scarred yellow cliffs, eroded and gouged by wind and water over countless ages of time into a bleak harsh beauty that matched her mood. It was going to be difficult to forget this place.

She was disturbed from her thoughts by the sound of a voice calling her name. Startled, she looked back toward the road. A white Jaguar was parked behind her own car, and two figures were climbing up the slope toward her, a man and a woman. The woman, unmistakable because of the long blond hair blowing in the wind, was Kate. But the man was not Rhys; he was too short and stocky for that.

Uncertainly Diana waved back, not at all sure she wanted her solitude invaded, particularly by anyone connected with Rhys.

Kate was out of breath by the time she reached Diana. Gracefully she sank down on a boulder, pushing her hair behind her ears and smiling. As the man joined them she said, "Diana, this is Robert Smith. He's been with Rhys for years. Robert, Diana Sutherland."

The two shook hands, a peculiarly formal touch in such a landscape. Diana saw a sturdily built man of perhaps sixty, his hair neatly slicked down, his hazel eyes friendly in a strongly boned face. "I'm a combination of cook, manservant and general factotum for Mr. Morgan," he said easily. "Nice to meet you, Miss Sutherland."

He and Kate exchanged a look, and Kate said earnestly, "Diana, we've been trying to track you down for the last couple of hours. There aren't that many guest houses in Woody Point, so we soon found out where you're staying. The lady there said you often came here to paint. She also said you were planning to leave tomorrow morning."

"That's right," Diana said economically, wondering where all this was leading. She did not have to wait long to find out.

Kate leaned forward. "Diana, we're here to ask you a favor, Robert and I. We want you to stay for a few days longer. You see, we both think Rhys needs you—"

This had gone far enough. Incisively Diana interrupted. "Sorry, Kate, the answer's no."

"At least hear me out."

"No, Kate. I won't change my mind."

"Please—"

"Look," Diana said, not bothering to hide her impatience. "I've seen Rhys twice this week, and both times I've been shown the door. So don't talk to me about need. Rhys has done very well on his own for thirty-eight years and no doubt will do so for another thirty-eight."

Robert spoke up; he had the traces of an English accent in a surprisingly deep voice. "That's where you're wrong, Miss Sutherland." There was something in his manner that unwillingly commanded Diana's attention. "I know Mr. Morgan well—we first met nine years ago in London—and I'm desperately worried about him. For as long as I've known him he's poured himself, body and soul, into his career. Well, he's lost that now. And the upshot is that he's turned his back on music altogether—won't go near the piano, won't entertain the thought of conducting or teaching or composing, all of which he's more than capable of doing. He's cut off his own lifeblood, Miss Sutherland, and he's dying in front of our eyes."

"You're exaggerating," Diana said sharply, aware of an underlying uneasiness that he might not be.

"I wish I were."

"Then why me?" she demanded, impressed by his

sincerity despite herself. "What do you think I can do that you or Kate can't do?"

He cleared his throat delicately, looking down at his blunt fingers spread on his knee. "Well, you see, Miss Sutherland, I've known about you for some time. . . in a general way, that is. No specific details; please don't misunderstand me. Mr. Morgan has had a number of, er, relationships with women in the past. But when he goes on tour he carries the photograph of only one woman with him—and that woman happens to be you. I recognized you immediately."

Diana stared at him, her fingers clutching at the rough edges of the rock she was sitting on as if the world was shaking under her. "That can't be true," she whispered.

"I pack his suitcases and look after his hotel room. It's true."

Wanting to look anywhere but into those shrewd hazel eyes, she blurted, "I don't know why he does that, Robert, but I can assure you I mean nothing to him."

"I don't know why he does it, either, but it's the reason that I'm here. I can't get anywhere with him, nor can Kate. We're gambling on the chance that you can."

"He won't let me in the door again—I know he won't."

"That's where I come in," Kate piped up. "If I say I want you to visit, he'll let you in." Briefly her eyes clouded. "I've been ill, you see. So he gives me a lot of leeway."

"This is crazy!" Diana burst out. "What do you expect me to *do*?"

"If we knew, we probably wouldn't be here," Robert said grimly.

With the sense that she was fighting a rearguard action, Diana added, "Anyway, I can't stay here indefinitely. I have family and a fiancé at home."

"A fiancé!" Kate echoed in dismay.

"Yes, a fiancé. So don't get any romantic ideas, Kate. Whatever was between Rhys and me is over and done with. Which makes this whole idea of yours even more ridiculous."

"At least give us a week," Kate pleaded. "Surely Rhys is worth that much to you? Seven days out of a lifetime—it's not much."

It didn't sound very much when put that way. After all, she had told Rhys earlier today that she was his friend; it now appeared her words were to be put to the test. And any lingering suspicions she had had that Kate loved Rhys or Rhys Kate, at least in any romantic sense, had somehow been dispelled during the course of this conversation.

Moodily Diana kicked at a rock, starting a miniature rock slide down the hill. As she watched the stones skitter and bounce, into her mind there came an image of Rhys's face with its new hardness and the memory of his voice, cold and controlled. Was there any possibility that Kate and Robert could be right, that she, Diana, held the key to the man hidden behind those barriers? If indeed he existed.... "I'll stay until the first of the week," she said grudgingly. "But that's all."

Kate clasped her by the hand, tears in her speedwell-blue eyes. "Thank you. I'm sure you won't regret it."

Diana was not nearly so sure. In fact, she was regretting her words already. She said dryly, "I'd better go back and tell my landlady I've changed my mind and that I'm staying after all. She'll wonder what on earth I'm playing about at."

"Oh, but you'll stay up at the house, won't you?" Kate said quickly. "It would be much better—"

"Oh, no," Diana replied grimly. "If I'm going to try my hand at this crazy venture, I'm going to need some time to myself. The last thing I want to do is stay in Rhys's house."

Kate bit her lip, daunted by the decisive bite in Diana's words. Conceding defeat, she said, "Okay, but why don't we follow you down to make sure everything's all right?"

Half an hour later Diana was to wonder if Kate had anticipated what would happen. For at Diana's request for an extension of her stay, Stella said blankly, "It's not possible, dear—I'm so sorry. Not ten minutes after you left I had a call from a couple who've just arrived in Deer Lake, and they've booked your room for the next four nights."

"Then you'll have to stay with us," Kate offered quickly.

"Aren't there other guest houses?" Diana said to Stella.

"Booked up solid for the next two weeks," the older woman replied with a kind of gloomy relish.

Cursing herself for getting into this mess, Diana

said, not very graciously, "Then I guess I will have to accept your invitation, Kate."

The girl smiled guilelessly. "Good! We'll come and get you tomorrow morning." She sketched a wave in the air. "Bye for now. And thanks."

Diana knew there was one other thing she had to do that evening: phone Alan. She owed him the truth about what was happening. Consequently, after getting a sweater from her room, she walked down to the phone booth, charging the call to her home number. His voice when it came over the line was relaxed and warm. "Hello?"

"Alan? It's Diana."

He was delighted to hear from her, and they chatted for a couple of minutes before Diana said abruptly, "Alan, I have to tell you what's happening." She took a deep breath. "Which means I have to tell you the name of Belinda's father, because it concerns him."

"Oh?" His voice was more guarded now.

"Yes. You've heard of Rhys Morgan, haven't you?"

"Good God! The pianist?"

"That's right. He's her father."

"You're moving in high circles, my girl."

"I suppose so. The thing is, he won't be performing anymore. . . ." Briefly she described the events of the past few days, including Kate's and Robert's pleas and her own reluctant acquiescence.

"You mean you said you'd do it?"

"Yes."

"Diana, I think you're getting in out of your

depth. With all due respect to you, it sounds to me as though the man needs professional help. Being your brother's keeper is all very well, but there are times it can do more harm than good—and this sounds like one of them to me.''

She had grown so accustomed to Alan's giving her free rein that his opposition threw her off balance, even more so when he added, ''I think you should come home now, before you get any more deeply embroiled.''

''But I promised Kate—''

''That's another thing; what do you really know about her? It sounds to me as though she has problems of her own.''

He was putting his finger on doubts she herself had had. *Oh, damn....* She said briskly, ''Three or four days won't make much difference one way or another, Alan. Rightly or wrongly, I did promise Kate and I feel I should carry through on that. But I'll be in Montreal by the first of the week—and that's a promise, as well.''

''I see.'' A slight pause, during which she had time to wish she could see his face. ''Probably some of this is nothing more than pure old-fashioned jealousy,'' he said finally. ''I don't like your being around that guy. I don't care how miserable he is.''

''Alan, truly you don't have to worry on that score,'' she said as forcefully as she could.

''Yeah, I know,'' he said heavily. ''Sorry about this, Di. If I wasn't so tied up at work I'd come over and keep you company, but it's impossible right now. Listen, your mother told me a letter came from Belinda. Do you want me to send it on to you?''

''No, I don't think you'd better do that,'' she said hastily, wanting no traces of Belinda in Woody Point. ''I'll give mom a call and get her to read it to me. I'll be back soon, anyway.''

They talked a little longer, each carefully avoiding the subject of Rhys, before saying goodbye. As Diana walked back up the hill to Stella's, she vowed to herself that if she made any kind of a breakthrough with Rhys before Sunday, she would leave. She owed far more to Alan than she did to Rhys.

WHEN THE TAP CAME at her door the next morning around ten, Diana was dressed and ready. ''Come in, Kate!'' she called brightly.

The door swung open and Rhys entered, his big frame dwarfing the dimensions of the room and looking out of place among all the doilies and flowering plants. He pushed the door shut behind him. ''Ready?'' he said.

She stood at bay amid her suitcases and painting gear. ''I was expecting Kate.''

''Were you, now?'' he said unpleasantly. ''I decided to come instead. Come on, we're going for a drive first.''

''Why this sudden urge for my company? Yesterday you couldn't wait to be rid of me.''

''Because there are a few things we need to discuss. And your bedroom is hardly the place for that.'' Sardonically he eyed the bright coverings on the bed. ''Unless there's anything else you have in mind?''

She willed herself not to blush and bent to pick up her portfolio. As she did so he said in quite a different voice, "Have you done any painting the last couple of days?"

She nodded stiffly.

"May I see them?"

Short of being childish, she could hardly refuse. She undid the ties on the folder and in silence extracted the two watercolors, propping them up on the dresser. For what seemed like a long time he stood looking at them. Then he said, "Somehow, God knows how, you've captured the pitilessness of time. Its inexorability. Ashes to ashes and dust to dust. And on a piece of paper not two feet square." With complete sincerity he added, "They're two fine pieces, Diana."

She smiled in acknowledgment, knowing she valued his opinion. "Thank you."

"They more than justify what I did ten years ago."

Her chin snapped up. "How can you say that?"

"You'd never have made such strides saddled with a husband and family."

She had made them as a single parent, she thought wryly. But she could scarcely share that with him. "We'll never know that, will we?" she said, their brief moment of accord shattered.

As he picked up her cases, she followed him downstairs, enduring Stella's bright-eyed interest as she said goodbye. Rhys, she couldn't help noticing, was very sweet to Stella. *Widows must be a specialty of his,* she thought sourly, wondering with a cramp of apprehension what he would have to say once they were alone.

He seemed to be in no hurry. Taking the tableland turnoff he drove for several miles, through the coastal fishing village of Trout Brook and eventually pulling up by the shores of a vast lake. Its waters were whipped into wavelets by the sea winds, while overhead smoke-gray clouds scudded by. Turning off the ignition, he shifted in his seat to face her. He was wearing an open-neck shirt, its sleeves rolled up to reveal tanned forearms corded with muscle. In the close confines of the car he seemed very near; she caught a drift of his after-shave lotion and with a sudden agonizing flash of memory knew it to be the same brand he had used so long ago. "Now," he said, "whose idea was it that you visit Kate?"

"Why don't you ask her?"

"I already did; she says it was hers. But I'm not sure I believe her. Kate can be very malleable."

"Are you suggesting it was my idea?"

"The thought crossed my mind."

"Well, you can forget it! I felt sorry for Kate; that's why I accepted her invitation. And I feel even sorrier for her if you make a habit of disbelieving every word she says."

"That's a red herring, Diana, and you know it." Lazily he draped his arm across the back of her seat, leaning forward. By pure force of will she refrained from shrinking away from him. "So it was nothing to do with my *beaux yeux*."

"You flatter yourself, Rhys."

"Do I? I wonder...." His free hand reached up to

cup her chin and she could not prevent her involuntary move backward. His thumb and one finger tightened on her jaw. "Just one kiss—for old time's sake," he drawled.

She put both hands up to push against his chest. His other arm whipped down from the back of the seat and somehow he had encircled both her wrists, holding them captive. "Let go, Rhys," she choked.

"I don't think so—I haven't had an opportunity like this for a long time."

His words were veiled in mockery but there was something far more dangerous in his eyes, something cold and calculated that made her, against all odds, try to break his hold on her. "Stop it!" she seethed. "I'm not seventeen anymore. So stop treating me as if I am."

His last words were, "I don't think age has anything to do with it," before he levered her chin up and bent his head to kiss her full on the mouth.

Rigid with an emotion that was a mingling of outrage and sheer terror, she felt his lips touch hers. They were warm, very sure of themselves.... Terror conquered everything else, for they were like the first taste of water after an interminable drought, an exquisite release, a rescue from the dead weight of the years.

Blind with fear, her strength augmented, Diana jerked her wrists free and pulled away from him, drawing in her breath in a great gasp. She fumbled for the door handle, and at the same moment both of them saw that her hands were shaking uncontrollably.

He moved back in his seat. "It's all right, Diana, you don't have to run away. I've found out all I wanted to know." The calculation she had seen earlier had gone and in its place was raw emotion; he made no attempt to mask his quickened breathing. "The old chemistry's still there, isn't it?"

"For you, maybe," she spat.

He laughed softly. "You're not fooling either one of us. How long did you say you were staying at the bungalow?"

Her voice sounded surprisingly self-possessed. "Don't push me, Rhys—I can still change my mind."

"I don't think you will, because that would upset Kate. And you wouldn't want to do that, would you? I must admit your visit could hardly have come at a more opportune time—I'm bored to death. You'll be a most welcome distraction."

And this was the man Kate and Robert thought she could help! If it had not been so dreadful, it would have been funny. If Kate had been with them right then and there, Diana would have reneged, no matter what the effect on the other woman. She said tautly, "I'm not as naive as I used to be, Rhys. Over the years I've learned to look after myself. If you try any more of the strong-arm stuff I'll leave, regardless of Kate."

"You wouldn't be daring me, by any chance?"

"No! I just want you to leave me alone. I'm Kate's visitor, not yours."

"In that case," he said smoothly and to her infinite relief, "I'd better tell you a bit about Kate so you're not going into the situation blind." He pulled the keys out of the ignition and took a sweater from the back seat. "Let's walk."

As they got out of the car the wind seized Diana's hair, whipping it around her head, and she was glad of the protection afforded by her jeans and Lopi sweater. They began walking along the shore of the lake, the angry slap of the waves a continual accompaniment to Rhys's narrative. "Kate is an orphan," he began, "and as far as we're both aware, I'm her only living relative. Last summer she married Barrie Pemberton, a bush pilot with an Arctic air company—he's eight years older than she is. I went to the wedding and there's no question it was a love match. But apparently they soon ran into trouble—I got this secondhand, you understand, from another pilot who was a friend of theirs. Kate's a dear, but she's not exactly what you'd call a liberated woman. Half the time she's scared of her own shadow, and I think she must have depended on Barrie a great deal. She hated his spending so much time away from home, and of course she had a point—flying cargo or passengers in the North can be pretty dangerous. So she wanted him to settle down to a desk job, but he wanted to keep flying. When she got pregnant, I gather Barrie did finally start considering other alternatives. He still had a contract to fulfill, however, so he had to keep flying.

"Anyway, they had a hell of a row before his last trip. He took off late one Monday night about four weeks ago with a planeload of supplies for an Inuit community, and he's never been heard of since. The search-and-rescue operation's been called off—they never found a trace of the plane or of Barrie.''

"I remember hearing about that on the radio," Diana said. ''Poor Kate—how awful not to know what happened.''

''When she heard the news that he was missing, she was distraught. On top of everything else, she felt guilty because they'd parted in such anger. The days went by with no results from the search—not a word on the plane or Barrie. A week after he disappeared she was upstairs doing something or other, and she saw a police car drew up outside. Thinking it was news of Barrie, she started running down the stairs. She tripped and fell and as a result lost the baby.''

Diana's footsteps had been slowing as she listened, for she had been expecting something like this. Forgetting that she was frightened of Rhys and angry with him, she put a hand on his sleeve, her gray eyes appalled. "How terrible. . . .''

''Yes. But that's not all.'' He stood still, facing her, the wind disordering his thick dark hair. ''When she came to after the anesthetic in hospital, she'd lost her memory. She remembers nothing of Barrie, their quarrel, his disappearance or the baby—just a complete blank. That was when the medical people got hold of me, because someone had to take responsibility for her. They say it's only a temporary thing, that her mind simply couldn't cope with the double loss of husband and child, so she's blotted it all out. Sooner or later, they assure me, something will trigger a response and she'll remember everything. In the meantime she's as you see her: sweet, gentle. . . and lost.''

Diana was still gripping his sleeve, a small part of her brain registering the rough texture of his sweater. "So the other day when the plane flew overhead...it must have reminded her of Barrie?"

"I think so. Yet not enough to bring about a total recall."

"Oh, Rhys...." As he brought his hand up to cover hers, she stared at him in perplexity. The Rhys who had taunted her in the car, whose coldness and self-sufficiency had repelled her, was the same Rhys who had traveled across the country to help a woman in need. Whose gentleness with Kate, and whose concern for her, she could only admire. He was a man of contradictions, whom she was no nearer understanding now than she'd been in the past.

This time when he leaned forward to kiss her she remained still and passive, the question deepening in her eyes. It was as if the telling of Kate's troubles had gentled him. His lips sought rather than demanded, and because of this, and because of the effect of his story, her own defenses were lowered. She moved a little closer to him. His arms went around her. The wind wrapped her hair about his head, tenuously binding them together.

Then for Diana everything dropped away except the pure magic of an embrace that was at once an echo of the past and yet a reality in the present. Rhys's skin had been chilled by the wind; as his mouth moved against hers, it warmed and softened and her own lips parted in a response as inevitable as the ocean tides. There was the first tentative touch of his tongue. Welcoming it, she let her hands slide up his chest and bury themselves in the silky hair at his nape. His arms tightened their hold so that she was pressed against him and she felt the first throbbing of his arousal. In her own loins was the accompanying ache of need, the imperative call of a desire buried for years, now too strong to deny.

From the windswept sky and the torn gray clouds there fell the first drops of rain, making dark patches on the rocks and bouncing off the surface of the water. It was Rhys who raised his head first, his blue eyes brilliant with a mixture of passion and laughter, a laughter she had thought was gone from him. A raindrop trickled down his cheek as he said, "This is one way to dampen our ardor, so to speak. Did you call this up, sea witch?"

She smiled back, her cheeks flushed with color, her lips tremulous from his kiss. "Not I, sir."

His own smile faded and he said hoarsely, "God, you're beautiful, Diana," pushing her hair back from her face, his eyes devouring her.

If anything, her color deepened. Her lashes dropped, hiding her expression.

"We must go," he said. "We'll get soaked." But still he held her, as if he was afraid she might disappear in the wind if he let go. His voice so low she had to strain to catch the words, he muttered, "You shouldn't have come back, Diana. What's between us is too strong—we'll burn each other out. We're better off apart; you know that as well as I do. Because when we're together—" he kissed her hard "—this is what happens, and we can't fight it."

Still lost in the sensuous wonder of a kiss that had

for the first time since their separation made her feel wholly a woman, desired and desiring, she looked up at him wordlessly. She knew there was something of the same trust in her eyes as might have been in Kate's. It was raining harder now, and suddenly he grabbed her hand. "Come on, let's run for it."

They headed for the grass embankment and raced across it toward the car, the thud of their footsteps carried away on the wind. Diana was filled with a primitive joy, as though she could run forever and soar on the wings of the wind like a bird. When they reached the car she fell into her seat and slammed the door, laughing at Rhys as he joined her. "Beautiful!" she exclaimed, knowing she did not need to explain to him what she meant.

He brushed her cheek with his finger as delicately as if it were the feather of a bird's wing. "Beautiful, indeed. And now we're going home, Diana, because if we don't, we'll be making love in the front seat of the car and that wouldn't do." He started the car and turned on the wipers. "Talk to me," he ordered. "Tell me some of the things you've been doing since I first knew you."

This was by no means an easy request, since she felt she could not reveal Belinda's existence. It was difficult to parry Rhys's surprise when he learned she had always lived in Montreal and even had an apartment in her parents' house. "I somehow saw you taking off with a backpack and roaming Europe," he commented, giving her a quick sideways look.

"I've done a fair bit of traveling one way or another," she said truthfully. "But up until two years ago Will was in Montreal, so that was a strong factor in keeping me there.''

This appeared to satisfy him, and the talk drifted to other subjects. When they arrived at the bunga-low, Kate was the one who showed Diana to her room. It was at the far end of the house, distant from Kate's room but across the hall from Rhys's, Diana realized with a touch of fear. Now that she was away from him, she was horrified by her behavior on the beach. In retrospect it seemed at best indiscreet, at worst wanton—particularly in view of her engage-ment to Alan, a fact she had not shared with Rhys. She had never responded like that to Alan, she real-ized numbly, nor did she think she ever would; yet she loved Alan and she no longer loved Rhys. This visit was madness; she must leave as soon as she decently could.

In the meantime Kate had perched cross-legged on the bed as Diana unpacked. ''I'm glad you're here,'' she said. ''I was afraid you might change your mind at the last minute.''

''I probably should have,'' Diana replied dryly.

''Nonsense. It'll work out, you'll see. I thought you and I could spend the afternoon together, then this evening I'll go to bed early and leave you with Rhys.''

Kate's assumption that leaving her and Rhys alone together would somehow produce a miracle seemed naive in the extreme to Diana, although she kept her doubts to herself, not wanting to spoil Kate's pride in her planning. ''I must show you where the music room is, too,'' Kate went on. ''Afterward, if it's still raining, could I see some of your paintings?"

"Of course you may."

The afternoon passed pleasantly enough. Kate was both sensitive and articulate, although it was noticeable to Diana how her conversation related strictly to the present. There were no remarks like, "Five years ago I did such and such," or "When I was growing up I knew so and so." In view of what Rhys had told her on the beach, that was only natural. However, Diana found herself wanting to protect Kate, to shield her from any more distress. If helping Rhys would help Kate, then Diana was prepared to do her best to reconcile Rhys with his musical abilities.

CHAPTER EIGHT

AFTER THEY HAD EATEN DINNER and while Rhys was talking to Robert in the kitchen, Diana went down the hall to the music room. Outside the clouds were dark and lowering, squatting sullenly on the plateau of Gros Morne and veiling the tableland with mist, while rain still spattered against the windows. She switched on one of the lamps and wandered along the laden bookshelves, impressed by the comprehensive collection of musical literature. The photographs gave her a pang, for several dated back to the time when she had first met Rhys. His vibrant confidence and his will to excel were both to be read in the lineaments of his handsome, more youthful face, yet he had been a year older than she was now.... With the tip of one finger she traced the stubborn line of his jaw, sighing unconsciously.

"I hope you're still not bemoaning the past."

Her hand dropped to her side. As a sudden surge of adrenaline coursed through her veins, she knew she was ready for this encounter; welcomed it, even. She turned and smiled in deliberate provocation. "You mean, do I regret having met you?"

"Something to that effect."

"No, Rhys, I don't regret that." With a faint sense

of wonder, she knew she was speaking the absolute truth as she went on, "You gave me three days of perfect happiness. I wonder how many women can look back on their lives and say they had that."

She could tell he had not expected so forthright an answer. "Other men have matched that experience for you since then."

Smiling brilliantly, she evaded his implied question. "You were the first. And," she added, glancing back at the photograph, "you were certainly the first person to demonstrate to me how completely one must devote oneself to one's art if one wishes to succeed. Oh, I saw the same devotion in Will—but it took your departure after those three days to make me really understand it." Again that touch of provocation in her smile. "A valuable, if cruel, lesson."

"It's because of that lesson that you are where you are today," he said insistently.

Despite Belinda...? "Perhaps," she acknowledged. "The other lesson I learned, of course, is that one can never give up the struggle. The gift of talent is for a lifetime and the expressing of the talent is for a lifetime, too."

"Unless it becomes a physical impossibility to do so," he replied sharply, his face hardening.

The preliminary skirmish was over; this was open warfare. "But in your case that is not so."

As if to give credence to his words he walked over to the piano, leaning on its polished surface, his reflection distorted on the gleaming black wood as he held out his scarred left hand. "How many times do I have to tell you that for my purposes this hand is virtually useless? Sure, I can still play—and probably better than nine-tenths of the population. But I will never again be able to play to suit my own standards or those of the audiences who have heard me the past few years. The agility is gone. The strength is gone. And they're never coming back." In a gesture of total frustration he banged the lid with his fist. "Do you hear me? Never!"

Deliberately she walked over to him, lifting the lid of the piano. "All right," she said, "so you can never be a concert pianist again. But you said it yourself—you can still play far better than most people. I'd be inclined to say better than ninety-nine percent. So you can play for your own pleasure, can't you? Or for mine—I'd love to hear you play again."

He straightened, standing so close to her that she could feel his breath fanning her cheek. "No!" he exploded.

"Why not?" she taunted. "Because you can't stand not to be the best? Not to be perfect?"

"You hit it right on." He had grabbed her arm, although temporarily neither noticed the contact, being too caught up in their clash of wills. "I can't stand to hear myself fall short of what I used to be able to do as easily and as effortlessly as breathing. When I sit down at that piano bench, the only thing I hear is my own failure. My inability to create the beauty and elegance I know is there. It's a bastardization, Diana, and I won't be part of it."

"Then you're still living in the past, with the image of yourself as you used to be! That self is gone, Rhys." Her mouth softened, her eyes pleading for understanding. "And it must be desperately hard to adjust to the fact that it's gone—don't think I'm blind to that. But you've got to come to terms with that loss, accept new and different roles—"

"Court buffoon?" he sneered.

Her temper flared. Disdaining to answer him, she said, "You know as well as I do that you have talents in other directions. You've done some composing in the past; there's that whole area. And there's teaching, passing on to the musicians of the future the fruits of your own experience, just as Will did with me."

"But would you have respected Will's judgment if he had only been able to turn out third-rate stuff himself?"

It brought her up short. "You don't want to be helped, do you?" she said, her angry gray eyes searching the unrelenting lines of his face. "You want to be left alone to feel sorry for yourself—"

This time she knew he was gripping her shoulders, for he was shaking her. "It's not like that," he said hoarsely. "Can't you understand? It's very simple, Diana—I quite literally cannot bear sitting down at the piano, trying to play, when all I hear is a mockery of what I should hear."

Feeling how weak her plea was even as she spoke, she said, "Somehow you've got to get over that, Rhys."

His fingers loosened their hold. "Join the crowd," he said ironically. "You must have been listening to Robert and Kate. What nobody seems to realize, no matter how often I say it, is that that part of my life is over. Dead and gone and not to be resurrected."

He was almost convincing her.... "But what would you do instead, Rhys? What other choices are there?"

He stirred restlessly. "If I knew that, there'd be no problem. The trouble is my whole life up until now has been devoted to one thing."

Perhaps he was right and Kate and Robert were wrong, Diana thought, impressed in spite of herself by his reasoning. Perhaps he would find another field of endeavor and devote to it the same drive and energy he had devoted to music. She said tentatively, "I suppose if I suddenly found myself unable to paint, or in the position of producing works that I knew were inferior, I'd be lost, too. I'm sure I would be."

"Then you do understand."

She gazed at him, her perplexity very evident on her mobile features. "I suppose I do. I'm sorry I shouted at you, Rhys."

He grinned suddenly, and she felt her heart turn over in her breast. "I think I did my fair share of the shouting," he said.

"So you did," she agreed primly.

He kissed her quickly on the cheek, an almost brotherly kiss of gratitude and comradeship. "Tell you what—why don't I light a fire and get you a drink?"

Knowing she wanted to prolong the closeness, she said, "That would be lovely."

In no time the flames were leaping up the chimney in the stone fireplace. Pulling down a couple of cushions from the hearth, Diana sank down on the rug, abstractedly admiring the play of colors in the fire's heart. When Rhys came back with her martini she smiled her thanks, content to be silent. But he must have been thinking back over their conversation, because he said quietly, "Diana, did Robert and Kate set up this visit of yours? So you could add your voice to theirs?"

Cross-legged on the floor, she looked up at him gravely. "Yes, they did."

"I thought so. What I'm interested in is why you agreed to do it."

"I must have thought I could help."

"I see. Was that the only reason?"

"For old times' sake, as well, I suppose," she said lightly, having no intention of sharing with him Robert's revelation about the photograph.

He sat down beside her, staring moodily into the flames. "We can't go back into the past, Diana. We're two very different people now."

Not sure what he was driving at, she hugged her knees and kept silent. She was wearing the same white pants and navy blouse she had worn on her first visit here, the blouse's loose fit and high collar disguising her figure yet subtly hinting at the curves beneath the thin fabric.

His head swung around, twin points of flame dancing in his blue eyes, at odds with the seriousness of his expression. "We can't go forward, either, you and I—there's no future for us, Diana. When I said earlier the timing was as wrong now as it was ten years ago, I meant every word of it. I've got nothing to offer a woman right now."

Her heart began to beat in heavy uneven strokes. Striving for normality, she murmured, "I'm sure you have a great deal to offer—but that's really nothing to do with me.''

He did not seem to hear her. ''So we're back where we were that first time. History repeating itself.'' He took a long drink from his glass. ''Do you know what I'm asking?''

She shook her head wordlessly.

''I want to have an affair with you. But just that, and no more.''

In her agitation she sat up straight, her back to the hearth; in the firelight her figure was outlined through her blouse. ''You certainly believe in plain speaking, don't you, Rhys? Do you think I'm likely to agree when you as much as told me you were bored and looking around for a distraction?'' She grimaced. ''You can't think very much of me.''

''I shouldn't have said that, because it bore very little relationship to the truth. The truth lies in that kiss on the beach, Diana—surely you haven't forgotten that?''

''No. But—''

''You know as well as I do that the physical attraction between us is as powerful now as it's ever been, if not more so—at least on my part. You're a mature and beautiful woman now, and I want you in my bed. Tonight. In this house.''

She moved away from him, her eyes huge in a face in which tension, outrage and an incredulous spark of humor were warring. ''Do you go around propositioning every woman you meet like this?'' she demanded.

''Hardly.'' There was an answering flicker of

humor in his expression before he sobered. "I haven't led a totally celibate life since we first met, but then I'm sure you haven't, either. But I've never met another woman who affects me as you do. That you'll have to take on trust, Diana, because I have no way of proving it to you." He drained his glass. "How long are you planning to stay here?"

"Only for three or four days."

"I said history was repeating itself, didn't I? Only this time it would be you who'd leave, rather than I."

For a wild sweet moment she was tempted. Four days with Rhys...and four nights. There would be the passionate glory of his lovemaking, of being showered with all the gifts his body and mind could bring her. Head bent, she closed her eyes, her hair falling forward to hide her face. As if in a dream, she seemed to feel his hands moving over her body to cup her breasts, moving farther to smooth her hips, and the blood leaped in her veins. She wanted it; oh, yes, she wanted it. She would be a fool—and a liar—to deny it. But because she wanted it did not mean she could have it.

She raised her head, conflict all too visible in the clouded gray eyes. "What's the point in my saying I don't want you? None whatsoever. We'd both know I was lying. But, Rhys—" she gazed at him steadfastly "—we're not going to become lovers again."

"You threw yourself at me at seventeen. But now, at twenty-seven, an independent successful woman, you're acting like a frightened virgin. Why, Diana?"

Because of Belinda, her heart cried. *Because our last affair left me with a child, your daughter. And while I love her with all my heart, I cannot risk such a thing happening again, in all its pain and loneliness and fear.* "I've grown up in the meantime," she said coldly. "I'm not quite so impetuous or so foolhardy."

"How long since you last made love with anyone?"

"That's hardly your business!"

He leaned forward. "Come on, tell me the truth—how long? A beautiful woman like you...the men must be around you like bees around honey."

Not men, she thought with a sudden stab of shame. Only one man—Alan. Who loved and trusted her and whom she had agreed to marry. Sickened that she could even have been tempted by Rhys's offer, she opened her mouth to tell him about Alan. But he had had enough of words. In one swift moment he was beside her, kissing her as if he could never have enough of her. When she tried to push him away, palms flat on his chest, she lost her balance, half-falling sideways. Then she was on her back on the rug, her hair spread on the pillow, and his weight was on top of her.

It was heaven and hell at the same time. Heaven because of the host of sensations beleaguering her: the movements of his lips against her own, the hardness of his rib cage on her breasts, the heaviness of his thighs across her legs. Hell because in front of her closed eyes all she could see was Alan's face. With all the willpower at her command she strove to remain passive and unresponsive, like a piece of wood in his arms or a stone statue rather than a living breathing woman.

When he raised his head there was naked fury in

his eyes. "Stop trying to fool me, Diana. Me of all people—I know you're not frigid."

He had punctuated his words with hard angry kisses and she had to fight for breath. "Let go, Rhys," she seethed. "All this will prove is that you're stronger than I am—which we know anyway." She writhed ineffectually under his weight. "Let me go!"

"When I'm ready." He levered himself up slightly, and for a moment she thought she was to be freed. But all he had wanted was to free his hand. Watching her face as a scientist might watch his subject during an experiment, he deliberately inserted his hand under the loose hem of her blouse, sliding it up the smooth concavity of her belly to find her breast in the flimsy bra and then letting it climb the silken slope of her flesh to the tip.

Willpower, reason, shame—they all fled at the insidious pressure of those probing fingers. Betrayed by her own needs, she felt her breast swell to his touch, the hardened nipple telling him all he needed to know. He was pushing her blouse up from her waist and she arched her back to help him as the flickering firelight fell on her bare skin, casting a shadow in the hollow between her breasts. He unclasped her bra so that there was nothing between his hand and her firm flesh, and she thought she would faint with the pleasure of it. When his head lowered and his lips teased her nipples, first one, then the other, she whimpered with delight, her hands buried in the thickness of his hair to hold him there and prolong the pagan sensations flooding her whole body. In unconscious invitation her hips moved under him, and in direct response she felt him fumble with the button of her slacks. Somehow she managed to open his shirt, running her palms across the curving ribs and up the muscled flatness of his chest to find the dark mat of hair that covered his breastbone. It was all so familiar, so well remembered, as if the long years since they had last made love had never intervened....

He had been kissing her, a deep kiss in which tongue had touched and played with tongue, and teeth had gently nibbled lips, a sensuous toying with each other that had become almost unbearably arousing. Now Rhys raised his head, his eyes burning, and said thickly, "Oh, God, Diana, I can't wait for you any longer." Kneeling on the rug he put his arms around her, letting his eyes linger on her swollen breasts and flushed cheeks. Then he began to lift her. "We'll go to my room."

Dazedly she blinked up at him, feeling the heavy pounding of his heart beneath her cheek, hearing his voice as if it came from a long way away. Rhys... this was Rhys, and she was half-naked in his arms, the softness of her breast lying against the tangled hair on his chest. She tensed, her eyes widening in appalled recognition of what they were about to do. "No, Rhys," she whispered, wriggling frantically in his hold. "No, we mustn't...oh, please, put me down."

Starting to walk toward the door, he looked down at her. "It's all right, Diana, don't feel ashamed—your body is beautiful."

"You don't understand...it's not that. Rhys, I can't make love to you, I can't!"

Something of her desperation must have reached

him. His footsteps slowed. "Why not? What's wrong?"

She shoved her face into his chest, unable to face those all too penetrating eyes. How could she tell him about Alan, when she had so blatantly responded to his lovemaking only minutes before? But she had to, she had no choice. She heard herself say, "I—I'm engaged, Rhys. Engaged to be married." Not even to herself did she sound convincing.

His body went very still. "What did you say?"

"You heard. Put me down, please."

His answer was to tighten his hold. "I don't believe you."

"You must—it's true."

"Look at me!"

Slowly she looked up to find him raking her figure with his eyes, his expression one of mingled anger and frustration. She tried to pull her blouse together while a flush stained her face. "It's true, Rhys," she repeated in a small voice. "I should have told you sooner, I suppose, but I didn't think...this kind of thing was going to happen."

"Oh, didn't you?" Unceremoniously he dumped her on her feet. "How very convenient to be able to produce a fiancé just at the critical moment. Why aren't you wearing a ring?"

"He hasn't given it to me yet," she said weakly. At the open derision on his face, she cried, "It's true! His name is Alan Ingram and he's a mathematics professor at McGill." It took actual effort not to add, *and he's very fond of Belinda,* because for so long that had been such an important part of her feelings for Alan.

Rhys ran his fingers through his hair, disdaining to do up his shirt. "Whether it's true or not, you've certainly managed to kill any urges I had to make love. Which I imagine was your aim. Good for you, Diana." His voice was savage. "Do you do this kind of thing often? Get a man so aroused he scarcely knows what he's doing and then play the outraged virgin?"

He was so far from the truth that there was an edge of hysteria in her laugh. "Oh, of course," she said sarcastically. "That's how I get my thrills."

Suddenly ashamed, she spread out her hands in appeal. "I'm sorry, Rhys. Truly I am."

"Yeah? Well, you'd better get out of here and go to bed. My normal civilized behavior doesn't seem to operate when I'm around you." There was finality in the way he turned away from her. "Good night, Diana."

She hesitated, torn by a desire to explain further yet knowing at the same time how impossible it would be for him to understand her at all when he was ignorant of Belinda's existence. "Good night," she answered tonelessly, and left the room.

She scarcely glanced around her bedroom. Pulling off her clothes she fell into bed, feeling as sore all over as if she had been beaten. Her eyes closed and almost immediately she was asleep.

CHAPTER NINE

IN THE MORNING the sun was shining, and as usual Diana awoke full of renewed optimism. Now that Rhys knew about Alan, there would be no repetition of the scene in the music room, she thought. And now that she herself more clearly understood Rhys's revulsion against the world of music and all it represented in his eyes, she would perhaps be able to alleviate some of Robert's and Kate's concerns. She could probably go home tomorrow, for after all, her mission was accomplished. She had talked to Rhys, as she had promised Kate. She had enough faith in him to believe he would sooner or later come up with an alternative to music. In fact, she was more than half-convinced that not only would he survive this crisis, he would emerge from it stronger and wiser.

That there was a large element of self-deception in all this—as far as the scene in the music room and her own ardent response to Rhys's lovemaking were concerned—she chose to ignore. In a couple of days she would be back home, where she belonged, with Alan and with Belinda, and her life would settle back into its normal comfortable grooves. Her relationship with Rhys would be, as it had been for so long, a thing of the past.

Wearing close-fitting purple trousers and a voluminous white smock top bound in purple silk, a slightly outrageous outfit that the seventeen-year-old Diana would not have had the confidence to wear, she made her way to the kitchen. She had plaited her hair into a single thick braid that hung over her shoulder and was bound with purple ribbon; her eye makeup was mauve. She looked a bit like an exotic and rare butterfly, and as she entered the room she saw amused appreciation in Rhys's eyes. "Good morning," she said cheerfully.

"Good morning. You're looking very gorgeous." He glanced down at his cords and cotton shirt in faint deprecation. "I feel rather like the drab male of the species."

"You'll pass," she said lightly, knowing that drab was the last word she'd ever apply to Rhys Morgan. "Mmm, something smells good."

"Coffee, bacon and scrambled eggs. Grapefruit on the table. What are your plans for the day?"

"Maybe Kate and I could go somewhere. I'd like to see more of the park before I leave."

"I'm not sure Kate's feeling too well. But you could check with her after breakfast."

As they sat down together at the table and began to eat, it seemed as though there was an unspoken agreement between them not to mention the events of the night before, and for this Diana was grateful.

Once the meal was over, she excused herself and went to Kate's room, tapping softly on the door. "Are you awake, Kate?"

"Come in," Kate called drowsily.

As Diana entered she saw that Kate was still in bed, the covers pulled up to her chin, her fair hair loose on the pillow. "Rhys said you're not feeling well."

"It's nothing serious. A headache, that's all."

Now that she was closer to the bed, Diana could see the pallor in Kate's cheeks and the bruised shadows under her eyes. "That's too bad. I'd hoped we could go out together today."

"Maybe tomorrow. Although with these headaches I usually feel miserable for a couple of days. I've had trouble like this for as long as I can remember." Her fingers plucked at the sheets and a frown appeared on her forehead. "I remember that," she fretted, "but I can't remember other things. Why can't I, Diana?"

Speaking as soothingly as she could, Diana said, "I'm sure when you're ready you'll remember everything you need to, Kate. In the meantime I think the best thing you can do is rest and relax."

Like a biddable child, Kate said obediently, "I suppose you're right. It's just that...it's as though there's a big steel door in my brain and every now and then it opens just a crack and I get a glimpse of what's behind. Then it slams shut and I'm left wondering if I imagined it all."

Diana took her hand, putting all the conviction she could into her voice. "If there are things you don't remember, it must be for the best. I'm sure everything will work out in the end."

Kate gave her a weak smile and said with the childlike simplicity that Diana had already noticed was one of her traits, "I like you, Diana. I'm glad you came here—for me, and because Rhys needs the company, too.'' She turned her head into the pillow. ''Why don't you go somewhere with him today, instead?''

Not on your life, Diana thought, contenting herself with saying, ''Maybe. In the meantime, have a good rest.''

She stole out of the room, pulling the door shut behind her, and for the first time saw Rhys standing there in the hall. He must have heard every word they had said.

He patted her shoulder. ''You handled that well, Diana. It's not always easy to know how to deal with these flashes of memory that she has. But the main thing is to keep her as calm and relaxed as possible— or so the doctors say. I hope they know what they're talking about.''

She was pleased by his praise, not so pleased when he added, ''By the way, I liked her suggestion that you and I take off for the day. Why don't we?''

''I don't think that's a very good idea.''

One eyebrow lifted sardonically. ''It's all right. I'm not planning to take you off in the woods somewhere and seduce you.''

She flushed. ''I didn't think you would. . . .''

''Good. I'll get Robert to pack us a picnic. Can you be ready in half an hour?''

''What about Kate? We can't just leave her.''

''Robert's here all day, and she'll probably sleep anyway. Bring your sketchbook or your camera—I'll take you to Western Brook Pond.'' He grinned. ''It's far more spectacular than its name would imply.''

A day exploring with Rhys—what harm could it do? She'd be leaving for home in a couple of days at the most. "All right then."

"Maybe change into jeans and bring a Windbreaker, because the flies can be bad."

They set off not long afterward, driving straight to the ferry dock, and fifteen minutes later were chugging across the bay. The air was crisp and clean with the tang of the ocean to it; gulls wheeled and dipped in their wake. The pattern of cliffs and hills shifted as they neared Norris Point, the little fishing village that was the ferry's destination. Purposely emptying her mind of anything but her pleasure in the outing, Diana began to enjoy herself. She sensed that Rhys must have made the same decision, for he was a perfect companion. Yet nothing could quite obliterate the sexual awareness between them. It added an edge to Diana's enjoyment, heightening her awareness of color, scent and sound, creating just enough tension between her and Rhys so that their movements and their conversations were given a slight extra significance. Both of them, she was sure, knew this; neither acknowledged it, and this in itself added excitement.

They drove up the shore until the bay opened into the sea at Rocky Harbour. The tide was out and the rock-strewn flats stretched out in a long curve from the shore to the lighthouse at Lobster Cove Head.

"A lot of the park employees live here," Rhys commented. "The main campground isn't that far away. It must be a bleak spot in the winter—imagine the winds that would blow in from the sea."

They found a little restaurant and had coffee with

some excellent homemade muffins, then continued on their way up the coast. The road followed the shoreline, passing through more small fishing villages, many of the houses with fenced yards.

"The fences are to keep the horses out, not to keep anything in," Rhys said. "Kind of a reverse function."

"Horses?"

"There are herds of half-wild horses all over Newfoundland. We should see some today—in fact, look between those two houses."

Following his pointing finger, she saw three chunky, dark brown horses with long black tails and manes peacefully cropping the grass.

"They leave sheep loose here, too. So if you want any kind of a garden, you have to have a fence."

On their right were the barren slopes of the Long Range Mountains. "Precambrian," Rhys said briefly. "Nearly a billion years old. Once they would have looked like the Rockies, which are a relatively young mountain range."

Between the mountains and the sea was a coastal plain consisting of low-growing shrub and bogs and crisscrossed by brooks. Along the shoreline itself grew stunted spruce and fir, twisted by the wind into a dense mat of vegetation. Tuckamore, Rhys called it, pointing out to Diana a small herd of sheep clustered on the shale beach.

Eventually he pulled off the road into a parking lot, where ahead of her through the windshield Diana could see a huge gap in the mountains, steep cliffs on either side of it. "We'll walk in so you can get a better view," he said, swinging the haversack that held their lunch onto his back.

At first they followed a winding narrow trail through the woods. The air was very still, the only sounds the thin twitter of birds hiding deep in the undergrowth. Many of the trees were gnarled and bent, hung with festoons of gray green old-man's beard, and even today, in bright sunshine, there was an eerie quality to the woods. But then the trail reached the muskeg and changed into a plank walk that wound its way across the bog past a lake edged by reeds, where swallows swooped and dived and beavers had built a dam. The bog itself, Diana discovered by testing it, was wet and spongy, the soil black. Rhys identified the plants for her as bakeapple and cranberry, cinquefoil and sphagnum moss. He showed her sundew plants and pitcher plants, both insectivorous, the latter with tubelike leaves in which water gathered to drown unwary flies trapped within. "I didn't realize you knew so much about the outdoors," Diana said, touching the tip of her finger to a sundew leaf and finding it sticky.

"I've got in the habit of going for long hikes every day since I came here. And it's much more interesting if you know something of the area—its geology and wildlife and plants. The park people are very helpful. They encourage visitors to learn as much as they can."

They had been moving ever closer to the cliffs. The last part of their walk was through trees and alder bushes alongside a salmon river, until finally they emerged onto a stone beach. There was a small wharf and some piled-up oil drums and the most breathtaking view Diana had seen for a long time.

They were on the shores of a lake, Western Brook Pond. The water at the edge was shallow, and without waiting to see if Rhys was following her, Diana jumped along a line of rocks that were above the waterline until she was as far from the shore as she could go. Then she stood still, drinking in the magnificence of those gaunt vertical cliffs. They were incredibly high and sharp edged, with their sides gouged by waterfalls. Silent in their immensity, they were eternally separated from each other by the deep cold waters of the fjord.

In front of her the swallows swooped, incongruously light and mobile. Behind her she heard Rhys say quietly, "It was carved out by the glaciers, millions of tons of ice against the living rock. There's a herd of caribou living on the barrens at the far end of the pond, they say, ten miles from here."

She said softly, "I'm so glad I saw this."

"Do you get the urge to paint it?"

Her head on one side, she considered his question. "I'd have to stay here for several days first—see it in all kinds of weather, watch the water and the clouds and the sky." She nodded slowly. "Then I could, yes."

"But you can't stay here for several days. You have to go home to your fiancé."

Her feet clinging to the rock, she turned to face him. "Yes...yes, of course." Alan seemed a very long way away.

"Are you sure he exists. . .outside of your imagination, that is?" Rhys asked harshly.

She took a grip on herself; it was as if the place had cast a spell on her. "Certainly he exists," she said overloudly. ."But he's a city person, and somehow it's difficult to visualize him here."

She had never articulated that before, but it was true. Alan thrived in Montreal, needing a background of people even though he himself might not always mingle with them. He liked all the comforts of civilization, all the cultural benefits of a big city. His sole forays into the outdoors were to ski in the Laurentians, an activity he pursued with a fanatical recklessness and a drive to excel that had won him countless competitions. It was a side to his character that had always rather intrigued Diana. However, he did not, she knew, go to the mountains to admire their beauty. Far from it. He went solely to get down the slopes in the least possible amount of time.

Unconsciously she sighed, unaware that Rhys had been watching the play of expression on her face. He spoke first. "You said he's a professor at McGill. So Montreal will continue to be home for you. It's funny, Diana—I never pictured you as being a sedentary creature. I figured once you were through art school, you'd be gone. Wandering on the four winds."

A dangerous topic, because he knew nothing of Belinda, nor of the restrictions that having a child could place upon one. She stared up at him while the water lapped at their feet, wondering for the first time in nearly ten years if she had done the right thing to keep silent about Belinda. This man standing so close to her, the breeze stirring his thick dark hair, had a nine-year-old daughter of whose existence he was totally ignorant, had apparently never suspected. What difference would it make to him to know he had fathered a child of quicksilver intelligence, whose inborn musical ability must surely rival his own, whose long black hair and deep blue eyes proclaimed her parentage more clearly than any marriage certificate could have done? Had Diana robbed both of them? Belinda of a father and Rhys of a daughter?

"What's wrong?" he asked sharply.

She passed a hand across her brow, her eyes full of bewilderment. "Nothing. Someone walking over my grave, that's all."

"What were you thinking? You look as though you've just been hit over the head."

It was too late now, she thought confusedly. Ten years ago she had chosen a certain course and now she had to stay with it. But, oh, God, had it been the right one? Would knowing about Belinda give Rhys back some meaning to his life, now, when so much else had fallen in ruins around him? The enormity of her lie—for a lie it had been, even if one of omission rather than commission—suddenly struck her and she swayed on her feet.

"Diana!" With his feet stretching from rock to rock, he picked her up in his arms and carried her back to shore. Seating her on the ground, he pushed her head down between her knees.

Gradually her vision cleared and the nightmare sense that she had done him an irretrievable wrong receded. "Sorry," she mumbled. "Don't know what happened."

He went down to the lake and dipped his handkerchief in the water, wringing it out and bringing it back to wipe her forehead. She closed her eyes, the touch of his fingers infinitely soothing. "We'll find a place in the shade so you can lie down, and after a while we'll have something to eat," he murmured. "We can take our time on the way back."

He could not possibly suspect the truth, she was sure of that, and she began to relax. When he found a patch of grass dappled with shadows from the alder bushes, she lay back, using her Windbreaker as a pillow. She felt very tired. It was good to close her eyes and forget everything for a while. . . .

She slept soundlessly and dreamlessly, although when she awoke her muscles were cramped from lying on the hard ground. Stretching lazily she looked around. The sun was no longer high in the sky, and when she looked at her watch she realized she had slept for nearly two hours. The haversack was lying beside her. There was no sign of Rhys.

Beyond the fringe of bushes she heard the sound of children's voices and the splash of water and then a man's deeper voice. Suddenly curious, she got to her feet. Peering through the leaves she saw Rhys down at the shoreline, his hiking boots lying on the beach, his trousers rolled up to his knees. Three children, two boys and a girl, were clustered around him; it was their voices that she heard. He was teaching them how to skip rocks on the surface of the lake, and even as she watched he picked up a flat piece of shale from the ground and gave it to the little girl—a girl perhaps a year or two younger than Belinda. He showed her how to hold it between her thumb and index finger and how to draw her arm back for the throw. The child, her brow puckered in concentration, braced her feet and swung her arm, and once, twice, three times the rock bounced on top of the water before sinking to the bottom.

The little girl jumped up and down in excitement as her brothers immediately tried to better her accomplishment. She grabbed Rhys's hand. "Let's do it again!" she shrilled.

Obligingly he bent to look for another rock, and the child squatted beside him, both absorbed in their task. With a lump in her throat, Diana turned away, wishing she hadn't woken up in time to see this. In her mind's eye was etched forever the images of Rhys's smile, the child's trust, the unspoken intimacy between them.

Doggedly she began to unpack the haversack, spreading the food out on the cloth Robert had provided. By the time she had finished, the children's parents had returned from their stroll along the beach and were chatting with Rhys. Diana waited, reluctant to join them; in a few minutes they were all saying goodbye, and Rhys was coming up the slope toward her. She busied herself quite unnecessarily with the food.

"You're awake," he said somewhat redundantly. "Feel better?"

She glanced up at him quickly, her smile fixed. "Yes, I do, thanks—I slept for ages. You must be hungry."

"Starving! Here, I'll open the wine. Try some of this cheese, Diana, it's delicious."

Their remarks remained commonplace, Rhys not referring again to her temporary faintness. They walked back to the car and then drove farther up the shore to a sand beach where they saw seals lying on the rocks in the sun and swimmers braving the cold sea waves. But for Diana the magic had gone from the day, and she raised no demur when Rhys finally suggested they head home. The bungalow felt like home to her when they got there; she was glad to go to the privacy of her bedroom and then to have a long hot shower before changing for dinner. Kate joined them at the table, looking very frail in a pale blue housecoat, her presence ensuring that the topics of conversation were cheerful and ordinary, which was fine with Diana. When Kate excused herself around nine, Diana did likewise, going to her room and closing the door.

She tried to read for a while, but the words on the page failed to hold her attention, and she had slept too long in the afternoon to be able to sleep so soon again. Still wearing the dress she had had on at dinner, a vivid pink knit that did full justice to the curves of her figure, she crept down the silent hallway to the music room, almost sure Rhys would not be there. Nor was he. With a lift of relief she pulled the door closed and turned on the light, hoping to find something more interesting to read.

Her high heels sank soundlessly into the carpet. The whole house was very quiet, almost as if she was the only person in it, and on impulse she crossed to

the windows and pulled the heavy floor-length draperies, shutting out the impenetrable blackness of the
night.

The lid was still raised on the piano. Idly she
brushed her fingers over the keys, admiring their
ivory smoothness. She would never be able to play
very well, but as a child she had taken lessons and as
Belinda's mother she had revived a little of her skill.
Now she opened the piano bench to see if there would
be anything in it that she could play.

Instead of the neatly arranged music books that
she had somehow expected, the bench was stuffed
with an untidy mass of papers, nearly all of them
with staffs and ledger lines and inked-in musical
notes. The occasional scribble of handwriting, usually a tempo marking, was undeniably masculine.
These papers, she was sure, belonged to Rhys. But
what did they represent?

She began sifting through them more methodically, separating them into piles, until it gradually
became clear that they were his own compositions.
He had written titles above some of them, while on
others were such terse annotations as "waltz,"
"sonata," "étude." One pile, significantly larger
than the others, appeared to have orchestral nota-
tions as well, and although she was not knowledgeable enough to assess it very thoroughly, it appeared
to be the scheme for a piano concerto. Temporarily
putting it to one side, forgetting that she had origi-
nally come here to find a book that would send her to
sleep, she sorted through the shorter compositions till
she found one that seemed relatively uncomplicated.

Propping the papers up on the rack, she very softly began to pick out the notes. Rhys had scrawled at the top, ''Allegro molto vivace,'' and indeed it was a lively and bright melody, full of unexpected leaps and runs. She had trouble with the rhythm at first but after three or four attempts was able to play the piece through, even adding a few chords with her left hand. It was a pity Belinda wasn't here—she'd have no trouble with it. And would she find it as inventive and rollicking a piece of music as Diana did?

Next she picked out some sheets labeled simply, ''Adagio,'' and more confidently began to play them. The melody line was exquisite, plaintive and sad yet with a sureness to each note that bespoke a complete mastery on the part of the composer. Entranced, she played it through again and then again, adding more of the harmony each time so that it gained richness and depth.

She had begun by playing very softly, picking out notes with only one finger. Now, totally caught up in the music, she was using both hands and the pedal, and when the handwriting directed, ''Forte,'' she obeyed, the chords reverberating throughout the room. So she should not have been surprised when the door was flung open and a voice said furiously, ''What the hell do you think you're doing?''

She jumped and her hands hit a wrong note. Wincing a little at her own mistake she swiveled on the bench, her gray eyes full of excitement. ''Rhys! When did you find time to do all this?'' With a sweep of her arm she indicated the music sheets scattered on the floor. ''I had no idea you'd been composing. This adagio movement is absolutely beautiful!''

His words dropped like stones into the silence. "You will pick all that up and put it away...and don't ever take it out again.''

The smile faded from her face. "But, Rhys, it's beautiful...''

He took a single threatening step toward her, his hands bunched into fists at his sides. "Did you hear what I said?''

To give herself courage she stood up, feeling the piano bench hard against her knees. When she spoke, her voice was commendably calm. "Yes, I heard you. But I don't think you can be serious. You must know far better than I the excellence of what's here.'' Encouraged that he had not interrupted her, she warmed to her theme. "Don't you see what this means?''

"Why don't you tell me?'' he said silkily. "I must admit that all it means to me is that you've been poking your nose into something that does not concern you. Trespassing on my privacy.''

She flinched. "Maybe so. Maybe I shouldn't have looked in the bench, and when I did look, maybe I should just have closed it and gone away. But I didn't—and I'm glad I didn't,'' she finished defiantly.

Another step closer. At least the bench was between them, she thought with false bravado, hearing that same dangerous smoothness in his voice. "Do tell me why.''

She leaned forward earnestly. "Don't you see?

This is your second career right here—you don't need to look any farther. As a composer you won't be denying all the years that have gone before. You'll be using them, drawing upon them for inspiration and experience. Oh, Rhys, it's so laughably simple!''

''Have you quite finished? You've managed to surprise me, by the way, Diana—I didn't realize you had such an evangelical streak in you.''

''There's nothing evangelical about it—it's pure common sense. I can't understand why you didn't think of it yourself.''

''I did. Some time ago. And abandoned it as I abandoned everything else that had anything to do with music.'' He was towering over her, the savagery that he had previously held in check now unleashed. ''How many times do I have to tell you that I'm through with music?''

Although inwardly quailing, outwardly she held her ground. ''I did believe you last night, because I understood the analogy you used to my painting—I know I wouldn't be able to turn out inferior works. But there's nothing inferior about these, Rhys.'' She picked up the sheets from the stand, holding them in front of her for emphasis. ''These deserve to be played by someone with far more ability than I and to be heard by far more than two or three people. You can't turn your back on them as if they don't exist—you can't!''

He pulled the sheets from her hand and tore them in two, the sound shockingly loud in the room. ''Then I'll destroy them so that they don't exist.''

''No!'' Forgetting all caution, she rounded the

bench and grabbed his wrist before he could further damage the papers, in her agitation quite unaware of how beautiful she looked with her flushed cheeks and eloquent eyes, her bosom heaving in the close-fitting dress. "You're destroying yourself, Rhys!"

"If I am, then that's my choice. It's not one you or anyone else can make for me. But I don't think I am destroying myself, Diana—to stay with music would be to do that. I will *not* be second-rate!"

"These aren't second-rate!"

"What do you know of it? Have you ever studied composition or form? Of course you haven't. You're no more competent to judge these than I would be to judge an art exhibit. So for God's sake just drop any ideas you might be harboring that I'm another Chopin or Beethoven."

"Oh, Rhys. . . ." She let out her breath in a long sigh of frustration, biting her lips as she sought for another way to convince him. But before she could say anything, his free arm had gone around her, his fingers digging into the small of her back. In a pure reflex action she loosened her hold on his wrist, fear clouding her eyes. Then he was kissing her, all his pent-up anger in the burning strength of his mouth, the steel strength of his arms.

Like a wildcat she fought him, trying to wrench her head free, her fists beating at his ribs in futile fury. But he was far too strong and was determined to have his own way. Viciously she kicked out at his shins, trying to grind the heel of her shoe into his ankle. With a muttered oath he shoved her roughly away from him, then picked her up bodily and carried her across to the couch. "Put me down!" she hissed, humiliated that she could be so helpless in his grip.

He grinned wolfishly. "Okay," he said, dumping her unceremoniously on the chesterfield so that her skirt fell above her knees, baring her long slim thighs.

"Oh...!" Pulling her skirt down with one hand, her eyes brilliant with pure rage, she tried to lever herself off the soft sinking cushions. But Rhys had flung himself on top of her, his body knocking the breath from her lungs so that she fell back, feeling as though she was suffocating as his big frame cut off light and air and freedom of movement. Helpless to struggle, buried in the yielding cushions, smothered by the fierce demand of his mouth clamped on hers, she felt her head begin to spin, and panic was swallowed up in a swirling dizziness.

She must have gone limp beneath him. The next thing she knew the weight had gone from her chest and she was gulping in air through her mouth. Shivering, she opened her eyes. Rhys was bending over her, concern battling with the remnants of anger in his face. "I'm sorry," he said abruptly. "I was far too rough."

She tried to stop the trembling of her limbs, not wanting him to see it, but a deep shudder caught her unawares.

"Oh, Diana...I'm sorry," he said, lowering himself onto the couch again. Despite herself she flinched away from him and he added roughly, "It's okay— just let me put my arms around you and keep you warm."

There was a world of difference between this embrace and the one that had gone before. Gently he drew her closer to the warmth of his body, pressing her head into his chest and putting one leg over hers. Then he held her, one hand stroking her hair softly and repetitively.

With a tiny sigh of surrender she gave herself up to him, and the tremors that had been rippling along her limbs gradually stilled. In an almost trancelike state she became aware of a whole battery of sensations. Physically, there was the simple comfort of warmth and of being held. But more than that, there was an almost childlike sensation of safety, of being protected and secure. Nothing could harm her here, she thought drowsily. She snuggled closer to him, rubbing her cheek against his shirt. "Nice," she murmured, trustingly letting one arm slide over his ribs to hold him close.

She couldn't see his face. If she had she would have seen the tightness in his jaw, the half humorous, half agonized look of frustration in his eyes as he schooled himself to remain still and passive, his hands loose on the soft fabric that covered her body. But almost asleep as she was, she must have felt something of the struggle: a tightness in his breathing or a tension in the fingers on her hair. Unexpectedly she raised her head.

His mouth was a taut line, willpower fighting instinct. Without words she knew instantly what was wrong, and she felt an uprush of such compassion and generosity that any other consideration fled. Without a trace of shyness she brought her hands up to his face, pulling his head down and kissing him full on the mouth. Her lips were soft and womanly yet more than hinting at a passion that could be every bit as powerful as his own; and even as she did it she knew she was doing the right thing, the only thing.

She felt the response run through his whole frame, a shudder of desire that quickened her own blood. His mouth took the initiative, moving against hers in deliberate arousal. His hands, which had been slack on her dress, began caressing her, searching out the secret places of her body with a desperate hunger, roaming her breasts and hips and thighs until she molded herself against him, lost to anything but her need of him. He pushed her dress from her shoulders, kissing the creamy hollow in her throat, then edged the wide neckline even lower until her naked breasts were revealed, firm and blue veined, aching for his touch. He lowered his head to kiss them, his tongue teasing the pale silken skin and with controlled eroticism gradually nearing the swollen rosy tips.

She couldn't bear it. Like fire racing through her veins, her need of him exploded into flame. Somehow he had found the zipper in the back of her dress, and as he pushed the fabric to her waist, then her hips, then her knees, until she was wearing only the flimsiest of briefs, she was undoing his jeans, his buckle cold against her bare flesh. Finally he rolled on top of her, and this time it was sheer heaven to have him there, to feel his weight crushing her breasts, his mouth drinking deeply of her own. And all the while there was his throbbing masculinity against her thigh, making its own instinctive demand of her.

Rhys lifted his head, levering himself up on his elbows so that his eyes could travel the length of her body from her tumbled hair and swollen breasts to her narrow waist and the lacy white briefs. It was a look every bit as arousing as an actual caress, and her whole body quivered in response. A small gesture, in one way, although a very blatant one in another. She saw the same shudder of desire pass over his face and felt it echo in the core of her body.

Yet something in her wanted to prolong the exquisite torment of this moment before he claimed her as his own. That he would, she had no doubt; it was inevitable. She said softly, her face full of wonder, "It feels so unbelievably good to be with you again, Rhys—so right. And I want you so much. Is it the same for you?"

"Of course it is." He smiled suddenly, bending to kiss one breast, then the other, gently rubbing his head along the valley between them. "Can't you tell?"

She had forgotten how in the past their lovemaking would often spontaneously dissolve into laughter, just as quickly returning to passion again. She heard him say, "We belong together, Diana, you and I, in a way that's unique in my experience—I'm not sure I can explain it. It's not rational. It's not just sexual, either. It's a sense of rightness, just as you said."

Because the muscles in his arms were corded with strain, she put her hands on his shoulders, drawing him down to her again, knowing she had had enough of words. But although he lifted the heavy weight of her hair and nibbled at her neck until she quivered with delight, he had not finished talking. "Stay here with me," he said urgently, his lips tracing the slender line of her throat. "You don't have to go back to Montreal."

She froze in his arms, her eyes dilated with shock; she had an actual physical sensation of falling, falling through space, to land with a mind-jarring thud on the hard ground of reality. Crumpled, bleeding inwardly, a victim of her own delusions, she thrust her fist against her mouth to prevent herself from crying out.

Scarcely aware of Rhys's weight and blind to the sudden hardening of his features, she whimpered, more to herself than to him, "What have I done? Oh, God, what have I done?"

His words had the shock of cold water thrown in her face. "Technically speaking, we've done nothing."

In a sudden sharp gesture she turned her head away from him, staring at the muted blues and golds of the velvet upholstery as if nothing else in the world existed. "You don't understand...." Silent tears began to course down her cheeks. "I forgot about Alan!" Her anguished gray eyes, drowning in their own tears, sought his face, and her voice was raw with self-contempt. "I never even *thought* of him—I threw myself at you as if he didn't exist."

Rhys made no attempt to hold her or to comfort her. "Perhaps you should pay attention to what that's saying to you." She looked at him so uncomprehendingly that he added impatiently, "You must have slept with him. Is it the same between you and him as it is between us?"

There was a ring of absolute truth in her simple reply. "I've never slept with him."

Rhys's eyes narrowed. "Don't you know what that says to me? If you and I were engaged you'd be in my bed, no question of that—and you'd be willing, too, wouldn't you, Diana?"

"It's different...it's not like that." She fumbled for words. "Alan wants to make love to me, I know, but he's willing to wait." She added with sudden intensity, knowing it for the truth, "He's a fine person, Rhys, and he's been very good to me. You'd like him, I know you would."

"But do you love him?"

"Of course I do. I wouldn't have agreed to marry him otherwise."

"Then what are you doing here?"

As her eyes traveled down their naked bodies, still lying so intimately together on the soft cushions, her cheeks were scorched with humiliation. "I don't know...I feel so ashamed of myself, Rhys," she whispered.

"Yet you said only a few minutes ago how right it felt to be in my arms."

"Yes, I did." Two more tears trickled down her face. "How can anything that feels so right be so wrong? So dreadfully wrong?"

Gently he wiped her cheek dry with his finger. "Perhaps because it's not wrong, Diana. The wrong would be in your marrying a man whom you don't desire."

"You don't know that!"

"I can guess it, though." He smiled faintly.

"You're a very direct and passionate woman, Diana. You know what you want and you go after it. And there's nothing wrong with that. I don't know what your life's been like the past ten years or for what reasons you've become involved with Alan—I'm sure they were good ones. But I suspect that that spark of, oh, call it mutual attraction, sex, lust, desire, whatever you like—is missing. And that means that sooner or later you'll be in trouble, the two of you."

There was a horrible logic to what he was saying. Alan's kisses had been pleasant, an agreeable extension of their friendship, but they had never had the cataclysmic effect of a single one of Rhys's. So did that mean she shouldn't marry Alan? Then into her mind there dropped an image of Alan and Belinda bent together over a puzzle, neat fair head close to silky black one; of him swinging the child into his arms last Christmas and of Belinda's shrieks of excitement. "Put me down, Uncle Alan, put me down!"

She heard herself say coldly, "You're wrong, Rhys. Alan and I are very happy together. It may not be the same as...as what happens between you and me. It *isn't* the same. But that doesn't mean the whole relationship is invalid."

"Diana, you're—"

"I'm not finished," she interrupted. "I don't understand what happens every time we come near each other; maybe your word 'lust' is the right one. But I do know this—it hasn't brought me much happiness. Oh, sure, I had three days ten years ago. And then you were gone and I was left to pick up the pieces. To get over you as best I could." Her voice had risen in spite of herself as the anger and resentment she had felt for so long spilled out. "And now you're saying the same thing, using the same excuses. The timing's not right, you said. Well, the timing'll never be right for you, will it, Rhys? So what am I supposed to do? Go to bed with you now? Have another three-day affair and then say, 'Goodbye, it's been nice knowing you'?" She drew a ragged breath. "No, thanks! I did that once and I won't do it again."

"It wouldn't have to be a three-day affair." His mouth twisted. "This time I won't have to leave to go on tour."

She had to end this.... "What are you trying to do—appeal to my sympathies?" she snapped.

"You know damn well that's the last thing I'd do." He swung himself around so that he was sitting up, facing her. "What I'm endeavoring to say is that we could give ourselves a chance. You're twenty-seven now, not seventeen. An independent woman. You don't have to go back to Montreal. Stay here with me—and let's just take it day by day and see what happens."

For a split second she was tempted, abandoning herself to the thought of what it would be like: the days spent roaming the countryside with Rhys, the nights spent in his arms. But then reality intervened and the brief golden dream was shattered. The one thing Rhys did not—and must not—know about her was that she had a child who needed her, for whom she was the only parent. And besides that, there was Alan.

She sat up, reaching for her dress and pulling it over her head. "I can't, Rhys," she said quietly yet with utter conviction. "It's impossible. No matter what you think, I do love Alan. And I owe him a great deal, so I can't act as though he doesn't exist. I feel badly enough about what I've done, as though I've already betrayed him."

"You're very loyal." No emotion in his voice.

"Well, naturally. He's my fiancé. How could I be otherwise?"

"He's a fortunate man. I hope he knows that."

"He loves me very much, Rhys. And deserves far better than what I've done tonight." She stood up, smoothing the dress over her hips. Rhys got slowly to his feet, too, standing very close to her. She looked up at him, her expression serious and intent. "Which is why I'm going to leave tomorrow, Rhys. I shouldn't have come here in the first place, but I thought I might be able to help you get back to your music. I don't think I can do that. I don't think anyone can. And I know I mustn't stay any longer—it would be wrong for everyone concerned. Don't worry, I'll find some kind of an explanation that will satisfy Kate."

"Kate is the least of my worries right now." His eyes were hooded, dark as night and just as unreadable. "I admire your loyalty, Diana; it's a rare commodity these days. But I still think you're making the wrong decision."

"I'm making the only possible decision." Very briefly she rested her palm against his cheek, knowing this was her real goodbye, that anything she might say tomorrow morning would be artificial compared to it. "Goodbye, Rhys," she said softly. "Take care of yourself, won't you? I..." Her eyes were suddenly sparkling with unshed tears. "No matter what, I still care what happens to you."

Before he could reply, she had picked up her shoes and left the room, her bare feet soundless on the thick carpet. The door closed behind her.

CHAPTER TEN

DIANA HAD MEANT to wake up early the next morning so that she could phone the airport, pack her few belongings and be on her way before lunchtime. However, when she surfaced from the depths of a profound and dreamless sleep and looked at the little bedside clock, it said eleven-thirty. Impossible.... She blinked and looked again, but the tiny gold hands remained obstinately at the eleven and the six. Quickly she got out of bed and dressed, pulling on her white slacks and embroidered blouse. It would be nice to get home and have a few more clothes to choose from, she thought wryly.

She padded down the hall to the kitchen. Robert was busy at the stove, a workmanlike white apron over his gray flannel trousers and blue shirt. He was stirring a saucepan from which arose a delicious odor, and when she peered into it he explained, "Homemade vegetable soup. I have a small garden behind the garage, so they're nearly all fresh vegetables."

"My father's a great gardener. Mmm, it smells good. Where's everyone, Robert?"

"Miss Kate's outside resting in the sun. I'm not sure where Mr. Morgan is."

"He's right here," a deep voice said, and in spite of herself Diana gave a start. Hoping Robert hadn't noticed, she said brightly, "Oh, good morning."

" 'Good afternoon' is more exact. Sleep well, Diana?"

There was nothing in the lazy voice but polite inquiry. Why then was she blushing? She buried her face in the fragrant steam. "Yes, thank you."

"Good. It's a beautiful day."

It was unlike Rhys to make small talk, so she looked at him sharply. He was staring out the window, his hands in his pockets. He didn't look as though he had slept well, Diana decided, for his eyes were sunk in their sockets and there were new lines graven in his cheeks. But when he turned to face her, there was something in his expression that forbade anything other than routine surface conversation. She said banally, "I must call the airport."

"Are you leaving, miss?" This from Robert, his spoon stopping its rhythmic stirring of the soup.

"Yes, I have to get back."

"We'd hope you'd be able to stay longer."

"I'm afraid that's impossible, Robert. May I make myself a cup of coffee? I'll drink it outside with Kate and tell her I'm leaving."

"You'd better find out if there's a flight first," Rhys said prosaically. "You'll probably have to go back via Halifax."

Putting the kettle on the stove, she took refuge in small talk. "Do you know the number?"

"Come with me."

She followed him down the hall to the music room,

a room she would have preferred not to visit again. Averting her eyes from the sofa, she saw a beige telephone on the desk. "The book's in the top drawer," Rhys said, apparently quite unaffected by their surroundings.

"I could have used the phone in the kitchen."

"So you could. But Kate might have come wandering in, and I want you to give her some kind of a decent explanation rather than surprise her like that. I have the feeling she's rather attached herself to you."

He was probably right, she realized with a twinge of guilt. Reaching for the drawer, she was about to open it when the telephone rang, its shrill summons making her jump.

With only a fractional hesitation Rhys picked up the receiver. "Hello?... Yes, this is Rhys Morgan."

Diana wandered over to the bookshelves, trying not to listen. But Rhys's sudden "*What* did you say?" made her head swing around, and she could not help hearing the rest of the conversation. "You mean he's alive? My God, we'd given him up for dead.... I see. Yesterday, eh?... Have the doctors there explained to him what's happened to his wife?... No, I suppose that's natural. When could he be released?... That soon? Is it possible for me to talk to him?... Thanks...."

He put his hand over the mouthpiece, saying abruptly to Diana, "Barrie's alive. Turned up at some little outpost last night and they flew him into Calgary—it's the hospital calling. Apparently he's not in too—"

He broke off. "Hello, Barrie? God, man, it's good

to hear your voice." His own was rough with emotion. "Yeah, the nurse told me that. What sort of shape are you in?... The survival training paid off for sure, didn't it?... Okay, how much have they told you?... Well, that's about it, Barrie. There was the shock of your disappearance and then the week or so of waiting for word from the search teams. As you probably know now, they didn't find a thing. Then one day the police came to your house, actually to tell Kate the search was being called off. She saw them from the upstairs window, must have thought they had news of you and went running down the stairs. The rest you know. She tripped and fell and had a miscarriage, and that, coupled with the strain of the previous few days, caused her to lose her memory. She doesn't remember you or her marriage or the pregnancy. She does get glimpses of earlier days sometimes, but they usually only serve to confuse her—a plane flying overhead will upset her, for instance. But the doctors have assured me it's only a temporary thing and that there'll be no permanent damage. I brought her here because it seemed best for her to have a change of surroundings and easier for me to keep an eye on her."

A long pause while Rhys listened intently. "You may be right—have you checked it out with the doctor who was seeing her before she came here?... I see. When can you come?... I don't know if I can arrange that or not, Barrie. Robert's here all the time, of course, but—just hold on a minute."

Again Rhys covered the mouthpiece with his hand, speaking directly to Diana. "Barrie wants me to fly out to Calgary right away and bring him back here. He's pretty weak, and the doctors say there'll be a delay in his release if he has to travel alone. Naturally he's very anxious to see Kate again, hence the rush. Diana, will you postpone your departure just for a day or two? I don't want to leave Kate with only Robert for company, and she certainly can't go with me."

What choice did Diana have? "Of course I will," she said fatalistically.

Briefly he squeezed her shoulder. "Good girl.... Barrie? Look, I'll call the airport and see what I can arrange, and I'll call you back as soon as possible. What's your number?" He scribbled the numerals on a piece of paper. "Okay, I'll get back to you. And listen—don't worry. Everything will work out some-how, I'm sure. The main thing is that you're alive.... I'll be in touch. Goodbye."

He replaced the receiver and said quietly, "You know, I still can't quite believe it's true, that after all this time he's alive."

"It's wonderful news, Rhys."

"Yeah...but I wonder how Kate will react. They seem to think in Calgary that seeing him again might bring back her memory."

"That could be very traumatic for her."

"And for him, too.... Thanks for saying you'll stay, Diana. I think having another woman for com-pany is good for her. Look, would you mind going out and sitting with her now while I make all the ar-rangements?"

"Of course not." Diana smiled at him, but he was

already flipping the pages of the telephone directory.

In the kitchen she briefly outlined to Robert what had happened, which disturbed his normal phlegmatic attitude enough that he added more salt than he had intended to the soup. Then she went out into the garden. Rhys was right—it *was* a beautiful day, with the sun blindingly bright and hot on her exposed skin.

When she walked across the grass, Kate smiled at her lazily. "Hello, Diana. I thought *you* were going to be the one to spend the day in bed today. Were you up late last night, you and Rhys?"

No guile in the question, not a hint of innuendo. "Yes, we stayed up talking until some disgraceful hour this morning," Diana responded lightly. "How are you feeling today?"

"Much better, thanks. Have you been getting anywhere with Rhys? You were in the music room last night, weren't you?"

For a moment Diana totally misunderstood the drift of Kate's question, and hot color rushed to her cheeks. Then she caught herself. "No, not really, Kate," she said steadily. "He refuses to play at all, because he says it will be second-rate, and I can understand that. And when I pressed him about composing or teaching, he lost patience altogether."

Kate sighed, the sun gleaming in her pale hair. "I was afraid of that, although I hoped that as an old friend you might have been able to accomplish something. He won't talk to me about it." She smiled ruefully. "He's very sweet and forbearing, mind you—but very obstinate."

Diana chuckled. Kate was no fool, for all her gentle ways. "I rather doubt that I'll bring the subject up again," she remarked. "I was told in no uncertain terms to mind my own business." She lay back on the lawn chair, closing her eyes and feeling the sun beat on her eyelids. It was difficult talking to Kate, knowing as she did about Barrie's imminent return.

Shortly afterward Rhys joined them, announcing casually to Kate, "I have to make a short business trip. I'm leaving this evening and I'll be back the day after tomorrow. Diana's promised to stay until I get home. The two of you will be all right together, won't you? Robert will drive me to the airport, so you can have the car while I'm gone."

"Are you sure you trust us?" Kate said blithely.

Rhys's eyes were on Diana when he answered quietly, "Yes, I'm sure."

Diana lowered her eyes and said, knowing he would understand, "I'm glad you were able to make the necessary arrangements."

He left around six, hugging Kate and kissing her on the cheek, not touching Diana at all. "See you in a couple of days," he said abruptly with a curt nod before striding over to the car where Robert was waiting. The two women waved as the car drove away, Diana trying to act naturally even though his coldness had hurt her.

The two days passed pleasantly enough. They lay in the sun, helped Robert with the meals, hiked up the mountain to the lookout in the cool of the evening, went to a movie at the park information center. Kate was undemanding company, incurious about

Diana's background and for obvious reasons silent about her own. It was very much a relationship based on the present moment, and as such it was peculiarly satisfying. Yet the whole time Diana was aware of her own uneasiness, knowing that in only a matter of hours Kate's past was going to confront her inescapably in the form of the husband whose existence she had blanked out. How would she react? Would she be happy to see him? Or would all the grief and bitterness come back and overwhelm her again?

It was late morning when Robert left for the airport to get Rhys and Barrie. After lunch—a leafy green salad with sliced meats, followed by raspberries and cream—Diana was too restless to sit down. "Let's go and weed the garden," she suggested. "There was rain during the night, so the ground should be soft."

Kate was agreeable, so the two of them settled to the task. There was enough cloud cover so that it was not uncomfortably warm and enough of a breeze to keep the mosquitoes and blackflies away. The earth smelled damp and rich. Kate worked quickly and efficiently, so much so that Diana was sure she must have had a garden of her own at some point in the past. However, like so many subjects that came up, it was forbidden territory. Particularly so today, Diana thought, hauling up a thistle with vicious strength and wincing as the spines dug into her fingers. There was no point in bothering Kate with unnecessary questions today, for Barrie's unexpected return would be more than enough for her to deal with.

The slow minutes went by. Kate loaded the weeds

onto the wheelbarrow and dumped them on the compost pile, raking them out flat. Diana hoed along the rows of carrots and beets, then used the wheelbarrow herself to remove the pile of rocks she had accumulated; Robert claimed the rocks multiplied underground, and he might be right, she thought as she unloaded them near the wall at the back of the property. A gull swooped down to investigate, its sleek plumage and cold yellow eyes at variance with the mournful pitch of its cry. And then she heard the noise she had been waiting for all afternoon: the crunch of tires on the gravel driveway, the smooth purr of the Jaguar's motor. Rhys—and Barrie—had arrived.

She straightened slowly, realizing for the first time that her back was aching. "That sounds like Rhys," she said, her voice a little higher-pitched than usual. "Shall we go and meet him?"

"You go ahead—I want to finish this row. I expect he's more interested in seeing you than me, anyway."

"None of that, Kate Pemberton!" Diana responded, half serious, half joking.

"He's certainly never looks at me the way I catch him looking at you sometimes," Kate responded placidly. "Off you go or he'll be wondering where we are."

Diana leaned her hoe against the wheelbarrow and walked slowly toward the house, so preoccupied by the prospect of Barrie's arrival that she gave no thought to her own appearance. She kicked off her boots at the back door and went into the kitchen, where she stripped off her socks. It took the quick spark of emotion that flashed through Rhys's eyes to make her realize that her shorts were very brief and that her cotton shirt, bent over as she was, revealed rather more of her breasts than was wise. For an equally brief moment she found herself admiring Rhys's height and lean muscular build in his well-fitting summer suit. He looked cool and, in a totally masculine way, very elegant. Not until he began speaking did her attention switch to the man at his side. "Diana, this is Barrie Pemberton. Barrie, Diana Sutherland."

Her outstretched hand was shaken with considerable force; the man's palm was rough and callused. Trying not to wince, she said, "Hello, Barrie."

"Rhys has told me you changed your plans in order to stay with Kate the last couple of days," he replied. "Thank you for that."

He was two or three inches shorter than Rhys, with unruly red hair and a curly red beard framing a face weathered to a mahogany brown. He was painfully thin, and across his forehead was the jagged white line of a new scar. His eye sockets were dark and bruised looking; his right wrist was in a cast supported by a sling. Normally, she could imagine, he would be powerfully built, but because of his recent ordeal he had lost so much weight that his shirt hung loosely on his frame.

"Shouldn't you be sitting down?" she asked.

"Where's Kate?" was the abrupt response.

"She's in the garden. . . we've been weeding. Would you like me to fetch her?" Anything to remove that look of intolerable strain from his dark brown eyes.

He took two steps toward the back door before Rhys's hand clamped on his shoulder. "Hold it, Barrie—it might be better if she came indoors. I'll go and get her. You stay here."

Diana could see the effort it took for Barrie to halt his impetuous rush for the door. Rhys had seen it, too, for he said evenly, "Take it easy; I'll be back in a minute."

As Rhys left the room, Diana stood by helplessly, wishing there was something she could do or say to relieve the tension. But it was Barrie who spoke. "Sorry about inflicting this on you, Diana." He rubbed his eyes, his hands not quite steady. "I might as well tell you, I'm scared to death. I love her so much—I should never have gone on this last flight."

"But at least you're home safely, and surely now she'll be all right."

"I hope to God you're right." He broke off because Rhys had opened the back door and was ushering Kate in. The girl slipped out of her muddy shoes. She, too, was wearing shorts with a faded cotton shirt, her fine pale hair pulled back into a ponytail, a style that made her look about eighteen. She looked relaxed and happy, for she was smiling at something Rhys must have said. There was nothing in her outward appearance to indicate her recent illness or her amnesia.

Beside her Diana heard Barrie's harsh indrawn breath. Then he had left her side and was striding across the floor toward his wife. "Kate," he said in a voice quite different from the one he had used a moment ago. "Darling Kate. God, how I've missed you."

Kate had not noticed him before. Now she stared at him, and for an instant so fleeting it might have been imagined, her face convulsed with emotion. Pain? Anger? Guilt? Then her features smoothed to tranquillity and her blue eyes emptied, to hold only a faint puzzlement. "I beg your pardon?" she said politely.

It stopped Barrie dead in his tracks. For a moment he swayed, and Diana thought he was going to fall. But he took hold of himself, saying with a manful effort at lightness, "Kate, it's Barrie. I know I've lost weight but surely I don't look that different."

She smiled uncertainly. "Am I supposed to know you?"

"Of course you are!" he burst out.

Kate took a step backward; Rhys was standing beside her, between her and the back door. "Well, I'm sorry, I don't," she said coldly.

Barrie's chest was heaving as if he'd been running, but when he spoke he sounded reasonable and calm. "Darling, I know about the baby...they told me at the hospital. I'm sorry about it, more sorry than I can say, because I feel responsible. If I hadn't gone on that last trip it wouldn't have happened. But you're more important to me, Kate. If I'd lost you, I would have gone out of my mind."

The girl looked from him to Rhys, her face a study in bewilderment. "I don't know what you're talking about," she said. "I think you must be out of your mind to talk to me this way—I've never even seen you before. Rhys, what's going on?''

Rhys dropped a comforting hand on her shoulder, and Diana saw a tremor pass through Barrie's emaciated body as Kate cowered against her cousin. Rhys said matter-of-factly, ''Take a good look at Barrie, Kate. Are you sure you don't know him? He's not the slightest bit familiar to you?''

Obediently Kate stared at the red-haired man, who bore her scrutiny with a stoicism Diana could only admire. ''I'm positive I've never seen him before,'' she said finally. ''I—I don't understand, Rhys. Why is he acting so strangely?'' She clasped her mud-stained hands in front of her, and there was a thin edge of fear in her voice. ''And why am I supposed to know him?''

It was too much for Barrie. He took a single step toward her. ''Because I'm your husband!'' he said hoarsely. ''We met two years ago. We were married last summer. You were carrying my child. Kate, you've *got* to remember!''

There was real fear in Kate's manner now. ''You *are* crazy,'' she cried. ''I don't know who you are or why Rhys brought you here, but I'm telling you once and for all, I don't know you!''

As the two of them faced each other, Rhys and Diana might not have been in the room. Barrie suddenly reached out and grabbed Kate by the arm, pulling her toward him. ''I love you, Kate. For God's sake, don't torture me like this. Can't you even say you're glad that I'm alive?''

''I really don't care,'' she said raggedly, her normally sweet-natured face distorted by a mixture of anger and fear. "Please take your hand off my arm and leave me alone. I—I'm going to go and wash my hands and get ready for supper."

Numbly Barrie let his hand drop to his side, watching as Kate ran past him out of the kitchen and down the hall, making no move to follow her. Abruptly he pulled out a chair and sat down, burying his head in his hands.

Across his stooped figure Diana's eyes met Rhys's, hers wet with tears. Rhys said quietly, "I was afraid this might happen."

"You mean you guessed that she might not recognize Barrie?"

"I thought she might not." He grimaced. "It's one case where I wish I'd been wrong."

Barrie must have heard this quiet interchange. He looked up, his face ravaged by shock. "You did warn me," he said dully.

"I tried."

"But I didn't listen. I was convinced you were wrong and that Kate would come rushing into my arms." His laugh was a travesty of humor. "I could hardly have been farther from the mark, could I?" He straightened in the chair. "So what do we do now?"

"There's nothing we can do right now," Rhys said firmly. "She's upset and we'll have to let her calm down. I'd suggest that at dinner tonight we all play it cool. You're just a friend who's recovering from a bad plane crash and you're here to recuperate."

"You're running a convalescent home, Rhys,"

Barrie said with the first touch of amusement Diana had seen in him. His faint smile changed his face, making him look younger and more carefree—the Barrie whom Kate must have known.

"Looks like it, doesn't it? Which brings me to my second piece of advice. I'll show you your room, Barrie, and I think the best thing you can do is have a rest. We've been on the go since some ungodly hour this morning."

Barrie levered himself up. "Okay." As if he couldn't help himself, he blurted, "Is she going to be all right, Rhys?" and Diana could see him brace himself for the reply.

"I don't know, Barrie," Rhys said with painful honesty. "I think the only thing we can do for now is go from day to day. You're not fit to go back to work right now—"

"I handed in my resignation as a pilot, anyway—shutting the stable door after the horse is gone," he said bitterly.

Diana said gently, "Try not to blame yourself too much, Barrie."

He gave a rueful grin. "Easier said then done. Sorry, Rhys—you were saying?"

"You can stay here for as long as you like. There's lots of room. In time Kate will come to accept you... as a new friend, if nothing else. And when you get back to Calgary you may have to seek medical advice."

Barrie stretched to relieve the tightness in his muscles. "I hear every word you're saying and it's damn good advice. But what I really feel like doing is taking her in my arms and holding her and never letting her go,'' he said grimly. "Don't worry, Rhys—I won't. I've got that much sense left. You're right, I'm going to hit the pit. See you later, Diana.''

When the two men left the room Diana sank down on a chair, for the strain of the scene had told on her. In a couple of minutes Rhys came back. He looked at her unsmilingly. "I think I'd better give you the same advice,'' he said, putting his hands under her elbows and bringing her upright. "Go to bed and have a rest, Diana.''

He was standing very close to her. He had taken off his jacket and loosened his tie, and she could see the steady beat of the pulse in his neck. Unconsciously she swayed toward him, unsurprised when she felt his arms go around her and pull her closer so that her cheek rested against his shirtfront. When she looked up at him, their kiss was as inevitable as the summer tides and just as powerful, lifting her up from darkness and pain and casting her on a shimmering golden shore. Again she had that terrifying sense of rightness, that certainty that this was where she belonged. Terrifying because it had to be false. She did not belong with Rhys; she never had, she never could. He had said so himself, and she herself knew it to be true. Her life lay in Montreal, with Belinda and with Alan.

She pulled free, her traitorous body immediately aching for that warm sweet contact, that press of limb on limb. It was all too much....

Knowing she was going to cry, too proud to let Rhys see, she muttered, "I'm going to my room,'' and hurriedly left him, part of her brain noticing that he had not attempted to stop her. Closing the bedroom door behind her she let the tears flow, not sure for whom she was crying. For Kate? For Barrie? Or for herself? It didn't seem to matter. Falling facedown on the bed, letting the tears soak into the pillow, she eventually fell asleep.

CHAPTER ELEVEN

WHEN DIANA AWOKE it was nearly six. She felt heavy eyed and lethargic, so she stripped off her shorts and top and went into the shower, letting the hot water beat on her neck and shoulders and against her closed eyelids as the steam enveloped her. Stepping out, she pulled off her shower cap and wrapped a towel around her before she went back into the bedroom to get her clothes.

Rhys was standing by the bed; the door into the hallway was closed. Her heart gave a single leap, then settled into a steady pounding. As if they had never intervened, ten years disappeared and she was back in his friend's apartment in Montreal; she had taken a shower and had emerged from the bathroom wrapped in a towel, just as she had today. But on that occasion he had walked up to her and his hands had pulled at the towel so that it had dropped to the ground, and then he had gathered her naked body in his arms, carrying her over to the bed, and there they had made love....

Her lashes flickered as she wondered if he was remembering the same occasion. She said foolishly, "Were you looking for me?"

"Dinner's nearly ready. Robert's made a soufflé, so he wants everyone at the table on time."

It was painfully obvious that he had no recollection of the event at all. "Very well. It'll only take me a minute to get dressed." Pointedly she glanced at the door, willing him to leave.

He seemed in no hurry, however. Walking over to the far window he gazed out across the waters of the bay to the hills beyond. "I also wanted to ask you a favor—another one," he said.

To have him here in her bedroom, so near and yet so drastically far away, was a torment. "You do choose your moments." As he glanced over at her, she clutched the towel a little tighter. "I'm getting your carpet wet."

Deliberately his eyes turned back to the window. "It won't take a minute. The next two or three days are bound to be a bit tense until Kate accepts Barrie as just another visitor—or else by some miracle remembers who he is. I'm asking you to stay a little longer, to give her some support. Would you do that?"

"I have to get back, Rhys. I've already stayed longer than I planned."

"I'm aware of that. It's only a matter of a day or two, Diana. Surely your Alan can do without you for that much longer?"

Put like that, it did sound silly for her to quibble, particularly as she knew that Alan was very busy at work; she had phoned him while Rhys was away. Yet she could not altogether smother the clear cold voice in her brain that warned her of danger. "For Kate's sake I'll do it," she said, praying she wouldn't regret her decision.

"But not for my sake?"

"Hardly."

"You disappoint me."

"That I doubt. And now, Rhys Morgan, if you want me to be ready for Robert's soufflé, you'd better leave." She purposely kept her voice light during this exchange, for she had no wish seriously to provoke him.

In a leisurely way his eyes surveyed her from head to foot. "It seems a pity."

She would *not* blush. "Doesn't it," she said dryly. "Out."

He began walking toward the door. With his hand on the doorknob he paused, looking back at her over his shoulder. "Do you remember the last time I saw you after a shower? It ended a little differently than this, didn't it?" A sardonic lift of his eyebrow, and then he left the room, the door closing with exaggerated quietness behind him.

She let out her breath in a sigh that expressed both anger and amusement. Trust him to have the perfect exit line... and he *had* remembered.

With one eye on the clock she began to dress. She had one outfit that she hadn't worn yet, a cotton dress in a tiny floral print on a soft turquoise background, fashioned with elbow-length puffed sleeves and a ruffled skirt edged with white lace. She put on dainty white sandals, drew her hair into a loose knot with soft curls around her face, and added a pale pink lipstick and a dusting of delicate blue eye shadow. Very romantic, she thought mischievously. Rhys would appreciate it.

As if she had conjured him up, there came a tap at her door. She opened it and smiled up at him. "I'm ready. . . two minutes early," she said pertly.

There was no questioning his expression as he looked her up and down; she remembered only too well how passion and laughter could mingle on his face. "You look delightful. Mind you, you looked delightful ten minutes ago, too."

Suddenly serious, he added in a low voice, "You know, Diana, more and more I'm coming to think that you and I belong together, that I'd be crazy to tamely let you go back to Montreal."

"That's not what you said a few days ago."

"It's not, is it?"

"I think you're being a dog in the manger. You didn't want me for yourself, but when you found out about Alan you didn't want him to have me, either."

"Would that it were that simple, my dear."

She stirred uncomfortably. She had no idea what he was getting at, and for the sake of her peace of mind she thought it was better so. With a sense of reprieve she heard the harmonious chime of the dinner bell. "Dinner's ready," she said brightly and redundantly.

"I'd better go and get Kate. She's no doubt hiding in her room until the last minute."

In the dining room Diana found Barrie nursing a drink as he waited for the rest of them. He had changed into a lightweight beige suit that even more clearly than his previous outfit showed how much weight he had lost. He looked tired and very tense.

"Did you sleep?" she asked sympathetically.

"No. Too worked up. Where's Kate?"

"Rhys is getting her." Although she was not a woman normally much given to touching men she didn't know, she found herself laying her hand on his sleeve. "We'll all help as much as we can, Barrie."

"I know that. Thanks, Diana." Then his expression tightened as Rhys and Kate entered the room, and across the table he and Kate regarded each other warily. He nodded stiffly. "Hello, Kate. I'm sorry if I got off to a bad start with you—it won't happen again."

She was wearing a very plain apple-green dress and had wound her hair into a braided coronet around her head. Of the two women it was she who looked the older. "I'd rather it didn't. I didn't like it," she said stiltedly.

As Rhys poured the wine, the other three sat down at the oval oak table and the meal began. Robert's soufflé was light and fluffy enough to satisfy even his own high standards. The delicate flavor of the asparagus in hollandaise sauce complemented it perfectly, as did the crisp hot rolls and the tossed salad. At first Diana and Rhys carried the major part of the conversation, while Kate and Barrie studiously concentrated on eating. However, the atmosphere gradually relaxed. Although it was obvious that Barrie's main interests were in things mechanical, he had seen Diana's Calgary show. Perhaps because of a certain detachment he was able to give her one or two interesting insights. He asked her—it was a common enough question—whether she worked in fits and starts or in a more or less regular routine.

"I try to keep to a routine, Barrie, particularly in the winter. Because morning's my best time of day, I endeavor to put in a good four or five hours then. It's less regular in the summer, when I'm able to get out more. I'm afraid if I waited until inspiration struck, I wouldn't get much done."

"Have you done many paintings here?"

"A few. Not as many as I should have. I've always noticed that if I stay away from painting for too long, it's difficult to get back to it. Almost as if I get scared of it, afraid I won't be able to do it; that I'll have lost the touch. Totally irrational, because so far, touch wood, I never have. But it's a very genuine fear."

"I used to have something of the same feeling about the piano," Rhys commented. "Before every performance I'd sweat blood, terrified that I'd get out there on the stage and not be able to play a note. Like you, it never happened...thank goodness!"

"Will you play something for us after dinner?" Barrie asked. "I haven't heard you for over a year."

Diana's eyes flew to Rhys's face, and because she was so attuned to his moods she saw the momentary tightening of his lips, the flicker of an indefinable emotion cross his features. His scarred hand gripping his wineglass he said evenly, "Sorry, Barrie. Since the accident I've completely given up playing, even for close friends."

Barrie looked momentarily taken aback. "I hadn't realized the accident had affected you that badly. I'm sorry to hear it. So tell me—you must be contemplating some kind of new direction? A new career?"

"I suppose I'll have to." The words had a finality about them that indicated the subject was closed.

Thoughtfully, Barrie buttered another roll. The candlelight was kind to him, blurring the ravages of his recent ordeal. When he spoke, although he addressed Rhys, Diana sensed intuitively he was directing his remarks toward Kate. "I'm in something of the same position," he said. "I've been a bush pilot now for seven years and loved every minute of it up until this last flight and the crash. But it's a hard life if you have a wife and family—you're away a lot, your hours are irregular, you can get stuck up north and be late back, you can run into mechanical trouble or bad weather. The things that can go wrong are endless. I'm finally coming to the conclusion that it's not fair to subject someone else to that kind of uncertainty. Would you agree with me, Kate?"

She was obviously surprised to be questioned directly. "I—I don't know," she stumbled. "I suppose you're right."

As if Rhys and Diana were no longer in the room, Barrie leaned forward, his dark eyes intent on her heart-shaped face. "That kind of life is fine for someone who's young and single. But marriage has to mean an altering of priorities. There's another person to consider—her needs and concerns. It's taken me a long time to understand that. Too long."

Kate's features were strained, and when she spoke it was with a kind of desperate courage. "Earlier today you said that I was your wife," she blurted. "I can't be, Barrie, I'd *have* to remember that. I don't understand why you're making such a mistake; maybe it's something to do with the plane crash you went through. But I wish you wouldn't talk to me that way. It only confuses me.''

Baffled, he sat back in his chair, and Diana said quickly, ''So you're contemplating a change of jobs?''

Gratefully he accepted her lead. ''Yes. The question is what. Flying's been my whole world, all I know. The thought of a desk job, indoors all day, drives me nuts.''

''What exactly happened when you crashed, Barrie?'' Rhys asked. ''Unless you'd rather not talk about it?''

''Hell, no, I don't mind.'' Barrie tugged at his beard ruefully. ''Talk about a catalog of errors, though. I was supposed to be taking some medical supplies up to an Inuit village and was late getting away because they couldn't straighten out the paperwork for the cargo. The weather report wasn't encouraging, but I decided to risk it anyway—my first mistake and a bad one, as it turned out. Two or three hundred miles off into the bush and miles from any settlement, I ran into the worst electrical storm I've ever seen. I took a wide detour to try to avoid it, which is one of the reasons the search-and-rescue people never found me—I wasn't on course. Second mistake. Anyway, to make a long story short, the tail of the plane was struck by lightning and caught fire. I knew I had to land; the only choice was on a lake. It was getting dark, and by the time I found one big enough the fire had really taken hold. I loused up the landing, and that was the third mistake.''

Diana listened with a kind of horrified fascination, her vivid imagination picturing the burning plane spiraling through the dusk over the harsh tundra landscape, all rocks and bogs and stunted trees. "I think it's a miracle you managed to land at all," she interjected.

He grinned, leaning back as Robert served him dessert, a fresh-fruit compote. "It's a miracle I got out of it alive. That landing could have served as a classic illustration for a beginning pilot of all the things not to do. The upshot was that the plane hit nose first and sank. The water was like ice, of course, because summer comes late up there, but luckily I'm a pretty strong swimmer and I made it to shore."

"Did you salvage anything from the plane... besides yourself, that is?" Rhys asked. Kate, Diana noticed, was listening to Barrie's narrative in a frowning silence, her fingers absently playing with her cutlery as she picked at her food.

"Not a thing. I had my hunting knife and a waterproof container of matches—I never travel without those. But my compass was smashed. I was really hampered by this—" he indicated his sling "—and I was pretty groggy, too, because I'd hit my head on the windshield. So it took me three times longer to do anything than it normally would. The weather was foul, cold and wet, a driving rain that seemed to get through any kind of a shelter I could rig up. I don't think I was ever completely dry the whole time I was out there. And if it wasn't rain, it was mosquitoes and blackflies."

"I've heard they're bad enough sometimes to drive animals—and people—crazy," Diana ventured.

"I can believe it. In the evening I'd sometimes light a smudge fire to keep them away, but during the day there wasn't much I could do."

"Did you have any idea where you were?" she asked.

"A general idea, yes. But with no compass it was hard to get an accurate sense of direction. I know I missed at least two Cree settlements where I could have got help, although even with a compass it would have been difficult to have hit them right on—they're just pinpoints in the wilderness."

"What did you eat?" Rhys asked.

"Not much! It's one way to diet, although not one I'd recommend. Berries. Tea made out of bark or lichens or the leaves of shrubs. That was about it. I was getting pretty weak by the end."

"How did you get help?"

"I'd like to be able to say it was sheer skill that saved me," Barrie grinned. "But it wasn't—it was sheer luck instead. I literally stumbled into the camp-site of three Indians on a hunting trek. I wasn't in great shape, so they hauled me on a travois to their village, where there was a two-way radio. The next day a plane flew in, and that was that." He stirred his coffee reflectively, and for a moment his eyes flickered over the peaceful civilized room and the faces of his three listeners. "It seems like a dream now, an almost-forgotten nightmare. I think the worst part was the loneliness. That and the uncertainty. The fear that I might be going around in circles or that I'd pass out from hunger and exhaustion before I could get help and that no one would ever know what had happened to me.''

Kate spoke for the first time. ''Something must have kept you going,'' she said, a note almost of hostility in her voice.

He looked at her, and for a moment his heart was in his eyes. Quickly she glanced down at her plate, her fingers clenched on her spoon. ''Something—or someone—must have,'' he agreed quietly. ''Whatever it was, I give thanks for it. Because otherwise I wouldn't be here today.''

There was a short silence, on Barrie's part, at least, full of things unsaid. With startling suddenness Kate pushed her chair back. ''I'm very tired. If you'll all excuse me, I think I'll go to bed.''

Barrie had half risen. ''Kate—''

''Good night.'' Hurriedly she left the room.

Rhys put out a restraining hand. ''Take it easy, lad. I don't think you can rush her at this stage.''

Barrie was staring after her. ''She was the one who kept me going, of course,'' he said tonelessly. ''She and the child. But will I ever be able to tell her that?''

''I'm sure you will. But it's going to take time.''

As Barrie collapsed in his chair, Diana was reminded that only a few days ago he had been lost and near starvation in the bush, his sole strength the thought of his young wife—who now did not even recognize him. She in turn got up. ''I'll go and see if she's all right,'' she murmured, catching Rhys's quick appreciative nod as she left the room.

Tapping on Kate's door she called softly, "Kate, may I come in?"

Still fully dressed, Kate opened the door and said, "Oh, it's you. I thought it might be that man."

"Barrie, you mean?"

"Yes. I wish he'd never come here, Diana." She began to pace up and down, her face set and tense. "He bothers me with all this talk about my being his wife. It isn't true! I just wish he'd never come."

"But he *is* here, Kate, and the house isn't big enough for you to avoid him all the time. Besides, he's Rhys's friend. Can't you just make the best of it? After all," she added mendaciously, "he probably won't stay that long—only until he's recuperated."

"I suppose I could," Kate said grudgingly. "I certainly don't want to offend Rhys. I owe him too much for that." With more conviction she added, "I will try, Diana. I promise I will."

"Good." Touched as much by Kate's earnestness as by the faint shadows of weariness under her eyes, Diana impulsively kissed her on the cheek, hugging her briefly. "Sleep well, Kate. I'll see you tomorrow."

"I'm glad *you're* here, Diana. You know that, don't you? I really feel as though you're my friend. And I know Rhys is glad you're staying longer."

"Mmm...I must go back to the others. 'Night."
After she'd closed the door behind her, however, Diana did not immediately rejoin the two men. Kate's avowal of friendship had done no more than put into words something she already knew. But it

was one more thread in the web that was binding her more and more closely to Woody Point. First Rhys and the shattering news of his accident. Then Kate with her tragic loss of memory. And finally Barrie, who had survived an ordeal that would have killed a lesser man, only to find his wife and unborn child lost to him.

She had had no intentions of becoming entangled like this. Moreover, the longer she stayed, the more difficult it was going to be to free herself. But free herself she must.

She would stay another two days, she decided, as a support for Kate while she adjusted to Barrie's continued presence. Then she must leave. She would make her reservations tomorrow....

THE NEXT TWO DAYS did not greatly improve matters between Kate and Barrie. Kate made an effort to be pleasant to him, the trouble being that it was noticeably an effort. Barrie on his part reined in his innate impatience and tried to respond to her overtures as he would have had she been any chance-met stranger. They circled each other warily, and only occasionally did the real Kate break through in a moment of spontaneous friendship and warmth that must have offered Barrie tantalizing glimpses of the woman he had known. He treasured those glimpses, although Diana sensed they also increased his frustration. He was a man of action, restless and strong willed, now faced with a situation where all he could do was play a waiting game. Already it was telling on him.

Diana was to discover it was also telling on Rhys.

He came looking for her late on the afternoon of the second day; to a certain degree she had been avoiding him, for she still had not found the courage to tell him she was leaving the next morning. He said without preamble, "Are you busy for the next couple of hours?"

"No, why?"

"Come for a drive with me. I need to get out of here."

She had been doing some desultory sketching, the results of which were clearly demonstrating her lack of motivation, so she was glad to abandon it. "Just let me get something on my feet." As was her habit in summertime, she was barefoot.

"Wear sneakers—we might go for a walk."

It was not until she was lacing up her footwear in the bedroom that she realized she was humming to herself, happy because Rhys had sought her out and wanted her company. In a spurt of recklessness, knowing she would be gone from here by this time tomorrow, she decided to enjoy herself.

However, as she ran out the front door to meet Rhys by the car, her resolve began to seem rather irrelevant. In the rays of the westering sun she saw his face thrown into relief: there was anxiety in it and unhappiness and the marks of a sleepless night, and she chided herself for not having noticed before. She had been caught up in her own pleasure when he had asked her to come with him, but when she thought back on it, she didn't think she was imagining that there had been a note of desperation in his voice.

Taking her place in the car she asked, "Where are we going?"

"Where would you like to go?"

"The tableland. It fascinates me."

In a silence that was strangely comfortable they drove to the parking lot where the trail wound down to the river. Rhys pocketed the keys. "Game for a climb?"

"Sure."

They crossed the road and began to pick their way over the tumbled sharp-edged rocks, not always going in a straight line, for they had to avoid streambeds and crevices, but always climbing. At first the slopes were scattered with pearl-white everlasting flowers, goldenrod and spiky mauve asters, interwoven with the pungently scented ground juniper. But the higher they went the more sparse the vegetation became, until there was nothing but a world of rock. The only sound was the splash of a stream that had emerged from the side of the mountain, its waters numbingly cold.

Diana's heart was pounding from the exertion, but she was lured onward both by Rhys's tall figure always ahead of her and by the recurring illusion that the next crest would be the top of the mountain.

Finally Rhys called a halt, reaching down a hand to pull her up the last steep fissure. She stood at his side, panting to get her breath back.

They seemed to be standing on the edge of the world. Behind them the slopes receded and dropped into a ravine, where the dwarf birch and alder grew knee-deep. Far below them the road lay like a straight brown ribbon, while the river, more adventurous, left a silver trail of S-shaped curves. To their left the orange light of the setting sun, in a splash of colors Diana could not have found in her palette, was reflected in the smooth mirror of the ocean. But it was the view ahead of them that held Diana's fascinated gaze the longest. They had climbed higher than the opposing range of mountains, and its crest stretched as far as the eye could see in an undulating pattern of plateaus and valleys, the plateaus golden in the sun, the valleys deep shadowed and mysterious. There was no wind, no cry of birds. They were alone in the silence, like gods surveying what they had created.

Eventually Diana found her voice. She said very softly, for it seemed almost sacrilegious to break the quiet, "Thank you for bringing me here, Rhys. I'll always remember it." She sat down on a rock, and as he sat beside her she propped her chin on her knees and asked equally softly, "What's wrong?"

His eyelids flickered, and for a moment she thought he was going to deny that anything was the matter. Then he said, "You see too much, Diana."

"I don't think so. Tell me what's bothering you."

He stared moodily out over the valley, his profile clear-cut against the western sky. "Everything. Nothing. Hell, I don't know." He grimaced shamefacedly. "I've been in a black mood all day. You seem to be the only person I can bear to have near me."

It was, in its way, a compliment, and she took it as such. "So tell me about it," she invited again.

"Well, there's Kate and Barrie. I'd hoped Kate's

memory would come back when she saw Barrie. But it didn't, and God knows how or when it will. I don't know how long Barrie can take the situation the way it is—having a wife who isn't a wife, loving a woman who doesn't even know him. And I know he's desperately worried about the future. He says he'll do any kind of work that'll suit Kate, but personally I can't see him lasting at a desk job, pushing papers around all day while other people do the active outdoor things.''

There were no easy answers for anything Rhys had said. Unless Kate regained her memory, for Barrie the picture was black indeed. For Kate it was not much better, since she would be condemned by her own psyche to a kind of half-life, rootless and without love.

"Then there's you and I." Her head swung around to stare at him, her gray eyes wary. "I want you to stay. But I don't think you're going to."

Her lips stiff, she said, "I've got a reservation to fly home tomorrow morning."

He nodded slowly. "I figured something like that was up. Is there any way I can make you change your mind, Diana?"

"For what, Rhys?"

"That's the trouble—I don't know." He looked at her soberly. "All I know is that I don't want you to leave. Having you here by my side seems so natural. So right."

Remembering the last occasion when that word had been used, she winced. "I have to leave, Rhys," she said in a low voice.

"I suppose so.... One part of me wants to rant and roar and hold you here by brute force, and to the devil with the consequences. The sane, rational, civilized part of me knows I can't do that. So don't look so worried; you're in no danger."

His profile was turned to her again, a strong dark silhouette that she knew she would carry home with her and, like the mountains, never forget. He had said she was in no danger; she wasn't sure she would agree with that. "Is that all?" she asked. "Or is there more?"

"Isn't that enough?"

"So there is more. Tell me...."

For a moment she thought he was going to refuse. Then he buried his head in his hands, so that when he spoke, his words were muffled. "You're the only person I can say this to—if I don't tell someone, I think I'll go crazy. I'm lost without my music, Diana. Lost.... I go from day to day and the hours pass, but there's no meaning in it, no purpose that I can find. I don't know what the hell I'm going to do...."

It was a cry for help, all the more convincing because it came from Rhys, who had always been strong and invulnerable, sufficient unto himself. Praying she would not fail him yet having no idea what she was going to say, she tentatively rested a hand on his arm. "And there's no way you can get back to it?"

"None. Something stops me every time. I don't know what and I can't fight it—it's stronger than me."

"Everyone's heard of writer's block," she offered, her heart aching for him. "There's no reason why musicians shouldn't suffer from the same kind of thing."

"I don't know if I can explain to you what music meant to me." At least he was looking at her now, and she gave him an encouraging smile. "I've never felt I could change the world; I'm not naive enough to think that. But when you look back over the course of history with all its cruelty and oppression and wars, there are those few who shine: the artists and musicians, the poets and philosophers. It's in them and their striving for perfection that I see the only hope for the future."

He paused, marshaling his thoughts. "For me music has always been a means of communicating my deepest feelings, of bringing people together. Sometimes at the beginning of a concert when I'd first come out onstage, I'd look out over the audience and see a gathering of totally disparate people, separate individuals. But the music would weld them together. However briefly, it was a unifying force, not a diversifying one. Our society is so splintered and separate today, we need that kind of unity. The kind of beauty that for a short while lifts people out of time." He fell silent.

She knew exactly what he meant, and nodded as she said, "The true artist is the one whose work can express something universal, that people from all walks of life can relate to—and that perhaps widens their boundaries at the same time."

"Well, I've lost that," he answered. "I can't do it

anymore. Since I was fifteen I've poured my whole life into music. You know that as well as anyone. Sure, one of the reasons I sent you away ten years ago was for your own sake, for your development as an artist. But the other was because of my total commitment to the world of music. I wouldn't allow anyone or anything to stand in my way. And now that it's gone, I'm realizing what the cost has been. I feel empty, Diana—like a shell you'd find tossed up on the beach, no longer occupied by a living creature. There's no meaning left in my life, no purpose. I might as well be dead.''

There was such savagery in his voice, and under it such despair, that Diana was terrified. Stricken to silence, she could only increase the pressure of her fingers on his arm, hoping to communicate to him her understanding and concern. But the terror would not go away. What if he were alone, she found herself thinking. Would he be tempted to fling himself down one of the ravines? Or on the way home to drive his car over one of the cliffs, thereby ending what the accident had started? She couldn't bear to think of it. . . .

Yet she recognized that he was not a man as ordinary men are. He was a creature of passion and brooding intensity, with the bone-deep sadness of the Celt ever ready to attack him and pull him down into the depths. Because of this, he was vulnerable; not even his great inner strength could always hold back the demons of despair and destruction. She heard herself say, "Rhys, you won't do anything. You wouldn't. . . ." She couldn't put her fears into words.

Instead of answering her directly, he suddenly stood up. "We'd better go," he said roughly, "or we'll be stuck up here after dark. The sun's about down."

"Rhys—"

"I'm sorry I burdened you with all this, Diana. It wasn't very fair of me, particularly as you'll be leaving tomorrow." He took her hand with impersonal strength. "Here, let me help you down the steep part."

For him the subject was closed; for her the fear was just beginning. She knew better than to say anything more, but as she scrambled down the face of the mountain, loose rocks tumbling and bouncing ahead of her, her thoughts were in a jumble. She had to leave tomorrow; it was impossible to do otherwise. Alan wanted her back and in a couple of days Belinda would be home from music camp. She had no choice. . . . But to leave Rhys alone in his depression? To abandon him when he needed her? She stopped dead in her tracks for a minute, staring blindly at an ocher-colored boulder. He did need her. For some reason she was the one with whom he could share his unhappiness. To her, and her alone, he had revealed the real man who lay behind the impregnable facade.

"Hurry up, Diana—it's getting dark," Rhys said impatiently.

She forced herself to concentrate on what she was doing, for a moment's inattention could easily lead to a fall and the last thing she needed right now was a broken ankle. By the time they reached the foot of the slope night had fallen in the valley, and high in the sky the first stars shone palely. Rhys unlocked the car doors and they got in. From the overhead light she could see his face, its expression grim and withdrawn, and again fear brushed her with its dark wings. How well did she really know him, this dark-haired man? What was he capable of doing, to others or to himself? She didn't know... but she was afraid. Would she one day in the future pick up a newspaper and read that the celebrated pianist Rhys Morgan had died in a climbing accident? Or would she hear on the radio of yet another car accident, only this time his would be the name that would come over the air?

"Stop staring at me like that, Diana," he said irritably.

She struggled for composure. "Sorry," she muttered. "I—I'm worried about you, Rhys."

"Look, I should never have told you all that. Forget it, okay? I'll be all right."

If only she could believe him... but deep in her heart she didn't. "Very well," she said submissively. "Are we going to be late for dinner?"

His smile held something of normality. "We'd better hope it's not another soufflé."

The meal for Diana was an ordeal: everyone pretended on the surface that things were fine, while underneath the tensions crackled and the silences mocked the empty meaningless words. It was a relief to go to her room, ostensibly to pack but in reality to sit by the window gazing out into the darkness, the stars in their cold uncaring brilliance themselves a mockery. She leaned her forehead against the cool glass, sick with fear, and gradually there coalesced in her brain the single, simple thought that if it were not for Belinda, she would stay here. But Rhys's own daughter was the one person who stood in the way of his obtaining such help as Diana could give. It had a cruel kind of irony....

And then it happened. As if Belinda stood in front of her, Diana could see the silky dark hair, the intent face as the child's nimble fingers flew over the keyboard. And superimposed over this image there was Rhys's face, ravaged by his inability to get in touch with the music he loved and needed. Belinda could do it. Belinda could bring Rhys back to his music.

CHAPTER TWELVE

HER HEART THUDDING, Diana sat up straight, stunned by the direction her thoughts had taken. Was she crazy? What was she contemplating? After all these years to bring father and daughter together? She must be out of her mind.... But crazy or not, the idea would not go away, for it had a mad logic all its own. If Rhys were to hear Belinda play, he would recognize in her the talent that had driven him for so many years. She would be his hope for the future, the meaning he had lost. And who could tell? Maybe in a literal sense Belinda could lead him back to the piano. Maybe he would undertake to teach her. To play for her, where he wouldn't play for anyone else.

Sleep was impossible. Abstractedly Diana paced up and down the room, examining the idea from all angles. One look at Belinda would be enough for Rhys to realize the relationship—no question of that. But what of Belinda? Would she recognize Rhys as the father she had never known? Would it harm her if she did, to realize a world-famous pianist was her father?

And what of Alan? He was to be Belinda's step-father. How would he feel about the risk entailed in bringing Rhys and Belinda face to face? Would he understand how necessary it was? That for Rhys it might represent the only means of salvation?

Her mind not at all on what she was doing, she folded her clothes into her suitcase, tidied the room and eventually got into bed. But for a long time she lay awake, too keyed up to sleep, while the pros and cons waged back and forth in her brain. But nothing could alter two basic premises: she was afraid for Rhys; and Belinda could save him. On these two thoughts, she finally did sleep.

She had thought she would be the first one up in the morning, but Robert was ahead of her, plugging in the coffee percolator as she went into the kitchen. When she began to speak, she knew the decision had been made. "Robert, where's Rhys?"

"Gone for a walk, miss. Said he'd be back in half an hour to see you off." Beneath Robert's imperturbable British aplomb she sensed disapproval at her departure.

"Robert, I'm coming back. Not for three days, though. I—I have something to do. Will you keep an eye on him for me, Robert, while I'm gone? I'm worried about him."

"So am I, miss. I'll do that, certainly." He added delicately, "May I ask what your plans are?"

"I can't tell you now, Robert. But I think it will work. When I come back, I'll want to get into the house without Rhys's seeing me. I'll phone you from the village, and hopefully we can arrange something." She smiled apologetically. "It all sounds a bit melodramatic, doesn't it? But it *is* important, Robert."

"I'm delighted to hear you're coming back, and I'll do anything I can to help," the man said formally. Cocking his head, he added, "That sounds like Mr. Morgan now. Would you fancy an omelet, miss?"

"Sounds delicious. With cheese?"

So when Rhys came in the back door he was met by a peaceful domestic scene. Diana immediately thrust a glass of orange juice in his hand. "You're up early," she commented lightly, although with a sinking of her heart she knew from one look at his face that he could hardly have slept at all last night.

"Thanks. It's a fine day for flying. When are you leaving?"

"I should get away by eight-thirty. I have to return the car I rented, and I haven't paid for my ticket yet."

Kate wandered into the kitchen, wearing a long loose robe and rubbing at her eyes. "Morning," she yawned. "Good, you haven't gone yet, Diana."

Barrie, fully dressed, was next to arrive on the scene. Kate was standing by the stove, chatting to Robert; Barrie's eyes, full of naked hunger, were drawn to her as if she were a magnet. Full of compassion she knew he would probably resent, Diana said cheerfully, "Good morning, Barrie."

"Hi, Diana. Great day for flying."

In a brief moment of intimacy, Rhys grinned at Diana; she was the first to look away. Hurriedly she finished eating, went to her room and put on her makeup, smoothing her hair into a chignon and fastening on opal drop earrings that Alan had given her for her last birthday, her rose-colored dress drawing out the pink fire in them. She looked at herself in the mirror with the strange feeling that she was leaving part of herself here, that only the sophisticated outer shell of Diana was getting on the plane to Montreal. Giving herself a little shake, she picked up her case and her leather folder of art supplies and went back into the kitchen.

Feeling like a hypocrite because she knew she was coming back, she suffered Barrie's quick hug and muttered thanks. Kate's kiss on the cheek was tearful and she murmured, "I'll miss you. But you'll write, won't you?"

"Of course I will." Diana shook hands with Robert, who gave her an almost military salute, his face carefully blank. Then she heard Rhys say, "I'll see you out to the car."

The one goodbye she had been dreading.... He put her gear in the trunk and slammed down the lid, then came around to where she was standing. Resting his hands on her shoulders he said evenly, "Goodbye, Diana. Do you think it will be another ten years before we meet again?"

She swallowed, knowing it would be only a matter of days. "I...hope not. Take care of yourself, won't you, Rhys? Please?"

His hands tightened their grip. "If I didn't know better, I'd almost think you care what happens to me."

"I do," she said with helpless honesty. "You know I do."

"I know you're leaving to marry another man, that's what I know."

"That doesn't mean I have to be indifferent to you," she cried. "Oh, Rhys, what's the good? We've been through all this before." Before she could lose her courage, she stood on tiptoes and kissed him full on the mouth, her eyes misted with tears. "Bye," she muttered, turning and opening the car door and getting in as quickly as she could. She turned on the ignition and jerked the car into gear, reversing in a shower of gravel. In the rearview mirror she saw him still standing there. He didn't wave.

She drove to Deer Lake as fast as she could, got rid of the car and checked in her bags at the airlines counter. Because it would be an hour and a half earlier in Montreal, she thought her chances were good of catching Alan still at home. Contacting the operator, she placed the call. His voice when he answered sounded very faraway. "Hello?"

"Alan, it's Diana. I'm at the airport in Newfoundland, and I'll be arriving at Dorval from Halifax at two-ten. Any chance you can meet me? If not I can always get a cab."

"Sure I'll meet you—try to keep me away! Give me your flight number, Di."

She gave him the necessary information and rang off with his "Looking forward to seeing you" ringing in her ears. She was looking forward to seeing him, too, she thought stoutly, wishing she didn't have so many misgivings about telling him her plan concerning Belinda and Rhys. Surely he'd understand. . . .

After leaving the tiny airfield at Deer Lake and the larger Halifax airport set as it was in the woods, it was strange to fly in over the vast urban sprawl of Montreal island. She saw the downtown skyscrapers, the Expo site and the mushroom circle of the Olympic stadium, and then the rows of streets and warehouses and railway tracks came closer and closer and the ground was rushing up to meet them. The plane bounced twice. There was a roaring in her ears as the flaps were lowered. As they taxied over to the terminal she checked her watch: dead on time.

Because she was nervous, it seemed to take forever to go up the escalators and along the moving sidewalk to the main terminal, where the luggage would be unloaded. She looked in vain for Alan's face among the crowds around the baggage carousels, then jumped when he came up behind her and flung his arms around her. "Hi, Alan—you scared me!"

His answer was to kiss her thoroughly and at some length. For Diana it was a strange experience. There was the well-remembered feel of his arms and the scent of his after-shave, familiar and known; but mixed with that was a series of tiny shocks. He was a little shorter and far leaner than Rhys, nor was he as strong. He smelled different. And most devastating of all, there was none of the fiery magic in his kiss that she had always found in Rhys's. She felt as though she was being split in two, her old loyalties and affection toward Alan opposed by the new raw memories of Rhys. With neither one could she feel comfortable or at home.

All this had passed through her mind very quickly. Nevertheless, when Alan released her there was a quizzical look in his eyes, and she knew he had sensed something of her equivocation. Being Alan, he approached it obliquely. "Great to have you back—I missed you. Your luggage will be coming to the third carousel. Let's go and wait over there." Keeping an arm around her shoulders he steered her through the crowds, where her ears picked up scraps of conversation in French and English. The announcements over the loudspeaker were in French, as well; she was home again. Two Indian women floated past in gold-embroidered saris. A Chinese family was having a high-pitched conversation with one of the security guards, and two very British-looking businessmen stalked by. "Jet travel is marvelously fast, but it does leave one disoriented," she said apologetically. "You wouldn't believe the contrast between here and Deer Lake."

"You were very taken with the scenery there?"

A nice safe topic. She expounded enthusiastically on the beauties of the tableland and the grandeur of Western Brook Pond, on the herds of wild horses and the friendliness of the villagers. Alan retrieved her luggage and they left the baggage area, emerging onto the concrete sidewalk, where the heat hit Diana like a blow. Wilting visibly, she said, "No fresh sea breezes here."

"We've had record highs the last few days, and no rain. I'm in the eighth row in the parking lot, by the way. Do you want me to bring the car over here?"

"Heavens, no. We can walk."

As the traffic slowed for them at the crosswalk, Diana was assailed by exhaust fumes and the dry gritty dust swirling in the wind created by the passing cars, a wind that was artificial, bringing no relief from the stifling oppressive heat. At Rhys's bungalow the air had been crisp and clean, laden with the ever present tang of the sea. . . .

Alan drove a Japanese sports car, its dashboard replete with gadgets, dials, computers and flashing lights. He had not had it long, and when he had first bought it she could only compare him to a small boy with a new toy. Remembering this now, she felt an upsurge of affection for him and smiled at him spontaneously. "It's good to see you again."

He leaned over and kissed her, his eyes tender behind his gold-rimmed glasses. "Good to have you back." He put her luggage in the trunk and opened the door for her, then got in the driver's seat. He took off his glasses and cleaned them, a sure sign that he was nervous. "I've got something for you. Hope you'll like it."

"Oh?" Not until he extracted a small square jeweler's box from his pocket did she realize what it was going to be. Unconsciously her fingers dug into the soft leather of her purse.

He opened the box, taking out the ring; it was a single ruby flanked by two diamonds, set in gold. "Perhaps I should have waited until this evening—it would have been more romantic, I suppose, to have given it to you in the moonlight on Mount Royal. But I didn't want to wait, Diana." He took her hand in his, and she felt the slight tremor in his fingers. "I love you and I want you to be my wife."

This was one of the reasons she had come home,

wasn't it? Alan's claim on her had been important enough to drive her out of Rhys's arms.... She smiled at him gravely. "I want to marry you, Alan."

She felt the circlet of gold slide on her finger, surprisingly cool on her flesh, felt him kiss her again. It all seemed to be happening at a distance and to someone else.

Alan sat back in his seat. "I've done it!" he said exultantly. "I guess I was a bit worried, Diana—thought you might have changed your mind or had second thoughts after meeting this Rhys Morgan again."

"No," she murmured. "I knew I would be coming home to you. The delays were because of Kate...but I explained that to you on the phone." Now was the obvious time to tell him about her proposed return to Woody Point with Belinda. But she had hesitated a fraction too long and he was speaking again.

"Why don't I take you straight home now? I know your parents are anxious to see you—your father's still on holiday. Then perhaps we could have dinner together tonight?"

She smiled gratefully, knowing that she did want to go home to her own apartment, where the familiar surroundings might help rid her of this strange feeling of detachment. "Lovely. Do you know if Belinda's written again?"

"There's another letter for you, yes. And she'll be home a day earlier than expected. Your mother had a phone call. Apparently two of the camp leaders were taken ill and couldn't be replaced, so they're having to send some of the children home early."

So the first thing she must do when she got home was make reservations for the return trip. She would tell Alan about it this evening; that would give her more chance to fill in the details, describe Kate and Barrie, explain about Rhys's catastrophic loss of everything that had given his life meaning. Alan would understand that she had to do this one last thing; of course he would.

Having made that decision, she was able to talk more naturally as the car sped along the autoroute, and before long they had turned off and were driving along the hilly tree-lined streets of Westmount. Alan parked in the driveway behind her father's car and got out to get her luggage.

"You'd better come in," she said easily. "Mum will want to congratulate you in person. She won't be able to wait until this evening for that."

It was Diana's mother who opened the door for them and immediately flung her arms around her daughter. "Darling! Lovely to have you home again. Come in, Alan. Did you have a good flight, Diana? Alan, you'll stay for supper, won't you? Here's your father, darling."

Roger Sutherland had listened to his wife's chatter for more than thirty years and could smile at it now as placidly as when he had first met her. He was in his late fifties, a neat balding man whose amiable undemanding nature had ensured he would never rise above the department-head level in the company he worked for. He had neither the ruthlessness nor the drive to make it to the top and was, moreover, perfectly content to remain where he was until he retired. Now he kissed his daughter's cheek, as always with that faint look of amazement that he, plain Roger Sutherland, could have produced such an exotically beautiful and talented creature as Diana.

Diana surveyed both her parents lovingly. Nellie Sutherland was short and undisguisedly plump. She went on crash diets periodically, encasing her ample hips in corsets and worrying over every calorie. For two or three weeks she would make herself and her husband miserable by serving quantities of unsugared grapefruit and infinitesimal amounts of everything else; during these stringent regimes, Roger would sneak up to Diana's apartment for snacks to keep himself going. Then between one day and the next she would decide she was fine as she was, that nature or heredity or fate had intended her to be plump and that it was useless for her to argue against any or all of them. The household would settle back to normal and Roger could enjoy roast beef and all the trimmings again.

She was looking at Diana with the critical appraisal of an expert. "You've lost a little weight, haven't you, dear? Didn't they feed you well in Newfoundland?"

Alan spoke up. "It must be love, Nellie. Diana's agreed to marry me."

Nellie's eyes flew to Diana's left hand, catching the sparkle of the new ring. "Darlings!" she cried. "Oh, Diana, I'm so happy for you."

There was a flurry of congratulations, of hugs and kisses and back slapping. Nellie was unashamedly crying and had to stop to blow her nose. "It's just that I'm so happy," she sniffed. "Roger, there's a bottle of champagne left from Christmas, isn't there?"

"Your diet..." her husband murmured, a gleam of hope in his eye.

"Darn the diet!" Nellie cried extravagantly. "My daughter's engagement is more important than mere calories."

Roger winked at Diana before hurrying off to fetch the champagne. It was lovely to be home again, Diana thought, smiling at Alan. Rhys and Woody Point seemed a long way away....

It was nearly two hours later that Diana went upstairs to her apartment to change for dinner. Alan had left to go to his own place and get out of his work clothes and would pick her up in a hour or so. She sat on the bed, looking at the telephone. Earlier, downstairs, surrounded by all the confusion of a family reunion, Rhys had seemed very remote. Now that she was alone, however, his problem loomed as large as ever. Without stopping for further thought she picked up the phone and dialed the travel bureau that always made her flight bookings; a few minutes later she put down the phone. In two days' time she would be back in Woody Point....

She and Alan had a window seat in a restaurant on the top floor of one of the downtown skyscrapers. Dusk was falling, the sky blurring from pale gold and eggshell blue to a luminous black that gathered into itself the reflection of all the myriad lights of the city. Far below the neon lights glittered, red as the ruby on her finger, green, yellow and blue. Bright raw colors flashing their urgent messages to the cars that drove by, themselves lit up in gold and red. The rectangular windows of other skyscrapers were laid out against the sky in neat rows, like playing cards on a black table. And behind all those many lights pulsed the hidden life of the city, a heartbeat that never completely stopped.

They ate mousse of quail liver and scallops *tartare*, followed by paper-thin crepes filled with fresh strawberries and whipping cream. Diana was sipping her cognac, feeling it slide warmly down her throat, when Alan gave her the opening she had been more or less waiting for all evening. "Do you have any plans for the rest of the summer, you and Belinda?"

She swished the amber liquid in the glass, then looked across the table at him. "Yes, I do, Alan. For reasons that I'll explain to you, I want to take her to Woody Point."

He sat up a little straighter, his eyes calculating. "I assume her father won't be there?"

"He will be. And that's the—"

"Diana! Have you gone out of your mind? That's playing with fire, isn't it, to take the child where she would be all too likely to meet her father? Let alone the chance of his seeing her and making the connection."

She said as calmly as she could, "This evening we've talked about everyone else but Belinda's father, haven't we? My parents, Belinda, Kate and Barrie. But not him." She let a little more of the cognac rest on her palate before swallowing it. "I want to tell you about him, Alan, if I may. I'm trusting you to keep this information confidential, of course.''

His expression enigmatic, he gave her a brief nod.

''I already told you his name is Rhys Morgan and that he is—or rather, he was—a concert pianist.''

Still not giving anything away, Alan said coldly, ''I've heard of him, naturally. I've even heard him play on a couple of occasions—an outstanding talent.''

''I also told you that last spring he was in a car accident and injured his hand so badly that he'll never play again on the concert stage.''

''Yes. It's strange I hadn't already heard about it.''

''I hadn't heard about it, either. According to Robert, his manservant, the publicity was just about nil, at Rhys's expressed request.''

''That would be pretty hard to take when you're at the very peak of your career, as he was,'' Alan said reflectively.

She said warmly, ''Exactly! I'm so glad you can understand that, Alan. He's lost without his music. It's left an immense void and there's nothing to fill it.''

''So what are you planning to do—plunk Belinda down in front of him and say, 'Oh, by the way, Rhys, I forgot to tell you, you've got a nine-year-old daughter'? Show a little sense, Di.''

She held tightly to her temper. ''You haven't let me finish explaining. You see, he won't go near the piano now. Because he can't play as he used to be able to, he won't play at all. I think, and Robert agrees with me, that this is wrong. He can't let all those years go to waste! As a teacher or as a composer and conductor, he could be happy again, I'm convinced of it. He would be a marvelous teacher, Alan. And while I was there I found manuscripts that he'd composed, both for piano alone and for piano and orchestra.''

''You seem very sure of yourself, considering that you're talking about a man whom you've known altogether for less than two weeks.''

''I am sure.'' She shrugged helplessly. ''I can't tell you why. I just know in my bones that I'm right.''

''So what are you proposing?''

At least he was listening.... ''I tried two or three times to get him to play, and Barrie asked him to, as well. No go. So what I want to do is take Belinda over there and have her play for him. If anything will do it, that will.''

''He'll guess who she is right away. From what I remember of the man, Belinda is the image of him.''

''I suppose so....'' She fiddled with her coffee spoon.

''There's no 'suppose' about it, Diana! Once he sees Belinda, he'll know she's his daughter. How are you going to deal with that?'' Before she could formulate a reply he ruthlessly pressed his advantage. ''And what of Belinda? She's a very intelligent little girl and a very sensitive one. I should think it's highly likely that she'll guess who Rhys is within five minutes of meeting him. Are you going to tell her who he is beforehand? Or are you just going to let her walk into that situation without a word of warning?"

"I don't know yet!"

"Then you'd better do some very hard thinking."

As she glared at Alan across the table Diana wondered if this was how he looked when he was tracking down a mathematical problem: cold eyed and implacable. In a pleading gesture she rested her hand on his, and the ruby flashed in the light. "Alan, I think we're having our first quarrel," she faltered.

His face softened, but only very slightly. "Yes, we are." He pressed her fingers. "I'm very fond of Belinda. I don't have to tell you that. I don't want to see her hurt, Di, and if you pursue this mad idea of yours, she will get hurt. It's inevitable."

"It's not a mad idea!"

"I fail to understand why it should be so important to you whether Rhys Morgan ever plays the piano again or not. So important that you'll jeopardize your daughter's peace of mind, even her whole future."

"You're exaggerating the dangers, Alan."

"Am I? Have you considered how Rhys is going to react? Apart from his precious piano playing, that is," he added sarcastically. "He's going to find out that ten years ago he fathered a child. Has it occurred to you that he might try to get custody of Belinda?"

She paled. "He wouldn't do that."

"How do you know? From the little I've read about him, he sounds like a strong-willed character, quite capable of going after anything—or anyone—he wants. Remember that he got to the very top of his profession, Diana, and you don't do that by being a nice guy all the time.''

''He couldn't get custody—she's lived with me ever since she was born.''

''Only because you deliberately kept the knowledge of her existence from him. And don't think he wouldn't use that.''

''You're making him out to be some kind of monster,'' she whispered.

''I don't think so. I'm only trying to make you look at some cold hard facts before you do something you might regret—and pay for—for the rest of your life. You and Belinda.''

That Rhys might try to take Belinda from her had never occurred to her, certainly. Shaken to the roots of her being, she found it impossible not to wonder if Alan was right. Was she being foolish? Acting impulsively without considering any of the repercussions?

Her doubts and confusion must have shown in her face. Relenting a little, Alan said more gently, ''I'm sorry if I've been hard on you, darling, and I know it's never much help to say it's for your own good. But for heaven's sake, take your time over this one, because the aftereffects could be disastrous. That's all I'm trying to say.''

She acknowledged his apology with a little nod, temporarily quite unable to counter any of his arguments. It was Alan himself who caused her to remember the peculiar urgency of her plan. He said, somewhat less insistently, ''You still haven't told me why Rhys's future is so important to you, Diana.

Before you left, do you remember my saying I might regret getting the two of you together again after all these years? That you might get involved with him all over again? Is that what's happened?''

Trying very hard to be honest, she said slowly, ''I'm not in love with him, if that's what you mean. I couldn't have accepted your ring if that had been true. But seeing him again did affect me; I can't deny that, Alan. Maybe there's always some kind of bond between a woman and the first man she makes love with, I don't know. But what really brought me back here to get Belinda is something more than just a tie with the past. The last evening I was there—'' She broke off, her brow puckered. ''Yesterday evening. It seems ages ago already.... We went for a walk together, Rhys and I. Actually what we did was climb halfway up a mountain. I could tell he was...unhappy, so I asked him why. He was upset about Kate and Barrie; that's a miserable situation. But there were other things besides that.'' She looked at Alan, her gray eyes troubled. ''He wanted me to stay, Alan. Not to come back to Montreal. But I refused—I knew I had to come home to you and to Belinda. He knows I'm engaged to you, even if he doesn't know about her.''

''I see. I wondered if you'd told him about me.''

''I did, yes.'' Her mind winced away from the circumstances, from the memory of her and Rhys lying naked in each other's arms. With an effort she picked up the thread of her narrative. ''The final thing he did was to tell me how totally lost and purposeless he feels without his music and how he can't bring himself to go back to it. Normally he's a very self-sufficient man, Alan—not at all the kind of person who goes around sharing all his troubles. Strong to the point of introversion, perhaps. But that evening for some reason he shared his feelings with me.''

Her voice was very low, her eyes downcast, so that Alan had to lean forward to catch what she was saying. "I'm afraid for him. I had this dreadful premonition that he'd be found at the foot of the cliff someday or dead in his car. And that while it would look accidental, I'd know—and so would Robert—that it wasn't.''

"So you think he's contemplating suicide. I'll tell you what I think—I think you're letting your imagination run away with you. Or else he's done a damned good job of playing on your sympathies.''

"Would I for a minute be contemplating taking Belinda over there if I thought it was all a figment of my imagination?'' she said heatedly.

"I'm not sure, Diana. I'm beginning to wonder if you're not deluding yourself, and that behind all this you simply want to see him again.''

"You mean I'm making it all up? Really, Alan!''

"Not making it up, just rationalizing something you want to do anyway.''

She snapped, "That's nonsense. If I didn't know you better, I'd say you were jealous.''

Although he kept his voice down in deference to their surroundings, there was no mistaking his anger. "You're right—I am. I don't want you going back there, Diana. I want you here with me, where you belong. You are, after all, my fiancée.''

"That doesn't mean you own me!"

"It merely means my wishes should at least be considered."

Suddenly appalled, she said, "Alan, we're still fighting. What's happening to us? We've never done this before."

He had been gripping the edge of the table. With a conscious effort he relaxed his fingers and managed a smile. "We haven't, have we? Look, let's get out of here."

They left the restaurant, went down on the elevator, carefully not looking at each other, and walked to the parking lot. The brief respite had given Diana the chance to think. Alan's objections were sensible and sound, and she could well be making the worst mistake in her life by bringing Belinda and Rhys face-to-face. But balancing that was her deep intuition that Rhys was in trouble and needed help that only she could give. He would not ask for it; he was too proud for that. So it was up to her to take the initiative.

As they were driving home she said quietly, "Alan, I know I'm taking an awful risk, but I have to take Belinda to Newfoundland—I don't really have any choice. But we shouldn't be gone for very long...."

There was silence for a few minutes while Alan skillfully wove in and out of the heavy traffic; perhaps, too, she thought, he didn't want to risk another outburst. Finally he said, "Very well. I just hope for the sake of everyone concerned—me, you, Belinda, Rhys—that you're doing the right thing. When will you go?"

She would almost have preferred that he rant and rave rather than preserve such an icy calm. "The day after tomorrow. Belinda gets back in the morning."

"Then I probably won't see you again before you go. You'll phone me from there and let me know how things work out?"

"Of course I will." She rested a hand on his knee. "I have to do this, Alan. And it doesn't change the way I feel about you. Please believe that."

"I haven't got much choice, have I?" he said heavily. "I'll be glad when it's all over and you're back where you belong."

It was the second time he'd used that word "belong." One of the things she'd always appreciated in her relationship with Alan was his ability to allow her independence and a considerable degree of freedom of movement. Had their engagement subtly altered that, giving him claims on her that she had not anticipated? She sighed, feeling the beginnings of a headache and knowing that this was not the time to discuss it. There'd been enough disagreements for one evening.

He pulled up in front of her parents' house and without turning off the ignition leaned over and kissed her hard on the mouth. "Take care of yourself. Give me a call when you get there."

"Alan—"

"Good night, Di."

She got out of the car, hearing him drive away before she'd even left the sidewalk. The headache had become a pounding reality, and as she slowly climbed the stairs to her apartment she found herself wondering with a sickening flood of panic if anything but disaster would stem from the meeting of father and daughter, a meeting she would be solely responsible for bringing about. Perhaps Alan was right. Perhaps she was being headstrong and thoughtless.... Oh, God, if only she could look into the future and get some kind of assurance that she was doing the right thing. As she stood under the outdoor light fumbling in her purse for her key, the ruby flashed its mocking red fire.

CHAPTER THIRTEEN

MORNING FOR ONCE brought no relief for Diana's uncertainty. She looked pale and heavy eyed, far from the picture of a happily engaged woman. It was an oppressively hot day, the air humid and heavy with the threat of thunder. In an effort at least to look cool, Diana put on the same gray linen suit she had worn to the lawyer's office that day when she had first decided to trace Rhys, setting this whole train of events in motion. But she didn't want to think about that.... She dropped in to see her parents and have a midmorning coffee, holding out her hand so her mother could admire the ring again and giving a suitably edited version of her dinner date with Alan. With rather overdone casualness she managed to say, "I think I'll take Belinda away for a few days before school starts. I'd like to take her to Newfoundland, actually. The scenery was just gorgeous, and I could do a little more painting there. If she wants to go, that is."

"She'll want to go if you're going," Roger Sutherland said dryly. "She worships the ground you stand on, and well you know it."

Diana had always recognized the close bond between her and her daughter, knowing it probably stemmed from the fact that she had been Belinda's only parent. Nellie piped up, "She's very fond of Alan, too—he'll be a fine stepfather for her. Here, dear, have a piece of coffee cake. I made it this morning."

Relieved for her father's sake that the diet was abandoned for now, Diana bit into the warm yeasty bread flavored with cinnamon, sticky with brown sugar and raisins. "It's either feast or famine with you, mom," she joked. "This is delicious. I'll have to bring Belinda in for a piece."

"That's really why I made it," Nellie said decorously, cutting herself a generous slice and buttering it. "Now, Roger, don't you say a word."

As she finished her coffee, Diana regarded her parents affectionately. She would always be in their debt, she knew; staid and respectable though they might appear, when she had discovered she was pregnant ten years before they had taken her in without demur, had looked after her during her pregnancy and then, when Belinda was older, had cared for the child during the day so that Diana could go back to art school. They had asked no questions and cast no blame, and for that alone Diana would be undyingly grateful to them. Remembering how unbearably unhappy she had been at first, she knew their discretion and love had been a saving grace. She got up, kissing them both. "Must go, I don't want to be late. I'll see you later."

She was to meet the bus from the music camp outside the Queen Elizabeth Hotel at noon. Ten minutes after the hour the sleek blue-and-silver vehicle drew up to the curb, and the sidewalk was soon crowded with parents and children, musical instruments and suitcases. Belinda was the fourth one off the bus, her long black hair swinging as she jumped down and ran toward her mother, flinging her arms around her. "Hi! I had a great time. I got a certificate from Madame Lacasse and she thinks I need a more advanced teacher. She wrote you a letter."

Diana hugged Belinda fiercely, feeling the delicate bones, the smooth skin, the excitement quivering through the child's body. "I missed you," she said as lightly as she could; she had always been aware of the danger of smothering her only child with too much love. "I'm glad you had a nice time. Why don't we go to Tony's for lunch, and you can tell me all about it."

Tony's specialty was smoked-meat sandwiches, to which Belinda was very partial; for all her fragile appearance, she had a healthy appetite. Leaving the cases at the hotel, the two of them walked the three or four blocks to the restaurant, dodging the noon-hour crowds on the sidewalks of Ste. Catherine Street. After only a brief wait they were seated, whereupon Belinda devoted her whole attention to the menu.

Belinda was very like both Rhys and herself in that respect, Diana thought, for she had the gift of total concentration. But mainly she was Rhys's child. Having seen him so recently, Diana felt a poignant sense of recognition as she gazed across the table at her daughter's bent head with its smooth black hair, her clear blue eyes focused so intently on the tantalizing selection of sandwiches, her long thin fingers holding the menu. She was a beautiful girl already, with the promise of greater beauty to come. Perhaps because of her outstanding musical ability she could show a poise beyond her years but in the twinkling of an eye could easily revert to an energetic, somewhat hoydenish nine-year-old.

The menu and the waiter having been dealt with, Belinda began to tell Diana about her stay at the camp—the friends she had made, her discovery that she could do the butterfly stroke and a backward flip, and the new piano pieces she had studied. She broke off suddenly to exclaim, "Hey, where'd you get the new ring? It's pretty. One of the violin teachers had one with the same kind of stone in it."

Glad of the opening, Diana said, "Alan gave it to me. He wants to marry me, Lindy."

"That's good," Belinda said casually. "I like Alan. Do you want to read *madame*'s letter?"

"Well, yes. But you do feel all right about Alan and me?"

"Sure. He's fun. Would he live with us?"

"Yes, he would." Until now Diana had given no thought to any of the practical arrangements such as where they'd live, whose furniture they'd use, what she'd use as a studio. Suddenly she foresaw all kinds of complications ahead.

She was brought back to the present when Belinda thrust Madame Lacasse's letter in her hand. It spoke of Belinda's abilities and self-discipline in glowing terms and went on to suggest that a teacher of high caliber would be essential if the child was to progress.

It was impossible for Diana not to make the connection with Rhys; it seemed as though fate was giving her a nudge. Quickly, before she could change her mind, she said, "How would you like to go away again for a few days—with me this time? I thought we might go to Newfoundland."

Belinda's smile was dazzling. "When can we go?"

"Tomorrow?"

"Yeah! How will we get there?"

"We'll fly and then rent a car. I just came back from there, Belinda, and I think you'll like it—we'll stay with some friends in a little place called Woody Point. The man who owns the house has a beautiful piano. I'm sure you'll enjoy playing it."

Trying to answer all of Belinda's questions, she sent up a quick prayer that she was doing the right thing. Right or wrong, the die was cast...and right or wrong, she had not told Belinda that the man in question was her own father.

THE FLIGHT TO NEWFOUNDLAND went without a hitch. The airplane was on time, the rented car was waiting for them and the weather was sunny, the air pure and fresh after the stifling heat of the city. With all these good omens, Diana should have been relaxed and carefree; instead, as they drove along the arm of Bonne Bay, passing the road to the tableland and catching their first glimpse of Gros Morne, she grew more and more jittery.

She still had time to turn back. Or she could take the ferry and keep going as far as Rocky Harbour and stay there. Then they were going along one of the narrow streets of the village and Belinda was saying approvingly, "It's a neat place. Where are we staying?"

"Up on the hill. But I have to make a phone call first."

She had tried to plan their arrival to coincide with the time of day when Rhys was usually out. Parking by the phone booth, Diana said, "Won't be a sec," and ran across to it. The coin slipped into the slot and carefully she dialed Rhys's number. Robert would be expecting her to call either today or tomorrow—surely he would answer?

"Hello." It was Robert.

"Robert, it's Diana. I'm here in the village."

"I'm very glad you've come back, miss. Mr. Morgan hasn't been himself since you left."

"What do you mean?"

"Oh, prowling around the house like a caged animal. Can't settle to anything. Last night he went out in the car about nine-thirty and didn't get back until three. I was nearly ready to call the police because I thought he must have had an accident. He said he'd just been driving around, though. He told me to stop worrying. But I was afraid that—well, anyway, I'm glad you're here."

"Where is he now?"

"The three of them went out after lunch. They should be back in about half an hour."

"Then I'll come up right away. I want to be in the music room when he gets home."

"You can park the car behind the house, miss. I'll be waiting for you outside."

"Okay. I'll be there in a minute." Quickly Diana replaced the receiver and went back to the car. She said breathlessly, "We'll go up now. Robert's the only one home. He's the manservant. Belinda, I'd like you to do me a favor. When the man who owns the house gets home, which should be in about half an hour, I'd like you to be playing the piano. And if he comes into the room, I'd like you just to keep on playing. Would you do that?"

"I guess so.... Why?"

"I can't explain right now, Lindy. All I can say is that it's very important."

"I should do some practicing every day anyway," Belinda said philosophically. "Is that the house?"

Diana turned into the gravel driveway, breathing a sigh of relief that there was no white Jaguar in sight. There was only Robert, coming down the steps to meet them. He directed her around the side of the house, where she parked the car in the shade and she and Belinda got out. As the child stepped into the sunlight, Robert's welcoming smile congealed on his face, his normally impassive features expressive of shock and speculation. Diana said quickly, "Robert, this is my daughter, Belinda. Belinda, this is Mr. Smith."

Robert had recovered enough to shake Belinda's hand and say politely, "Welcome to Woody Point, miss. I hope you'll enjoy your stay."

Her vivid blue eyes smiled up at him. "I'm sure I will," she said confidently. "Mom said you had a swimming pool and a piano, so I'll have lots to do."

"Do you play the piano, miss?"

Another shock for poor Robert, Diana thought wryly, interjecting, "Yes, she does, Robert, and I promised her I'd show her the music room right away. Do you mind if we go there first?"

She could see his brain working as he made the various connections. "Just let me get your luggage, and we'll go right along."

The music room was bathed in sunshine, the smooth black surface of the piano gleaming in the light. Belinda gave a little gasp of delight, for the name of the company, written in gold letters on the side, was world renowned, and she had never before had the chance to play on its instruments. Her mother and Robert and the mysterious man for whom she was supposed to perform were all forgotten. She walked across the carpet and very carefully lifted the lid, brushing her fingers lightly across the ivory keys. Then, like a girl in a dream, she sat down, automatically adjusting the seat to her height. First she struck a single note, middle C, listening with her head on one side to its purity and resonance. Then she started playing scales, slowly at first, listening intently, them more rapidly as her fingers loosened up. A series of chords, covering the entire keyboard. More scales.

Knowing nothing short of an earthquake would disturb Belinda now, Diana nodded to Robert, and unobtrusively he left the room, leaving the door ajar. She herself went to stand in one corner behind the music stands, where her beige dress blended into the shadows. Now that the moment had come, the moment that had perhaps been inevitable since that

evening so long ago when she had worn her long
white dress to a concert and had fallen under the spell
of a man's blue eyes, she felt almost calm. What
would happen, would happen. She was the instigator, for she had brought Belinda here. But events
were now beyond her control. . . .

Belinda was playing a Chopin waltz when Diana
heard the faraway slamming of car doors and then
the sound of voices—Kate's high sweet tones, Barrie's deep rumble, what sounded like a sharply
spoken question from Rhys and Robert's murmur of
reply. Robert, she knew, would ensure that Kate and
Barrie stayed out of the way; it was no surprise when
she heard the single fall of footsteps approaching
down the hall. She moved back into the shadows as
far as she could get.

The door was shoved open and Rhys strode into
the room, his face hard with anger, his blue eyes
brilliant. Eyes that flew to the piano, where a slight
black-haired girl was seated, her slim fingers flying
over the keys, her whole body absorbed in what she
was doing. The sunlight shone on her hair, which had
the patina of satin.

He stopped dead in his tracks, his hand still on the
doorknob. The color drained from his face, leaving it
ashen pale under its tan. Momentarily he closed his
eyes, giving his head a little shake. But when he
opened them again the girl was still there and the
pure, exquisitely chosen notes still floated in the
golden air.

Rhys let go of the door, and from her corner Diana
saw him shudder. His sudden indrawn breath was

shockingly loud as he walked toward the piano, Belinda the magnet to which he was irresistibly drawn. He was close enough now to see the dark lashes, the fine-boned wrists, the soft curve of mouth that was a younger replica of her mother's. Dragging his attention away from the child's face with an effort of will that Diana could only guess at, he began watching the nimble fingers. Slowly, almost imperceptibly, Diana could see him being drawn into the music. She held her breath, knowing that this was the crucial moment, praying Belinda would not inadvertently do or say the wrong thing.

Rhys started to speak, clearing his throat first to bring his voice to normalcy. "Your fingering could be improved upon in the arpeggio there," he said huskily.

For the first time Belinda realized someone else was there. Unintentionally she struck a wrong note, wincing at the discord. Looking up, her mind obviously still much more occupied with the music than with the man, she said, "How? Show me."

Diana waited with bated breath to see what he would do. For a moment he hesitated, his mouth a set line. Then he reached down and repeated the passage, his fingers as agile on the keys as if he had been practicing daily. Belinda watched intently. "Like this?" she said, playing the notes rather more slowly.

"That's right. Only keep your wrist a touch higher." After he had adjusted it to his satisfaction, she went through the whole passage again, more confidently this time, and then again.

"That does feel better," she said. "You know this bit here?" She played a short section. "I always have trouble with the modulation."

"Why don't you try slowing the tempo just a touch and then playing that first chord almost in a staccato fashion? Here, let me show you what I mean."

The two dark heads were bent over the keyboard, Rhys's arm brushing Belinda's shoulder. The minutes ticked by as the waltz was dissected, bar by bar. But Diana was scarcely aware of the passage of time, for she knew now that her plan had worked: Rhys was playing again. From her knowledge of him, always more instinctual than rational, she knew that something in him that had been drawn far too tight for far too long was slowly relaxing; he was coming home after a long exile.

They came to the end of the waltz and Belinda got up, giving Rhys the seat so he could play the whole piece through for her. When he finished she clapped spontaneously, her elfin features alight with pleasure, her face almost on a level with his. He seemed unable to find anything to say now that the impromptu lesson was over. Belinda, however, rarely suffered from that complaint and now said artlessly, "Is this your piano?"

He nodded, watching the swift play of expression on her face.

"And your house?" Again a nod. "You're very lucky to have such a beautiful piano." With scarcely a pause she prattled on, "I've seen your picture on record covers, haven't I? You're Mr. Morgan, aren't you?"

He found his voice. "That's right—Rhys Morgan. And who are you?"

"I'm Belinda Sutherland. My mother's a friend of yours. She's an artist. She brought me here for a visit."

Right on cue Diana stepped out from her corner and said steadily, "Hello, Rhys."

"Hello, Diana," he replied quietly. "This is a. . .a very unexpected pleasure."

She smiled, her cheek muscles stiff, her eyes unconsciously pleading with him not to say anything that would upset Belinda. Surely by now he would have realized that to Belinda he was simply Rhys Morgan, a famous pianist? "I knew Belinda would enjoy meeting you. She's never been fortunate enough to hear you play in person, before today."

"I see," he said heavily, the two small words fraught with meaning.

So he had realized Belinda did not know his true identity, Diana thought wildly, knowing she must say something. "This is Belinda's first trip to Newfoundland."

"I hope you can both stay for a few days."

"Thank you, that's very kind of you," she replied inanely, taking shelter behind stock phrases because the whole situation was so impossible to cope with otherwise.

"Will you give me more lessons?" This from Belinda, the rather overdone casualness of her voice belied by the hands tightly clasped in front of her. "Madame Lacasse said I needed someone better to

teach me now. Though I don't s'pose she meant anyone as good as you.''

Rhys's expression softened. "Yes, I'll do that,
Belinda. Why don't we set a time each day...how
about ten o'clock in the morning?''

The child's smile was so dazzling that it was
obvious to both adults she would have agreed to
midnight if Rhys had so chosen.

He went on, "In the meantime why don't you
play for me for half an hour now—some of your
best pieces and some of the ones you're working
on? That way I'll have an idea where we should begin.''

Belinda sat down obediently, thought for a minute
and then began to play. Perching on the arm of the
chesterfield, Diana watched the two of them, although oddly it was Alan of whom she was thinking—Alan and his warnings. She had largely ignored
them, intent upon bringing about this meeting of
Rhys and the child whom he had instantly recognized
as his own. The meeting had accomplished its purpose: he had played for Belinda and had agreed to
teach her. And now, inevitably, Diana was left to
wonder what the cost would be....

Eventually Belinda finished playing and regarded
Rhys warily, a patch of color high in each cheek. He
said seriously, "You did well, Belinda—you're ex-
ceptionally talented. There are some areas we can
work on, but we'll talk about that tomorrow, okay?''
As if he couldn't help himself, he reached over and
patted her shoulder, a spasm of some undefinable
emotion crossing his features. When he spoke, how-

ever, his words were prosaic. "Do you want to go for a swim in the pool?"

"Yes, please.... Will you come, mom? I'll show you how I do the back flip." Turning back to Rhys she added in explanation, "I learned it at music camp."

So it was that half an hour later Diana found herself lying on a lawn chair at the edge of the pool, dark glasses hiding her expression as she watched Rhys and Belinda cavort in the water like a couple of otters. She was unable to prevent herself from feeling faint stirrings of jealousy and unease that Belinda had taken to Rhys so readily.

Beside her Kate murmured. "She's a lovely child, Diana. I'm surprised you never mentioned her on your last visit."

If Kate was wondering about the physical similarities between Belinda and Rhys, she was keeping her questions to herself. Diana replied untruthfully, "Oh, I guess I was on a holiday from parenthood. One needs a break occasionally."

Kate sighed sharply. "You're very lucky. I wish I—" She broke off, her expression bewildered. "For a moment I thought I'd had a child...but that's absurd."

On the other side of her Barrie sat up. "I'm going for a swim," he said roughly, loping across the grass, shedding his shirt and diving in.

Kate added more casually, "You know, at first I didn't like Barrie at all—he scared me. But I'm getting to know him better now, and I like him more and more. Particularly since he's dropped all that nonsense about my being his wife."

Her heart torn for both of them, Diana said evenly, "I'm glad to hear that, Kate. He certainly looks much better than he did."

"Robert's trying to fatten him up." Kate stretched gracefully, her body slim as a wand in a one-piece leaf-green suit. "I think I'll go in, too. Are you coming?"

"No, I'm just going to sit here." Diana had no desire to be part of the horseplay in the pool; she had been so keyed up to face the meeting between Rhys and Belinda that she felt tired and out of sorts now that it was over.

Then, as Kate joined the others, she saw Rhys pull himself out of the water and pad across the grass toward her. His chest and limbs glistened with moisture; his wet hair was slicked to his head, emphasizing the rugged masculinity of his features. He said abruptly, "Come and join us."

"No, thanks."

His eyes raked her body in its diminutive bikini. "Motherhood certainly didn't spoil your figure," he said, so quietly that only she could hear him. As she flushed, unable to think of an answer, he leaned over and swiftly gathered her into his arms.

Her temper flared as the accumulated anxieties of the past couple of days found an outlet. "Put me down!"

"You're going for a swim."

"I don't want to!"

"Temper, temper," he mocked. He shifted her slightly in his arms so that her breast lay against the wet mat of hair on his chest, the warmth of her hip against the concavity of his belly. "She's my child, isn't she?"

There was no point in denying it. "Yes, she is."

"I knew it the moment I laid eyes on her."

His arm tightened and for a moment she thought he was going to kiss her in front of them all. For the second time she hissed, "Rhys, put me down."

He grinned nastily. "How's your fiancé? I see he came up with a ring."

"Don't be so crude. Rhys, everyone's looking at us. Will you please put me down?"

"I bet he didn't want you to come over here. But you always were headstrong, Diana—I hope by now he's getting used to that. Or is he still cherishing the illusion that he's the boss?"

"Alan treats me as an equal," she said furiously. "Unlike some people I could mention."

He laughed heartlessly, carrying her over the edge of the pool and jumping in, still with her in his arms. When she rose to the surface she fought free of him, sputtering and pushing her wet hair back from her eyes. Belinda's head bobbed up beside her. "Race you to the end of the pool, mom."

They stayed in the pool for an hour or more, got changed for dinner and ate a leisurely meal. Then Diana took her daughter for a short walk down the road. Belinda was rather quiet, however, perhaps overtired from a combination of travel, time delay and excitement, and they soon went back to the house. Belinda got ready for bed without any of the standard arguments; she was sleeping on a cot in Diana's room. She murmured drowsily, "Night,

mom. Don't let me oversleep and miss my lesson tomorrow, will you?''

''I don't think it's very likely. Good night,
dear.''

In no time Belinda's breathing had settled into the
deep steady rhythm of sleep. Tired herself, Diana
read for a while, then got up to change for bed. She
had pulled her dress over her head and was standing
clad only in her bra and panties when her door
opened silently and Rhys stepped in.

She couldn't risk waking Belinda. She clutched the
dress to her, her gray eyes stormy. But he had eyes
only for the sleeping girl. He walked over to the cot
and stood looking down at his daughter, and for a
moment there was such naked longing in his face that
Diana felt her heart quicken in her breast. Trying to
imagine how she would feel were she in his shoes, she
was almost overwhelmed by a suffocating uprush of
fear that she had made a terrible mistake in bringing
the two of them together, only to separate them again
in a matter of days.

Staring at Belinda as if he would imprint her features on his brain forever, Rhys whispered, ''She's a
beautiful child.'' Very slowly, as if the movement
hurt him, he looked over at Diana. ''Although not as
beautiful as her mother.''

Seared to her soul, she heard him add, ''Get
dressed, Diana. We're going for a walk.''

Without the strength to argue, forgetting any self-
consciousness, she pulled the dress on again, buttoning its front closure. It was a slim-skirted outfit of
dark green cotton with military tabs at the shoulders

and flapped pockets, its intentionally masculine styling emphasizing her very feminine curves.

They left the room together, Diana slinging a cardigan over her shoulders as they went out the back door. It was dark enough that moths were fluttering on their fragile brown wings around the light; a new moon carved a pale arc in the velvety sky. In silence they walked across the grass away from the house toward the jagged black line of woods.

CHAPTER FOURTEEN

WHEN THEY REACHED the tree line Rhys stopped, half-turning so that he was facing the waters of the bay, black as obsidian, and the mysterious humped backs of the mountains on the far shore. It was very quiet. They were too far from the bay to hear the waves, and there was no wind to stir the warm air.

He was leaning one arm on the branch of a tree; as Diana's eyes grew accustomed to the darkness she could distinguish the dark pits of his eyes, the shadowed planes of his cheeks and the gash that was his mouth. She had some idea of what was to come. She could have taken the offensive, she supposed, but somehow she didn't think it would make much difference.

So it was Rhys who broke the silence. "Why didn't you tell me, Diana? Ten years ago, before she was born."

"For so many reasons, Rhys. For one thing, I'd lied to you. I'd presented myself as sophisticated and experienced and older than I was—"

"I remember that," he replied grimly. "So you'd taken no precautions against pregnancy?"

"None whatsoever. How could I have? I had no idea what was going to happen when I went to the concert that night."

"But you didn't get pregnant the other time."

"Other time?" For a moment she didn't know what he meant.

"You'd made love with a student, you told me."

"Oh. . .that was a lie, too."

"So you were a virgin. I should have known that."

"I was very determined that you shouldn't know." She paused, then plunged on, knowing only absolute honesty would serve her now. "I wanted you so much, Rhys, that I was determined to let nothing stand in the way. And then later I paid the price for it, in the classic female sense. I discovered I was pregnant."

"You should have told me." His voice was a mixture of anguish and rage. "I knew you'd lied about your age—the rest wouldn't have mattered."

"It mattered to me. A question of pride, I guess. But it was more than that. I was in love with you then—I'd told you that, as well. But despite the fact, you sent me away. You wouldn't let me come with you or write to you or see you again—for ten years, you said." She picked at the bark on the trunk of the tree. "I was only seventeen, Rhys. After you'd gone I was so hurt and angry and unhappy that for weeks I went around in a daze. The last thing I was likely to do was get in touch with you when I found out I was pregnant. Your career was all-important; you'd made that very clear. I wasn't quite so naive as to think you'd want a pregnant girl friend hanging around your neck."

He took a deep breath. "I see. How did you manage?"

"My parents were wonderful. I moved back home,

had the baby and then a couple of years later went back to art school while my mother looked after Belinda. Our apartment is in their house.''

"So that explains why you stayed in Montreal all those years.''

"Yes. A child ties you down.''

"Did it never occur to you later on to let me know I'd fathered a child?'' he demanded, the anger surfacing again. "I could have helped.''

"I was managing all right,'' she said stubbornly. "And usually you were off in New York or Paris or Vienna—how could you have helped?''

"You've got it all worked out, haven't you?'' he said with barely suppressed violence. "How many people know I'm Belinda's father?''

"Will and Celia guessed, I think, but I made them swear never to say anything. I told Alan just a couple of days ago before I came back here. No one else.''

"Not even Belinda?''

"No.''

"She'll have to be told.''

"Why, Rhys? In a few days I'll have to take her back to Montreal. School will be starting, and her visit with the famous Rhys Morgan will be a thing of the past.''

"You're not getting away with that, Diana.''

His voice was perfectly level, but she found herself shivering. "What do you mean?''

"I mean Belinda is my daughter. Now that you've finally seen fit to let me know she exists, I'm not going to simply let her disappear from my life. What kind of man do you think I am?''

Alan had warned her.... "I have to go back to Montreal," she said sharply.

"Then let's go back as man and wife."

Shocked, she stood rooted to the spot. "We can't do that!"

"Why not? People are doing it all the time, some of them for a lot less reason than we have."

She fought for composure. "Rhys, I don't want to marry you—I'm engaged to Alan. He's very fond of Belinda and she of him. It's all arranged."

He gave an ugly laugh. "Then it can be un-arranged. Do you think I'm going to let someone else act as a father for my child?"

"You don't have any choice."

"That's where you're wrong, my dear. I've already lost nine years of my daughter's life—you cheated me out of those."

"What else could I—"

"Be quiet! I've missed seeing her take her first steps, learn how to talk, go off to school, start to play the piano—I'll never know any of that. But I won't be cheated out of the rest, Diana. Not by you or Alan or anyone else."

Although she was trembling all over, she managed to make her voice ice-cold. "So what are you propos-ing?"

"You and I will marry and Belinda will live with us. It's very simple."

"And what if neither she nor I want to do that?"

"*She* will—I can guarantee you that."

The last of Diana's composure shattered. "You're trying to steal my child! You can't *do* that."

"Cut out the histrionics. I'm not trying to steal her at all. Do you think I'm blind to how much she loves you and you her? What kind of a fool would I be to try to disrupt that?" He took a couple of steps closer to her, his manner softening. "You've done a fine job of raising her, Diana, and I'm sure it wasn't always easy. All I'm saying is that I want to share the burdens and the joys—be a real father to her. If I've been deprived of her all these years, then equally she's been deprived of me."

He was right...oh, God, how right he was. "She has Alan," she said obstinately.

"Alan may be an estimable man, but he is not Belinda's father."

He was standing so close to her now that she could see the thick fringe of his lashes; his irises had absorbed the blackness of the sky. "I don't know what else to say, Rhys. Quite apart from Alan, you and I can't get married just because it's convenient and might be good for Belinda—there's a lot more to marriage than that. We don't love each other. How long do you think she'd be happy if we weren't getting along? We just can't do it!"

Something in her tone of voice, perhaps the note of desperation, must have reached him. He rested his hands on her shoulders, kneading her tense muscles as if he was gentling a frightened young animal. "Hush a moment," he murmured, "and relax. You're all worked up."

She tried to move away, but there was steel strength in those probing fingers. It was easier to stand still, letting her forehead rest on his shoulder as her anxiety and frustration began to seep away. Strangely enough, of all they had said it was his words of praise that came to mind. "I'm glad you think I did a good job with her," she whispered.

"She's a delightful child." His face was resting against her hair and his arms were around her now, his hands running up and down her back in a soothing hypnotic motion. She closed her eyes.

When, a few moments later, she felt his lips brush her cheek, it seemed only natural to raise her face to his. His kiss began almost tenderly and further lowered her guard. An enticing warmth spread through her body. Her hands crept up to encircle his neck.

As if that had been a signal, his mouth demanded more of her. She felt his teeth teasing her lips, the first touch of his tongue. The warmth burst into flame, urgent and fiery bright. Her fingers probed the nape of his neck, the hardness of his scalp under the thick dark hair, even as her body willingly and joyously pressed itself to his. She felt the throb of his drive, real and insistent, making a demand as old as time, and her own blood pulsed in her veins in an acquiescence just as powerful.

Somehow they were lying on the dry sweet-scented grass, she half on top of him as he undid the buttons on her dress and pushed it away from her body. In the blackness of night her flesh was a pale gleam, the valley between her breasts a dark hollow. Briefly he was content to have the silky fabric of her bra covering her; through it he stroked the fullness of her flesh to its tip, with his lips tracing the tautness of her nipple. But she had been opening his shirt, and with swift impatience he unclasped the flimsy shred of nylon and flung it aside, pulling her down to lie across him, the pink-tipped softness of her breasts and smooth milk-white skin in sensual contrast to the bone and sinew and tangled hair of his chest.

Her hair fell forward to envelop them both as he began kissing her again, fiercely and hungrily, and her response was just as unrestrained. His hands had been cupping her face, tangled in her hair; now they left, and she raised her weight from him as she felt him fumble with the fastening of his trousers and then slide them down his hips until he was lying beneath her naked. Her own lacy briefs, the last barrier between them, he pulled roughly from her. Then he drew her down to him again, molding the long indentation of her spine, smoothing the curve of her hips, clamping her legs with the heaviness of his thigh so she could not escape had she wanted to.

But she had forgotten reality, forgotten fiancé and daughter. Oblivious to everything but the pulsing rhythms of his body and her own needs, she buried her face in his shoulder, her nostrils filled with the musky scent of his skin and its tantalizing warmth. She ran her fingers through the rough hair that went from the hollow of his throat to his navel, and because he was caressing the secret places of her body, the places that only he had known, she allowed her hands to slide lower in a mixture of boldness and shyness that broke the last shreds of his control.

He groaned her name and then they rolled over. Above her head the stars whirled and spun. He had brought her so close to the peak of desire that when he entered her she cried out, lost in the white heat of her body's rhythms, filled with him: completely herself yet at the same time completely one with him as could happen no other way. Together they reached the crystal clarity of the pinnacle and together fell down the far side to lie spent in each other's arms.

It was a long time before either of them spoke. Diana felt utterly secure cradled in Rhys's arms, as though she had come back to her true home after an absence of many years, and at first she had no desire to move. But gradually she became aware of other sensations—of grass scratching her spine, of a rock digging into her hip and of the coolness of the night air on her skin. Then Rhys shifted his position, muttering an expletive. She giggled. "What's wrong?"

"I think I'm lying on the point of an arrowhead." After searching through the grass he held up a sharp-edged piece of granite and grinned at her in the darkness. Hugging her roughly he muttered into her ear, "God, I needed that, Diana. I don't know what it is about you—it was like coming home again." His words so closely allied her own feelings that she felt a quiver of superstitious dread. He nestled his face in her neck. "You smell nice," he murmured. Because he was tickling her, she pushed him away; he grabbed at her and they wrestled for a few moments, Diana laughing breathlessly until she was subdued.

Then he took her left hand in his and began pulling at one finger. "Ouch! What are you doing?" she exclaimed.

"Taking off that ring. You won't be needing it anymore."

"Rhys, stop!" It was suddenly no longer funny. She clenched her fist to impede him, saying agitatedly, "Don't do that."

Leaning up on one elbow so that his body hovered over hers, he said with deliberation, "You're not engaged to him anymore, Diana, you're engaged to me."

"What are you talking about?"

"You and me. We're going to get married—remember?"

"Oh, no, we're not." She pulled away from him, searching on the ground for her dress.

"We certainly are." He reached out for her, but she had scrambled to her feet, shaking out her dress. He got up himself, holding his trousers, and no power in the world could have stopped her from admiring the long lean lines of his body silhouetted against the hills and the sky. Horrified by her own duplicity, she pulled on the dress and knelt to find her undergarments. When she stood up, Rhys was fully dressed; she shoved her bra into her pocket and said tremulously, "Are you ready?"

He came closer. "Not yet, Diana. You think I'm joking, don't you? I've never been more serious in my life, believe me. I want you for my wife."

"You want to be Belinda's father—that's what you want."

His breath hissed through his teeth. "Have it any way you want, we're still going to get married."

"I'm sorry, Rhys. It's my turn to say no now and your turn to be the one who gets left behind. I won't marry you—and Belinda and I will be leaving here in a couple of days."

There was a long pause. "So you're out for revenge, are you?" he said finally. "Ten years ago I did it to you, so now you're going to do it to me. I'd thought better of you, Diana."

Was it true, what he was accusing her of? Did that long-ago desertion still rankle so much that now she was seizing upon an opportunity to get her own back? She pushed her hair back from her face. "I don't know about that. All I know is that I can't marry you. It wouldn't be right."

"But it's right for us to make love?"

She hung her head, knowing she had no answer for him, despising herself for having fallen so easily into his arms. "I can't seem to help it with you," she stammered. "But that doesn't make it right, nor does it mean we should get married."

"If I can't persuade you one way, I'll persuade you another. One thing I'm adamant about is that Belinda be told who I am. We'll do that tomorrow, after her music lesson."

"I don't want—"

"For God's sake, Diana!" he exploded. "Credit the child with a little intelligence—she's probably guessed who I am already. All she had to do was look in the mirror."

It was another breach in her defenses. "That still doesn't mean we have to get married," she said coldly.

"There's something else you haven't taken into consideration."

She hated it when he used that tone of voice. "Oh?"

"Yes. We've just made love, right? So there's a chance you might be pregnant again."

Her face froze with shock and she gasped in dismay. "No!"

"Why not? It happened last time."

For a moment she wondered if she was going to faint. He grabbed her arm, giving her a little shake. "You hadn't thought of that, had you? So what are you going to do, go back to Alan and wait until you find out one way or the other? And what if you are—will you marry him anyway?" He answered his own question. "You won't, Diana. I know you well enough for that."

Sick and dizzy, she did the only thing possible and flailed out at him, pulling her arm free. "That's why you made love to me, isn't it?" she cried bitterly. "So you could have a weapon to hold over my head. You're despicable, Rhys Morgan! I wouldn't marry you if you were the last man on earth."

She whirled and began running down the hill, fighting to keep her balance, her ears strained for the sound of his pursuit. But when she reached the back door she was alone, and mercifully the kitchen was empty. She fled to her room, flung her clothes on the floor and fell into bed, unable even to release her emotion in a storm of weeping because of Belinda. Fists clenched in the pillow, she fought for calm.

She had no idea how much time passed before she

heard the back door open and close and then the soft
fall of footsteps go past her door; it was a long time
after that before she slept.

"MOM, ARE YOU AWAKE?"

Diana raised her head, wincing at the sunlight
streaming in the window. "I am now."

"What time is it?"

She squinted at her watch. "Eight-thirty."

"I could go and get some breakfast now, couldn't
I? I don't want to be late for my lesson."

"Robert's up, I'm sure." Against her will she
heard herself ask, "You're looking forward to the
lesson, are you?"

Belinda's face lit up. She was wearing a clean
blouse and shorts and had painstakingly braided her
hair into two pigtails, Diana noticed. "Oh, yes! Wait
until I tell Madame Lacasse who I've had lessons
with."

Diana's heart sank—another complication.
"Whom, not who," she corrected automatically.
"I'll get up in a while, okay?"

"Okay." As Belinda tiptoed out of the room,
making far more noise than if she had walked normally, Diana pulled the covers over her head, wanting only to shut out the new day and all the pitfalls
that lay ahead.

It was after ten when she got up, and the door to
the music room was closed. She made a cup of coffee
and carried it outside to the patio that overlooked the
pool.

Barrie was sitting in one of the wooden lawn

chairs, morosely poking at the flagstones with a stick. He gave her a crooked grin and said bluntly, "You look as bad as I feel."

"Thanks a lot," she responded dryly.

"Rhys acting up? I figured he might as soon as I cottoned on to who Belinda was." As her eyebrows flew up, he added impatiently, "Well, she is his daughter, isn't she? They're as alike as two peas in a pod."

"Yes." While she rather appreciated Barrie's lack of subtlety in bringing the problem into the open, she found she did not want to discuss it further. "He's giving her a music lesson right now, so at least I've accomplished that much," she said dismissively. "What about you, Barrie? How are things going?"

"Hellish," was the succinct reply. "Oh, Kate's very sweet to me and takes me out for walks and insists I eat three square meals a day, as if I was some kind of an invalid in my dotage. But as far as anything else is concerned, she might as well be my little sister. She's completely buried any possibility that I might be her husband, and if I as much as put my hand on her shoulder she kind of freezes, as if I'd done something indecent." Viciously he jabbed at the earth with the stick. "But I *am* her husband, not her brother! I tell you, Diana, I think I'll go nuts if she doesn't soon remember who I am."

"Maybe when you go back home to Calgary she'll have a better chance of remembering."

"As things are now, the last thing she'd do is go anywhere with me. Now if I were Rhys...she'd follow him wherever he wanted to go. I don't mean she's in love with him, because she's not; at least I'm spared that complication. But she does seem to trust him in a way she certainly doesn't trust me.''

''Perhaps it will just take more time, Barrie—you haven't really been here that long, and she's far more open to you than she was.''

''I can stay another two or three weeks, I suppose. But I've got things that need looking after in Calgary—all the insurance claims for my plane, contracting my regular customers...and doing something about finding another job.'' He sighed, staring down at his feet. ''I got a letter yesterday from a flying buddy in Edmonton. He says there's a desk job coming open there in a couple of months and that I'd have as good a chance as any and better than most of getting it. But it's pure administration. Indoors eight hours a day, five days a week, pushing papers around. I always swore I'd never let myself get caught in that trap, but I don't know what alternative there is. I can't go back to flying; it was too hard on Kate, I see that now. And if she stays the way she is, I'll have to stick pretty close to home.'' He was snapping the stick into pieces. ''I suppose I could send for an application form. That's not really committing myself, is it?''

''It would at least keep it open as an option,'' Diana said gently. ''In the meantime, maybe something better will come along.''

''Maybe,'' Barrie responded without much conviction.

The conversation became more general, Barrie telling her about one or two of his more hair-raising adventures in the north, Diana describing a painting expedition she had gone on a couple of years ago with some friends, in which she had been flown to a remote spot in northern Ontario and had spent most of her time evading the amorous intentions of the pilot.

The back door opened behind them, and Kate's voice called out gaily, "What's the joke, you two?"

Diana patted the empty seat beside her, trying not to notice the mingled pain and frustration in Barrie's eyes as he watched his wife walk across the grass toward them, her body slim and graceful in a brief pair of shorts and a top. "Come and join us."

Kate smiled at them both impartially. "Rhys would like to see you in the music room, Diana. Robert and I could hear the two of them playing in there—it's like a miracle."

Diana felt her nerves quiver as she stood up; it was a miracle for which she was about to pay the price, she thought painfully. "I'll see you both later."

She went indoors, pausing by the mirror in the hallway to push a wisp of hair back from her face. She was wearing navy blue shorts and a mannish white blouse, her hair in a ponytail, her feet bare; the overall effect was anything but that of the mother of a nine-year-old. With her chin well up, she walked into the music room.

The lesson had apparently resumed. Rhys was playing a short passage, then Belinda repeated it. Rhys again, then Belinda, once, twice, three times, until Rhys pronounced himself satisfied. Then they moved on to the next few bars.

Diana doubted if they had even noticed her come in, so intent were they both on what they were doing and so close was the rapport between them. Although she went to stand by the window, her gaze kept returning to the piano, to the child's elfin features that were a very feminine version of the man's at her side, to the burnished wood of the piano in which their reflections wavered, to the long rank of ivory keys and the four hands passing over them. She took a piece of paper and a pencil from the desk and, propping the paper on a book, began to sketch them. With the side of the lead she was shading the long sweep of Belinda's hair, when a shadow fell over the paper: Rhys. Looking down at the two figures she had so swiftly and skillfully captured, "Will you give me that?"

Her pencil stilled. "It's only a very quick sketch—"

"I'd like to have it."

She handed him the sheet in silence. As he took it his fingers brushed hers, purposely, she felt. In agonizing recall she remembered those fingers brushing other parts of her body, probing and exploring, carrying her to the heights of passion. She flinched away, her lashes falling to hide her eyes.

"Can I see it, mom?" Rhys carried the sketch over, handing it to Belinda, who studied it with her head to one side. She grinned up at Rhys. "You and me look a lot alike."

Diana had been given her cue. "I...we have to talk about that, Belinda. You know I've never told you much about your father...only that we met the one time and we've never seen each other since then and that it wasn't possible for us to get married. Not even your grandparents knew who your father was. Nobody did, least of all your father himself. I told you all that.''

Belinda was sitting very straight at the piano, her hands clenched in her lap, her clear blue eyes fastened unwinkingly on her mother. Thoroughly unnerved, Diana fumbled for words, her knowledge that Rhys was listening just as intently not helping at all. She ended up by saying baldly, ''The reason that you and Rhys look so much alike is—'' the words came in a rush ''—he's your father.'' There. It was said, and the silence of ten years was broken. But how was Belinda going to react?

''That's good,'' Belinda said matter-of-factly, smiling up at Rhys. ''I thought you were, you see, but I guess I was scared to ask, in case you weren't.''

''You mean, you already knew?'' Diana asked faintly.

''His little finger is a bit crooked, just like mine—I noticed it when we were playing scales. At school in science class we had some stuff about heredity, so I thought that might mean we were related. Besides both being able to play the piano.''

Diana sat down in the nearest chair, for her legs would no longer hold her up. She said straightforwardly, ''I want to make sure you understand that Rhys didn't know you existed until we came here, Lindy. So you must never think that he didn't bother with you all these years. He couldn't, because he didn't know about you.''

Had she looked up, she would have seen both gratitude and respect in Rhys's expression as he looked over at her. He said very softly, "Thanks, Diana," and she nodded in mute acknowledgment.

"He was probably very busy getting to be famous, anyway," Belinda remarked forgivingly.

Rhys winced. "I did put my career first in those days, Belinda, and that was unfair to your mother. But I've paid for that mistake, because I realize now how much I missed by not knowing about you sooner." He smiled, easing the tension a little. "I'm going to have to make up for lost time."

Belinda betrayed the first hint of real anxiety. "You won't just disappear again? I'll be able to keep on seeing you?"

He looked her straight in the eye and there could be no doubting his sincerity. "I promise you will. We haven't worked that all out yet, your mother and I, but I promise I'll do my best to be a good father to you."

What did he mean, Diana wondered, by saying it wasn't all worked out? Surely he wasn't going to tell Belinda that he'd proposed marriage and been turned down? "We'll have to arrange visiting rights," she said with businesslike briskness. For the first time it was beginning to occur to her that by bringing Rhys and Belinda together she had inadvertently opened up a continuing relationship between Rhys and herself. Because of Belinda, they would have to remain in contact and inevitably would see each other from time to time. She wasn't sure how she felt about that....

Unmistakable anger had flashed across Rhys's face at the mention of visiting rights. He said coolly, "That wasn't quite what I had in mind, but we can discuss it later." He glanced at his watch. "Robert will have lunch ready. Why don't we go to the dining room?"

Belinda got up from the piano bench and tucked her hand in Rhys's, a wordless little gesture that, to Diana at least, said volumes. As Diana preceded them out of the room, she found herself remembering Alan's warnings and linking them to the hint of steel in Rhys's voice a moment ago. Although Belinda now knew the identity of her father, that had settled nothing, she knew; it was not in any way an ending, but rather a beginning. But a beginning to what?

CHAPTER FIFTEEN

OVER THE NEXT FEW DAYS Diana deliberately effaced herself as much as possible, allowing Rhys and Belinda to spend a lot of time together. The music lessons stretched to two hours; the afternoons were spent playing in the pool or sightseeing or going for long walks on the beach. The evenings were for Diana and Belinda, because Rhys more and more often was shutting himself in the music room. He was working feverishly, so Belinda informed her mother, on the first movement of his piano concerto—the one that Diana had unearthed on her earlier visit. He had also composed three or four delightful études especially for Belinda, which she took great pride in playing.

This schedule also meant that besides seeing less of Belinda than usual, Diana saw very little of Rhys. Under the circumstances, she felt, it was just as well, for she wanted no repetition of what had happened up on the hillside the other night. It was a memory she wanted to bury as deeply as possible, dismissing it as an aberration, a temporary insanity. So she swam in the pool in the mornings, she painted the sea caves along the Green Garden Trail in Gros Morne National Park and hiked the tableland. And as often as she could, she acted as a buffer between Barrie and Kate.

The slow days passed, deceptively quiet and peaceful. Diana finished what she knew was a major painting and, in the hiatus that such an accomplishment always brought, found herself at a loose end one sunny afternoon. Kate and Barrie had taken Belinda fishing; Rhys was working, the music room door firmly closed. Taking a book and a blanket from her room she wandered up toward the woods, her feet carrying her in the opposite direction to the one she and Rhys had taken over a week ago. Following a narrow trail through the tall bracken she wound her way up the hillside, going very slowly, for it was hot. To her left she saw a little clearing in the trees, the grass sprinkled with daisies, their white and yellow faces lifted to the sun. Scratching her legs in the process, she made her way over to it and spread her blanket on the ground, stripping to her bikini and lying down on her stomach, bra straps undone. Propping up her book, she began to read.

A robin was caroling monotonously nearby, the same succession of notes over and over again; she was reminded of Belinda's practicing. A sparrow scratched in the underbrush, and tiny flocks of chickadees called back and forth as they busily canvassed the spruce trees for food. Otherwise the summer afternoon drowsed in the heat, the leaves hanging still on the trees. She rested her cheek on her arm, and her lashes drifted shut. The robin's song grew farther and farther away as her breathing deepened and she slept.

THE MAN WHO CAME up the hillside a little later moved as stealthily as an Indian for all his size. He saw the broken-off ferns where Diana had left the trail before he saw her; for a moment he was frozen to stillness at the sight of her. The curving lines of her body were relaxed in sleep and dappled with sunlight, while her hair was a pale cloud about her face. Beside her a book lay open on the blanket. Very carefully he eased his way through the tall bracken. . . .

She was dreaming, a slow sensuous dream bathed in the delicious heat of the sun. She was being stroked as if by the warm sure hands of the wind. They caressed her neck, pushing aside the heaviness of her hair. They traced her spine to her hips and the silken length of her thighs. They lifted her boneless body and cupped the fullness of her breasts and she gave herself up to them, rejoicing in her nakedness.

The barrier between sleep and wakefulness was crossed unnoticed. When she saw Rhys's nude body hovering between her and the sun, it became part of the dream and she opened herself to him, her lips soft from his kisses, her eyes slumberous with desire. There was no haste this time, nor did they speak. Slowly and inevitably their bodies' rhythms claimed them both. And when they joined together, the gathering tension was just as slow and inevitable, their wordless communication as beautiful and as intricate as the translucent fronds of the ferns. But it had to end. Her slender fingers, tensile, strong, drew him down to her and fiercely held him close; her breathing panted in her throat. He shuddered once, twice, then his head dropped to lie against her tangled hair, his fingers lying loosely at her throat where the pulse drummed.

The bruised edges of the ferns had released a sweet scent in the air, and the robin still sang, although it

sounded farther away now. Diana was drifting off to
sleep again when she heard Rhys murmur into her
ear, "Diana...beautiful Diana. I don't know what
this is between us, whether you can call it love or
not.... I only know I don't want you to leave. I want
you at my side, I want to sleep with you every night
and wake up in the morning and find you there...."

As if a cloud had covered the sun, her mood darkened, swinging from peace and fulfillment to an inex-
plicable fear. Her eyes flew open, and symbolically
the first thing she saw was Alan's ring flashing red in
the sun, like an accusing eye. Bloodred, she thought
wildly. *Alan, oh, Alan, what have I done to you?
And what have I done to myself?*

Tears flooded her eyes and suddenly she was weeping, harsh tearing sobs that crowded her throat and
racked her body. She twisted in Rhys's arms so that
her face was hidden in the grass, not wanting him to
see her, wishing she had never laid eyes on him again.
"Go away," she whimpered. "Please—go away!"

His answer was to hold her closer, as if by the
touch of his hands he could draw the pain from her.
Frantic from an inward battle in which anger warred
with pain, and guilt with fear, she struck out at him
with elbows and fists. "Let go of me!"

He grabbed her flailing arms. "Stop it, Diana—
calm down."

But she was beyond reason now, her eyes turbulent
with rage. "Let go!" she spat, kicking out at him
and, at his grunt of pain, managing to twist one wrist
free. Half-sitting up, she pulled away from him,
forgetful that she was still naked, her one desire to

hurt him as she had been hurt. "Why did you make love to me this time? Trying to make doubly sure that I was pregnant?"

The minute she had said the words she wished them unsaid, for she had never seen such contempt in a man's face before. "You little bitch—is that the way your mind works?" He let go of her other wrist as though the contact was repugnant to him. "Let me tell you why I made love to you. Because you looked so unbearably beautiful lying asleep in the sun. Because I wanted you as I have never wanted anyone else in my life before. Because I craved the intimacy, the excitement, the joy that I knew I could find in your body and equally that I could give back to you. I wanted to give and receive, to hold and be held, to be close to you, a woman, in the most precious and elemental way that exists. But you don't understand that, do you? Oh, no—to you it was cold-blooded and calculated. Something cheap and tawdry. An attempt to tie you to me by impregnating you." In one lithe movement he got to his feet, pulling on his trousers and grabbing his shirt as if he could not be gone from her soon enough.

Sick at heart she fumbled with her own clothes. "Rhys, I'm sorry—I shouldn't have said that. But I—"

"No, you certainly shouldn't." He thrust his feet into his moccasins. "I presume you can make your own way back to the house? After all, we don't want anyone to suspect we've been together, do we? They might make the mistake of thinking we're in love. . . and nothing could be farther from the truth, could it, Diana?"

Unable to think of a thing to say, she watched him push his way through the undergrowth and disappear from sight down the path. The bracken grew still again and the sound of his footsteps was swallowed up in the forest's silence. He might never have been with her. . . .

She lay back on the blanket, pressing the heels of her hands against her eyes to hold the tears back. There was no use in crying. The damage was done. She had cheapened herself in Rhys's eyes, and once again she had betrayed Alan. Whomever she came close to she hurt, she thought dully. She was no good to Rhys or Alan. Rhys had only to touch her and she fell into his arms; to Alan, who loved her and wanted her, she was unable to respond. There was no sense in it, no rhyme nor reason. All she knew was that she could not go on like this, torn between lust for one man—an ugly word, "lust," she thought with de- tachment—and loyalty toward another. Somehow she had to resolve it. But how?

SHE WAS NO NEARER to answering the question three days later, when it was time to leave Woody Point. This was partly because Rhys had been studiously avoiding her. He spent a lot of time with Belinda, and whenever he was with Diana it always seemed as though there were other people around, as well. One part of her was relieved by this: she didn't think she could deal with another sexual confrontation. But another part of her was piqued that he should shun her so blatantly.

On the morning of the day she and Belinda were

due to leave, Diana took her coffee outside and sat on the low stone wall that paralleled the driveway at the front of the house, where the vast panorama of clouds and hills and water was spread in front of her. She hadn't slept well and knew she looked far from her best; she could have done without the lightning-quick scrutiny of Rhys's discerning blue eyes. "Good morning," she said in a carefully neutral tone.

His own voice was just as impersonal as hers when, without ceremony, he said what he had come out to say. "Belinda has given me your phone number and address, and I'll be keeping in touch with her regularly by phone and letter. My own plans are a bit up in the air at the moment—I don't feel I can abandon Kate and Barrie, for one thing—so I'm not sure when I'll be able to see her next. Certainly for Thanksgiving, if not before. If you were to put her on the plane in Montreal, I'd meet her in Halifax."

Diana listened in silence, her coffee forgotten. This was not a discussion, she realized; she was being told what Rhys's plans were with regard to Belinda. And furthermore, he was making it painfully clear that those plans did not include herself. *She* was not invited for Thanksgiving.

"We'll also have to talk about Christmas. Perhaps we can all get together for that." Diana must have winced, because he added with savage emphasis, "I've missed all the other Christmases with my daughter. I won't miss this one."

There would be no end to the contacts with him, Diana thought sickly. Whenever the phone rang in her apartment, it might be Rhys. When she picked up the mail at the door, there might be a letter from him. At the very least he would want input into Belinda's musical training, and this would probably extend to other facets of the child's life as she grew up. Diana would never be free of him...and it was her own actions that had brought this about.

"Have you nothing to say?" Rhys demanded.

She bowed her head submissively, unable to meet his eyes. "You seem to have it all worked out."

"Diana." He put a hand under her chin, forcing her head upward. "Look at me." Although she met his gaze, there was something in her expression of an animal caught in a trap seeing its captor for the first time. Unconsciously his fingers tightened on her jaw.

"You're hurting," she muttered.

He released her abruptly. "Sorry. And I'm sorry if I sounded dictatorial—I'm not sure how else to deal with it. I already love Belinda and I think it will be important for both of us that we keep in contact. The trouble is you've made it so obvious that you don't want me back in your life. That you're determined to marry Alan, no matter what." His face hardened. "The next time I see you, you'll probably be his wife. I wish to God I could get over this feeling that that's the worst thing in the world for you to do."

From the door Kate's voice floated across to them. "Rhys, telephone!"

"Damnation." He stood up, his fists clenched at his sides. "I won't be a minute. Wait here...I haven't finished yet."

She did wait until he disappeared into the house. Then she got up quickly, dumping the rest of the coffee, now lukewarm, out on the ground and going around to the back door. There was nothing more to be said between her and Rhys....

After she had finished her packing, Robert carried out their suitcases, taking a minute to shake her hand formally and to thank her for her success as far as Rhys's music was concerned. Then he stood back as the others gathered around. Kate kissed Diana on the cheek, whispering, "I'll miss you." Barrie gave her a quick hug and a gruff "Take care of yourself."

"You, too, Barrie. And all the best." Trite words to express all that she hoped for him and Kate, but it was the best she could do. From the corner of her eye she saw Belinda fling her arms around Rhys and saw Rhys kneel to give her a fierce hard embrace, the morning light glistening on the two silky dark heads so close together. She felt a lump in her throat. Rhys had said he loved Belinda. The feeling was clearly mutual. There was a tremor in Belinda's voice as she said, "Bye, Rhys. Thank you for all the music you wrote for me. I'll practice really hard every day."

"I know you will. And I'll send you some more music in my first letter—that's a promise. You promise you'll write back?"

"Of course I will!"

He patted her shoulder and then turned to Diana, the smile slowly leaving his eyes. Taking her by the shoulders he kissed her full on the mouth, without haste, and her body trembled to his touch. When he raised his head, he said in a voice so low that only she could hear, "We shouldn't be saying goodbye like this, Diana—it's all wrong. You know that as well as

I do. You just won't admit it.'' He must have seen her gray eyes cloud over in rebellion. Before she could speak he kissed her again, not releasing her until she was breathless and pink cheeked, horribly conscious of their audience. "I'm the only man who can kiss you like that," he said in a rough undertone. "Remember that, Diana—and remember me."

He stepped back and she hurriedly tried to gather her wits. "Ready, Belinda?" she said brightly. "Hop in, dear." They both got in the car and to a chorus of goodbyes Diana drove away.

Twisted in her seat, Belinda waved frantically until Rhys was out of sight. Then she slumped down, her little chin quivering, tears trickling down her cheeks.

Driving slowly, for the roads in the village were narrow and frequently doubled as playgrounds for the children, Diana sought the right words. "He'll phone you and write to you, dear, I know he will. And you'll see him in October if not before."

"October's ages away. Why couldn't we have stayed longer? School doesn't start until Wednesday."

The road had widened and Diana sped up a little. "We need a day or two at home before school starts to get your clothes ready and buy some scribblers and pencils."

"I could have had two more lessons."

Belinda was normally a tractable and happy-natured child; this overt rebellion was not like her. Diana said carefully, "It's always hard leaving a place where you've had fun. But once you're back home you'll be glad to see nannie and grandpa again and Alan and all your friends."

"What are you marrying Alan for?" Belinda burst out. "You should marry Rhys instead."

This was worse than Diana could have anticipated. "I'm engaged to Alan, darling. He's been my friend—and yours—for a long time."

Belinda hung her head. "I do like him. But he's not like Rhys."

"Of course he isn't; they're two very different people. It's not a competition, Lindy. You don't have to stop liking one because you like the other. There's room in your life for both of them."

But Belinda was not to be deflected by any kind of philosophical discussion. "Why did Rhys kiss you if you're engaged to Alan?"

Diana's hands tightened on the wheel. She said weakly, "I think he was grateful because I'd brought you to meet him, that's all."

"It didn't look like that to me," Belinda said stubbornly. "If you married Rhys we could all live together."

"Well, I can't marry Rhys," Diana replied, the first touch of sharpness in her voice. "I'm engaged to Alan and that's that." Her manner softened. "I'm sorry you're upset, Lindy. But adults can't always rearrange their lives as easily as you seem to think they can." Purposely changing the subject she said, "Is that an eagle over the water there? No, it's an osprey, isn't it?"

Belinda made an indeterminate sound that could have been either assent or dissent, and for the remainder of the journey to Deer Lake they drove mainly in silence. But at the airport she seemed to brighten, the meal on the plane further cheering her up. Diana began to relax, as well, and it seemed that by the time they reached the bustle and confusion of Dorval their relationship was back on its normal footing.

Although Alan had known their flight time, he was not among the crowds at the arrival gate. Diana was conscious of being somewhat relieved; she wasn't sure she could have depended on Belinda's reaction. She hailed a taxi, which within forty minutes had them home at the apartment.

The rest of the day passed busily, shopping for school supplies and having dinner with Nellie and Roger. Knowing it was impossible to keep it a secret any longer, Diana broke the news to her parents of Rhys's identity as Belinda's father. "It makes no difference to my plans with Alan, of course," she finished firmly.

"Of course," Nellie repeated guilelessly. "Although really, Diana, it would be very convenient if—"

"I've just been through all that with Belinda. No more, please." Diana felt a little guilty as she saw Nellie's downcast expression. She knew her mother was an incurable romantic who had undoubtedly already begun weaving a delightful tale of reconciliation and love between the handsome sophisticated pianist and her own beautiful artistic daughter. Alan's dual role as a mathematician and inventor of toys had never really appealed to Nellie.

Belinda looked very tired when they went back upstairs and she raised no objections to an early bedtime. She had been asleep for nearly half an hour when the telephone rang.

Momentarily paralyzed, Diana stared at the instrument as if it had suddenly turned into a snake about to bite her. What if it were Rhys? What would she say? She picked up the receiver, her mouth dry. "Hello?"

"Welcome home, darling. How are you?"

It was, of course, Alan. She said brightly, "I'm fine, and you?"

There was faint irony in his reply. "Fine, too. Sorry I didn't get to the airport—I thought it might be better if you both got settled in a bit before I made an appearance."

"That was probably a good idea. Belinda was upset at having to leave Rhys," she answered slowly.

"I see." A heavy pause. "May I drop over for a while, Di? Or are you too tired?"

She *was* tired, but the thought of postponing seeing him did not appeal to her. Better to get it over with.... "No, I'd like to see you."

"Be there in half an hour." He rang off.

She showered quickly, for traveling always made her feel grubby, and put on a linen caftan, its simple unadorned lines giving her an air of dignity and furnishing her with a courage she felt she was going to need.

She was mixing one of Alan's favorite cocktails when she heard his footsteps on the stairs. An ice cube slipped from her fingers and fell on the floor, skidding under the table. She bent to pick it up, wishing she was anywhere but where she was, knowing she was dreading telling him the truth but unable to do anything else. Behind her the door opened; she had unlatched it earlier.

"What on earth are you doing under the table?" His voice was relaxed, amused.

Forgetting the ice cube she stood up, the heavy folds of her gown swirling about her legs. He looked just the same. Gold-rimmed glasses over quizzical pale blue eyes, neat brown hair, tidy even features. Over one arm he was carrying a sheaf of cream-colored roses. Proffering them he said, "I know this is a bit like carrying coals to Newcastle, considering your father's garden, but they reminded me of you."

Without the slightest warning to either one of them, she burst into tears. Alan dropped the roses unceremoniously on the counter and put his arms around her, holding her head to his shoulder, murmuring words of comfort into her ear. She stopped as quickly as she had started, giving one last sniff. He pressed an immaculate white handkerchief into her hand. "Give a good blow and then come and sit down and tell me what that was all about," he said with a spurious calm that didn't deceive her.

The roses and the cocktails were left in the kitchen. Diana curled up in one corner of the chesterfield, Alan facing her yet a little apart from her, his eyes watchful behind his spectacles. She began tugging at the ring on her finger, saying unevenly, "I'm going to have to give this back to you, Alan."

With one hand he stayed her. "Hold it—how about telling me first what's going on?"

She looked at him, her breath still hiccuping in her throat. "I'm so ashamed of myself, and I can't even explain how it happened. It just did. While Belinda and I were in Newfoundland I...I slept with Rhys, Alan.'' She twisted the ruby back and forth. ''Not just once. Twice.'' Risking a glance at him, she saw that he had paled. Whatever he had been expecting, it had not been this. She rushed on, trying to remove his hand from where it rested on the ring. ''So you see, I have to give this back. There's no use in my saying I'm sorry, or that I never meant it to happen....''

He swallowed hard. Obviously needing to know the worst he demanded, ''Are you in love with him again?''

''No!''

''Did he ask you to marry him?''

''Yes, but only after he'd seen Belinda.''

''Maybe you should.''

''No. I—no.''

As Alan got up and began pacing restlessly around the room, Diana could almost see his mathematical brain struggling with the attempt to make order out of a number of horribly unpalatable facts. ''I'm jealous as hell,'' he said finally. ''Hurt. Angry. All of those things. But you mean too much to me, Di, for me to meekly hand you over to someone else. Particularly someone who over and over again seems to cause you nothing but heartache and distress.'' He drew a deep breath. ''I'd like you to keep on wearing my ring. Let's give ourselves a couple of weeks to cool down, and then we can assess the whole situation again. How's that?''

''It's more than I deserve.''

"I don't feel like debating that one way or the other right now," he said with a wry smile that didn't quite make it to his eyes. "How about that drink you were making?

Although he stayed another hour or so it was something of an ordeal for both of them, for the conversation was stilted, any mention of Rhys carefully avoided. When he got up to leave he kissed her briefly on the cheek, otherwise not touching her. "I'll give you a call in the next couple of days, Di. Sorry about this evening—I've been lousy company."

"I'm not much better." She felt a rush of affection for him, knowing he was dealing with her confession the best way he was able to. "Thank you for the roses."

Another quick kiss and he was gone. She latched the door behind him and, too tired to think about anything with any kind of coherence, went to bed.

TWO DAYS LATER, when the phone rang around five in the afternoon, Diana was sure it was going to be Alan. She picked up the receiver and said brightly, "Hello!"

"Diana? It's Rhys."

The world rocked on its axis, then slowly righted itself. "Oh. . .oh, hello."

"You sound surprised. You were expecting someone else?"

"Yes," she said, quite incapable of evasion. "Where are you?"

"Woody Point, where else? Is Belinda home?"

Her tongue felt as though it was stuck to the roof

of her mouth. "Yes, she is. It was the first day of school today."

"May I speak to her?"

"Just a minute, I'll get her." With exquisite care she put the receiver on the table and went down the hall to her daughter's room. "Linda? It's Rhys on the telephone. He wants to talk to you."

The child catapulted off her bed, where she had been reading. "Hurray!" she cried. "Can I use the phone in your room, mom?"

"Sure." So Belinda wanted privacy to talk to her father. Diana swallowed her hurt, knowing it was childish, and went into the kitchen, starting to prepare supper with rather a lot of unnecessary banging of pots and pans. And all the while she knew that the small hurt Belinda had inflicted was merely masking the larger one: that Rhys had not wanted to talk to her, had not even asked how she was. She was honest enough with herself to admit that the sound of his voice on the phone, coming so unexpectedly, had made her heart skip a beat and had turned her knees to water. *Why*, she wondered numbly, staring at the bag of potatoes as if she had never seen it before. And the answer clicked neatly into her brain, as if it had been waiting on the sidelines for just this opportunity. Because she loved him. That was why.

Aghast, she stared out the window, blind to the green tracery of elm branches that were waving gently in the breeze. She loved Rhys.... Perhaps, deep down, she had never stopped loving him, and it had taken their reunion this summer to bring it all out in the open again. That was why the lightest touch of his hand set her trembling, why the sound of his voice across the miles that separated them had the power to turn her world upside down. She loved him. She loved Rhys Morgan.

It was fifteen minutes before Belinda came racing into the kitchen, her face aglow as she recounted at top speed everything she had said to Rhys and Rhys to her. Belatedly Diana tried to pull herself together, murmuring the appropriate responses as she began to peel the potatoes, her mind on anything but what she was doing.

The evening passed slowly. Alan didn't phone, for which Diana was grateful. It was enough to have to cope with this revelation about her own feelings, a revelation that had, she realized now, been staring her in the face for days, without having to deal with what it meant in terms of Alan.

Her reprieve was brief, however. She spent the next morning in her studio, where, as always, work had a calming effect on her. Then she gave Belinda lunch, returning to the studio after the child had gone back to school. She was combining several of the sketches she had done in Newfoundland, and from them the outline of a painting that intrigued her was beginning to emerge. The door bell must have rung several times before she heard it.

Wiping her fingers on a rag, still very much preoccupied by what she had been doing, she went to the door. "Alan," she said foolishly. "Oh...come in."

She was wearing a paint-stained smock over blue jeans. "I've disturbed you at work—sorry," he said.

"I had to drive someone to Trafalgar Heights, and as I was so near I thought I'd drop by."

Abandoning any thoughts of further work, she steeled herself for what lay ahead. "I'm glad you did," she said evenly. "I need to talk to you."

Something in her tone of voice must have alerted him. "That sounds ominous," he said with attempted lightness.

She leaned against the counter. "Alan, Rhys phoned here yesterday. Not to talk to me, to talk to Belinda. But just hearing his voice like that—I was expecting it to be you, you see—made me realize something I should have realized sooner. I was blind, I guess."

She hesitated briefly. "I'm in love with him, Alan. I don't think I ever stopped loving him. I just buried it so deeply that it took the visits this summer, and my own reactions, to unearth it." Flashing a quick glance at his set face, she plowed on. "I'm not about to rush out and marry him—it doesn't mean that. What it does mean is that I can't possibly marry you."

He had been standing very still as she spoke, his hands thrust deep in his pockets, his eyes staring down at the floor. Now he looked up. "Do you know, I've been half-expecting this? Ever since the first time you went to Newfoundland. I think I knew even then what a gamble it was and that I might be the loser."

"I'm so sorry," she said in a low voice. "When I told you I loved you, I was sure I meant it. It's just that—"

"Don't try to explain it or justify it, Di. It's not one of those things we can always arrange to suit ourselves, is it?"

This time when she held out his ring he took it, shoving it in his pocket without a glance. She faltered, "Will we still see each other sometimes? You've been such a good friend to me, Alan. I don't want to lose touch with you."

"Nor I with you." He made an attempt to pull himself together. "After all, we're not teenagers anymore, are we, that we have to storm off to opposite sides of the globe? Look, I'm off to a conference in Toronto in a couple of days, and then classes start the following week. Why don't I give you a call when things have quietened down a little?" Starting toward the door he added, "Maybe by then you and Rhys will be married."

"I don't think so," she said very soberly.

Something in her mien must have touched him. Swiftly he crossed the room, putting his arms around her and squeezing her hard. "Whatever happens, Di, I wish you all the best," he said huskily. "Take care of yourself, won't you? And say hello to Belinda for me."

He was hardly out of the door before the tears started to flow. Sitting on one of the stools by the counter, she leaned her head on her arms and cried her eyes out, crying for Alan, whom she had hurt, and for herself, who loved a man who held her in contempt.

CHAPTER SIXTEEN

OVER THE NEXT couple of weeks Diana flung herself into her work with something of the fanaticism she had shown in earlier years and perhaps with something of the same motivation: to exorcise Rhys from mind and body. She never answered the telephone when Belinda was home. Rhys was phoning regularly and she was painfully aware that he never asked to speak to her. Although with the passage of time she had discovered she was not pregnant, she scarcely knew whether to be glad or sorry.

In her painting she found an escape from all these emotions whose intensity and confusion could only frighten her, making her aware of how vulnerable she was. She would never be free of Rhys, she knew that now. As a seventeen-year-old she had thrown herself into a love affair, hungry for experience. Now, as a mature woman, she loved Rhys just as passionately and just as unwisely. It brought her no happiness. In fact, loneliness and depression were her constant companions as the mellow September days drifted by, ripe as a fruit for the plucking and, by Diana, almost unnoticed.

For some time she had dealt with a gallery in Old Montreal, where a showing of her work was sched-

uled for the middle of October. Michel Cormier was
the owner of the gallery, and he and his wife Jeanne
had been friends of Diana's for several years. It was
one of those relatively rare relationships in which
business and pleasure had been combined to happy
effect. Her Newfoundland pieces had so aroused
Michel's Gallic enthusiasm that he was pressuring her
for more, planning on printing a last-minute adden-
dum to the catalog. So she was doubly motivated to
spend as much time as possible in the studio.

It was Michel himself who, toward the end of the
month, insisted on her taking a break. "We have
tickets for the chamber group coming to Place des
Arts, Jeanne and I, and we want you to come with us.
Perhaps you wish to bring a friend?" He paused delicately, for he knew of Diana's broken engagement.

"No, no friend," she said firmly. "But I'd love to
come."

As it happened, Jeanne had come down with a
late-summer cold by the time of the concert, so
Michel and Diana went alone. In an effort to combat
her own depression Diana had taken particular care
with her appearance, dressing her hair high on her
head and wearing a Mexican gown of navy blue, its
square neckline bordered with orange braid, its long,
slightly flared skirt embroidered with orange and
yellow and white flowers.

Michel picked her up in a taxi, for he was an impatient man who could never be bothered to hunt for a
parking lot. *"Charmante!"* he exclaimed when he
saw her. "Like one of those birds—how do you call
it? A parrot?"

She laughed outright. Slipping easily into French she said, "I'm not sure that's a compliment, Michel! But I'll take it as such. How's Jeanne?"

"Miserable. Whichever doctor finds the cure for the common cold will make a fortune."

She smiled at him affectionately. Michel was only an inch or two taller than herself; he was possessed of a luxuriant black mustache and what Nellie Sutherland would primly call "sex appeal." He flirted outrageously, and because Diana knew he adored his lovely auburn-haired wife, she felt quite safe in responding to his undeniable charm and often caustic wit.

Downtown they joined the crowds thronging around the semicircular dome of Place des Arts and once inside crossed the cool white-tiled lobby with its brightly colored abstract paintings. The concert was in the Salle Wilfrid Pelletier. Diana subsided into her seat, studying the program with interest. "This is a good idea, Michel," she said spontaneously. "I've been spending too much time shut up in the studio."

"It is because I am such a slave driver, *n'est ce pas?*" He patted her hand. "I am glad you enjoy yourself."

In the intermission they left their seats to make their way to the bar, where Michel, with a dispatch Diana could only admire, rapidly procured two drinks. *"Salut,"* he said, touching his glass to hers.

It was one of their rituals. *"Salut-là!"* she responded, smiling at him. Behind him, in the crowd's restless pattern of movement, she sensed rather than saw someone approach them and glanced over his shoulder. Audibly she gasped in shock. It was the one face she would not have expected to see here, the face of a man who should have been hundreds of miles away. That he was intent on speaking with her was obvious.

She summoned all her willpower and managed to say with some degree of composure, "Hello, Rhys. This is a surprise." Which, she thought grimly, was the understatement of the year.

He was not alone, she saw now, with a further effort of will trying to hide the hot stab of jealousy that pierced her. For the woman with him was beautiful in a way quite different from Diana's own undeniable beauty. She was very small, particularly standing beside Rhys, and delicately made, with a sweep of lustrous black hair seemingly too heavy for her slender neck. Her eyes were the shade of delphiniums, somewhere between blue and purple, and were thickly fringed with dark curling lashes. She had, Diana had to admit in all fairness, a delightfully warm and friendly smile. But Rhys was speaking, and she forced herself to pay attention to him.

"Diana, I'd like you to meet Huguette Danville. Huguette, Diana Sutherland."

Diana hastily introduced Michel, identifying him as the owner of the gallery where she dealt, and for a few moments the conversation was general, revolving around a discussion of the music they had just heard. Then Michel and Huguette switched to an animated discussion in French of a ballet production each had seen a couple of weeks before. Moving a little aside,

Rhys said mockingly, "Stepping out on your fiancé again?"

Anger flashed in her eyes. She said frigidly, "Alan and I are no longer engaged."

"Really? Now why would that be?"

She glanced at him accusingly. "You already know about it, don't you?"

"Belinda did happen to mention it on one of our phone calls, yes," was the casual reply. "But of course she didn't know why."

"I don't think the reason need be any of your concern." Moving to the attack she demanded. "What are you doing in Montreal? Belinda didn't tell me you were here."

"As yet, Belinda doesn't know. I arrived only this morning."

It hadn't taken him long to find Huguette.... She said sweetly, "Shall I tell her I saw you? Or is this a clandestine visit?"

With a certain satisfaction she saw an answering anger flare in his eyes. "You do have a way with words, don't you, Diana? There's nothing clandestine about this. My piano concerto is to be performed here before Christmas, and Huguette will be the soloist. This evening is simply giving me the chance to get to know her a little. I planned to phone you tomorrow morning to see if I could come and visit Belinda in the evening."

"Of course," she said stiffly, adding with a slight emphasis on the first word, "She'll be delighted."

He drew a finger lazily down her cheek, his sardonic gaze catching the involuntary flutter of her lashes at the contact. "Don't be bitchy, Diana."

After that comment it was perhaps fortunate that the houselights dimmed, summoning them back to their seats. Rhys added briefly, "I have your address. Seven o'clock be okay?"

She nodded and managed a civil goodbye to Huguette. Rhys, she noticed, did not suggest they all meet after the concert. He probably had other plans, she thought miserably, hating herself for being so jealous yet knowing it was beyond her power to control it.

"You look very cross," Michel said amiably. "For me it was a great pleasure to meet Monsieur Morgan. One hears so much about him. And his companion...." He rolled his eyes. "*Ravissante!* You have known Monsieur Morgan since a long time?"

"You could say that," she responded dryly, settling in her seat and rather ostentatiously burying her nose in the program.

"He reminds me of someone, but who?" Diana held her breath as his forehead wrinkled. Then she heard his sudden hiss of breath. "*Mon Dieu!* It is your Belinda!"

Very quietly but with crystal clarity she said, "Michel, if you breathe that to another living soul I'll remove every one of my paintings from your gallery and tear them up. So help me!"

In his face she saw his innate sophistication struggle with blank amazement and even a trace of humor. Theatrically he placed his hand over his heart. "Your secret is safe with me," he intoned.

"Good."

Clapping began around them as the performers filed back onstage. Diana knew she could trust Michel implicitly, but his rapid recognition of a relationship she had kept secret for nine years made probable all kinds of problems ahead. For he would not be the only one.... *Damn Rhys,* she thought viciously. Why did he have to come here? It was far too close to home. Far too dangerous.... *Damn him, damn him.*

Her anger was with her the rest of the evening, the austere beauty of a Beethoven string quartet passing over her unnoticed, and it persisted through the next day, not helped by Belinda's wide-eyed happiness at the thought of a visit from her father. He was punctual to a fault, for at seven sharp the white Jaguar parked at the curb outside the house and a few moments later his footsteps could be heard ascending the staircase.

While Diana stood back a little, Belinda ran to open the door. As Rhys seized the child in his arms and swung her high in the air, she forgot all the dignity of her nine years and squealed with delight. "I can play both the pieces you sent me—want to hear them?"

"Sure I do." He hugged her hard, an expression of such open tenderness on his face that Diana felt tears sting her eyes. Irritably she blinked them back. This was no time for sentiment.

Rhys put Belinda down and came farther into the room, holding out his hand. "Hello, Diana."

Reluctantly she put her hand in his, feeling the latent strength of his handclasp, the warmth of his palm. "Hello," she said, attempting to sound casual, succeeding in sounding merely unwelcoming. Purposely she had refused to change her clothes for this visit, so she was still wearing her smock and jeans, her hair in two pigtails, her face bare of makeup. She added with more assurance, "If you don't mind, I'm going back to the studio. Michel, whom you met last night, is having a showing of my work in October, so I'm very busy. Belinda will look after you, I'm sure."

It was, in its way, a deliberate throwing down of the gauntlet, her response to all the phone calls in which he had barely acknowledged her existence. "Touché," he murmured, a hint of laughter in his eyes. "However, once Belinda's in bed, there are a couple of things I'd like to discuss with you. If you're not *too* busy, that is."

She flushed in annoyance at the barely disguised sarcasm in his voice. "I'll be in the studio. You can show him where it is, okay, Belinda?"

She shut herself in the studio, forcing herself to ignore the sounds of the piano and the interwoven dialogue of the two voices, Belinda's clear and high-pitched, Rhys's deep and resonant. But try as she might, she could not concentrate on the canvas in front of her, for her brain kept beating the refrain, *Rhys is here, Rhys is here.* And overriding the anger and hurt was a treacherous glow of joy. To have him here in her apartment, which had been home to her for ten years, seemed a momentous event. Did he find it equally significant? Or was it for him simply a chance to see Belinda in her normal setting, Diana's presence of only peripheral interest?

The canvas was an unfinished portrait of the fisherman she had talked to in Woody Point, whose face had remained in her memory in almost photographic detail. She had caught to perfection the weather-worn skin and in the faded blue eyes the memory of a thousand cold November mornings spent on the heaving gray waters of the sea. Now she was working on the flannel shirt around the sunken flesh of his throat. A relatively easy task, but it simply wouldn't go right, so after her third attempt she gave up in disgust, cleaning her brushes and settling at her desk to do some long overdue paperwork. She owed an installment on her income tax and knew if her accountant was to see the present neglected state of her ledgers he'd be horrified. She grinned to herself. Her accountant was a very proper, fussy bachelor of fifty-odd whose life was dominated by credits and debits. He was always faintly scandalized that an artist—and a woman, at that—could make as much money as Diana did.

She was frowning over a collection of tattered receipts that looked as though they had been in intimate contact with the contents of her paintbox when there came a tap at the door. "Come in," she called absently, then smiled at Rhys in rueful acknowledgment of the confusion of her desk. "Do you do things like this?" She held up a much-folded receipt daubed with cadmium orange and annotated with an illegible scrawl. "I haven't a clue what this was for. I always think I'll remember and I never do."

Rhys chuckled. "I just pass the whole mess over to

my accountant and let him worry about it. He thinks all musicians are mad anyway.''

''Maybe we have the same one,'' she said darkly, gathering up all the receipts and shoving them back in the drawer.

''Belinda's in bed. She'd like you to say good-night.''

''Okay.'' She stood up and yawned unselfcon-sciously, stretching the kinks out of her back. Before she could guess his intention he had put his arms around her and was kissing her, and the shock ran right through her. For a moment she was rigid, neither resisting nor acquiescing. Then, pliant as a stem of grass in the summer wind, her body curved itself to his and the present moment became the whole world. The firmness of his lips and the questing of his tongue. The hardness of his chest under his thin shirt and the insistent heavy beat of his heart.

When he slowly released her she stood very still in the circle of his arms, her gray eyes bemused. He tweaked one pigtail, saying with a lightness denied by the hard rhythm of his breathing, ''You smell of paint.''

From the bedroom down the hall Belinda's voice called, ''Mo-om!''

Diana gave herself a little shake. ''That's Belin-da,'' she said unnecessarily. ''I must go.''

''I'll come with you.''

She was very conscious of him following her down the narrow hallway. Belinda was under the covers, only her bright-eyed, pink-cheeked face showing.

Diana kissed the petal-smooth skin. "'Night, darling. Sleep well."

"G'night, mom. G'night, Rhys—I'll see you on Friday."

He ruffled the child's hair. "It's a date."

So Rhys was still to be in Montreal by the end of the week. And this evening he had arrived in his own car, which augured a lengthy stay. Again Diana felt the slow burning of anger. She led him into the living room, with its pleasant air of informality and comfort, and pulled the door shut behind them; she did not want Belinda hearing what she had to say. Without offering him a chair she said flatly, "Rhys, how long are you planning to stay in Montreal?"

He wandered over to the far wall to examine a tempera panel she had done three years ago, entitled *Girl on a Swing*. It was Belinda, her black hair streaming in the wind, her child's body given up to the exquisite joy of soaring through the air on a summer's day. "I'm moving here," he said abruptly. "I've bought a house on the next street. Do you have any other paintings of Belinda?"

"You've bought a house?" she echoed blankly.

He was still examining the painting, his back to her. "Yes. Rather a nice one and in excellent shape. We've already got some of my stuff moved in. Kate and Barrie are helping, and Robert's in his element, of course, because for years he's been wanting me to settle down and lead a normal life."

Allowing herself to be sidetracked, Diana asked. "How's Kate?"

"The same. Drifts through the days. Barrie's got

her an appointment with a specialist in a couple of weeks. He may need one himself by then; the poor guy's going around the bend.'' He stood back from the painting, head on one side. ''It seemed best that they come here with me, at least for now, and actually Barrie's getting leads on a couple of jobs around here.''

She said very carefully, ''Are you planning to settle here, Rhys?''

He turned to face her, infuriatingly casual. ''That's the general idea.''

''Why?''

''On the practical side of it, my concerto's been commissioned by the symphony here, and I could be in line for the conductor's position in a year's time. But the main reason, obviously, is Belinda.''

''So without as much as a 'by your leave,' you're going to move in practically next door.''

He regarded her sardonically. ''It doesn't sound as if you think much of the idea.''

''I don't.'' She fought to subdue her temper, knowing that to lose it would not help matters. ''Look, Rhys, all these years no one but me has known you were Belinda's father. And outside my immediate circle of family and friends, a lot of people don't even know about her—''

''You mean you've kept her hidden away? As though she was some kind of disgraceful secret?''

''You're putting the worst possible interpretation on it! Do try to understand. In the last two or three years I've become quite well known around here, and it has seemed expedient to me, for instance, to keep her name out of any of the publicity. It would be such a juicy tidbit for the press, wouldn't it? 'Artist's illegitimate daughter....' Belinda doesn't need that."

"You're behaving like an ostrich! You can't hope to keep that kind of thing a secret indefinitely."

"I've done very well—until you came along."

His eyes narrowed. "Now just what do you mean by that?"

"It took Michel exactly two minutes to figure out that Belinda, whom he knows, must have been fathered by you, whom he'd only just met. I don't want you in Montreal, Rhys. I don't want people making that kind of connection behind my back."

Her voice had risen in spite of herself. He said with a dangerous calm, "Let me get a couple of things straight. Over the years I've kept a close watch on your work, and this—" he indicated the tempera panel on the wall "—is the only painting I've ever seen of Belinda. Are there others?"

"One more in my room. What was I supposed to do—do a portrait of my daughter and then put it on sale for the whole world to see?"

"Including me. That would have been one way of letting me know I had a child, wouldn't it?" His voice was quiet and level, but it didn't take much discernment to see he was furiously angry.

"I have a perfect right to guard my own private life," she snapped.

"And what happens when your show opens next month? Does Belinda go to the opening?"

"No! How could she?" she retorted defensively.

"So you *are* keeping her hidden. It sounds like some kind of Victorian novel—the housemaid's mistake," he snarled. "What happens at school? Don't they ever ask where her father is? And why her grandparents on her mother's side have the same last name that she does? For God's sake, Diana!"

In an exhilarating flood of adrenaline she lost her temper. "It's all very well for you to turn up like this and start criticizing me, Rhys Morgan!" she seethed. "Since she was born I've done the best that I could. And if I've made some mistakes—well, I never set myself up to be perfect. Not like some people I could mention!"

In two strides he was standing so close to her that she could feel his breath fanning her cheek. "I don't—" he began, then just as impetuously checked himself, letting out his breath in a long sigh. Adopting a more reasonable tone he continued, "Look, Diana, I didn't come here to quarrel with you. Nor did I realize quite the extent to which Belinda's life was circumscribed. That can't go on—you must know that as well as I do. And there's only one way to correct matters that I can see, which is for you and me to get married."

She blinked and took one instinctive step backward. "No way," she said forcefully.

Something flickered in his eyes and was gone as quickly as it had appeared, leaving her with the puzzling sensation that it had been pain. "Stop and think for a moment, Diana, and I'm sure you'll realize you have virtually no choice. For one thing, I'm staying in Montreal; that's not going to alter.

The arrangements are all made for the concerto, Huguette has started work on it and the first orchestral rehearsal will be in a month. The second thing that's not going to change is my relationship with Belinda.'' He rested a persuasive hand on her shoulder, where her muscles quivered at his touch, and looking straight into her eyes went on, ''I can understand why you didn't get in touch with me ten years ago, and you've done a fine job of raising Belinda. But I do know about her now. You can't change that. And if you attempt in any way to keep her from me from now on, I'll fight you every inch of the way.''

His vehemence had shaken her, as perhaps he had intended it should. ''That doesn't mean we have to get married,'' she said stubbornly.

''It does, Diana. I want to take her to the opening of your show. She certainly will want to attend the premiere of the concerto. And on a more prosaic basis, I want the three of us to go to places like the Botanical Gardens and St. Helen's Island and Mount Royal together. I'm not going to hide my daughter— I'm proud of her.''

She felt perilously close to tears. ''So am I. But—''

His mouth tightened. ''You really hate the idea of marrying me, don't you?''

''Yes. No. I don't know....'' She spread her hands in helpless appeal.

He said coldly, ''We're not two children. We both have careers that are important to us, and we'll both be free to pursue those careers. Marriage won't make the slightest difference to that.''

With Alan she had cherished her independence; with Rhys it was quite a different matter. She didn't want Rhys to talk of independence; she wanted him to tell her he loved her. "Does that mean you'll be free to pursue Huguette as well?" she said shrewishly.

"Jealous, Diana?"

"No!"

"You don't have much of a leg to stand on. You, after all, were out with a married man the other night."

"Michel and Jeanne have been my friends for years. Jeanne happened to have a bad cold; that's why she wasn't there." Because it seemed important to know, she added, "What about Huguette? Is she married?"

"She's separated from her husband and having a very hard time," he said shortly. "I'll be seeing a great deal of her over the next three months, so you might as well get used to it."

"How nice," she responded with saccharine sweetness, knowing she was behaving appallingly but unable to help herself. "Perhaps I can get in touch with her husband and we can commiserate with each other."

There was no gentleness in the hand that clamped on her shoulder this time. "Let's get one thing straight," he said grimly. "When you're my wife, you'll be exactly that. You'll sleep with me and not with anyone else."

"Does the same rule apply to you?"

"Of course it does. After all, we've got a nine-year-old daughter to consider."

"So you'll be faithful to me for appearance's sake if for no other reason?"

He glared at her. "You really can be a bitch when you want to be, can't you? You know damn well that I can't keep my hands off you when I come within ten feet of you. Or are you in danger of forgetting that?"

She tried to back away but he was too quick for her. His kiss was an assault, expressing all his pent-up anger and frustration. She fought to be free, twisting like a cat in his hold, trying to scratch him with her nails, kicking him futilely with her bare feet as rage and pain exploded into violence. Somehow she wrenched her head free, gasping incoherently, "I won't marry you—I won't!"

With one hand he caught both her fists. "Yes, you will...and what's more, you'll like it." Very slowly, holding her mesmerized with his blue-flamed eyes, he rested his other hand on her breast, smoothing the flesh with deliberate sensuality. "Won't you, Diana?"

She bit her lip, her gray eyes agonized, wishing with all her heart she could repudiate his claim, knowing it was useless even to try. She could deceive neither him nor herself. Conceding him at least a temporary victory she begged, "Please let go, Rhys."

To her surprise he immediately did so. Watching her closely he said, "Tomorrow I'll find out about getting a license. I'm not sure of the regulations here, but hopefully there won't be much delay."

Feeling very tired, she sank down on the arm of the nearest chair, her shoulders slumped in defeat. There was no way out; she knew that. For Belinda's sake, and because Rhys was the kind of man he was, this marriage had to occur. A loveless marriage, she thought dully, for Rhys did not love her and she could not do the loving for both of them. Once married, she would be with him day and night, tortured by a continual proximity that, because it would be only physical, would be a travesty of intimacy. She did not see how she was going to bear it. She loved him, and it was in the very nature of that love to want all of him, body and soul. The former would be hers, she was in no doubt of that. But the latter? Not so...not so.

In a last-ditch attempt at defiance she said, "I don't want to get married in Montreal. Someone will find out and there'll be reporters and pictures in the paper—I couldn't stand that."

"There are three million people in this city, Diana. I hardly think it's likely anyone will pay attention."

"Anyway, it would be on the records. Someone would just have to look it up," she persisted obstinately and with no particular logic.

He sighed sharply. "All right. I'll look after it somehow. Until the arrangements are made, why don't we keep this between the two of us? And in the meantime, I'd like you and Belinda to come and see the house on Friday—you could both stay for dinner. I purposely bought a house nearby so she could be near her grandparents and keep going to the same school."

"You were very sure of yourself—or, I should say, sure of me."

He did not bother to acknowledge this. "Any time after six on Friday—Belinda has the house number. I'll let myself out." A curt nod and he had turned on his heel and left the room. A moment later the back door closed on its latch.

So that was that, Diana thought numbly. Apparently she and Rhys were getting married. When or where she didn't know, but it didn't seem to matter much. Knowing Rhys, she would be willing to bet it would be soon. Then she would be Mrs. Rhys Morgan, with the legal and social sanction to live under his roof, share his bed and acknowledge him as the father of her child. The odd thing was that she felt absolutely nothing. Neither dread nor anticipation, pain nor joy. Just a vast spreading indifference toward whatever might happen. . . .

CHAPTER SEVENTEEN

Diana saw nothing of Rhys for the next few days. But she did have other visitors. The morning after Rhys's proposal she concentrated on her portrait of the fisherman to the exclusion of everything else and in less than three hours was standing in front of it in critical appraisal. It was finished, she knew. Did it express what she had wanted it to? Nothing ever quite did, she thought wryly, which no doubt was one of the reasons why she was driven to keep on painting.

Very much aware of the vacuum that always followed the completion of a work, she began cleaning her brushes, and when the door bell pealed she was delighted. An hour ago she would have been furious, but now it was a welcome diversion. The smile was wiped from her face, however, when she opened the door.

Kate almost fell across the threshold. She was weeping, clutching a handful of sodden tissues, her delicate features swollen and distorted.

"Kate! What's wrong? Here, come and sit down." Diana steered her over to the kitchen table, gave her some fresh Kleenex and filled the kettle while Kate blew her nose.

"Oh, Diana, I'm so glad you're home," Kate wailed, scrubbing at her already red nose as a child might have done. "Barrie and I have had an awful fight." Tears welled up in her eyes again.

"Let's have a cup of coffee and a muffin and you can tell me about it," Diana said calmly.

"He keeps saying I'm his wife," Kate hiccuped. "He said that the first time I met him, remember?" She raised horrified blue eyes to Diana. "It can't be true, Diana. I couldn't have forgotten something like that, could I? He even said we were going to have a baby." She buried her face in her hands and her fine pale hair fell forward. "I'd *have* to remember that!"

Inwardly cursing Barrie yet at the same time understanding all too well his frustration and hurt, Diana said soothingly, "Getting upset like this isn't going to help, Kate, dear."

Raising her head, oblivious to what Diana had said, Kate went on, "He's been offered a job in North Bay and he wants me to go with him. But how can I? I like him, but—oh, why can't I *remember*?"

Unable to think of a thing to say, Diana poured the coffee and put out the muffins with butter and some homemade jam. While Kate was adding cream and sugar to her cup, the telephone rang. "That's probably Barrie," Kate said dispiritedly.

Diana barely managed to say hello before Barrie's voice came crackling over the line. "Diana? Is Kate there?"

"Yes, she is."

"I thought she'd come to you. I'll be over in a minute to get her."

"Maybe you should wait for a while, Barrie. She's still quite upset."

She could hear him sigh as clearly as if he was standing right beside her. "Damnation—it's all my fault. I lost my cool, and I know I shouldn't have. But I've got this job offer, Diana, and it's right up my alley." His voice warmed. "I'd be responsible for setting up a small northern airline service—all the administration, hiring pilots, buying equipment. Even a bit of flying myself, although nothing like in Alberta. It's exactly what I've been looking for. I'd be home more of the time, but it wouldn't be like an ordinary desk job—much more exciting and interesting. But it's in North Bay. I can't go without Kate and she says she won't go."

"When does it start?"

"They'd like me there right now. The end of the month is the deadline."

"When's the appointment with the specialist?"

"Next week. But I'm beyond expecting miracles from any specialist. I think the best thing is for Kate and me to be alone together. But if she won't... damn it all, we can't keep living off Rhys. He's been great, but there's a limit."

"I don't know what to say, Barrie. But right now Kate and I are having a coffee and then I have to go downtown—maybe she'd like to go with me. So don't worry about her, all right?"

"Okay. Thanks, Diana. Tell Kate I'm sorry I yelled at her." Another sigh. "If I didn't love her so much, I wouldn't care." In a valiant effort to change the subject he added, "You and Belinda are coming for dinner later in the week, aren't you? I'll see you then.''

Diana replaced the receiver and repeated his message to Kate, adding brightly, ''Why don't you come downtown with me, Kate? I have to go the gallery and run a couple of errands, and it's a lovely day.''

''All right, that would be nice,'' Kate said without much enthusiasm. But the outing did her good. When Diana dropped her off around three o'clock in front of the imposing brick house that Rhys had bought, she looked much more her normal self and waved gaily as she ran up the walk. ''See you Friday!''

As she drove away, Diana knew nothing had really been solved. But at least Kate was in a better frame of mind. As for herself, it was becoming more and more difficult to think of anything else but Friday evening, when she and Belinda would go for the first time to the house where Rhys was proposing they would live. And when she herself would, presumably, find out what his plans were as far as this marriage was concerned.... She had the uneasy feeling she would be glad when it was all over.

Belinda had no such qualms. At five o'clock on Friday afternoon she was ready, shoes polished, hair brushed until it shone, even her fingernails cleaned. For the next hour she proceeded nearly to drive Diana crazy, so impatient was she to leave.

Finally it was time to go. Belinda had discovered they could cut through a little lane between the two streets, so they set off on foot, Diana with a crocheted shawl over her cranberry-red silk dress, its full skirt whispering as she walked. Garnets twinkled at her earlobes, while a matching clip held her hair in a smooth knot; her shoes were the thinnest of leather straps on very high heels. If she was to be defeated by Rhys's iron will, she thought as a touch of irrepressible humor temporarily overcame her nervousness, she would at least go down with flying colors.

That it had been worth the effort she knew the minute Rhys opened the door. His eyes swept over her in one quick comprehensive glance, and he said, almost as if Belinda wasn't there, "Each time I see you, Diana, it's as if I'm seeing you for the first time again—so young and fresh and beautiful." He bent and kissed her lightly on the mouth, a mere brushing of his lips that nevertheless brought a flush to her cheeks and a spark of irrational joy to her heart.

Then he turned his attention to Belinda, ushering them both indoors. The vestibule was magnificent, with inlaid oak flooring and leaded glass around the paneled doors, the high ceiling and sweeping oak staircase giving an impression of space and airiness. Rhys said easily, "I'm afraid things are far from settled yet. Not all the paintings are unpacked, for instance. No carpet on the stairs, and some of the draperies aren't quite to my taste. But there's the whole winter ahead for that." Belinda was solemnly shaking hands with Barrie and he added softly, "Besides, I'm sure you'll want some of your things here."

She raised troubled gray eyes. "Rhys, are you sure—"

"Indeed I am. In fact, I want you to keep next Friday free. And don't worry, we won't be getting married in Montreal. Could your parents look after Belinda?''

"I'm sure they could. But what—''

Smoothly interrupting her and plainly having no intention of answering any further questions, he asked, "How about a sherry or a cocktail?''

To an outsider looking in, the dinner would have seemed a pleasant gathering of congenial friends. Robert had excelled himself as far as the food was concerned. The wines were faultless, and the conversation flowed with seeming ease. But Diana was all too aware of undercurrents and unspoken tensions. Kate looked tired and distrait, and she only picked at her food. Barrie had a tendency to lapse into a frowning silence, his mind on anything but what he was eating. And she herself was suffering from a recurring sense of unreality.

Rhys had as much as said that next Friday they would be married. Which meant that in a week she would be the mistress of this huge house and the wife of the handsome dark-haired man at the head of the table, his head now bent to hear what Belinda was saying. What did she really know of him, she thought in a panic, swallowing a mouthful of chocolate mousse that might as well have been anything for all the attention she was paying to it. He was a stranger to her. Yet a stranger who held her in thrall. . . .

They moved into a small sitting room after the meal, where Robert brought the adults Spanish coffee and Belinda a frothy milkshake. The fire that was crackling in the marble hearth was a cheerful note now that the evening had drawn in. Kate had grown increasingly silent, and Barrie, who had been surreptitiously watching her, finally said, "Are you tired, Kate?"

She smiled at him guardedly. "I have an awful headache," she confessed. "Would you mind very much if I go upstairs? Perhaps I'll take a couple of aspirins."

"Can I do anything to help?"

When she unexpectedly patted his hand, he flushed. "No, it's all right. Excuse me, please." She smiled at everyone else and left the room.

Diana sood up, as well. "It's long past Belinda's bedtime, so we'd better be going. Thank you, Rhys, it's been a lovely evening."

"I'll drive you home."

They were standing in the hall while Rhys fetched Diana's shawl when from outside came the approaching wail of a siren, rising and falling in a crescendo of sound. Diana shivered. "There's a hospital near here, so you hear quite a number of ambulances. I never seem to get used to them."

Rhys put the shawl around her shoulders, his hands lingering, then patted the pockets of his light gray suit for his car keys. Through the leaded glass came a distorted flash of red as the ambulance screamed past.

There was a rattle of high-heeled shoes on the stairs. From halfway down Kate's voice shrilled, "What was that? It's the police—why are they here?"

Barrie took a step forward. "It's only an ambulance, Kate."

It was doubtful if she even heard him. Her face was

pale and strained, her eyes turned inward to a vision only she could see. "It's the police," she muttered, her hand clutching the newel post nervously. "I must let them in." With startling suddenness she resumed her headlong rush down the stairs, her full skirt swirling around her knees.

It all happened so quickly that none of the little group of watchers in the hall below was able to prevent it. Her heel skidded on the smooth oak. Her ankle turned. She flung out her arms to save herself, but they met only empty air, and with a cry of fright she pitched forward. With a sickening thud her head struck the banister and her limp body tumbled to the foot of the stairs.

Barrie was the first to move. "Kate!" he cried, falling on his knees beside her.

Rhys said swiftly, "What's the name of the nearest doctor, Diana?"

"Dr. Wardell, just down the street." She reeled off his number from memory, for he was Belinda's doctor and on more than one occasion she had had to call him on the spur of the moment. Barrie had straightened Kate's crumpled body, and gently Diana spread her shawl over her. Kate's eyes were shut and already there was a swelling visible over one eye.

"Why don't you get a blanket from one of the bedrooms upstairs?" Barrie suggested. "And maybe a facecloth from the bathroom. We could put a cold compress on her forehead."

Impressed by his air of calm and remembering that as a bush pilot he must be used to dealing with emergencies, she ran upstairs. The first room she came to was obviously the master bedroom; there was a sweater she recognized as Rhys's draped over one of the chairs. Across the foot of the wide bed was a neatly folded blanket. Reaching for it, she happened to glance upward and her heart gave a sudden jolt, for she instantly recognized the oil painting over the bed. It was one of hers, a work she had done eight or nine years ago down on the Montreal waterfront. Even now she thought the play of light on the water and the shadows cast by the sheds were really quite well done.

Grabbing the blanket she went back downstairs, being careful to hold onto the banister. There was no time to ponder why Rhys should have a painting of hers in his bedroom or to wonder how long he had had it, for Kate was stirring slightly. Rhys had just come back into the hall, reporting tersely to Barrie that Dr. Wardell would drop in on his way home from the hospital. Belinda had her hand tucked in his; he had not forgotten her even in the confusion.

Kate's lashes flickered and she muttered something undecipherable under her breath. Then her eyes opened. "Barrie?" she whispered. "What happened?" Her gaze left him and flickered around the circle of watchers: Diana, Rhys, Belinda. "Why is everyone staring?" she muttered fretfully. Her eyes suddenly widened with terror. "I fell, didn't I? I fell...oh, God, what's happened?"

She was becoming more and more agitated, and soothingly Barrie stroked the sweep of her hair. "You fell, yes," he said matter-of-factly. "The doctor will be here any minute. Just lie still."

Something in his voice must have penetrated the

confusion in Kate's brain. Obediently she quietened, turning her head to lie against his sleeve. Into the silence the door bell chimed.

Rhys let Dr. Wardell in. The doctor was a stout florid man with the air of one who has seen everything and could therefore be surprised by nothing. He put his lizard-skin bag on the floor and knelt beside Kate.

As Rhys led Belinda back into the living room, Diana followed. "Oh, Rhys, do you think there's any chance Kate will be all right now? I wondered if she was beginning to remember about the baby."

"So did I. We'll just have to wait and see."

Diana clasped her hands in front of her. "If only she'd recover her memory!"

Belinda, rather subdued, had gone to sit on the chesterfield, picking up a beautifully illustrated book about the Arctic. On impulse Diana added, "When I went upstairs to get a blanket for Kate, I noticed you have one of my paintings in your room. Have you had it long?"

"Nine years."

"It was one of the first I did after Belinda was born," she confessed. "For over a year I...I couldn't paint at all. It was terrible."

"So I did that to you, too." For Rhys, there was an unusual hesitancy in the hand that he rested on her sleeve. "I'm sorry, Diana. More sorry than I can say. I behaved very badly toward you back then. I was so frightened of commitment—other than to music, that is—that I treated you as less than a person. I see that now, although I didn't at the time."

Her eyes met his and she said very slowly, resting her own hand on top of his, "It's all right, Rhys—I think we both made mistakes. But we've both paid for them, and they're in the past now, where they belong. Why don't we just leave them there?" Even as she spoke it felt as though a great weight was being lifted from her shoulders. This quiet exchange between her and Rhys had removed the burden of resentment, anger and hurt that she had carried around with her for years.

There was no time to say anything more, for Dr. Wardell had poked his head around the door. "I'm on my way," he said breezily. "I've given the young lady a very mild sedative and she's asleep now. Her husband is with her. I'm quite confident that when she wakes up she'll have complete recall of the period up to the plane crash and the miscarriage—that's usually the way these things go. Diana, it might be an idea if you went and sat with her for a while, as well—I understand you and she are good friends. Not that I anticipate any trouble, you understand." He nodded in a self-satisfied way. "Anyway, I'm going to drop in tomorrow morning on my way to the office. Good night."

Diana smothered a smile. She was used to him and put up with his mannerisms, knowing him for a highly competent physician. He addressed a few words to Belinda and then took his leave.

Rhys suggested casually, "There's a little dressing room off my bedroom. Why don't I settle Belinda there while you go and see Kate, Diana?"

Kate was in the bedroom across the hall from

Rhys's, her breathing soft and peaceful. Barrie was sitting close by the bed, his hand resting on one of hers. In a low voice Diana told him what the doctor had suggested, and then she pulled up a chair. The minutes ticked away, and the group was joined by Rhys. An hour passed.

Finally Kate began to stir—tiny restless movements of her hands at first. Then her head began rocking back and forth on the pillow, a frown marring the serenity of her features. Her lashes fluttered. Barrie bent forward, his grip unconsciously tightening on her fingers, all his anxiety and love naked in his eyes.

Kate opened her eyes, looking straight up at him. "You're back!" she whispered. "But they said you'd had a plane crash."

For once Barrie was at a loss for words. Kate was struggling to sit up, and awkwardly he propped her against his arm. She reached up and touched his face, as if to reassure herself that he was real. "You weren't hurt?"

"Oh, Kate...you've remembered," he said huskily.

"Remembered?" Her eyes widened, her features suddenly contorting with pain. "Barrie, I have something terrible to tell you." She turned her face into his sleeve. "I lost the baby. I fell down the stairs and I had a miscarriage."

"Darling, I already know about it. As long as you're all right...." He rested his chin on her head. "Don't cry, sweetheart. I'm sorry about the baby, of course I am...but we'll have other children. Just as long as I have you."

Kate drew a long shuddering breath. "We had a terrible quarrel, didn't we? When they came to tell me about the crash they didn't say you were dead, but I knew they thought you were. I felt so awful because I didn't think I'd ever be able to tell you how sorry I was. How guilty I felt sending you off to fly with that on your mind—I was sure the crash was my fault."

"It wasn't your fault at all, Kate, believe me—it was a combination of the forces of nature and my own errors in judgment. But that doesn't matter, because I'm here and so are you. We can begin again."

Kate raised her head, smiling at him uncertainly. "You look different—your beard is trimmed." Beyond him she noticed for the first time Diana and Rhys and the spacious elegant bedroom. "Where are we?" she faltered. "I don't recognize this place. I was in the hospital, wasn't I?"

She was becoming agitated again, and Barrie lowered his face to hers, holding her close. "You were in hospital, yes, darling. But that was two months ago. You lost your memory, you see."

"Two *months* ago?" Weakly she pressed her fingers to her eyes. "It can't be!"

"You had amnesia, Kate. The double shock of the plane crash and the miscarriage was too much for you—so you suppressed them, blanking them out completely. A couple of hours ago you had a fall on the stairs and knocked yourself out, and this is what triggered the recall."

Kate must have made some movement because he went on calmly, "But don't worry about it, Kate. We've got all the time in the world, now that we're truly together again." He buried his face in her soft corn-colored hair. "Oh, Kate, I love you so much."

"And I love you. Don't go away, will you, Barrie? Stay here with me. I don't want to be left alone."

"There's nothing I want more than to be with you."

By a kind of unspoken agreement Rhys and Diana got up quietly and stole out of the room, Rhys gently pulling the door shut behind them. Although her vision was obscured by tears, Diana could tell he was as moved as she by the reconciliation they had just witnessed. She murmured shakily, "I'm so happy for them."

"So am I. Diana, don't you think—"

Across the hall a plaintive little voice called, "Mom, is that you? I can't get to sleep."

Diana gave herself a little shake. "All right, darling, we're going home now. You'll drive us, won't you, Rhys?"

If Rhys was frustrated by his inability to complete his question, he gave no sign of it. "Certainly," he said coolly, and as he let Diana and Belinda off at the apartment ten minutes later, his only words to Diana were, "Keep Friday free, won't you? We should be back by midevening."

Back from where, she wanted to ask. And back to what? She murmured an assent, helping Belinda out of the car, and without further ceremony he drove away.

THE WEEK RUSHED BY. In the studio Diana drove herself mercilessly, a new work taking shape in her mind as she produced sketch after sketch. The "labor-pain period," she had always called this stage, nor did it ever seem to come any easier, no matter how many paintings she did.

In the meantime, Belinda was back and forth between the two houses, for her music lessons with Rhys had resumed. It was Belinda who volunteered the information that on two afternoons she had also played for a Madame Danville, "who's got hair like mine, mom. She's so pretty, and nice, too." More than ever determined to stay away from the other house as long as she could—but how much longer would that be, she wondered—Diana went back to the studio.

On Wednesday evening Kate and Barrie dropped in, Kate's first words being, "Where have you been hiding yourself, Diana?"

Diana had the grace to look ashamed of herself. "I've been meaning to get in touch with you both, but somehow the days have just gone by. How are you, Kate?"

There was really no need to ask, for Kate looked a different woman: radiant and with a new confidence in herself obvious in every word and gesture. Her sweet smile brightened her face as she linked her arm with Barrie's. "I'm fine! We came over to see you because we're leaving tomorrow morning for North Bay. Barrie has a new job there, setting up and running a bush-plane service."

"But no long trips anymore," Barrie interjected quickly. "I'll be leaving those for the pilots we hire."

"It sounds ideal," Diana said warmly. "I'm so glad it's all worked out. I think this calls for a drink, don't you?"

She was genuinely pleased to see the two of them looking so happy, so wrapped up in each other, so looking forward to their bright new future together. But it was a pleasure shot through with disturbing flashes of an emotion she recognized as envy. When she and Rhys were married, there would be none of that closeness, that sense of working toward a common goal. All Rhys had promised was mutual independence, with freedom for each to go his or her own way. Not for her and Rhys this shining vulnerable happiness, this delight in each other's company....

As if her thoughts had conjured up his name, she heard Kate say, "We'd hoped Rhys would be able to come over with us this evening. But he and Huguette are hard at it again—he's made a major revision to the cadenza and needs her right there to play as he goes along. It must have been midnight last night before they quit, wasn't it, Barrie?"

"It could have been, I suppose—we'd gone upstairs by then." He gave her an intimate little smile at which Kate blushed entrancingly, and again Diana felt that sharp stab of pain.

Why was Rhys bothering to marry her, she thought in sudden despair. He would be happier with Huguette, who could so easily share that whole side of life that was so important to him.

And then, relentlessly, her brain supplied her with the answer: he was marrying her because of Belinda. It was that simple. And, loving him as she did, it was unbearably hard to accept....

As though she had divined Diana's thoughts, Kate said gently, "I don't think there's any kind of a romantic attachment between Rhys and Huguette, Diana. It's a working relationship and a very good one—but I'm sure that's all.''

"Rhys can do as he pleases," Diana replied shortly.

Kate looked troubled. "Hardly. He told us, in strictest confidence, that you and he are to be married in the near future.''

"I think Rhys's idea of marriage is a little different from yours, Kate. I don't think it will alter our respective life-styles much at all. And why should it? After all, it's mostly for Belinda's sake that we're doing it.''

Kate leaned forward, unusual force in her voice. "I don't think that's so—at least on Rhys's part.''

"I'm sure it's so," Diana responded flatly. "I was a wide-eyed romantic at seventeen, Kate, and it was Rhys himself who ensured that I would never be that again. I'm sorry if I'm disillusioning you—but that's the way it is.''

Although Kate patently disagreed, she must have thought it wiser not to argue. All she said was, "At least give him the benefit of the doubt. Remember that in the last six months he's suffered an injury that ended his concert playing, he's met you again, he's discovered he has a daughter and he's embarked on a new career. You could hardly blame him if he's still reeling from the shock.''

Unconvinced though she might be, Diana did not want to hurt Kate's feelings. "Maybe you're right. No doubt it will all work out one way or another.... So you two leave tomorrow. You must both be excited.''

Before Barrie could speak, Kate said, "We are, and for so many reasons. But mostly because we've been given a second chance, Diana." She twisted the intricate gold ring on her finger. "Our marriage wasn't doing very well before the plane crash. I was trying to cage Barrie in, keep him safe—"

"And I was refusing to consider your needs," Barrie interjected. "Hell-bent on doing my own thing."

Kate smiled gravely. "I think we'll both do better now. Be more flexible, more understanding of each other."

"And raise dozens of little Pembertons," Barrie said irrepressibly.

They all laughed and began talking of other things. When Kate and Barrie left an hour or so later it was with promises to keep in touch and with mutual good wishes for the future. As the door closed behind them, Diana leaned her head against the wood, wishing her own future looked as bright and full of joy as Kate's. Kate might see Rhys and Huguette as simply a working partnership, but then Kate saw the best in everyone. Diana was not as easily convinced.

CHAPTER EIGHTEEN

THE NEXT DAY Rhys telephoned, a brief businesslike call to say he would pick her up around one the following afternoon. "Where are we going?" Diana asked, allowing some of her exasperation to show in her voice.

"To get married. I thought that was the general idea."

"You know that's not what I meant!"

"You'll see, Diana."

"And do I wear a long white dress?" she snapped.

"Hardly, if it's publicity you're trying to avoid. Anyway, remember what happened the last time you did that?"

All too well she remembered, the months and years that lay between disappearing as if they'd never been. Thoroughly out of sorts, wanting only to end the conversation, she said shrewishly, "I'll try to refrain from wearing sackcloth and ashes, at any rate."

"You do that," he replied tersely. "I'll see you tomorrow." A sharp click as the connection was cut.

She stared down at the receiver in something like despair. Why had she said that? It seemed as though he brought out the worst in her, and it was very little excuse to know that she was worried and confused and afraid of the future. So, perhaps, was he....

For the first time she tried putting herself in his shoes. He loved his newly discovered black-haired daughter and he couldn't tolerate that she be put in an equivocal situation. To avoid this, and to do what he felt was the right thing, he was determined to marry Diana. But that didn't mean he wanted to. Maybe he would have preferred eventually to marry Huguette. Maybe he felt trapped and afraid of the future, too....

Unable to bear the tenor of her thoughts, she slammed the receiver back on the telephone and went to bed, there to lie awake for what seemed like most of the night. Her last night to sleep alone, she thought, pounding at the pillow to try to give it some semblance of comfort. Tomorrow night she might not get much sleep, either, but for a different reason.... As if he were there, she could feel Rhys's hands on her flesh and she shivered with an emotion that was both anticipation and fear.

Because of rehearsals for the school play, Belinda did not come home for lunch the next day. Consequently Diana had ample time to get ready. Despite her remarks to Rhys, she had had no difficulty in deciding what to wear. Last spring, after selling three major paintings, she had found in one of the exclusive boutiques in Old Montreal a sand-colored suede suit, the skirt slightly flared and slit in the front well above the knee, the jacket Chanel-style. Later the same day she had bought a pure silk blouse, in palest cream with a high ruffled neckline, and a dashing wide-brimmed hat a couple of shades darker than the suit. It was one of those rare outfits that combined extreme elegance with comfort; if she was making a disastrous mistake in marrying Rhys, Diana thought, regarding herself in the mirror, at least she was doing it in style.

She was pulling on soft kidskin gloves when the door bell chimed. Giving herself one last glance in the mirror for courage, she went to the door and opened it, and in silence she and Rhys surveyed each other.

It was impossible not to feel a surge of pride that this was the man who was choosing to marry her. He was wearing a three-piece gray pinstripe suit, impeccably tailored, his white shirt emphasizing his dark good looks, the whole civilized garb adding to, rather than detracting from, his lean muscular build and the athletic grace with which he moved. The severe line of his mouth softened as he looked at her. "I'm glad you eschewed the sackcloth and ashes. I like this much better."

Impulsively she rested her gloved hand on his sleeve. "I'm sorry I said that—I didn't mean it."

As he bent and kissed her cheek, she caught the tang of his after-shave and the clean fresh smell of his skin. She would know him if she were blind, she thought dazedly, overwhelmed by a flood of such love for him that her knees felt weak. She felt his arm around her and she knew in her very bones that he was all she wanted or would ever want. *Oh, God,* she prayed incoherently, *help me make him happy.*

"Diana, are you all right?"

She nodded, her lashes hiding her eyes. "Mmm. . . I'm fine. I just have to get my handbag." She slipped out of the circle of his arm and went to her room, mentally berating herself. Cool independent Diana—what a myth that was! But it was an independent Diana he wanted, a woman who would not make demands on him or show that she needed him, and somehow that was the woman she must be with him. How, when a mere kiss on the cheek could make her faint with need, she didn't know. . . .

The face she presented to him when she went back in the kitchen was calm and composed again. She said lightly, "Am I still not allowed to ask where we're going?"

"Right." He grinned. "Ready?"

She gave one last look around the pleasant sunny little kitchen, knowing that the next time she came here it would be as Rhys's wife. For better or for worse her life would never be the same again. "Ready," she said evenly.

They drove in the Jaguar to the airport, where at the ticket counter Rhys got their boarding passes. "Why St. John's?" Diana asked, torn between curiosity and amusement.

"It seemed appropriate to get married in Newfoundland, and I have a good friend in St. John's who'll marry us in his church—I thought you'd prefer that to a civil ceremony. But there's an eight-day waiting period before you can get married in Newfoundland, which is why I didn't drag you to the altar last week."

She couldn't help laughing, and more than one pair of male eyes rested appreciatively on her as she walked at Rhys's side. "They're all envying me," he said darkly. "You do realize that I'm insanely jealous and that if one of them dares to speak to you—"

"You'll fall in a fit on the floor and have me incarcerated for life," she finished neatly.

Ushering her through the checkpoint ahead of him, he said cheerfully, "Thank God I'm marrying someone with a sense of humor."

It was impossible not to feel a lift of her spirits. Everything was going to be all right, she thought optimistically as she walked through the security check and picked up her handbag from the conveyor belt. The conviction stayed with her throughout the flight, throughout the taxi drive to the gray stone church on one of the steeply sloping hills that led up from the waterfront in St. John's.

Rhys's friend was a stooped scholarly man whose gold-rimmed spectacles reminded her briefly and poignantly of Alan. He treated the couple with an old-world courtesy, betraying no curiosity that they should have come so far to marry. When, in what seemed like a very short time to Diana, he led them into the sanctuary and began to speak the words of the marriage ceremony, his voice was slow, thoughtful and vibrant with conviction, allowing the words themselves to make their own impact.

Rhys slipped a narrow platinum band on her finger and they were pronounced man and wife. Then he kissed her, his blue eyes very serious, the touch of his mouth like a tangible symbol of the promises he had just made. Afterward they went to the study, where they signed the appropriate forms, Diana writing, "Diana Morgan," firmly and clearly. They were toasted in vintage port poured from an exquisite crystal decanter that came to light from behind an untidy pile of theological tomes. The bottle was carefully dusted off on the tail of the minister's gown before use.

From then on, the day began to have an aura of increasing unreality for Diana. She and Rhys taxied to a restaurant down by the harbor where the cuisine was as good as any restaurant in Montreal. They ate seafood and bakeapple pie and drank wine and liqueurs. A stroll, arm in arm, along the darkening streets, none of them familiar, perhaps never to be visited by them again. Another taxi ride, this time back to the airport; a delay of an hour in their flight time. During the flight back to Montreal each of them became more and more silent, and Diana more and more tired.

They drove home in the Jaguar to Diana's apartment, where Nellie and Roger were sitting at the kitchen table bickering amicably over a game of hearts. A lone dish of celery and carrot sticks on the table bore mute testimony to Nellie's dissatisfaction with her girth. Nellie jumped up as they entered, scattering her cards. "The last three tricks are mine. I have three trumps left."

"But I have two," Roger objected.

"I'm sure mine are higher. Hello, Rhys. How are you, darling?" This to Diana. "Have a nice day?"

"Oh, yes," Diana said politely, racking her brains in vain to think of something to add to this innocuous reply.

Fortunately Rhys came to her rescue. "We have to

ask your blessing," he said in his deep voice. "Diana and I were married today."

"Married!" Nellie shrieked. "Oh, darling, how lovely! What a handsome husband you have. Won't Belinda be thrilled, and isn't it nice you'll all be living so near? Roger, you haven't said anything. Aren't you pleased?"

"You haven't given me a chance to, Nell," her husband said with a twinkle in his eye, kissing Diana affectionately and shaking Rhys's hand. "I'm happy for you both."

Her mother, of course, was still bursting with questions, so Diana had to go over the day step by step. Finally Nellie said, "We'll stay here tonight, won't we, Roger, so you two can go to a hotel—this is your honeymoon, after all."

Diana's feet were hurting in their high-heeled shoes and she had not even considered arrangements for the night. The thought of a strange hotel didn't appeal to her at all; somehow she wanted to begin married life in a more mundane setting. But what would Rhys want? She said uncertainly, "I'd be quite happy just to stay here, Rhys. Then in the morning we can tell Belinda we're married."

"Fine with me," he said promptly, and she breathed a tiny sigh of relief.

With rather embarrassing rapidity Nellie picked up the cards and put on her sweater. "We'll leave you two alone then," she said brightly. "Come along, Roger."

Too tired to think straight, Diana said, "Good night mom, dad. Thanks for looking after Belinda."

With Nellie's "Sleep well" echoing in her ears, she sank down into a chair, pulling off her hat and shaking out her hair.

"You look exhausted," Rhys said gently.

"It's silly, isn't it, when all we did was sit most of the day. But I *am* tired."

"Traveling's tiring in itself. I should know, after all my years on the concert circuit." Before she could guess his intention, he was kneeling by her chair, undoing the straps on her shoes and easing them off, then rubbing her fine-boned feet with firm sure strokes.

"Rhys, you don't have to do that—"

"I know," he said equably. "Lean back and relax."

His head was bent as he concentrated on his task; the overhead light shone on his thick dark hair, and for a moment Diana wondered if she was going to cry. Leaning her head back, she closed her eyes and concentrated on the movements of his hands, infinitely soothing, until gradually the tensions of the day began to seep away. When he eventually stopped, she was able to smile at him more naturally. "Thank you. That was lovely."

He got up himself and helped her to her feet. "Now go and have a long hot shower—that's an order."

He had released her hands and was loosening his tie, a prosaic little gesture that again, inexplicably, threatened her with tears. "Rhys. . . ."

He was hanging his jacket on the back of the chair. "Mmm?"

She had no idea what she wanted to say. "I—make yourself at home, won't you?" she said lamely.

He shot her a quick glance, calmly undoing his vest. "I will. Off you go."

It was rather pleasant to be told what to do for once, she thought as she went into the bedroom and pulled a housecoat out of her closet. In the bathroom she bundled her hair into a shower cap and stepped under the stinging hot water. As it enveloped her she realized Rhys's prescription had been the right one; she felt a great deal better. Drying herself, she brushed her hair and put on the housecoat. It was a very plain blue one she had had for years, she noticed with faint amusement; somehow it seemed suitable for beginning such an atypical honeymoon. Belting it tightly around her waist she went in search of Rhys.

He was sitting in the living room reading a magazine, his shoes off and his feet up on the coffee table. When he saw her he put the book down and stood up, stretching lazily to his full height, his shirt pulled taut across the hard planes of his chest.

Diana said mischievously, "Your turn for the bathroom. It's just down the hall."

"Thanks." He yawned. "Back in a few minutes."

When he came back he was wearing only the trousers of his suit, his chest and feet bare. "Minor details like pajamas I seem to have forgotten—not that they'll be necessary." He smiled at her. "Ready?"

An intimate question for intimate circumstances. Diana felt warmth creep into her cheeks, which were already pink from the shower. It seemed a long time since they had made love on the hillside at Woody Point, a lovemaking that had ended in discord and, for her, unhappiness. But now there was no reason to quarrel; they were married. Rhys was her husband and as such was entitled to share her bed. Swept by a paralyzing shyness she fumbled with the belt of her housecoat, her eyes lowered.

He said, a thread of laughter in his voice, "This is all a bit overpoweringly domestic, isn't it? I feel as though I should have been married to you for months—except that I'm not sure where your bedroom is."

"It's next to the kitchen," she said awkwardly.

"Come on, then." An arm casually around her waist, he led her from the living room, flicking the light switch off as they left.

Her bedroom had always been Diana's retreat, the place she went when she didn't want to think about painting or when the responsibilities of being a single parent became too much. The carpet was thick and soft, while the color scheme was a restful blending of green, pale yellow and white, summer colors that even in the midst of winter gave an impression of light and space. Looking around him, Rhys said appreciatively, "Nice. Looks like you." He closed the door and began unbuckling his belt.

Diana found herself wishing she had got dressed again after her shower. At least removing her clothes would have given her something to do, she thought wildly. As it was she perched on the very edge of the bed, trying to look anywhere but at Rhys. He turned off the light and the room was plunged into a darkness that at first seemed absolute but gradually brightened a little from the reflections of the street lamps outside.

Rhys came toward her across the carpet. When she saw that he was naked, the age-old trembling began within her, an ache of desire edged with a fear that perhaps this time the magic would not work for them, that somehow marriage would have tamed their instinctive hunger for each other.

Holding her by the elbows he brought her to her feet. She felt his hands at her belt and must have made some tiny sound of protest, because he said softly, "Hush, sweetheart—everything will be all right."

"Sweetheart," he had called her, she thought wonderingly, standing quite still as he pulled the edges of her robe apart, his eyes traveling along the slender lines of her body from throat to ankle. Then the garment fell to the floor and she could hear in his quickened breathing the sound of her own blood racing through her veins.

"You're mine, Diana," he said, making no attempt to hide the exultant male pride in his voice. "My wife. I want you so much—it feels like forever since we last made love...." Fiercely he pulled her close, burying his face in her neck, his hands sliding over her body as if he would relearn all its curves and textures. There could be no doubt that he wanted her, and her fears disappeared, blown away like leaves in the wind. With her hands she drew his face to hers, her mouth eager for his kisses, conscious through every nerve ending of his closeness, his warmth, his strength. He had said she was his; equally she felt that he was hers, husband and ardent lover, bearer of passion and promise and joy.

He had been raining kisses on her mouth, as avidly as a man who has been starved. They fell back on the bed, urgency in every movement, hands never still. Their bodies were consumed by fires that could be extinguished only by a greater fire, a climax of heat and flame, white and searing, that by its very intensity would burn itself out. In the darkened room there was the rush of their breathing, fanning the flames. As she was encircled, Diana's last shreds of conscious thought were that Rhys could wait no longer and that she did not want him to. His agonized "Sweetheart..." mingled with her "Now, Rhys, now!" Gathered into the very heart of the fire storm, she gave herself up to the throbbing light that surrounded her, knowing Rhys was with her, melted to her, closer than he had ever been before.

The aftermath of such a conflagration could have been ashes: gray dust and the blackness of scorched earth. But it was not so. Indeed, although inevitably there was a return to the reality of two bodies lying together on a bed, of two separate people, the closeness remained in a different guise. Rhys's arms cradled her, his slow gentle kisses reassuring her she was still wanted. Then his head came to rest heavily on her arm and his dark-lashed eyes closed, his breathing becoming quiet and regular as he slept. Love welled up within her, and a deep protectiveness. Her arm curved over his shoulder. With her cheek resting against his hair, she, too, fell asleep.

Sometime in the early hours of the morning they awoke and made love again, this time with a slow silent sensuality as each relearned what pleased the other, made bold by the darkness and by the knowledge that they had all the time in the world. Diana gave freely of herself, in return discovering once more how sensitive and generous a lover Rhys could be. Shyly at first, then more openly, she asked for this touch, for that caress, finding that her diffident demands were encouraged and more than met. It was a mutual exploration of more than the physical, for it represented the gradual building of a trust between them—a trust that in itself could only serve to enhance their lovemaking. This time he brought her again and again to the very edge of fulfillment until finally he could hold back no longer and his shuddering body found its release in her.

When Diana awoke the next time it was daylight. She was lying on the far side of the bed, tangled in the sheets, naked, and for a moment could not imagine why this should be so. Then memory flooded back. Turning her head she saw Rhys lying beside her, flat on his stomach, his arms flung wide, his face vulnerable and relaxed in sleep, his dark hair ruffled on the pillow. Filled with a vast contentment, her cheeks warm as she remembered some of the things they had done in the night, she lay watching him, knowing that all her happiness lay in his hands.

Gradually the realities of ordinary living asserted themselves. The bedside clock said ten past eight. Belinda would be waking soon. It had long been their practice on Saturday and Sunday mornings, when there was no rush to get to school, to make crepes or omelets with a fresh-fruit salad for breakfast and to eat in a leisurely fashion at a small table they set up by the living room windows overlooking the side garden. Hating to disturb Rhys yet knowing she must, she pressed his bare shoulder. "Rhys?"

He woke instantly and the slow smile that irradiated his face as he saw her said far more than his lazy "Good morning, did you sleep well?"

"In between interruptions," she said wickedly.

As he reached for her, pulling her toward him, she nestled into his chest, the hair rough on her cheek. "We've got to get up," she murmured. "Belinda will be waking soon."

He rubbed her earlobe. "That's too bad—I could stay here all day."

Laughter bubbled up in her. "You're hopeless," she scolded.

With all their new knowledge his hands moved on her body and involuntarily she gasped with pleasure. "What did you say?" he asked innocently.

"Stop! Oh, Rhys, that's heavenly... I wish we didn't have to get up, either, but we do."

He hugged her hard. "Why don't you have the bathroom first? That way I can sleep a little longer."

She slid out of bed, walking around the end of it to find her robe where it had fallen to the floor so many hours ago. As she straightened with it in her hand she saw Rhys's eyes on her, and with a new kind of pride in herself she stood still for a minute, her slender body bathed in the early morning sunshine.

"You're so beautiful," he said huskily. "I don't think I'll ever have enough of you."

Her lips curved in a womanly mysterious smile as she slowly wrapped herself in the blue robe. The light was falling on him, as well, shadowing the hollows under his collarbones, delineating the strongly muscled arms and curving rib cage. "Nor I of you," she said softly.

Her heart was singing as she showered and dressed and went out into the kitchen. Shortly afterward Rhys joined her and she poured him a coffee, steaming and fragrant. Then they heard Belinda's door open. A moment later the child trailed into the room in her long nightdress, her hair coming loose from its single thick braid. "'Lo, mom." She gave Rhys, who was sitting at the table, the special smile she reserved for him alone. "You're here early," she said ingenuously.

Rhys looked over at Diana, who said, "Belinda, we've got some news we hope will make you happy." Lightly she rested her fingers on Rhys's shoulder. "Rhys and I were married yesterday."

The child's mouth fell open. Wide-eyed she looked from one to the other of them. "Married?" she squeaked.

"Yes." Unconsciously Diana was holding her breath.

"You mean we'll all live together?"

"That's right. In Rhys's house, eventually."

"And Rhys will go to parent-teacher meetings at the school with you, mom?"

There was a lump in Diana's throat. "You'd like that?"

"Yeah. . . . Most of my friends, their fathers go."

In his deep voice Rhys said, "I'd be happy to go, Belinda. And yes, we will all live together, and your mother and I will share a room. We'll live at my house, but there's no great hurry to get everything moved over there. It'll take a while."

"That's great," Belinda said, her beaming smile falling impartially on both of them. "What's for breakfast, mom?"

The last of the tension dissolved. "I'm just heating the frying pan for crepes."

Another thought had occurred to Belinda. Her blue eyes very wide, she said to Rhys, half statement, half plea, "I could have piano lessons from you all the time."

"You certainly may."

Belinda plunked herself down on the nearest chair and attacked her piece of honeydew melon with absentminded gusto. "Have you got any empty boxes, mom? I could start packing up my toys and books right away."

Diana began mixing the batter for the crepes, a small ordinary task that added to, rather than detracted from, her happiness. Body and mind at peace, she found herself wondering how she could ever have wanted to delay this marriage to Rhys. It was a perfect state, she thought dreamily. In this kitchen, under her roof, were the two people she loved most in the world. And by marrying Rhys, she had ensured that the three of them would stay together and that her happiness would continue, day after day, for the rest of her life.

CHAPTER NINETEEN

A MONTH LATER Diana was to look back on the certainty that marriage to Rhys had guaranteed a state of perpetual happiness as, at the very least, naive and at the most as incredibly foolish. Stupid and blind and unrealistic.

It was late October now, and on the hills that surrounded the city the trees were turning color—their last brave showing before winter stripped the leaves from their branches, leaving only naked skeletons to stand in the ice and the snow. But in Place Jacques-Cartier, where Diana was sitting on a bench in the sun, the ice and snow seemed a long time away. Outdoor vendors were still selling flowers, the jagged yellow petals of chrysanthemums and the tightly bunched heads of roses making vivid splashes of color against the gray cobblestones. A horse-drawn carriage clattered by. Pedestrians and tourists eddied along the narrow streets, past the old Renaissance-style *hôtel de ville* with its clock tower, and the monument to Nelson, their voices a mingling of French and English. On the breeze was borne the smell of the river.

This was the cradle of the city, as Diana well knew. The site of the little settlement of Ville Marie, found-ed over three hundred years before by Maisonneuve and his small band of followers, who had braved the long journey from France, the cruel climate and the constant threat of Iroquois attack for the greater glory of God. Not far from where she was sitting was the Seminary of St. Sulpice, parts of which dated back to 1680, its clock the oldest in North America. The spire of Notre-Dame de Bon-Secours pierced the sky nearby, the tall statue of the Virgin Mary on its roof stretching her arms out over the river, for hers was the sailors' church. Only a few streets away, in Place Royale, men had been flogged at the whipping post. At the waterfront had landed *Les Filles du Roi*, the King's Girls, carefully selected young women who had been brought out from France, each with a dowry, to marry the soldiers and workers and coureurs de bois. From the Château de Ramezay, with its dormer windows and its wrought-iron fence, governors from France had held sway, as well as army officers from Britain and America. Fires had raged here, and floods had inundated the narrow streets.

Diana loved coming here, loved the sense of history that never seemed to clash with the immediacy of the present. And she came often, for Michel's gallery was only a block away. Her show was over now, and considering the success it had been, she should have looked happier. Every one of the paintings had sold. The reviews had ranged from encouraging to ecstatic, and she had received three important commissions as a direct result of the show. But she did not look happy, and if she had been asked the reason for her discontent, she would have answered with one word: "Rhys."

Everything else was fine. Her parents were well, and Rhys could not have been nicer to them. The move to Rhys's house had been accomplished smoothly; the room on the top floor, which had been remodeled as Diana's studio, had better lighting than her old studio in the apartment, she would have been the first to admit. Because of the pressures of her show, she hadn't been able to do as much as she wished toward making the house into a home. But when she had apologized to Rhys for this, he had said easily, "I never meant to turn you into a housewife, Diana. The house will get looked after sooner or later, I'm sure—don't worry about it. After all, I'm in no position to complain. Look how little I'm home these days."

Which had left her with the feeling that he did not really care much about the appearance of their new home and that somehow she had blundered by apologizing. Independent women didn't apologize to their husbands because the housework didn't get done, she thought with a grim kind of humor. That, after all, was the whole point of being independent.

As for Belinda, she was flourishing under the new regime. Although she had never complained about the lack of a father, it was plain she preferred having one. Always touchingly careful of Diana's feelings, she nevertheless lit up whenever Rhys entered the room, and, according to him, her musical abilities were expanding by leaps and bounds.

So it always came back to Rhys. Although today

he had not done so, he generally worked at home during the days, shutting himself in the music room on the ground floor right after Belinda left for school and staying there until at least one o'clock. He would then go to the nearby racquet club and play forty minutes of squash, come home and have lunch and go back to work, this time until Robert served dinner. The early evening he usually kept free to be with Belinda; after his daughter went to bed he would not infrequently closet himself again until midnight.

It was an austere routine that Diana respected, knowing that hard work and long hours were behind most successes, be they in the fields of music, art or literature. But of necessity it was a schedule that left her and Rhys's little time together, particularly when coupled with the demands of her own career. As the days slipped by, gradually their initial closeness and warmth lessened. Not intentionally, nor by any open disagreements or quarrels. Rather from lack of time, that most precious of all elements.

There was another cause, Diana admitted to herself miserably, shifting position on the bench. Huguette. Under other circumstances Diana would have liked Huguette very much, for she was friendly, vivacious, very French in her mannerisms and her chic, bringing to her playing both an intuitive emotional ear and a high degree of musical intelligence. Her warmth and charm spread over all of them, never singling out Rhys—at least not in front of Diana. Yet she and Rhys spent many hours together, either in the Westmount house or at the studio Huguette rented downtown, where she gave lessons to a small number of university students. And it was indisputable that she shared far more intimately in Rhys's world of music than Diana ever could. Rhys had already told her that Huguette was newly separated from her husband; vulnerable as Huguette must feel, was it not inevitable that she fall in love with Rhys? And he with her?

As if her thoughts had conjured them up, two people stepped out of one of the restaurants near the old Bon-Secours market: a woman in a rust-colored dress, its full skirt billowing in the breeze, and a man in a business suit. Huguette and Rhys. Arm in arm they began walking along the sidewalk. Diana stayed where she was, her heart banging against her ribs. Rhys's head was bent to hear what his companion was saying; he laughed suddenly, making some quick riposte, and across the square Huguette's answering laugh rang out, confident and gay. They looked so right together, Diana thought painfully. So at ease with each other.

Numbly she wondered what on earth she would say or do if they saw her. But she need not have worried. As they approached rue St-Paul, Rhys hailed a taxi, opening the door for his companion and getting in after her. The taxi disappeared around the corner.

Diana got up from the bench and began to walk, with no particular destination in mind. There wasn't any reason why Rhys and Huguette shouldn't have lunch together, she told herself firmly. No reason whatsoever.... But couldn't he have invited his wife, as well, another part of her brain argued. He hadn't even asked her this morning if she had any particular plans for the day, mentioning only that he had an appointment with the conductor at ten. So now where were they going, he and Huguette?

As she walked along, she found herself thinking of Alan, wondering if he had suffered from these corrosive pangs of jealousy when he had known she was with Rhys. She hoped not. It was a painful and somehow degrading emotion—especially when, as in her case, there was no real basis for jealousy, nothing tangible for her to put her finger on. Rhys would not sleep with Huguette, she was sure of that....

But he might be in love with her, the devil in her argued. He might *want* to sleep with her. *After all, he's never told you he loves you, has he?*

And that was the final factor in her unhappiness, for no, Rhys had never told her he loved her. He desired her, no question of that. On the relatively rare occasions nowadays when they went out together socially, he gave every appearance of enjoying her company. He admired her artistic talent, respected her capabilities as a mother, liked her sense of humor. But he did not love her...and it was the absence of that one essential ingredient that, for Diana, was slowly poisoning the marriage, killing it before it had really had a chance to live.

Her footsteps slowed. She had crossed rue St-Sulpice and was standing outside Notre Dame church. Without making a conscious decision she walked up the steps and swung open the heavy door, stepping into the cool lofty interior. As always, it was a sight that dazzled her. The main altar was highly ornamented, with illuminated statues, carved and gilded fretwork and a blue-painted backdrop. Yet the whole effect was so light and airy that it was as if the angels themselves could lift one heavenward. She slid into a pew, letting her eyes wander over the stained-glass windows that depicted scenes from the early history of the city, and gradually her spirits grew calmer. The hushed silence, the flickering of the many candles, the sense of timelessness all soothed her and made her fears seem groundless. Everything would be all right, she thought with new confidence. All that she and Rhys needed was a little time together.

After a while she got up and left the church, catching the metro and then a bus and arriving home before Belinda did. Rhys wasn't home either, but resolutely she closed her mind to any implications that that might have.

Perhaps if he had come home, had sat and had a cup of tea with her, she would have been able to put her discontent into the right words and have gained the reassurance from him that she needed. But he didn't come.

When he finally arrived he was late for dinner, apologized hastily, bolted his meal and was off to what he vaguely called a rehearsal. It couldn't be a rehearsal of his own concerto, she knew, for he was still revising parts of the third movement. Yet it must be something important for him to miss his usual hours with Belinda. Perhaps Huguette was playing at the rehearsal, the little imp of mischief in her whispered. Perhaps that was why it was so important....

After Belinda was in bed, Diana sat up reading,

forcing her mind to remain on the contents of the book. It was after eleven when she heard Rhys's key in the lock. Seeing the light on, he came to the door of the living room and wearily pulled off his tie. "What a hell of a day," he said, yawning and flinging his jacket on the chair after his tie.

He did look tired. No one could drive himself as hard as he had lately without its having an effect. But Diana hardened her heart against his bruised eye sockets, the lines slashing his cheeks. "Where have you been?" she asked coldly.

"Symphony rehearsal—I thought I told you that."

"What are you rehearsing?"

"Huguette's playing Saint-Saëns's Second Concerto in ten days. Didn't I mention that to you?" He dropped into a chair with a sigh, draping one leg over the arm.

"No, you didn't."

Something in her tone of voice finally made him take notice. "What's wrong, Diana?" he said evenly.

Without subterfuge she said, "I was in Place Jacques Cartier at noon today. I saw you and Huguette coming out of the restaurant."

"So?"

Infuriated by his monosyllabic reply she said, "Had I known you were going to be in the area, I might have enjoyed having lunch with you. I am, after all, your wife. Or are you in danger of forgetting that?" She stopped abruptly, knowing she had already said far more than she should have.

With a visible effort at patience that served only to annoy her further he said, "Why didn't you tell me at breakfast this morning you were going to the gallery? I presume that's where you were. We could certainly have set up a lunch date.''

He was being so damned reasonable. ''Oh, I wouldn't have wanted to intrude,'' she replied nastily.

He rubbed his eyes. ''Come off it, Diana. I'm not in the mood for a row. All I want to do is go to bed and get some sleep. Are you coming?''

''I want to finish this chapter. I'll be up in a while.'' She stared blindly at the book in her lap, ostentatiously turning a page.

He stood up and she willed herself not to look at him. He said with silken smoothness, ''The book can wait. Come to bed, Diana.''

Twin flags of color in her cheeks, she retorted, ''I'll come when I'm ready.''

''No, you don't have that quite right. You'll come now.''

She gave up any pretense of reading and said incautiously, ''Give me one good reason why I should.''

''That's easy.'' He crossed the room and pulled her to her feet. The book fell to the floor. There was nothing tender or gentle about his kiss, nothing subtle. It was a raw primitive demand and she fought back the answering surge of her blood, holding herself rigidly. But then his hand found her breast, fondling it with calculated skill, using as a weapon against her her own vulnerability to his touch, her own admissions to him in the long dark nights of what pleased her. She tried to pull her head free, her hands pushing at his chest. But he was deliberately smoothing the curves of her hips, drawing her closer to him so that there could be no mistaking his intention. As he swept her up in his arms, carrying her over to the chesterfield, her last coherent thought was that at least she had this. That if they could not be close in other ways, at least their bodies had a language of their own and could weave a pattern of intimacy. It was not love. It was not permanent. But it was all she had, and once again she surrendered herself to it, recklessly and with all the abandon that he himself had taught her. . . .

But afterward, long after they were in bed, Rhys asleep beside her, Diana lay on her back gazing upward at the dimly lit ceiling, bitterly aware of the cost of that temporary intimacy. For a short while she had been held and touched and the barriers between them had melted; but now she was left with a loneliness all the more devastating because of their lovemaking. Black after white, she thought bleakly, with no shades of gray in between to ease the transition.

It would almost be better if they never made love, for then she would not have to cope with the cruel contrast between what happened in the privacy of their room and what happened the rest of the time. In her heart she acknowledged for the first time that in the past ten years nothing had really changed: she still loved Rhys, just as passionately and just as unwisely as she had then. But his first love was, and would surely always remain, his music. The music to which, she, by one of those ironies of fate, had reunited him. Her true rival was music; Huguette, beautiful talented Huguette, was merely a bodily personification of all that was lacking and would always be lacking in her marriage. For Rhys, Huguette must represent the synthesis of all he held dear: the abstract beauty of music and the real flesh-and-blood beauty of a woman. Diana could not compete with that.

Two tears slid down her cheeks, but the sensation of utter defeat that pervaded her was too deep for tears to assuage.

THE AUTUMN DAYS slipped by. Diana was working on a commissioned portrait, which was gradually taking shape to her satisfaction. She was as grateful for her career now as she had been ten years ago, for it gave her reprieve from day-to-day difficulties and eased the tangle of emotions in which she seemed to be inextricably caught. Toward Rhys she had adopted a stance of casual friendliness, as much for Belinda's sake as for her own. Not that he appeared to notice how she behaved. He had informed her tersely one day that he was having problems with the final allegro, so she could only assume that it was for this reason he spent so much time in the music room, not because he had any motives of avoiding her.

He was there one evening when the telephone rang. Diana was in the kitchen making fudge for a sale Belinda's school was having. Hastily removing the saucepan from the stove, she picked up the receiver. "Hello?"

"Diana? *C'est Huguette ici. S'il vous—*" She suddenly seemed to realize she was speaking in French. "Please, may I speak to Rhys?"

She sounded upset, not at all her usual lighthearted self. "Yes, just a moment, please," Diana replied politely, adding to Belinda, "Stir it a minute, dear. I'll be right back."

She hurried across the hall and tapped on the door, even through the thick panels able to hear the impatience in Rhys's voice. "Yes?"

She opened the door. He was seated at the desk amid a welter of manuscript paper, pen in hand, head propped up on his elbows. "What do you want?" Hardly a propitious remark.

"Telephone for you," she said levelly.

"Who is it?"

"Huguette."

He grimaced, his mind plainly still on what he was doing. "Did she say why she was calling?"

"No. Only that she wanted to speak to you."

He raked his fingers through his hair. "Okay, I'll be right there."

Diana was beating the fudge again when he came into the kitchen and picked up the receiver, using the long cord to go partway into the hall. "Huguette?" A long silence. "I see.... Yes, I'll come. Give me twenty minutes."

He came back into the kitchen. "I have to go out for a while. Don't wait up for me."

"You won't be here to try the fudge," Belinda said, disappointed.

"Save me a piece, Lindy, and I'll have it when I get back."

And when will that be, Diana wondered silently to herself as they pronounced the fudge ready and she poured it into the pan to set.

She kept herself purposely busy all evening, writing letters and bringing her account books up to date, not wanting to think about Rhys and Huguette. She was making a valiant effort to hold at bay a whole mixture of emotions, among them anger and hurt and disillusion, which, if she had allowed them to, would have overwhelmed her. She went to bed about eleven and grimly set her mind to sleep.

She must have slept, for when she suddenly found herself sitting up in bed it was pitch-dark and the bedside clock said two-fourteen. She looked over at the other pillow, and although subconsciously she had been prepared, it still came as a bitter blow to find herself alone in the big bed. Rhys had not come home.

With a quick flare of hope she wondered if it could have been the noise of his return that had awakened her. But although she remained locked in position, hugging her knees, her ears straining to pierce the darkness, the house lay quiet and still around her. No sound of a car or of a key in the lock or of a man's footsteps on the stairs. Only a dead silence that echoed and reechoed in the emptiness of her heart. Rhys had not come home.

Eventually she got up, knowing she would be unable to fall asleep again. Pulling on her warmest housecoat in an effort to drive away the chill that seemed to have penetrated right through to her bones, she went downstairs and into the kitchen, where she put on the kettle and made herself a cup of tea. Hugging the cup in her cold hands, she curled up in an armchair in the living room, her eyes avoiding the chesterfield.

As the slow minutes ticked by, the agonizing pain that had paralyzed thought slowly began to give way to anger, hot and reviving. How dared he do this? Did the marriage vows he had taken such a short time ago mean so little to him? To stay out all night, blatantly, without excuse—it was insupportable.

More time passed. As the clock on the mantel chimed three, its note incongruously sweet and pure, Diana's anger was shattered by fear. He had had an accident. He was lying in a hospital bed, unconscious and alone.... She got up and began pacing up and down, nightmare visions crowding her head. Should she phone the hospitals? The police? Should she waken Robert?

Gradually a touch of common sense reasserted itself. Rhys always carried identification on him; if he had had an accident, she would have been the first to be notified. Her steps slowed and again she huddled in the chair. There was nothing to do but wait.

As it happened her vigil lasted only ten more minutes. Through the tall windows that overlooked the street she saw the glow of the car lights and heard the purr of the Jaguar's motor almost simultaneously. A car door slammed. Footsteps came up the path and took the front steps two at a time. And then the sound she had envisaged, the turning of a key in the lock.

She remained where she was, knowing he must see the light she had switched on beside her. She had absolutely no idea what she was going to say.

The front door shut behind him. "Diana?"

She got to her feet. Now that the moment of confrontation had come she could feel the tension singing along her nerves. As he appeared in the doorway, the words burst out of her in a flood. "So you've decided to come home...how nice! Am I supposed to feel flattered?"

He passed a hand over his face in a gesture of utter weariness that made her even angrier. "Diana—"

"Having stayed this late, you might just as well have stayed until morning—or were you hoping to sneak in without my realizing?"

Her voice had risen. He said flatly, "Shut up. Unless you want the whole house to hear you."

"Then you'd better close the door," she said furiously.

His mouth hardened. With dangerous quietness he did as she had asked. "Look, Diana, I've had one hell of an evening—"

"*You've* had one hell of an evening! What kind of an evening do you think *I've* had, waiting for you, wondering why you were so late? I was even worrying about you, afraid that you'd had an accident—that was pretty silly of me, wasn't it?"

Although his fists clenched at his sides at her tone, his voice was creditably under control. "Let's sit down and talk this over sensibly. I'm sorry you woke up—"

"I'm sure you are."

"Will you please listen to me for a minute?" he thundered.

"Don't shout at me, Rhys Morgan!"

With a strength born of rage he propelled her to the nearest chair and forced her down into it. Towering over her he ordered, "Now stay there and keep quiet." He drew in a quick hard breath. "I'm sorry you were worried. When I saw how late it was getting I thought of phoning you, but I figured you'd be asleep and it would only disturb you."

"You mean you would have torn yourself away from Huguette long enough to telephone?" she interrupted, too angry to curb her tongue.

"You're determined to think the worst, aren't you?"

"What would *you* think if *I* stayed out until three-thirty in the morning with a man who didn't happen to be my husband?"

"Huguette's my friend and she was in trouble. I did what I could to help, that's all."

"So every time she wants her hand held you're going to drop everything and run over there—how charming," she said with heavy sarcasm. "Perhaps you've forgotten you've got a wife and a child?"

"At the moment I'd sure as hell like to forget I've got a wife," he lashed back.

If he had intended his words to hurt, he had succeeded. Too proud to let him see how much he had hurt her, she said with icy clarity, "If you want to move in with Huguette, go ahead. But you won't ever see Belinda again."

His eyes glittered with rage. For a moment she thought he was going to strike her and she shrank back in the chair. As if the only way he could keep his hands off her was to move away from her, he strode over to the door and flung it open. "I'm not going to spend the rest of the night trading cheap insults with you," he snarled. "Although I have to admire your talent in that direction. I'm going to bed."

"Don't expect me to sleep with you—not after you've spent the night with someone else," she stormed.

"I'm sleeping in my own bed, where I belong. You can sleep where you like."

"From now on I certainly will," she retorted wildly. "Why should I let a few words spoken in church stop me? They're certainly not stopping you."

"Oh, for God's sake!" he exploded. "You're talking nonsense, Diana, and you know it. Let's stop this ridiculous charade before we go too—"

"The only charade that needs finishing is our marriage," she said with vicious emphasis. "I can't imagine why I married you. Belinda and I did fine without you for ten years. We didn't need you then and we don't now."

"That's a lie."

"Oh, is it? I don't think so."

He banged his fist against the door frame in a gesture of such pent-up violence that she was momentarily silenced. "I've had enough of this—you're beside yourself."

"Perhaps I am," she said more calmly. "If so, I have reason to be. Tell me something, Rhys—" across the room her words fell like icicles "—why did you marry me?"

He had already started to leave, his back half-turned to her. Her question stopped him dead in his tracks. Very slowly he swung his head around and said heavily, "This will make you laugh, I'm sure. I married you because I loved you, Diana."

The room rocked on its foundations. "That's not true," she said, her voice barely a whisper.

He gave her a mocking smile that did not reach his eyes. "I thought it would amuse you. Good night."

"Rhys! You can't leave now—" But she was speaking to herself; he had gone. Alone in the room she sat riveted to the chair, staring blindly at the door through which he had passed. He could not have been telling the truth...it had been his last cruel joke. He didn't love her. He had married her because of Belinda. A marriage of convenience, a pragmatic gathering under his roof of his former mistress and his newly discovered child. Nothing more than that.

Then she remembered the look in his eyes as he had left the room, the look of an animal that has received a mortal blow and must hide itself away to lick its wounds. And she remembered all the cruel words she had flung at him in pain and anger.

Unable to bear her thoughts, she got up from the chair and began pacing up and down the room. It couldn't be true. He didn't love her. He didn't! If he loved anyone, it was Huguette. He had simply wanted to have the last word in a quarrel that had gone on too long—and in that he had succeeded, she thought with a desperate kind of humor.

On and on the argument raged in her head, until she was brought to her senses by the clock chiming four, a clear silvery summons to sanity. She could do nothing more tonight; increasingly she was afraid she had already done far too much, that her tongue, unbridled and fed by fury, might have done damage that would be irreparable. The only counterbalance she could find to this conviction was that for all the words that had been flung back and forth, Rhys had offered no concrete explanation of why he had remained at Huguette's until three in the morning.

She trailed up the stairs, exhaustion washing over her in a leaden tide. Perhaps she had been cherishing an inward hope that Rhys might hear her, might call to her.... The door to their bedroom, however, was tightly closed and from behind it there was only silence. She tried to whip her anger to life again but was unable to summon the energy even for that. Going past their door she came to the smallest of the three guest rooms. She closed the door behind her and lay down on the bed, pulling the duvet up over her for comfort as much as for warmth, and closed her eyes. But Rhys's face, hard and unforgiving, kept intruding on her vision, and in her ears rang the bitter words they had exchanged.

She burrowed deeper under the covers, as around and around in her head the thoughts kept churning, keeping sleep at bay far more effectively than any amount of noise or bright light could have done. The nerves in her legs twitched. Her head began to ache. She was first hot and then cold. It was with a sensation of pure physical relief that she eventually saw the first glimmer of gray light begin to appear through the open curtains. A new day...and one in which somehow she must persuade Rhys to sit down with her and deal with the impasse to which they had come. Yet how?

Her watch ticked past six o'clock, then six-thirty, and still she lay gazing out the window at the tangled branches of the maples now outlined against the dawn sky. Facts; what she needed were facts. Number one, of course, was that Rhys had stayed at Huguette's long past the bounds of propriety or common sense—yet why? She was as ignorant of that now as she had been during the long minutes of waiting for him to come home.

There was one way to find out, she thought in sudden excitement. She could go and see Huguette and ask her point-blank. And, oddly enough, she was sure she would be told the truth. From Huguette she would find out whether Rhys had been unfaithful to her, and if so, why. Then she would be in a better position to assess those last devastating words of his as he had left the room. And she would know what she was fighting against. . . or fighting for.

Fighting? The word had taken her by surprise. Last night in the heat of anger she had told Rhys she did not need him, that she should never have married him. She knew how wrong she had been. She loved Rhys and needed him as she needed the very air she breathed. And if she had to fight for that love, she would. Fight with all her strength and with every weapon at her command.

CHAPTER TWENTY

DIANA GOT UP shortly afterward, carefully smoothing out the bed so no one would know it had been occupied. She wanted neither Robert nor Belinda to discover where she had spent the night. Then she went downstairs.

The morning proceeded normally. Belinda got up for school at the regular time, carefully wrapping a big piece of the fudge in tinfoil and leaving it on the counter for Rhys. He came into the kitchen just before she was ready to leave, wearing his track suit and carrying his squash racket, and she solemnly presented it to him. He dropped a kiss on her head. "Thanks, sweetie. I'll eat it on the way to the club, and it'll give me lots of energy so I'll be sure to win." He peered at the box she was carefully loading into her schoolbag. "You mean the school gets all that and I only get one piece?"

As Belinda giggled, Diana realized she had been guilty of more than one lie the night before. Belinda needed Rhys just as much as she herself did. He mustn't be in love with Huguette, she thought in desperation, blindly tracing the pattern on the tablecloth. She surfaced in time to hear Rhys say, "If you like, I'll run you to school, Lindy, on my way to the club."

The child's face glowed—a treat, indeed. She kissed her mother goodbye and pulled on her jacket, and the two of them went down the back steps, leaving Diana sitting at the table. Rhys had not so much as looked at her, she thought sickly, let alone spoken to her. She might as well not have been there. And now he was gone, and she had no idea when he would be back.

For a moment her one urge was to give in to a storm of weeping. Grimly she fought it back, knowing that inadvertently she had been presented with the perfect opportunity to go and see Huguette. Taking out the phone book, she looked up her address: one of the side streets off Papineau in the Maisonneuve district. Hurrying upstairs she dressed in a smart jade green wool suit, for it seemed important that she look her best. Calling to Robert that she would be back in time for lunch, she ran outside and got into her car.

Huguette's apartment was in one of a line of brick houses very close together, with tiny patches of garden in front. It was on the second story, so Diana climbed the curving wrought-iron staircase that ended in a small balcony outside a brightly painted door. She took a deep breath and pushed the bell, for the first time wondering what she would do if Huguette was not home.

She need not have worried. In only a few moments she heard the pad of footsteps, then the sound of the latch being unlocked. Huguette's face peered around the door.

Whomever she might have been expecting, it was

clearly not Diana. Politely she erased the surprise from her face. "Diana—please come in," she said cordially. "I am just making coffee. You are in time for it."

"I know this is very early," Diana said awkwardly as she followed Huguette through a tiny hallway into the kitchen, which faced away from the street. Her brain recorded quick impressions as she went. A strong smell of stale cigarette smoke. A litter of empty glasses, coffee mugs and ashtrays, out of place in the otherwise spotless tidiness of the living room. The dark circles under Huguette's eyes, her face looking younger and more vulnerable without makeup. The aroma of freshly percolated coffee.

Diana perched on a stool by the counter, noticing how the artfully arranged posters and potted plants gave the small and rather ordinary kitchen a touch of distinction. Her coffee was given to her in a very attractive pottery mug; as she stirred in cream and sugar, there was a tiny expectant pause, and she knew she had to state her reason for coming. With a kind of desperate honesty she said, "Huguette, are you in love with Rhys?"

"*Mon Dieu....*"

She had burned her bridges now. "Or he with you?" Suddenly terrified of what answer she might hear, she buried her nose in her coffee mug. But just as quickly she raised it, for Huguette was laughing, a helpless warm tide of laughter that left Diana totally confused.

"This is so—how do you say—dramatic for so early in the morning! No, Diana, I am not in love with your husband. On the contrary—'' her piquant face sobered ''—I am far too much in love with my own husband.''

''But you're separated,'' Diana blurted. All her normal tact and discretion seemed to have deserted her this morning, she thought ruefully—not that Huguette appeared to mind.

''So I am. And that is the trouble and that is why Rhys was here half the night—which, I presume, is why you are here now.''

No point in denying it. ''Right.'' Her lashes dropped in shame. ''We had a dreadful fight when he got home. I said some terrible things. I . . . I even accused him of sleeping with you.''

Huguette reached out a hand and patted Diana on the sleeve. ''Ah, no, you have no worries there. Believe me, Rhys is not the slightest bit interested in any other woman in that way. Surely you must know that?''

Diana shook her head miserably. ''No.'' Now that she had started, it all came pouring out. ''I've been so jealous of you, Huguette. It seemed that you and Rhys were spending more time together than he and I were, and then when he was so late last night I jumped to all the wrong conclusions. . . . They *were* the wrong ones, weren't they?''

''*Certainement.* If you were thinking Rhys and I were having an affair—'' she gave the word its French pronunciation ''—then you could not have been more wrong. Let me explain to you, Diana, what has been happening so you will understand. Here, have more coffee.''

Something that had been held tightly inside of Diana for too long was relaxing. There could be no doubting Huguette's sincerity. And the genuine liking she had always felt for the younger woman, but which had been distorted by jealousy, was now free to surface. "But perhaps Rhys loves you?" she heard herself ask.

"Absolument, non. Impossible!"

"But. . . how do you know that?"

"It is very simple." Huguette spread her hands wide. "He loves you. It does not take much discernment to see that."

"It might not for you," Diana said warmly. "But I don't know that."

"He has never told you?"

"No." She flushed, then paled. "At least, never until last night. He told me then that that was why he'd married me. But I was too angry to listen. I thought the only reason we got married was Belinda, you see."

"Quel contretemps," Huguette murmured. "To me it was always so obvious. He talked about you so much and with so much pride and love in his voice. For me, you see, that was good, because I felt entirely safe with him—like a brother. Now with Guillaume, I feel quite different."

"Guillaume is your husband?"

"Oui. I want so much to be back together with him—and he with me, I am beginning to think. But we are both proud and stubborn, and whenever we are together we fight. A woman who was once his mistress, before we married, has come back to Mon-

treal to live and I thought they had resumed their relationship. He, in his turn, made ridiculous accusations about me. And so last night Guillaume was to come over and I invited Rhys to come, also, to act as... how do you say?''

"Referee?" Diana suggested dryly.

"Oui, c'est ça! And what a session it was. But I think it may have worked. You see, because Rhys was there, many things were said between Guillaume and me that needed to be said. Tonight Guillaume comes alone, and we will see.'' For a moment her face was strained and desperate. "I pray we have learned our lesson. Love is not like moonlight and roses, is it, Diana? Not always. It can be pain and jealousy and even hatred. We have both discovered that, *n'est-ce pas?*''

"Yes, I think we have. I know I have.'' Grasping for reassurance, Diana heard herself add, "You really do think Rhys loves me?''

"I am convinced of it. And I am sorry if anything I have said or done has caused you trouble. I would like to think we could be friends.''

"I would like that, too.'' They smiled at each other, and with a lift of her spirits Diana knew she had made a new friend. "I do hope things will work out between you and your husband, Huguette. And now, will you excuse me? I'm anxious to get home again, because I must see Rhys. I don't know if he'll ever forgive me for some of the things I said last night—it was as if the devil had got into my tongue.''

"It seems strange he has never told you he loves you,'' Huguette mused. "He must have a reason, I suppose. Because I would be willing to swear he does.''

Diana could hardly bear the surge of hope that welled up in her. She loved Rhys, and if by some miracle he should love her, why, nothing in the world could come between them. Yet it was a bittersweet hope; she was almost afraid even to contemplate it, for it opened in front of her a vision of felicity and joy that frightened her in its perfection. Again she said, this time more urgently, ''I must go. So much depends on what he says. . . . I'm scared, Huguette.''

''It will be all right, you'll see,'' Huguette said with a comforting lack of emphasis. ''Promise me one thing—you will come back and tell me what happens. And you will stay longer next time.''

''I'd love that,'' Diana responded with unforced warmth. ''Thanks so much, Huguette. And for you—*bonne chance.*''

The journey back seemed to take forever. The traffic was heavy, a car with a flat tire causing a tie-up of at least a block, and as Diana inched forward she was fuming with impatience. But eventually she reached their street and parked in front of the big brick house. There was no sign of the Jaguar, she noticed with a sinking heart; Rhys did not usually stay this long at the squash courts. She ran up the front walk, inserted the key in the lock and called Robert's name.

He came out of the kitchen, wiping his hands on a green baize apron. ''Yes, madam?'' he said with an unusual degree of formality.

She scarcely noticed. ''Robert, where's Rhys?''

''I'm afraid I couldn't say, madam.''

This time his tone of voice did penetrate; it was full of disapproval. "You mean you don't know or you won't tell me?" she asked, her eyes flashing dangerously.

"Mr. Morgan came back shortly after you'd gone out. He asked where you were, but of course I didn't know. He changed his clothes and left the house, carrying an overnight bag."

Robert plainly did not think much of all these comings and goings; Diana suspected he had an idea what was behind them and was torn between his old loyalty to Rhys and his more recent loyalty to Diana and Belinda. She said abruptly, knowing she had to take him into her confidence, "We quarreled last night, Robert, and it's very important that I talk to him. You don't have any idea where he might have gone?" She looked around her hopefully. "He didn't leave a note?"

Robert's voice warmed a trifle. "I don't believe so. He did make a phone call as soon as he got in."

She stared at him in perplexity. "Where could he have gone?" Her voice trembled. "You don't think he's left, do you, Robert? For good, I mean?"

"Surely not," Robert said, scandalized. "He'd tell you if he was going to do that."

"After last night, he might not. Oh, Robert, what am I going to do?"

"Now just keep calm, Miss Diana," he said paternally. "He won't be gone for more than five days—"

"Five days!" she echoed in dismay.

"Because he has a rehearsal then, and he's never missed a rehearsal in his life. So if worse come to worst, we'll simply have to wait for him to return. He could have driven up to the Laurentians, I suppose. . ." he finished doubtfully.

"He wouldn't go to Woody Point, would he?"

"He might have. It's always been the place he's tended to turn to in times of trouble."

"We could call the airport and find out if he bought a ticket," she said excitedly.

The airport, however, refused to divulge the information. Diana put the phone down, saying disconsolately, "I guess I'll just have to wait for him to come home. You really think he'll be back for that rehearsal, do you?"

"I'm sure of it."

"Maybe he said something to Belinda this morning when he took her to school." Diana cheered up visibly. "I'll ask her at lunchtime."

But all Belinda could produce in answer to Diana's careful questioning was that Rhys had promised her a present when he got back. "It's going to be a surprise," she crowed. "I wonder what it'll be."

So he *was* coming back. . . . Diana turned away to hide her expression, gripping the edge of the counter very tightly until she had herself under control. She hadn't realized until then the full extent of her fear that Rhys had simply disappeared from her life again, just as he had ten years ago. She said with intentional lightness, "Well, you shouldn't have too long to wait."

"Four days is all." Belinda heaved a sigh. "It seems like a long time, though."

It did indeed, Diana agreed inwardly, wondering

how she was going to live with herself for four long days. The memory of her accusations haunted her, accusations she now knew to be groundless. She needed to see him, she decided frantically. She needed to apologize to him for the hateful words she had hurled at him, and if she could find the courage she needed to ask him if he truly did love her. Maybe after last night he didn't. Maybe she herself had killed that love.

After Belinda had gone back to school, she found herself unable to settle down to anything. The few facts she knew—and pitifully few they were—circled in her brain. Rhys had left in the car with a small overnight case. He was to be gone four days, for if he had promised Belinda a present, he would carry through on that promise; of that Diana was sure. If that certainty was betrayed, then there was meaning in nothing, and her knowledge of Rhys was but a mirage.

She found herself standing in their bedroom in front of the closet that held his clothes. Business suits, evening suits—they were all there as far as she could tell. But a more casual blue tweed jacket, one that she particularly liked on him, was gone, as was his checked lumberman's jacket and his hiking boots. He could have driven up to the Laurentians, she supposed; however, it began to seem more and more likely that he had flown, both literally and metaphorically, to his habitual place of refuge in Woody Point, where he had always gained solace from the hills and the bay and the cool ocean winds.

She ran downstairs, calling to Robert that she

would be back in a couple of hours. Getting in her car she headed for Atwater Avenue and the airport.

When she arrived, her heart quailed at the size of the parking lot, row upon row of cars, none of them Rhys's. Her chin set with determination, she began methodically driving up and down the ranks of cars, searching always for the white Jaguar. White Buicks and Corvettes and Rovers. Green and maroon and gray Jaguars. Her hopes were beginning to fade, for she had covered more than two-thirds of the parking area, when on her left she saw it: Rhys's white Jaguar, with the familiar license plates. She braked, momentarily slumping over the wheel. So he had gone by plane. Her hunch had been right.

Behind her a horn blasted impatiently. Slipping the car into gear, she began searching again, but this time for an empty spot. She parked the car in the first one she saw and hurried toward the terminal. At the ticket counter she booked a seat on an evening flight to Deer Lake via Halifax, paid for it with her credit card and slipped the ticket folder into her handbag. Maybe she was crazy to do this. Rhys, after all, had left presumably to get away from her for a couple of days. But something in her far stronger than logic or caution was driving her to find him, and blindly she was obeying that compulsion.

It was a compulsion that was with her the rest of the day, as she made arrangements for her parents to come and stay in the house, glossing over the purpose of her trip to them, and as she packed a few clothes. It was with her in the plane as it droned through the darkness, and in the anonymity of the motel room at Deer Lake where she spent the rest of the night. It was with her in the car she rented the next morning to drive to Woody Point and was still with her as she wound up the hill to the bungalow. An unfamiliar car was parked outside the house. That the car-rental agencies were doing very well out of her and Rhys was her last coherent thought as she walked across the driveway and rang the door bell. Her mind blank, her body tense, she waited.

No answer. Only a dead silence from the interior of the house, a silence that bespoke emptiness and desertion. She pushed the bell again, but still no response. Trying the handle, she found the door was locked.

She ran around to the back, and this time the door yielded. She stepped inside, smelling the slight mustiness of a house that has been shut up. ''Rhys?'' she called.

Again no answer. Stifling a crushing disappointment, she went swiftly from room to room. The bed had been slept in, while across the chair was draped a blue tweed jacket. The thermostat was turned up. There was a used coffee mug and a couple of knives in the sink and a few provisions in the refrigerator.

So he had been here and had gone out; she might have missed him by a matter of minutes. She went to the back door and called his name as loudly as she could, but the wind tore the sound from her lips and tossed it skyward. Going back inside, she saw that his backpack was gone from its usual place in the porch, nor could she find his hiking boots. He had probably gone for the day. Once again there was nothing for her to do but wait.

In retrospect that was to seem like one of the longest days in Diana's life. She didn't want to go far from the house in case Rhys should return, nor was the weather conducive to being outdoors. Woody Point in November, she soon realized, was a very different proposition from Woody Point in August, and while the artist in her might respond to the massed gray clouds and the dark array of the hills, the woman in her, the wife who wanted her husband, shivered under the threatening winds and the squalls of cold driven rain. Until Rhys came back there was no welcome for her here, no peace. The keening of the sea gulls was the very voice of her loneliness, the icy fingers of the wind the first touch of fear.

Midmorning she went down to the village to get a few more groceries, hurrying back up the hill only to find the house still empty. In the afternoon she curled up in the armchair and slept fitfully for a while, for she had had very little sleep the past two nights. Around five she got up and occupied herself in the kitchen, making a stew in the pressure cooker; she took far more trouble than usual in an effort to pass the time. By now it was already growing dark outside.

With the coming of night the wind rose rather than diminished; it rattled at the windows as though seeking a way in and on the hillside whipped the black branches of the spruce trees to a frenzy. But it was when the rain started that Diana really began to worry, for it was not the warm misty rain of summertime but a downpour, streaming across the windowpanes, drumming on the roof. And somewhere Rhys was out in it.

Had he fallen and hurt himself? Was he lost? Surely there could be no other reason for his continued absence.... At seven she ate a small amount of the stew, making up her mind that if he had not returned by eight she would call the police detachment at Rocky Harbour. She couldn't bear much more of this waiting in the isolated storm-battered house. Even turning on the radio for the sound of another human voice brought her no comfort, for the announcer seemed to take great relish in describing the wind velocity and the predicted rainfall, issuing a gale warning to all small craft. She snapped it off and went to get herself an extra sweater from her suitcase, turning up the heat as she went.

She was in the bedroom when beneath the constant noise of the wind she heard the back door open and then thud loudly as if it had been slammed against the wall by the force of the gale. For a split second her feet were glued to the floor. Then, galvanized into motion, she sped down the hall to the kitchen.

Rhys had just managed to close the door. He was leaning against it, his breath heaving in his throat, his eyes closed. But he must have heard the soft fall of her footsteps. He looked up and she saw raw shock jolt through his body. "Diana," he muttered. "Diana?"

She was afraid he was going to faint. Running toward him, she put her arms around him to hold him up and felt the tremors that were convulsing his frame. His wet clothes were plastered to his body. His hair was soaked. One cheek was scraped raw, and blood had mingled with rain to stain the collar of his shirt pink. "Rhys you're wet through," she said urgently. "Come in, quickly."

She helped him into the kitchen, struggling under his weight and hooking a chair out from the table with one foot, easing him down into it. Then she knelt beside him, beginning to undo the snaps on his jacket. With one hand—a hand that was ice-cold, she realized in near panic—he stayed her. Rubbing dazedly at his eyes with his other hand, he muttered, "It really is you? I'm not dreaming?"

She raised his fingers, pressing them to the warmth of her face. "See? I'm real," she said shyly. "Oh, Rhys, I had to come—"

With what must have been the last of his strength, he put his arms around her and pulled her close, smothering her words against his jacket. "Sweetheart, sweetheart," he repeated over and over again, and she didn't think she had ever heard anything more beautiful than that repetitive refrain, so quietly spoken yet so heartfelt.

But he was shaking with cold and she knew something had to be done. Easing back from his embrace she said firmly, "Rhys, you've got to get out of those wet clothes. Let me help you to the bedroom—maybe a hot shower would help."

His smile could hardly be called a success, for his teeth were chattering, but she knew she would always treasure the memory of the soft light in his eyes as they rested on her worried face. "You're probably right," he murmured. "Can you help me up? My knees seem to have given out."

"Should I call a doctor?"

"Lord, no. He'd only tell me I acted like a damn fool, and I know that already. I did this—" he raised his hand to his cheek "—when a branch broke off the old pine tree on the crest of the ridge."

Together they staggered down the hall, Diana realizing how exhausted he was by the degree to which he was depending on her help. It was as much as he could do to make it to the bedroom. He collapsed onto the nearest chair, resting his head in his hands. She bent to unlace his boots, pulling them off his feet and then stripping off the wet woolen socks, working as fast as she could. "I'm causing you a hell of a lot of trouble," he mumbled.

"Nonsense. I'm so glad you're safe. That's all that matters."

His jacket had followed the socks to the floor and she was peeling the shirt from his shoulders. He caught at her wrist. "Do you mean that, Diana?"

She said steadily, her gray eyes direct, "I mean every word of it."

There was an odd note in his voice. "I believe you do."

As he stood up to remove his trousers, she hurried into the bathroom and turned on the hot tap, knowing it would gradually fill the air with steam. When he came in she was pulling two thick towels out of the linen cupboard. "Will you be all right?" she asked anxiously.

He was naked except for his briefs, and in places his skin was blue white with cold. "I'll be okay." He ran the tip of one finger lightly down her cheek. "One hundred percent better for finding you here.

Although if you want to dry my back afterward, I won't say no.''

She smiled uncertainly, not sure if he was joking, even under these circumstances unable to prevent herself from admiring the long muscular lines of his body. "Call if you need me."

From the bedroom, where she was drawing the curtains to shut out the rain-swept night, no longer nearly so threatening now that Rhys was with her, she heard the water sluicing over his body. She felt ridiculously like a new bride, perilously happy and frighteningly vulnerable, as if on the brink of some shining new discovery that could change the whole course of her life. For whatever they said and did in the next hour could indeed determine the pattern of their life together. Would they discover a mutual love so deeply rooted that it would furnish their house with certainty and contentment for the rest of their days? Or would she once again have that beautiful dream snatched away from her in yet another awakening to a reality in which she loved but was herself unloved?

The water had been turned off, leaving her with only the sounds of the wind and the rain. Then she heard his deep voice call, "Diana?"

Feeling horribly unsure of herself, she pushed open the door and was enveloped in steam. "You must be warm now!"

He grinned at her. There was color back in his face and his voice sounded stronger. "Much better. Are you going to dry my back for me?"

She found she was blushing, for he was completely

naked, little trickles of water running down his chest and legs. Wordlessly she took the towel he was holding out to her and, as he turned around, began to scrub furiously at his back. Within half a minute she was far too hot. Putting the towel down, she pulled her sweater over her head and resumed her task. But gradually, of their own accord, her hands slowed, until through the towel she was caressing rather than rubbing him, a slow sensuous movement that made her own body tingle with pleasure. Very slowly he turned to face her, his eyes falling deliberately from her flushed cheeks to the rise and fall of her breasts under the thin knit shirt she was wearing. "I can still hardly believe you're here." He drew her closer to him, holding her against his body. "It seems like a miracle!"

Filled with contentment she stood very still, feeling the dampness from his skin seep through her clothes. When he released her and his eyes had once again traveled down the length of her figure, he said with a hint of laughter, "You're wet through—you'll have to change your shirt."

She blushed, knowing her breasts were delineated by the damp fabric as clearly as if she wore nothing. Then she heard him say, his voice suddenly serious, "I want to see your body. Take off your clothes, Diana—will you do that for me?"

How could she refuse him? Every motion filled with grace and unconscious provocation, she pulled her shirt over her head, shaking out her hair, and slid her jeans down over her hips. Her bra and panties, strips of nylon and lace, fell to the floor. She faced him proudly, almost wantonly, for he could not hide that he wanted her, that he found her beautiful and desirable. He stepped so close to her that the tips of her breasts brushed his skin, a sensation so unbelievably sweet that she quivered with delight. She heard herself whisper shamelessly, "Please, Rhys—make love to me. Now." His answer was to take her breasts in his hands, bending his head to kiss each nipple. She pressed herself against him. "I want to be yours," she whispered. "Always yours."

"So you will be. As I will belong to you—and only you."

It was all the avowal she needed, and those were the last words they spoke for some time. His arms about her waist, he drew her into the bedroom and down onto the bed, pulling the covers over them both until they were in a tiny enclosed world that held only themselves. And there she gave so freely of herself, so lovingly and generously of all the secrets of her body, that his response was almost uncontrollably fierce, sweeping them both up into the frantic unbearable tension and the equally unbearable miracle of relief. When his body finally stilled within her, she found she was weeping.

"Sweetheart . . . what's wrong?"

"I'm crying because I'm happy." She clutched at his shoulders, her face strained with the intensity of her feelings, knowing the words had to be said no matter how he reacted. "Rhys, all I ask of life is to be held like this by you," she said in a low voice. "I love you so much."

"Say that again." A mixture of such incredulity and joy began to dawn in his eyes that she felt her heartbeat quicken.

"I said I love you." The words poured out. "I don't think I ever stopped loving you, not even through all those years when you were gone from me. At first I thought I hated you, and then I thought I was indifferent to you—and they were both lies."

"After the other night I was sure you hated me. And hated yourself for marrying me."

"I thought the same of you." Now that she had begun she couldn't stop. "I'm so sorry for some of the things I said that night, Rhys—I scarcely knew what I was saying, I was so jealous of Huguette."

"I gave you cause to feel that way," he responded soberly. "Not as far as Huguette was concerned, I don't mean that. She was a friend and nothing more. But I'm not very proud of how I've been behaving since we were married, Diana. Burying myself in my music, leaving you alone so much. It was escapism, pure and simple. I was so unsure of you—I was convinced you'd agreed to marry me only because of Belinda, you see. You seemed so cool and remote most of the time. . . ."

She ran her fingers up his stomach. "Except in bed," she said wickedly.

He laughed outright. "We were neither of us much good at disguising that, were we? But I'm beginning to realize we were very good at disguising other things—our true feelings for each other, for instance. I was hiding those even from myself. . . partly, I suppose, because so much had happened to me in such a short time. The accident and the injury to my hand, with the loss of a career I'd spent most of my life building up. You arriving on the scene, so beautiful and so unattainable. And then the discovery that I had a child, your daughter and mine. One thing on top of another.... I know I used composing as an escape, a way of losing myself and my own confusion for a while in a world of order, where I knew the rules."

"I can understand that. I don't think I'll ever mind your spending time on your music, Rhys. How could I, when I do the same thing with an easel and a paint-brush? What I minded was the thought of your spending all that time with Huguette. I'd more than half convinced myself you were in love with her."

"There was never the slightest danger of that, Diana. She's not you, you see. And it's you I want and will always want—only you."

Her eyes were shining with tears again. "I can hardly believe you're really saying that."

He reached over and kissed her, saying huskily, "I've got a whole lifetime ahead of me to convince you. I love you, Diana." He punctuated each word with a kiss. "I love you, I love you."

"I've never heard you say that before," she whispered. "I don't think I'll ever be able to hear enough of it."

Obligingly he repeated it. "I love you, Diana."

She laughed breathlessly. "I'd have traveled ten times as far to hear you say that."

"How did you know where I was, anyway?"

Briefly she described the events of the past day and a half, finishing up, "I could have waited until you got back, but it seemed too important to wait. Once I'd heard what Huguette had to say, I needed to hear it from you. So that's why I came." She hesitated. "Why did you come here, Rhys?"

"Because I needed to think, and this has always been the place I've run to. I was afraid I'd trapped you into a marriage you'd started to hate already, and yet, because of Belinda, I could see no way out for either one of us. I thought getting away from the whole situation, distancing myself, might give me a clearer view of what to do." He smiled crookedly. "I'd have been better off grabbing you and telling you I loved you, wouldn't I? I'm not scared of many things, Diana, but I was afraid of that. I thought you'd laugh in my face, and I couldn't have borne it. I think seeing you here today, realizing you'd come all this way to see me and to put things right between us—that's done more to convince me you love me than any amount of words could have."

She shivered reminiscently. "You looked so terrible when you came in the door."

"I've had quite a day. I hadn't slept for two nights, because all I could think of was you, so I was determined to walk myself into the ground so I'd at least get a decent night's sleep. I went much too far and I didn't pay nearly enough attention to the weather—with the result, as you know, that I got back well after dark and soaking wet. It serves me right. I broke every rule of the woods."

She nestled against him with a sigh of perfect contentment, running her hand down his ribs to rest on the hard ridge of his hipbone. "But you're here now and you're safe."

He covered her hand with his own, resting his face on her breast. "Tell me something," he murmured. "Why did you come looking for me this summer?"

"Because Alan wanted to marry me and something was holding me back. That something was you, although I didn't realize it then. I came because I wanted to assure myself that everything between us was over. Dead and buried. And at first I thought it was. That was when I agreed to marry Alan. But the more I saw of you, the more entangled I seemed to get—no matter how hard I fought against it." She stroked a lock of dark hair back from his forehead. "Now you tell me something—why did you buy a painting of mine so long ago and hang it in your bedroom? And why did you carry a photograph of me with you whenever you went on tour?"

"Because, music or no music, I couldn't get you out of my mind," he said roughly. "I didn't call it 'love'— I didn't know what to call it." He paused. "I think for years I was afraid of the word. Afraid of what it might do to me to admit that I loved you, that you were the one woman in the world I wanted to be with for the rest of my days. So all through those long years that we were apart I threw all my emotions into my career. As a result I made it to the top. . .and discovered once I was there that it was a damned lonely place to be."

"Lonely?" she queried. Of all the words she might have expected, it would not have been that one.

"Yes, lonely. Because you weren't there. I think that was when I started to realize how inescapably I was bound to you. All along I'd been reading every article I could find about you, seeing as many of your shows as I could—and telling myself it was only casual interest." He laughed shortly. "I couldn't have been more wrong."

She couldn't help smiling. "At exactly the same time I was telling myself our affair was a thing of the past. We were both wrong."

"And thank God for it." He kissed her lingeringly. "Just before the accident I was starting to make plans to get in touch with you again—"

"Really?"

"Oh, yes. That was the agreement we'd made, wasn't it? That in ten years' time we'd get in touch again. But the accident changed all that. I wasn't going to come and see you and have you feeling sorry for me. So, like an animal, I hid myself away to lick my wounds. You can imagine how I felt that day you arrived here."

"It's as though it was meant that we see each other again," she whispered.

"I think it was. Neither one of us could escape it." He smoothed the silken skin of her breast with his left hand, the scars white against his tan. "I'll never forget the first time I saw you, so young and beautiful in your white dress. I knew then that I had to have you. But it's taken me ten long years to understand that it was love that bound me to you—and in that time I so nearly lost you."

"We nearly lost each other." With supreme confidence she added, "We'll never do that again, Rhys."

"No, I don't think we will." He gathered her close. "We'll cherish our love, Diana, and it will give us all the music and the beauty we'll ever want."

Harlequin Presents

ALL-TIME FAVORITE BESTSELLERS
...love stories that grow
more beautiful with time!

Now's your chance to discover the earlier great books in Harlequin Presents, the world's most popular romance-fiction series.

Choose from the following list.

17 LIVING WITH ADAM   Anne Mather
20 A DISTANT SOUND OF THUNDER   Anne Mather
29 MONKSHOOD   Anne Mather
32 JAKE HOWARD'S WIFE   Anne Mather
35 SEEN BY CANDLELIGHT   Anne Mather
36 LOVE'S PRISONER   Violet Winspear
38 MOON WITCH   Anne Mather
39 TAWNY SANDS   Violet Winspear
41 DANGEROUS ENCHANTMENT   Anne Mather
42 THE STRANGE WAIF   Violet Winspear
50 THE GLASS CASTLE   Violet Winspear
62 THE MARRIAGE OF CAROLINE LINDSAY
    Margaret Rome
66 CINDY, TREAD LIGHTLY   Karin Mutch
67 ACCOMPANIED BY HIS WIFE   Mary Burchell
70 THE CHATEAU OF ST. AVRELL   Violet Winspear
71 AND NO REGRETS   Rosalind Brett
73 FOOD FOR LOVE   Rachel Lindsay
75 DARE I BE HAPPY?   Mary Burchell
78 A MAN LIKE DAINTREE   Margaret Way

FAV-CB-2

Harlequin ◆ Presents

ALL-TIME FAVORITE BESTSELLERS

Complete and mail this coupon today!

- -

Harlequin Reader Service

In the U.S.A.	In Canada
1440 South Priest Drive	649 Ontario Street
Tempe, AZ 85281	Stratford, Ontario N5A 6W2

Please send me the following Presents **ALL-TIME FAVORITE BESTSELLERS.** I am enclosing my check or money order for $1.75 for each copy ordered, plus 75¢ to cover postage and handling.

☐ #17	☐ #35	☐ #41	☐ #66	☐ #73
☐ #20	☐ #36	☐ #42	☐ #67	☐ #75
☐ #29	☐ #38	☐ #50	☐ #70	☐ #78
☐ #32	☐ #39	☐ #62	☐ #71	

Number of copies checked @ $1.75 each = $ _____
N.Y. and Ariz. residents add appropriate sales tax $ _____
Postage and handling $ .75
           TOTAL $ _____

I enclose _____
(Please send check or money order. We cannot be responsible for cash sent through the mail.)
Prices subject to change without notice.

NAME _____
                 (Please Print)

ADDRESS _____ APT. NO. _____

CITY _____

STATE/PROV. _____

ZIP/POSTAL CODE _____
Offer expires July 31, 1983   30356000000